D1086740

A MARRIAGE BELOW ZERO

broadview editions
series editor: Martin R. Boyne

A MARRIAGE BELOW ZERO

Alan Dale

edited by Richard A. Kaye

broadview editions

BROADVIEW PRESS – www.broadviewpress.com
Peterborough, Ontario, Canada

Founded in 1985, Broadview Press remains a wholly independent publishing house.
Broadview's focus is on academic publishing; our titles are accessible to university and college
students as well as scholars and general readers. With over 600 titles in print, Broadview has
become a leading international publisher in the humanities, with world-wide distribution.
Broadview is committed to environmentally responsible publishing and fair business practices.

The interior of this book is printed on 100% recycled paper.

PERMANENT   100%

Ancient
Forest
Friendly™

© 2018 Richard A. Kaye

All rights reserved. No part of this book may be reproduced, kept in an information storage
and retrieval system, or transmitted in any form or by any means, electronic or mechanical,
including photocopying, recording, or otherwise, except as expressly permitted by the
applicable copyright laws or through written permission from the publisher.

Library and Archives Canada Cataloguing in Publication

Dale, Alan, 1861-1928, author
        A marriage below zero / Alan Dale ; edited by Richard
A. Kaye.

(Broadview editions)
Includes bibliographical references.
ISBN 978-1-55111-983-0 (softcover)

        I. Kaye, Richard A., 1960-, editor II. Title.
III. Series: Broadview editions

PR4525.D122M37 2017   823'.8   C2017-906070-8

Broadview Editions
The Broadview Editions series is an effort to represent the ever-evolving canon of texts in the
disciplines of literary studies, history, philosophy, and political theory. A distinguishing feature
of the series is the inclusion of primary source documents contemporaneous with the work.

Advisory editor for this volume: Colleen Humbert

Broadview Press handles its own distribution in North America
PO Box 1243, Peterborough, Ontario K9J 7H5, Canada
555 Riverwalk Parkway, Tonawanda, NY 14150, USA
Tel: (705) 743-8990; Fax: (705) 743-8353
email: customerservice@broadviewpress.com

Distribution is handled by Eurospan Group in the UK, Europe, Central Asia, Middle
East, Africa, India, Southeast Asia, Central America, South America, and the Caribbean.
Distribution is handled by Footprint Books in Australia and New Zealand.

Broadview Press acknowledges the financial support of the Government
of Canada through the Canada Book Fund for our publishing activities.

Typesetting by Aldo Fierro
Cover design by Lisa Brawn

PRINTED IN CANADA

Contents

Acknowledgements

I would like to thank Kate Eickmeyer for her heroic, meticulous work on the notes to this volume. Special thanks to Margot Kotler, A.W. Strouse, Meechal Hoffman, Aaron Hammes, and Ken Nielsen for their extraordinary help with the notes and the preparations of the manuscript of this edition. I owe Erin Garrow and James Arnett a considerable debt for their superb excavation of most of the contemporary reviews of *A Marriage Below Zero*, all of them reprinted here for the first time. Special thanks to Hazel Lien, the archivist at Eastnor Castle, for her painstaking transcription of Lady Somerset's deposition, and to James Hervey-Bathurst for kindly granting me permission to quote from this extraordinary document. My colleagues at Hunter College and at the Graduate Center of the City University of New York (CUNY) have provided invaluable advice, particularly my always-insightful colleague Talia Schaffer, herself a scholar of neglected nineteenth-century novels. Deborah Epstein Nord and Priyanka Jacobs of Princeton University, along with other members of the Victorian Studies group at Princeton, offered some sage suggestions related to this volume. The extraordinary resources of the British Library, the Princeton University Library, and the New York Public Library were invaluable in allowing me to explore the historical and biographical context of Cohen's novel. I feel enormous gratitude, as well, to the Research Foundation of the City University of New York, which provided much-needed funding for this project.

Introduction

> The happiness of a married man depends on the people
> he has not married. —Oscar Wilde, *A Woman of No
> Importance* (1893)

Alan Dale's *A Marriage Below Zero* (1889) is the first novel in
English to address the subject of male homosexuality in explicit
terms. Written under a pseudonym by Alfred J. Cohen, a twenty-
seven-year-old British-born theater critic residing in New York
City, the novel is narrated by a young woman who discovers that
her husband is conducting an affair with a long-time male friend.
Most reviewers (see Appendix A) were outraged by Cohen's
subject matter, although a few critics praised the author for
addressing an urgent social problem that had burst into public
attention in several high-profile court cases and that had never
been treated fictionally before. For while a few anonymously
published Victorian pornographic texts had depicted same-sex
activity between men and several nineteenth-century novels
presented coded, semi-coded, or oblique homoerotic scenarios
between male protagonists, more than any other work of British
or American fiction that had preceded it Cohen's novel brought
sustained attention to what was emerging as a scandalous new
topic. "Sodomy" or "buggery" had been an occasional topic in
bawdy British poetry and fiction in earlier centuries and in underground pornographic texts. In the 1880s and 1890s, however,
the issue had become the focus of a changed legal and scientific
treatment of male same-sex eros. Increasingly throughout the
nineteenth century, male same-sex erotics represented not so
much a fall into disreputable or immoral activity but a crucial,
identity-forming activity.

This remarkably altered attitude toward same-sex erotic
behavior is reflected in *A Marriage Below Zero*, although,
somewhat paradoxically, because it is narrated from a woman's
perspective this first fictional treatment of homosexuality leaves
undisclosed the perspective of a homosexual male character.
The novel's heroine, Elsie Ravener, initially a self-described
"frivolous" middle-class young debutante, gradually learns of
her spouse Arthur's illicit affair with an older man, the "coldly
statuesque and hatefully ubiquitous" Captain Jack Dillington.

When Arthur abandons her for his lover, she pursues them on two continents. With protagonists who sometimes have some of the characterological thinness of figures in a nineteenth-century melodrama, the novel is a tragicomic fictional work that is also heavily indebted to the protocols of Victorian sensation fiction and urban newspaper reportage addressing urban "vice." Because it was authored by a British émigré but published in America, *A Marriage Below Zero* represents an unusual instance of turn-of-the-century Trans-Atlantic literature in which, as we shall see, the circumstances of recent British sex scandals are brought to lurid fictional life for American readers.

In some ways the subject of Cohen's novel is less homosexuality *per se* than the threat posed by homosexual relations to a conventional upper-middle-class marriage. As I have suggested, because of Elsie's limited perspective in the novel, we are never quite privy to the details of the male couple's private activities, something that proved a relief to one early reviewer of the novel, who wrote in the *New York World* that Cohen "does not permit his tumble-bugs to roll their ball of dung before the public. He only covertly insinuates that they do roll it behind the scene, not without some escape of the odor" (see Appendix A3, p. 196). Yet in framing its subject in terms of a woman's outraged viewpoint, *A Marriage Below Zero* reflected and contributed to the increasing interest of nineteenth-century readers in the romantic and erotic relations between men, a topic that was attracting intense attention in Britain, elsewhere in Europe, and to a far lesser degree in America throughout the 1880s and 1890s. Sodomy had been a serious crime in Britain, sometimes posing a real threat even to upper-class or aristocratic men such as the poet Lord Byron (1788–1824), whose travels outside of Britain in part were prompted by fears of prosecution at home for his intimate relations with men. During the first third of the nineteenth century, more than fifty men had been executed for sodomy, a punishment that held sway until 1835. That year saw the execution for sodomy of James Pratt (b. 1805) and John Smith (b. 1795), the last two men in England executed for that crime. In his 1836 article "A Visit to Newgate," Charles Dickens recalled observing these two condemned men along with an imprisoned blackmailer of "sodomites," Charles Swann, at Newgate Prison, which Dickens had visited as a reporter (see Appendix B1). Dickens's vivid account of the restless Swann, pacing the prison with a "military gait," and the condemned

Pratt and Smith, "motionless as statues," faces averted but one of them described as "pale," "haggard," and "ghastly," offers an unusually sympathetic perspective on "sodomitical" men. As in his other writing, Dickens implied that lower-class citizens were more vulnerable to social opprobrium. (Pratt was a groom, married with children, and Smith an unmarried, unemployed laborer.) In fact, the case had highlighted the issue of class prejudice in the criminalization of sodomy. In a striking but failed attempt at commuting Pratt's and Smith's death sentences, the magistrate who originally had committed the men to trial wrote a petition on their behalf, describing the men's offense as the "only capital crime that is committed by rich men but owing to the circumstances I have mentioned they are never convicted."[1]

At century's end, however, class privilege increasingly ceased to be a guarantee against prosecution for the crime. As we shall see, the Cleveland Street case, in which the discovery of a male brothel in London's West End ensnared upper-class men, helped bring an end to the once-assumed protections of social status. Meanwhile, numerous researchers, aligned with the methodologies of "sexological" science and sometimes committed to increasing tolerance toward those of unorthodox sexual tastes, devoted their attention to a range of new sexual "types," sometimes called "inverts." Such scientific approaches were not without the moralizing judgment of older disavowals of homosexuality. In his account of a young married man of "pederastic" inclinations, "Patient S," the pioneering sexologist Richard Krafft-Ebing (1840–1902) judged the youth to be prone to an "unusual, perverse, and even monstrous manner of sexual gratification," one that was a "congenital or acquired perversion of the sexual instinct, and, at the same time, defect of moral sense" (see Appendix D2, p. 252). This intensified late-nineteenth-century focus on same-sex "deviance" manifested itself not only in the areas of science, medicine, and law but also in the late-nineteenth-century popular press, which increasingly spent ink on court cases ensnaring men accused of vices now rendered legally actionable owing to the so-called Labouchère Amendment. That law, passed in 1885 and named after its chief architect, the politician and writer Henry Labouchère (1831–1912), called for a punishment of one to two

---

1 Quoted in Charles Upchurch, *Before Wilde: Sex between Men in Britain's Age of Reform* (Berkeley: U of California P, 2009), 112.

years of "hard labor" for acts of "gross indecency." Although seemingly less harsh than earlier anti-sodomy statutes, in rendering both private and public same-sex behavior a punishable offense the amendment actually expanded the scope of legal attacks on same-sex erotic behavior, although, as the historian H.G. Cocks has demonstrated, there were numerous sodomy trials throughout the nineteenth century that targeted both public and private male–male sexual activity. (Pratt and Smith, for example, had been executed for sexual behavior that took place in the privacy of a room of a boarding house.) "Labouchère's amendment, therefore, was not a radical break with the past," notes Cocks, "but part of a process which had begun a century before."[1]

Cohen's novel appeared precisely at the time when a familiar nomenclature for—and understanding of—male same-sex behavior that relied on classical and sometimes biblical models was struggling to catch up with the new scientific and legal construals of male–male desire. For example, the "aestheticism" that defined the late-Victorian, male-dominated, so-called art-for-art's-sake movement (which was based on the principle that art and beauty were all important) proposed that a love of the beautiful would elevate the species, particularly art that evoked male beauty that distinguished itself from female models of the beautiful. In an 1894 essay, Charles Kains Jackson (1857–1933) wrote ecstatically of a "New Chivalry" that would, by "inducing boys to be beautiful as well as girls," undermine an "Old Chivalry" that had overstressed female beauty (see Appendix C6, pp. 236–40). Part Platonic manifesto, part social-Darwinist program aiming for more perfectly evolved men, and part coded pederastic credo, the "New Chivalry" looked forward to an epoch that would welcome a "youthful masculine ideal" and the possibility of an elevated male camaraderie. (The article's semi-veiled homoerotic agenda proved incendiary, prompting the dismissal of Kains Jackson as editor of *The Artist and Journal of Home Culture*, the magazine in which the article first appeared.) Other writers hungered for a new language amidst a growing punitive atmosphere. "No one dares speak of it; or if they do, they bate their breath," wrote the

---

1 H.G. Cocks, *Nameless Offences: Homosexual Desire in the Nineteenth-Century* (London: I.B. Taurus, 2010), 17. "Unnatural crimes," furthermore, were regarded as among the most serious of the crimes of sodomy.

writer John Addington Symonds (1840–93) in 1891; "surely it deserves a name."[1] From 1889 to 1893, Symonds authored a memoir that spoke frankly of his own struggle as a married man with homosexual impulses, a work that was unpublished until it appeared in part in 1986 and only in full in 2017 (see Appendix C5). Symonds's writing on ancient Greece and the Renaissance looked to such civilizations for illustrious models of love between men.

The new sexological science diverged from aestheticism in its understanding of same-sex eros. In his account of "Patient S," Krafft-Ebing uses German terms for male same-sex activity for which the English equivalent is "male-love" or "pederasty" (see Appendix D2). Although coined in the 1860s, the terms "homosexuality" and "homosexual" had yet to gain widespread currency in Britain or America and did not appear in English until 1890. Although the word "homosexual" is often attributed to Havelock Ellis (1859–1939), the groundbreaking British physician who sought to bring tolerance in public attitudes toward men and women of same-sex preferences, he wrote in 1897 that "'homosexual' is a barbarously hybrid word and I claim no responsibility for it."[2] Those words appear nowhere in *A Marriage Below Zero* or in contemporary reviews of the novel. In gossiping about Arthur and Jack, Elsie's friend Letty refers to them as Damon and Pythias, the devoted friends of classical Roman myth (p. 67). This had been an age-old term for intense male friendship (Shakespeare's Hamlet salutes his friend Horatio with "Oh Damon dear" [3.2.297]). In his novel set in the South Pacific, *Omoo* (1847), Herman Melville (1819–91) had written of "extravagant friendships, unsurpassed by the story of Damon

---

1 John Addington Symonds, "A Problem in Modern Ethics," *We Are Everywhere: A Historical Sourcebook of Gay and Lesbian Politics*, ed. M. Blasius and S. Phelan (New York: Routledge, 1997), 92. Anxiety about terminology and same-sex erotic behavior dates back at least to 1828, when, in a parliamentary debate on whether to eliminate the capital crime of "buggery," future prime minister Sir Robert Peel (1788–1850) refused to use that word, referring instead to the "crime *inter Christianos non nominandum*" ("the crime not to be named among Christians") (Jeffrey Weeks, *Coming Out: Homosexual Politics in Britain from the Nineteenth Century to the Present* [London: Quartet, 1979], 44).

2 Havelock Ellis, *Studies in the Psychology of Sex* (London: F.A. Davis, 1897), 45.

and Pythias: in truth much more wonderful."[1] At the *fin de siècle*, however, the conjoined names had accrued pernicious associations of a too-close male–male companionship.

Contemporary reviewers of *A Marriage Below Zero* declined to give a specific name to the passion linking the novel's male duo. One critic declared that the novel concerned "[p]erverted animalism of an unnamable sort" (see Appendix A6, p. 198)—the reference to animality a tacit post-Darwinian acknowledgment of the new power of the natural sciences in gleaning knowledge of sexual behavior. Complicating Cohen's reliance on the sexological and legal comprehensions of same-sex eros as a congenital or innate trait is the novel's suggestion that influence plays a role in Arthur's devotion to Jack. "Exactly what was the understanding between them, I did not know," explains Elsie, "but that the older man was partly accountable for the delinquencies of the younger, I was perfectly persuaded" (p. 155). Sexology allowed for such an understanding; Krafft-Ebing had stressed influence in his discussion of his "Patient S," who claimed no feelings of sexual attraction toward other men until he was pressured into a sexual relation with "G" (see Appendix D2). Such a notion of homosexuality as reliant on erotic leverage links *A Marriage Below Zero* to such *fin-de-siècle* texts as Robert Louis Stevenson's *Strange Case of Dr. Jekyll and Mr. Hyde* (1886), with its depiction of a reputable man undone by his criminal double, and Oscar Wilde's *The Picture of Dorian Gray* (1890), whose titular protagonist is seduced into aestheticism by an older male and who in turn lures other men into dire circumstances. Yet Cohen's novel notably resists the gothic, supernatural tropes structuring these works, preferring an admixture of the melodramatic, the sensational, and (whether intentional or not) the comic.

A Marriage Below Zero was published in New York by G.W. Dillingham, a firm that specialized in popular fiction, theater-related works, and "penny dreadfuls," the cheaply produced predecessors of mass-market paperbacks. That "Alan Dale" was in fact Alfred J. Cohen seems to have been widely known, as a number of the contemporary reviews of *A Marriage Below Zero* bear out. Cohen had invented the pseudonym Alan Dale (initially "Allan Dale" and based on the character of Alan-a-Dale of Robin Hood lore) well before his scandal-courting novel appeared. While his novel's subject matter would have been unfamiliar and certainly

---

1   Herman Melville, *Omoo* (Evanston, IL: Northwestern UP, 1968), 152.

shocking to most of his contemporary readers, *A Marriage Below Zero* drew on familiar Victorian literary modes that tracked marital troubles and the travails of scandal-prone protagonists. Elsie's first-person account of marital woe recalled a host of sensation fictions dealing with adultery, from Mary Elizabeth Braddon's *Lady Audley's Secret* (1862), with its narrative of marital betrayal, to Ellen Wood's *East Lynne* (1861), a novel of a woman's adultery followed by the protagonist's spousal abandonment and domestic servitude.

Cohen also may have been offering an updated version of Anne Brontë's *The Tenant of Wildfell Hall* (1848), whose heroine details (almost entirely in a diary form resembling Elsie's first-person account) the torturous challenges of freeing herself and her young son from an abusive, alcoholic husband. In both formal and thematic terms, the work of fiction that *A Marriage Below Zero* most strongly resembles is Wilkie Collins's sensation novel *The Law and the Lady* (1875), which focuses on an enterprising wife's attempt to discover the details of—so as to demonstrate as false—her husband's possibly criminal secrets. But Cohen, eschewing the complicated plot of Collins's novel with its numerous subsidiary characters, offers in *A Marriage Below Zero* the stark simplicity of theatrical melodrama that he had experienced with daily frequency as a critic of the New York stage. His novel centers primarily on the triangular tangle of Elsie, Arthur, and Jack. Yet there is some shading in the narrative voice of the novel's heroine, who is depicted as a keenly observing, unworldly innocent in a way that recalls the heroines of the Victorian novelist George Meredith's fiction, who typically bring a rational skepticism and remarkable self-possession to tryingly incomprehensible circumstances.

Set in three urban settings—London, New York, and, in its violent denouement, Paris—*A Marriage Below Zero* is a novel of manners that dramatizes the ways in which conventional manners struggle to adjust to a new, threatening social phenomenon: the homosexual spouse. Put another way, *A Marriage Below Zero* is a failed or frustrated novel of heterosexual courtship and doomed homosexual devotion. In its opening pages, Elsie describes the suffocating social codes of a courting environment in which, to her dismay, women must acquire "feminine" wiles and engage in mindless chit-chat in order to snare eligible men. At the same time, the novel's relentlessly caustic, neo-Austenian view of the rituals of courtship as pointless and its revelations of the basic fraudulence of Elsie and Arthur's marriage suggests the value of the stage over the novel. Flamboyant confrontation, along with the threat of confrontation, is a key element in the plot of *A Marriage Below Zero*. Furthermore, the novel joined a number of fictional works at the *fin de siècle* that explored the social problem involving the imagined paucity of eligible males as well as the limitations of marriage for independent-minded, financially strapped females. In works ranging from George Gissing's novel *The Odd Women* (1893) to Grant Allen's New-Woman novel *The Woman Who Did* (1895), British novelists fretted over the fate of women who did not—or did not wish to—find a secure marital arrangement. The New Woman—a figure that evoked the roles of social reformer, educated free-thinker, sexual rebel, celibate pro-female activist, or enlightened feminist (and sometimes an amalgam of some or all of these roles)—stood at the center of such fictions.

The best of the "New Women" novels envisioned expanded options for women who were increasingly considered "redundant" in a Victorian society in which nearly half of the single female population had not found husbands. Even Gissing's naturalistic novel, as it relentlessly depicts hardship and the death of one of its young female protagonists, concludes with a group of women raising the dead woman's child. Because economic pressures required that many women find their futures outside the domestic sphere, the New Woman presented an alluring model of female independence and fortitude. Although Elsie has no vocation outside the home, *A Marriage Below Zero* does depict the ways in which social restrictions on women were waning. Thus Elsie's attempt at making Arthur jealous by inviting a male neighbor to her house leads to an awkward moment when Arthur returns home, in what would have been a severe infraction two decades earlier. Yet while Elsie is feistily rebellious in the face of her husband's disavowal of normal spousal duties, *A Marriage Below Zero* ultimately offers no solution to Elsie's dilemma beyond her exposure of her husband's same-sex secret. Nor does it suggest any providential or visionary compensation in freedom after (or outside) marriage for Elsie's grief. Bitterness is the prevailing tone, beginning with Elsie's ever-escalating sarcastic retorts to her husband in the first days of their marriage to the ugly denouement in a Paris hotel room. Yet beyond its allegiances to earlier literary models, *A Marriage Below Zero* evoked a set of widely covered cases in Cohen's native country, courtroom trials that helped to solidify, through their own melodramatic codes of public revelation, confrontation, and rebuke, an understanding of male homosexuality as a concern for a newly agitated citizenry, particularly "innocent" marriageable or married women.

"Oh God, There Is No Woman in This": *A Marriage Below Zero* and the Somerset and Russell Family Scandals

> I remember standing on the top of the steps of the house with the Duchess watching the men returning from some expedition, somewhat behind the others. W. Dalrymple & Henry walked with Walter's arms around Henry's waist, he leaning on Henry. The Duchess said to me "what a disgusting Boy that is" I said he is very mischief making besides being very insufferably tiresome, she said "It is an extraordinary infatuation...." —Lady Henry Somerset's Deposition, 1876[1]

In presenting his tale of a socially prominent English couple threatened by a homosexual relationship, Cohen probably was referencing a sensational case involving a well-known British family, the Somersets. Henry (1849–1932), known as "Penna," and Isabella (1851–1921), known as Isabel, were two members of the British aristocracy, although as the second son of the Duke of Beaufort Henry stood little chance of inheriting the kind of fortune his wife could count on. They saw their marriage collapse in a very public way with Lady Somerset's accusations concerning her husband's sodomitical relations with other men. At the time of the scandal, Lord Somerset held prominent positions as an MP and Comptroller of the Queen's Household. A protégé of then–prime minister Benjamin Disraeli (1804–81), he was an up-and-coming government official. Lady Henry was the daughter of the third Earl Somers (Charles Somers-Cocks, 1819–83) and the first cousin once removed of the novelist Virginia Woolf (1882–1941). (Isabel's mother and Woolf's grandmother were sisters.) The Somersets' 1872 marriage had been an extraordinary social event, attended by countesses, dukes, and earls. The poet Alfred, Lord Tennyson (1809–92), a family friend, was unable to attend but sent a basket of snowdrops, which Isabel carried during

---

1 Isabel Somerset's hand-written, un-paginated deposition has never been published in its entirety and was made available to me by Hazel Lein, the archivist of Eastnor Castle, the Herefordshire estate that remains in the hands of Lady Henry's descendants.

the wedding ceremony. Residing at Reigate Priory and in a house at Badminton, as well as at their London home in Charles Street, the couple was soon feuding. In March 1877, Isabel's cousin Walter Dalrymple, who probably met Henry at Isabel's wedding, came to call on Isabel at her London home. From this time on, Henry began a relationship with Dalrymple that would prove disastrous for Isabel. "In Feb 1877 we came to London—and Walter Dalrymple called on us in March," Isabel writes. "From that date he was constantly with Henry, he used to bring him to luncheon when I used to hear them refer to the evenings when he used to take down to the House of Commons with him—by degrees he was constantly in the house, going up to sit with Henry before he was up in the morning."

Much of what we know of the troubled Somerset marriage comes from newspaper accounts as well as letters and the legal deposition that Isabel submitted to the court (some of the contents of which are disclosed for the first time in this Introduction). In many ways this extraordinary document is far more an episode-laden sensation text than *A Marriage Below Zero*. The deposition reveals a wholly naive wife who initially is stymied in her wish for a child and yet eventually becomes a mother, only to find herself caught in a domestic drama consisting of purloined letters, a plotting mother-in-law, accusations of "child theft," and blackmail, with a cast of characters that include all-knowing servants, interfering relatives, an agitated prime minister, and an apparently concerned monarch, Queen Victoria. Evidently there is not just one lover for the philandering husband, as there is in Cohen's novel, but several. (Isabel laments that the "same four men separately or together [are] always in the House.") According to Isabel's deposition, shortly after their wedding Henry insisted on a *mariage blanc* involving separate bedrooms and an insistence on his part that there be no children, although this last vow was broken when Isabel conceived and gave birth to a son, Somey.[1] But the marriage foundered with Henry's abusive behavior and flagrant cavorting with other men. At one point, according to Isabel's deposition, she fell ill and Henry so ignored

---

1 These and other details are drawn from Isabel's deposition as well as two biographical studies of Lady Somerset: Ros Black, *A Talent for Humanity: The Life and Work of Lady Henry Somerset* (Chippenham and Eastbourne: Anthony Rowe, 2010), and Olwen Claire Niessen, *Aristocracy, Temperance, and Social Reform: The Life of Lady Henry Somerset* (London: I.B. Tauris, 2007).

her condition that relatives summoned a physician. In another incident, Henry, furious at the prying questions of Isabel's relatives, menaced his wife with a knife. "I shall live for the moment to have my revenge on you," he told her.

Isabel's testimony discloses her cruel baptism into a counter-world of unspeakable transgressions against her household, with a cast of outsized characters. Beyond the irascible Henry are the omniscient servants as well as various relatives, most of whom express disgust with Henry's actions. Henry's mother, witnessing Dalrymple's arm around her son's waist, declines to accuse her son of any impropriety but declares Dalrymple a "disgusting boy," while Henry's younger brother, Arthur, suggests to Isabel that she find evidence against Henry's friends—"or tell me where to find anything about them. I feel that all of this will end with our names being dragged through the Dirt."[1] With considerable revulsion, the deposition catalogues the parade of male cohorts that Henry brought into their home: "Mr. Orrid [sic], Mr. Dalrymple, Mr. H. Smith, Mr. Widderburn. I used to see coats & hats in the Hall and made a point of asking the footman who was there." Elsewhere we read of anxieties about Henry's flagrant behavior, with Orred admonishing Henry that if his intimacy with Henry Smith were revealed, "the world and the Somers would be agog.... Your devotion to HS is all very nice and Arcadian, but you are carrying it on to such an extent as to let it interfere with ordinary society."[2]

"To the long years of indifference & estrangement was now added my husband's hatred and aversion & threats to me," Isabel writes in the deposition. "I now began to attribute it to the influence of some *woman* racking my brains to think who it could be." Isabel discovered receipts for jewelry, which confirmed her sense of Henry's secret intimacies: "I saw a bill from the Jewellers in Oxford Street which contained an account for Diamond and pearl sleeve links, diamond and pearl studs, a pearl pin at £21 & a gold caskit price £36 I knew none of these were in Henry's possession. This I mentioned to Mama. And we wondered to whom he had given them." Finally, troubled that Henry had begun entertaining other young men at their house, in the spring of 1877, at her mother's suggestion, Isabel covertly examined correspondence between Henry and his male cohorts. Among Henry's letters was a note from Orred offering to introduce Henry to "a beautiful

---

1 Quoted in Niessen 53.
2 Quoted in Niessen 54.

youth ... just going into the F.O. [Foreign Office]," a sonnet from Wedderburn, and a missive from Smith beginning "Dearest and beloved Penna."[1] Upon reading one letter from Harry Smith, "wrapped around a photograph of himself" and ending with the clause, "A long kiss from your own Harry," Isabel exclaimed to her nurse, "Oh God there is no woman in this, this is too fearful to bear," to which her maid replied, "Oh, my lady, if you had not been so young you would have seen what all this was long ago."[2] Copying the correspondence in longhand, she returned the letters to Henry's desk. Isabel's mother counseled her daughter to seek legal advice.

Meanwhile, rumors were accumulating to the point that Prime Minister Disraeli wrote to Henry's mother expressing "disquiet over what I have heard of the disturbance in your family," reports, the prime minister confided, that "must greatly distress my Gracious Mistress," Queen Victoria.[3] Although alarmed, Henry's parents chose to view their son's behavior as prompted by, at worst, a mental defect or, at best, ungentlemanly deportment. The Duchess, Henry's mother, wrote to her daughter-in-law, "We have nothing whatever to say in defense of Penna and unless he is mad cannot understand his behavior," while the Duke admonished his son that "a man may get tired of his wife but your conduct is not that of gentleman."[4] All the while, Isabel struggled to find a language to describe her husband's offences. "I said what bad men Mr. Orrid [sic] & W.D. are I mean something very bad. W.D. is a real beast," Isabel explained to her mother, as reported in her deposition. "[My mother] said 'My Dear, do you mean bad in a horrible way.' I answered 'I do.'"

But the real tipping point occurred when Isabel learned that her husband had taken a male friend along to the nursery to see the couple's son, Somey. In the last paragraph of her deposition, its almost illegible handwriting suggesting her agitated state of mind, Isabel explains:

> On the 4th Feby (Monday) my child's nurse told me
> of Lord Henry's having brought up Mr Orrid [sic] to

---

1 Quoted in Niessen 55.
2 Correspondence between Lady Henry and Lady Somers (22 Dec. 1877), quoted in Niessen 50.
3 Cited in Niessen 59.
4 Quoted in H. Montgomery Hyde, *The Cleveland Street Scandal* (New York: Coward, McCann, and Geoghegan, 1976), 43–44.

see my son in his bed & I could not understand the reason for his having done so and on the 5th of February (Tuesday) having found the letter from Orrid to my husband advising him "if necessary to make me remove from Charles Street" I became frightened for my child's safety & sent for him to my mother at the Alexandra Hotel and left him with her & afterwards went there myself to sleep the night having been sent for while undressed by my parents who feared for my safety on account of my husband's rage & violence.

The agitated language makes it unclear whether Henry was aiming to eject Isabel from their home or to abscond with their son. In either case, it is clearly the threat of corrupting, extra-familial influence that spurred Isabel and her advisors into action. Technically, Isabel's decision to take Somey to a local hotel represented a violation of English law stipulating that husbands were the sole legal guardians of their children. Henry immediately filed a lawsuit against his wife for illegally absconding with Somey.

With that action, a nasty domestic dispute entered the public arena. Isabel's deposition recounts the verbal and physical cruelties visited on her by Henry as well as her discovery of his infidelities with other men. Under the 1839 Infants Custody Act (an expansion of the rights of women to have custody of their children), Isabel petitioned to prevent Henry from gaining access to their son until he reached the age of sixteen. The in-camera court judgment was an uneasy Solomonic compromise. "I cannot find fault with her," the judge declared in his judgment, but then added, "I quite enter into the feelings of Lord Somerset.... The child is to remain in the company of the mother but is not to be cut off from his father or the Beaufort family." Referencing the letters between Henry and his male cohorts, the judge acknowledged that they contain "a ... greater warmth of affection, than is to be found generally in other respects among men" but credited this to modern youth's tendency toward extravagant rhetoric.[1] Newspaper accounts invariably took Henry's side. "Those charges have been fully investigated and are found to be entirely groundless," complained the *Hampshire Telegraph and Sussex Chronicle*. "Under these circumstances it is monstrous that they should ever have been made, and Lord Henry is entitled

---

1 Cited in Niessen 63.

to the sympathy of his friends."[1] Other newspapers expressed dismay that a father might be denied contact with an only son and future heir.

Still, the effect of Isabel's testimony on the in-camera court appears to have been powerful, in effect countering Henry's formidable social and political connections, not to mention the dominating prerogatives that Victorian husbands commanded over their households. Henry was granted paternal access to his son, while religious piety restrained Isabel from seeking a divorce. The court judgment declined to disclose the identity of Dalrymple or those of Henry's other incriminated friends. Isabel successfully petitioned for Somey to be a "ward of chancery," ensuring that if in the future she felt concerns about her son's contact with his father or father's family, she could apply to the court to get their visitation rights amended. Henry resigned his position as magistrate and exiled himself to Morocco and then to Florence. In the years after the scandal, Isabel was socially shunned ("stranded in a back-water," in her words) for her accusations concerning a crime, as she put it, "only mentioned in the Bible."[2] Her first biographer noted that the liberal states-man and future prime minister William Gladstone (1809–98), once a family friend, refused to receive her in his home.[3] Isabel continued to oversee her household at Reigate Priory and then at Eastnor Castle, becoming in later years a pioneering social reformer on behalf of inebriate women. Henry appears to have been largely unrepentant about his romantic affairs with men and the dissolution of his marriage. In 1889, the year of *A Marriage Below Zero*'s publication, he published a book of poetic reveries on a former lover (or lovers), whose addressee's sex is cagily disguised through a second-person address. Entitled *Songs of Adieu*, the volume was panned in the *Pall Mall Gazette* by Oscar Wilde (1854–1900), who quipped that its author "has nothing to say and he says it."[4] That same year, Isabel traveled to America as part of her growing pro-temperance campaign.

---

1 *Hampshire Telegraph and Sussex Chronicle*, 9 July 1878.
2 Quoted in Kathleen Fitzpatrick, *Lady Henry Somerset* (Boston: Little Brown, 1923), 125. Isabel evidently is referencing the injunction in the book of Leviticus in the King James Bible that stipulates, "Thou shall not lie with mankind, as with womankind; it *is* abomination" (18:22).
3 Fitzpatrick 127.
4 Oscar Wilde, "The Poet's Corner IX," *Pall Mall Gazette* (30 Mar. 1889).

Given that they are both disconcerted first-person accounts detailing similar experiences, it is irresistible to compare Cohen's novel to Isabel's deposition. Yet it is the differences between the two "cases" that are the most striking. Whereas the errant Arthur of *A Marriage Below Zero* is an awkward, deceitful, and timid husband (Elsie's mother at one point notes his "bashfulness"), in Isabel's telling Henry is an obstreperous, menacing rake, openly contemptuous of his wife, recklessly doting on his male friends, and cognizant of his privileges as a well-connected nobleman. The deposition recounts how Isabel informed Henry that, after he declined to attend the races at Bath with her, a certain Mr. Baldwin told her, "don't you see he does not care for you, you have thrown yourself away." Isabel tells Henry, "Don't you see you must not expose me to have these things said," whereupon, Isabel notes, a "very angry" Henry spoke "very hotly" to her. Whereas Elsie gradually learns how her marriage represents a camouflage for an illicit secret life, Isabel discloses in her deposition that from the outset Henry was cruelly blunt with her, not so much about his precise reasons for having married her but about his lack of feeling for his wife:

> [Henry] told me a few weeks after my marriage that he
> had never been in love with me, but that the marriage
> was so advantageous that he had consulted a friend
> as to the expediency of marrying me—as at the same
> time he intended to become a clergyman—but that the
> opening of marrying me was so advantageous that he
> could not put it aside—that he still continued to resent
> in his mind my having previously refused him—but
> that he thought I suited him very well—to this I an-
> swered nothing.

It is a testament to the commonplace intimacy structuring rela-tions between Victorian men that even when Dalrymple moved into the Somersets' London home and Isabel discovered him breakfasting with Henry in his bedroom, she did not suspect that he was her husband's lover. By Isabel's account, Henry took pleasure in abusing her in the company of his friend:

> On the evening after his arrival I sat up till Henry came
> in, my maid was in my room and found Henry in his
> night shirt & Walter sitting there. I went back to my
> maid & said "What a bore that man is, one cannot have

a word with his Lordship night or day." During the two visits that he paid me at Eastbourne with Dalrymple, Henry's manner & treatment of me were so unkind that in the drawing room before Dalrymple I used to cry.

Two of the most conspicuous differences between Isabel's deposition and *A Marriage Below Zero* lie in the two husbands' differing libidinal appetites and in their attitudes toward their homes. Elsie laments her husband's absence from their Kew Gardens house and eventually discovers that he has kept a flat in London. Henry, on the other hand, threatened to take over his and Isabel's several properties. Unlike Arthur, who is devoted to his lover Jack, Henry evidently entertained several paramours, with whom he appeared at all hours. At the same time, Isabel refers to the system of "total neglect" to which Henry subjected her, writing that in January 1876 "it constantly occurred I did not see him for more than a quarter of an hour in the 24 hours." In answer to her complaint he told her that "many people would be thankful for the liberty you have," to which she answered, "I did not consider that liberty was the only thing a wife wanted." Henry replied, "Of course I should never divorce you—whatever you did, but I should lead you a miserable life." Henry, in Isabel's account, was fierce in asserting his patrilineal rights. "You do not treat me the way a husband should treat his wife," she wrote to him, prompting him to burst into her dressing room with the threat, "I tell you I would murder you if you took my child away from me."

Although one should be cautious about comparing a deposition in an actual legal case to a first-person work of fiction, it nonetheless is tempting, as I have suggested, to relate Isabel's account before the court to Elsie's narrative, particularly given the divergent depictions of the two misbehaving husbands. It is as if we see on display two contradictory models of the married Victorian "sodomite"—in 1878, a hyper-masculine profligate, emboldened by his aristocratic male privileges; in 1889 a timorous prig, whose eyes "were fixed dreamily upon two little fleecy clouds" (p. 91) instead of on his wife on their wedding day. (Their carriage ride afterwards reminds Elsie of a "funeral coach.") With Isabel's story one has a sense that Charlotte Brontë's Jane Eyre had wandered into the world of Samuel Richardson's *Clarissa* (1748). Certainly the two narratives confirm a much-noted divergence between the British aristocracy of which the Somersets were prominent members and the middle-class world of *A Marriage Below Zero*, a divide in which aristocratic mores on matters of sexual conduct largely dispensed with bourgeois proprieties of sexual conduct. Beyond the differences of class separating the real-life Henry and the fictional Arthur, these two-timing husbands speak to the changed legal atmosphere for men of same-sex inclinations. While male homosexual behavior at mid-century was already illegal, with the 1885 Labouchère Amendment same-sex acts were further criminalized. At the same time, the co-existence of these different kinds of sodomy-committing males would seem to confirm Cocks's critique of the first volume of the French theorist Michel Foucault's *The History of Sexuality* (1974). Foucault had contended that, whereas before the nineteenth century sodomy had been a crime to which an individual might succumb, at a certain point the "sodomite" or "homosexual" appeared as a recognizable type. An individual's sodomitical acts, Foucault claimed, came to define his identity in a highly significant way. Against this contention Cocks argues that there may have been varying kinds of sodomites or homosexuals throughout Victorian times, each of whom became more or less visible over time.

That *A Marriage Below Zero* provides a largely sympathetic account of its heroine's troubles surely reflects the sentiments of many British citizens who had learned of Lady Henry's domestic predicament. For although she initially earned the enmity of many of her social circle and her own family, with each sordid revelation of Lord Henry's infidelities with other males much of the public came to view Isabel as a blameless injured party in her husband's marital deceit and personal debauchery. There are a number of reasons that the Somerset case represents a shift in attitudes. First, the court's decision signaled a crack in upper-class privilege. In *The Decline and Fall of the British Aristocracy*, the historian David Cannadine cites the outcome of the Somerset case as indicating how "an aristocratic lineage no longer" provided "immunity" from the consequences of public ignominy.[1] Isabel's triumph in court also heralded an expanded legal authority for women seeking redress for the iniquities of neglectful, violent, or sexually misbehaving husbands. And while it may be tempting to see Isabel's reaction to her husband's behavior as a social purist's revulsion against same-sex vice, her primary objective was to question Henry's authority in the home once she grasped that her marriage was a cover for his illicit (if barely concealed) amorous behavior.

That Disraeli and apparently Queen Victoria had taken an interest in the family's scandal strikingly suggests that matters of criminal and legal import now had turned into matters of intense

---

1   David Cannadine, *The Decline and Fall of the British Aristocracy* (New York: Vintage, 1991), 381.

governmental concern. Of course throughout the nineteenth century, there were numerous sex scandals involving men who were caught having same-sex relations, but with the increased government attention came the possibility of intensified social-purity legislation. At the same time, Isabel's case helped to ensure that when the subject of homosexuality first emerged in popular consciousness in Britain it was invariably entangled with the idea of same-sex eros as a threat to female interests, the family, and the young. Significantly, there was a direct personal link between Isabel and one of the chief architects of what became the most pivotal piece of anti-homosexual legislation of the Victorian era. Her long-time friend, the crusading journalist W.T. Stead (1849–1912), sometimes considered the father of "investigative journalism," was a key figure in creating anti-homosexual legislation. In his series of 1885 articles published in the *Pall Mall Gazette*, "The Maiden Tribute of Modern Babylon," Stead exposed widespread prostitution involving women and girls. Stead's series and his unusual journalistic techniques (he once "kidnapped" a young girl to demonstrate the vulnerability of young women) became an international sensation.

Later that year, Stead's newspaper exposé led to the passage of the 1885 Criminal Amendment Act, which raised the age of consent for girls from thirteen to sixteen, a law that included the Labouchère Amendment, which criminalized acts of "gross indecency"—a category encompassing same-sex erotic behavior between men. The first public test of that amendment was the Cleveland Street scandal, which jolted the Victorian public into mindfulness of a disreputable London counter-world, a homosexual underground in which upper-class males solicited the erotic services of working-class young men, a headline-grabbing *cause célèbre* for social puritans and maverick populist journalists. Although, as the historian Katie Hindmarch-Watson has detailed, the London police for years had been monitoring the suspected "immorality" of boys working for the General Post Office, the focus on the illicit transactional sexual behavior of these young men reached a flashpoint in 1889 with the first of two high-profile British trials that coincided with the publication of *A Marriage Below Zero*.[1]

The Cleveland Street Case erupted on 4 July 1889 when a

---

1 Katie Hindmarch-Watson, "Male Prostitution and the London GPO: Telegraph Boys' 'Immorality' from Nationalization to the Cleveland Street Scandal," *Journal of British Studies* 51.3 (2012): 594–617.

London policeman discovered that a telegraph boy, Charles Swincow, was carrying an inordinate amount of money. Interrogated, the youth confessed to his role at a male brothel at 19 Cleveland Street in London's West End. Soon the police questioned other telegraph boys, ultimately building a case that drew on several government agencies: Scotland Yard, the Director of Public Prosecutions, the Home Secretary, the Attorney General, and even the office of the Prime Minister, Lord Salisbury (Robert Gascoyne-Cecil, 1830–1903), an extraordinary marshaling of public offices that suggested a national emergency. Once again the Somerset family was dragged into a public homosexual scandal. The *North London Press* named Henry Somerset's brother, Arthur Somerset (1851–1926)—the very same brother who once had asked Isabel if she could supply him with evidence of his brother's sexual indiscretions with other men—as a regular at the Cleveland Street brothel. Faced with likely arrest, Arthur fled to Paris in August 1889, just weeks before the indictment of two men for thirteen counts of procuring six boys "to commit diverse acts of gross indecency with another person." Somerset could have read about the ensuing scandal in Paris, where *Le Figaro* reported on the accused men's "tendresse étrange pour les jeunes télégraphistes."[1]

The British, Continental, and American press continued to cover what it dubbed the "West End Case," a trial that generated a tangle of sexual and class anxieties in that the controversy ensnared socially privileged men as well as working-class youths—from gentlemen "of superior bearing and apparently good position" (as one police report explained) to boys and soldiers.[2] The government was hardly vociferous in pursuing the case, probably because of the high social status of the accused but also owing to the low repute of so many of the boy accusers on whose testimony the police were forced to rely. Tellingly, in early October 1889 Arthur Somerset returned to England for his grandmother's funeral at the family estate in Badminton, and although police officers tracked him down there, he was neither arrested nor even detained, although a warrant for "gross indecency" ultimately was issued against him on 12 November 1889. Arthur was never tried or convicted, however, and the resolution of the case for the

---

1 "Strange tenderness for young telegraphists." Quoted in Theo Aronson, *Prince Eddy and the Homosexual Underworld* (London: John Murray, 1994), 146. Somerset ultimately settled in Hyères, France, residing there in penury until his death in 1926.

2 Quoted in Aronson 133.

indicted men—a compromise in which the accused pled guilty to acts of "indecency" but not to the far more serious charges of conspiring and procuring—undoubtedly resulted from pressure from influential individuals, perhaps members of the royal family, one of whose members, Prince Albert Victor (1864–92), Queen Victoria's grandson, was rumored to be a Cleveland Street client. In an impassioned 1889 letter composed in the midst of the scandals, the playwright George Bernard Shaw (1856–1950) decried the Labouchère Amendment, by which, Shaw wrote, "two adult men can be sentenced to twenty years penal servitude for a private act, freely consented to and desired by both, which concerns themselves alone" (Appendix C4, p. 222). Shaw's unpublished letter, intended for *Truth* magazine, a journal edited by Henry Labouchère, represented the lone defense of homosexual practices amidst the frenzy of outrage fomented by the Cleveland Street case. "After 1889," Cocks observes, "it was apparent that the disorderly urban world of the blackmailer and that of the legitimate politician or editor were not that far apart."[1]

Within a year of the publication of *A Marriage Below Zero*, yet another British marital scandal involving accusations of infidelity and sodomy roiled the upper reaches of English society, attracting widespread attention. Frank Russell, 2nd Earl Russell (1865–1931), the grandson of Lord John Russell (1792–1878), the former British prime minister, and the brother of Bertrand Russell (1872–1970), the future philosopher, had married Mabel Scott in 1890. The couple separated within months of their wedding and in 1891 the countess filed for divorce on grounds of cruelty. That claim was denied and the couple, although separated, remained legally married. But in 1894, concerned that her husband would not support her financially while they lived apart, Lady Russell petitioned for restitution of conjugal rights. When she aired charges of immoral behavior in an 1892 interview for the newspaper *The Hawk*, her husband sued her for criminal libel. During the ensuing twelve-day trial, the Scott family claimed that the earl had been sent down from Oxford for "immoral relations" with his math tutor. The charge of sodomy was explicit. In a remarkable development, Earl Russell claimed that his wife's charge of sodomy itself was so heinous an accusation that it constituted actionable marital cruelty. As the judge's summary to the jury explained, Lady Russell had accused her spouse of the "commission of as a serious a crime as a man could

1 Cocks 154.

commit."[1] After less than thirty minutes of deliberation, the jury found against Lady Russell. (At the reading of the verdict, Lady Russell was reported to have "uttered a loud shriek, audible even outside the court."[2])

The Russell–Scott legal imbroglio garnered extensive press coverage in Britain and America. Yet even in the wake of a legal judgment supporting the earl, many rallied in defense of the wife. In an 1891 article entitled "Sodom and Gomorrah Redivivus," the *Los Angeles Herald* described the trial proceedings as disclosing "an indescribable mélange of infamy" that chimed with details of the Cleveland Street case, while six years later, as the couple's legal ordeal entered a new phase, *The New York Times* reported that Lord Russell was "hissed by the crowds" as he left the Old Bailey courthouse.[3] The *Los Angeles Times* noted the arresting parallels between the Russell–Scott case and Cohen's recently published novel: "The developments in the scandalous divorce trial in London between Countess Russell and Earl Russell remind one strongly of an erotic novel published ... within the last year under the title, 'A Marriage Below Zero,'" reported the paper. "Many people who read the book probably thought it was a hypothetical or an impossible case; but the exposure of the inner workings of the Russell household

---

1 Quoted in Ann Sumner Holmes, "'Don't Frighten the Horses': The Russell Divorce Case," *Disorder in the Court: Trials and Sexual Conflict at the Turn of the Century*, ed. George Robb and Nancy Erber (London: Macmillan, 1999), 154.

2 Edward Marjoribanks, *Famous Trials of Marshall Hall* (London: Penguin, 1950), 95.

3 "Sodom and Gomorrah Redivivus," *Los Angeles Herald*, 2 Dec. 1891; "Lady Scott to Be Released," *New York Times*, 15 July 1897. In 1895, the countess filed an action for restitution of her conjugal rights. Again, her appeal failed, after which a series of pamphlets appeared that accused her husband of sodomy, including sexual relations with a cabin boy on the earl's yacht. The countess's mother was charged with libel. At her 1897 trial, she defended her actions by claiming that she had acted "for the sake of a good, sweet, honest and suffering woman." Unimpressed, the presiding judge called the pamphlets "a cruel libel, persistently published" and gave Lady Scott an eight-month jail term. On hearing the sentence in court, her daughter collapsed while screaming insults at her estranged husband. Although still married to Mabel, Earl Russell wedded a woman in Las Vegas, Nevada, prompting a charge and conviction of bigamy in a British court, for which he served a three-month sentence in 1891. (The conviction, however, paved the way for the earl's much-desired divorce from Mabel.)

shows that it is not entirely impossible, even in the *crème de la crème* of English aristocracy." Like all accounts of the trial, the paper was oblique about the specifics of Earl Russell's alleged transgressions, only hazarding that the trial proceedings read like "the last days of Sodom and Gomorrah" (see Appendix A11, p. 205).[1]

Clearly, *A Marriage Below Zero* had been published at the precise moment when the British and (to a lesser degree) the American public's concern over homosexuality as a matrimonial threat had reached an amplified pitch. The 1895 Wilde trials, in which the playwright ultimately was convicted of "gross indecency" under the Labouchère Amendment, further expanded the frontiers of criminal scrutiny of high-profile individuals, raising the curtain on previously ignored or countenanced erotic behavior. Some observers recoiled at what they saw as government overreach. Although his social-purity campaign had helped to win the passage of the Labouchère Amendment and while he now claimed that same-sex desire was "unnatural for seventy-nine out of eighty persons," Stead objected to Wilde's arrest as an excessive intrusion of the government into private affairs.[2] Owing to the Labouchère law, however, the covert pleasures of Clubland and the ideals of the "New Hedonism," the legacy in Victorian times of all-male classical culture, entered a new era where such activities and values were viewed as loathsome forms of "degeneration" and "gross indecency."

A Marriage Below Zero exposes the camouflage provided by marriage to men of same-sex leanings. Although in the opening chapters of the novel Arthur and Jack are depicted as a socially loathed pair, the two nonetheless are allowed into middle-class society despite the open secret of their unseemly relationship. "Why I heard the remark the other day that the only reason Ravener and Dillington went into society at all, was to borrow its cloak of respectability" (p. 80), Letty explains to Elsie in order to dissuade her from pursuing Arthur. When Arthur proposes to Elsie and they wed, the gentlemen who once shunned him suddenly treat him with civility and respect. Arthur himself is pleased by his new-found social acceptance. Elsie describes her baffled surprise at the inordinate pleasure he takes in newspaper accounts of their wedding. Thus *A Marriage Below Zero* calibrates how married women's interests are betrayed even as social appearances are maintained.

---

1 Untitled Article, *Los Angeles Times*, 3 Dec. 1891.

2 W.T. Stead, *Review of Reviews* XI (June 1895): 492.

Evident in the novel's notation of the contrasting physical traits of its male cohort (Elsie describes Arthur as "pretty" in appearance and Jack as repellently brutal) is the suggestion that the novel's male couple reproduces the gendered dynamic of a heterosexual couple, with Jack providing a compensatory hyper-masculinity for the feminine Arthur. Similarly, in Tolstoy's *Anna Karenina* (1877), Anna's lover Vronsky visits his military club and is teased by a transparently homosexual, physically asymmetrical pair, a youthful officer with a "feeble, delicate face" and his "plump," older lover, who wears a bracelet on his wrist (see Appendix B2, p. 209). Together they are known as the "inseparables"—a standard term of the period for a homosexual couple. (In her court deposition, Isabel had used this very phrase to describe her husband and a male friend.) As in Cohen's novel, Tolstoy's men of same-sex preferences are socially despised but tolerated—indeed, the two officers hold the same military rank as Vronsky. Cohen's Jack is also a military man—a captain—a detail that suggests the relative acceptability of men of same-sex preferences within a military environment. The stress in *A Marriage Below Zero* on Jack's primitive appearance evokes, too, a nineteenth-century tendency to construe sexual deviance in physiognomic terms—that is, as detectable through physical traits.

A Marriage Below Zero drew not only on this new "scientific" doctrine and the protocols of melodrama and sensation fiction but also on newspaper reporting in the era of William Randolph Hearst (1863–1951), the influential American publisher whose daily papers thrived on boldface headlines, lurid crime reporting, and populist political causes. As Matthew Rubery has demonstrated, nineteenth-century fictionalists took many of their formal techniques and subject matter from journalistic practice.[1] Cohen's position as an urban daily newspaper critic meant that he was immersed in muckraking, gritty newsroom protocols that fed on scandalous events. Readers were exhorted to believe that beneath the surface of city life a seedy, dangerous stratum of underground activities thrived. Revelations concerning urban vice found an echo in such underground narratives of Victorian sexual immorality as *Teleny* (1893), a work of homosexual pornography possibly authored by Wilde. In *The Sins of the Cities of the Plain* (1881), another pseudonymously penned pornographic work, the narrator "Jack Saul" declares

---

1 Matthew Rubery, *The Invention of Newspapers: Victorian Fiction after the Invention of the News* (New York: Oxford UP, 2009).

that "[t]he extent to which pederasty is carried on in London between gentlemen and young fellows is little dreamed of by the outside public" and noted that "[m]any of us were married; but that makes no difference," adding that "married men are not in request," their popularity, according to Saul, eclipsed by a widespread fondness for soldiers.[1] Throughout the 1890s, the American writer Stephen Crane (1871–1900) contributed a stream of sketches dealing with New York's "low life." Crane authored a naturalistic, best-selling 1893 novella, *Maggie: A Girl of the Streets* (first published in newspaper installments), which focused on a young New York City woman's fall into prostitution in the city's Bowery District. Nor was it only female prostitution that intrigued Crane. According to an anecdote recounted by Crane's biographer John Berryman and based on a document found among the papers of an earlier biographical account of Crane's life by Thomas Beer, in April or May 1894 in New York City Crane was approached by what Berryman describes as a "boy prostitute" who was "diseased" and who was begging for money. He was, as Berryman writes, "painted, with big violet eyes like a Rossetti angel." According to Berryman's account, Crane fed the young man and gave him fifty dollars, thereafter beginning a novel based on the boy entitled *Flowers of Asphalt* that began in a train station and that followed a youth who journeyed to New York City.[2] (No such novel by Crane has ever been located.) But the task of bringing the topical issue of homosexuality to fiction fell to Cohen, who situated his narrative amidst a closely knit British upper-middle class, where rumors have a reputation-destroying force and an aggrieved wife acts as an unwitting agent of a punitive new legal and scientific system.

Nineteenth-Century Sensation Fiction, Same-Sex Desire, and Late-Victorian Feminism

> To Mr. Collins belongs the credit of having introduced into fiction those most mysterious of mysteries, the mysteries which are at our own doors. —Henry James, "Miss Braddon"[3]

---

1 Jack Saul, *The Sins of the Cities of the Plain, or the Recollections of a Mary-Ann, with Short Essays on Sodomy and Tribadism* (New York: Erotica-Biblion Society [1881], 1888), 71, 64.
2 John Berryman, *Stephen Crane* (London: Methuen, 1950), 86–87.
3 *The Nation* 9 Nov. 1865.

As James's remarks on the sensation fiction of the 1860s suggest, in setting their novels in the familiar terrain of the middle-class home, novelists such as Wilkie Collins (1824–89) and Mary Elizabeth Braddon (1837–1915) drew on anxieties about threats to the domestic realm. Furthermore, sensation fiction, like the mode of melodrama to which it is linked, was an especially opportunistic mode of representation in that it exploited topical social concerns. In the face of public scandals, many feminist thinkers worried about the implications of new forms of male–male relations, seeing such developments as evidence of an erotic deviance that ignored or rejected women's marital and social interests. In Sarah Grand's *The Heavenly Twins* (1893), New Women are confronted with enervated, effeminate males, while her novel *The Beth Book* (1897) directly linked syphilis to decadent male authorship. Shaw, in his unpublished letter to *Truth* magazine (see Appendix C4), viewed the rising public panic about homosexuality as a distraction from women's economic concerns and other social issues, noting that the elaborate accusations of the lead prosecutor in the Cleveland Street case "would never have been dreamt of had he advanced charges— socially much more serious—of polluting rivers with factory refuse, or paying women wages that needed to be eked out to subsistence point by prostitution" (p. 225). Not only did the case detract from more pervasive social and economic problems, it helped to forge a rift between two marginalized groups that might have found common ground. In her study *Sexual Anarchy: Gender and Culture at the Fin de Siècle*, Elaine Showalter laments the failure of feminist women and homosexually oriented men of the 1880s and 1890s to forge an ideological alliance. That failure, Showalter suggests, represented a missed opportunity given that these two increasingly self-aware constituencies shared an interest in challenging prevailing gender fixities and outmoded sexual conventions.[1]

In a sense, *A Marriage Below Zero* renders comic some of the sources for that failure. Initially Elsie is delighted to learn that her suitor Arthur treats her seriously and with seeming directness—a welcome departure, she explains, from the supercilious males who initially court her. "Here I was talking with a man with as much ease as though he were one of my beloved feminine school-friends" (p. 71), she declares, in one of many declarations that come to assume ironic—and somewhat comic—meaning. There are early warnings: at social gatherings she notices that

---

1 Elaine Showalter, *Sexual Anarchy: Gender and Culture at the Fin de Siècle* (New York: Viking, 1990).

Arthur "seemed to be eagerly searching for some one in the crowd, and at last I saw his eyes rest upon his unprepossessing friend" (p. 71). Arthur himself acknowledges his unusual bond. "You have heard of Damon and Pythias," he tells her, and seeing her blush, proclaims, "I don't mind ... Make all the fun of us you like" (p. 71). Once married and ensconced in their Kew Gardens home, Elsie comes to see that her husband's unaffected behavior indicates that he has no physical feelings for her—that his attraction to her, to draw out the obvious implications of the novel's title, represents a negative desire, and thus their bond itself is "a marriage below zero" (a phrase that never appears in the novel). Whereas in an early and even mid-Victorian context male effeminacy had yet to accrue associations of same-sex desire, we can see in Elsie's misguided attraction to the effeminate Arthur a changed sense of what effeminate behavior in men indicates. What might have registered as an egalitarian ideal—a New Man comfortable in the Victorian domestic sphere and conversant with women—now poses perils to women and to the home over which females traditionally had so much shaping influence.

Elsie's proto-feminist alarm over her husband's erotic preferences is reflected in the writing of a number of advanced women thinkers of the era. Many feminist writers and their allies were troubled by what they viewed as the self-preening, anti-female postures of the male-dominated Aesthetic and Decadent movements. That these entwined movements' endorsement of Hellenic ideals conceived of women as inferior to men is evident in Charles Kains Jackson's "The New Chivalry" (see Appendix C6), which explicitly insisted on the inferior intelligence of women. An implied effeminacy on the part of some male aesthetes also disturbed a number of feminist advocates, although, significantly, before the public disclosures of the Wilde trials such writers seldom registered a direct connection between effeminacy and homosexuality. The South African writer Olive Schreiner objected to aesthetically inclined men as unnaturally self-indulgent: "The curled darling, scented and languid, with his drawl, his delicate apparel, his devotion to the rarity and variety of his viands whose severest labour is the search after pleasure," she noted in "The Woman Question" (1899), first published in *Cosmopolitan Magazine* (see Appendix D4, p. 257). Other progressive writers detected a similarly repellant effeminacy in certain "New Men." As Eleanor Marx and Edward Aveling wrote in their 1886 essay "The Woman Question," "The effeminate man and the masculine woman are two types from which even the average person recoils with perfectly natural horror of the unnatural."[1]

In the early years of the twentieth century, the "unnatural" disorder of same-sex desire—what Lady Somerset had described as a crime "only mentioned in the Bible"—would earn a new terminology. For the socialist visionary Edward Carpenter (1844–1929), the preferred terms were "homogenic love" and the "intermediate sex," new-fangled, non-judgmental nomenclature. In his 1897 essay "The Homogenic Attachment," Carpenter insisted that primitive cultures offered exemplary cases of male–male erotics (see Appendix C7). In John Addington Symonds's *A Problem in Greek Ethics*, the renowned critic sought to exalt same-sex eros by tracing it to Hellenic civilization (see Appendix C2). More enduringly, however, "homosexuality" and the "homosexual" emerged as a common terminology, the latter having first appeared in an English-language text in Charles Gilbert Chaddock's 1892 translation of Richard Krafft-Ebing's *Psychopathia Sexualis*.

By century's end, concern over sodomitical men entering marriage prompted *Reynolds's Newspaper* to publish a front-page article in 1895 entitled "Sex-Mania," in which the newspaper fulminated against the "most conspicuous devotees of unnatural offenses"—namely, "persons already married. The inference is obvious. They have led their unloved ... spouses to the altar from motives other than affection—position, money, influence. They have simply gone into the marriage mart and bought a female for commercial reasons" (see Appendix D3, p. 254). In such a way did the aims of the late-Victorian social-purity movement dovetail with a proto-feminist preoccupation with the dangers of deviant male sexuality, a notion that would endure into the next century. "There is an undeniable tendency in many homosexuals to look upon woman as an inferior," wrote Dora Marsden in the feminist journal *The New Freewoman* in 1913. "It is hardly to be presumed, then, that the men who entertain this instinctive aversion to women are absolutely uninfluenced by it when summoned by women to support their demand for independence."[2] Marsden conflates male homosexuality with an "instinctive" aversion to women—and, by implication, to the cause of women.

---

1 Eleanor Marx and Edward Aveling, "The Woman Question" (1886), cited in Showalter 175.
2 Dora Marsden, *The New Freewoman* 1 Sept. 1913: 15, cited in Showalter 175.

Alan Dale: A British Émigré Writer in the New York Theater

Born on 14 May 1861 in Birmingham, England, into a middle-class Anglo-Jewish family, the future drama critic Alfred J. Cohen was educated in Birmingham at King Edward's School, whose illustrious alumni included the Victorian scientific polymath Francis Galton (1822–1911) and the Pre-Raphaelite painter Edward Burne-Jones (1833–98). Although he passed the entrance exams that allowed him to attend Cambridge, there is no indication that Cohen ever attended university. According to the *Jewish Encyclopedia*, Cohen spent three years after secondary school studying the "dramatic arts" in Paris.[1] In the early 1880s he worked as a stenographer for Leander Richardson, a London-based American journalist for the *New York Dramatic Times*. Evidently impressed with his young assistant, Richardson brought Cohen to America in 1887. Cohen arrived in New York City when there was considerable traffic between the English stage and its American counterpart. However, there were obstacles to the British newcomer's ascent. Cohen's pseudonym "Alan Dale" was in all likelihood an attempt to disguise his Jewish background at a time when anti-Semitic sentiment might have been an impediment to a career as a newspaperman. Yet even with his pseudonym the increasingly influential critic sometimes found himself baited in the press for his ethnicity.[2]

For two decades Cohen flourished as a theater reviewer, a tenure that began at Joseph Pulitzer's (1847–1911) *Evening World*, which Cohen joined in 1887, a position he held until 1895. In his characteristically acquisitive fashion, William Randolph Hearst poached Cohen from Pulitzer's stable for Hearst's *New York Journal*. Here Cohen earned a formidable reputation as a sharp-tongued observer of the "Great White Way," a term for the Broadway theater district that Cohen helped to make popular, and as an innovator of what we would understand today as the "celebrity profile," interviewing, among others, Ellen Terry (1847–1928),

---

1 Cyrus Adler and Edgar Mels, "Cohen, Alfred J.," *The Jewish Encyclopedia* (New York: Funk and Wagnalls, 1906), http://www.jewishencyclopedia.com/articles/4460-cohen-alfred-j.

2 In the 16 May 1914 *Morning Telegraph*, for example, the journalist Deborah Duvetyne claimed that Alan Dale had "Mosaic lips" and that he had altered his birth name because it is "more euphonious than Cohen, the patronymic name of his fathers," a physiognomic insinuation magnified in an accompanying cartoon of Cohen as short, bearded, and hook-nosed.

Lillie Langtry (1853–1929), and Ida Rubinstein (1883–1960). "When he takes pen in hand the playhouses throughout the land tremble upon their foundations and the faces of actors burn white with fear," commented the *Dramatic Mirror*, while *Who's Who in the Theatre* noted that "[h]is criticisms probably carried more weight than any others in New York."[1] Cohen himself made one contribution to the American stage with a play that, like *A Marriage Below Zero*, dealt with scandalous subject matter. In 1918, his *The Madonna of the Future*, a comedy on out-of-wedlock childbirth, opened at New York's Broadhurst Theater. *The New York Times* hailed its "audacious ideas and brilliant lines," comparing its author to Wilde and Shaw, but hazarded that Alan Dale "overwhelmed his idea and situation in a flood of repartee and paradox."[2] The play closed after several weeks amid accusations of indecency.[3] There is no evidence that Cohen himself had any personal connection to the underground homosexual coteries of London and New York. Married to Carrie L. Frost and the father of one daughter, Margaret, Cohen died after a long illness at the age of 67 in May 1928, while traveling on a train from Plymouth to Birmingham on one of his frequent visits to his native country.

ALAN DALE DIES SUDDENLY; WON FAME AS CRITIC
Chicago Daily Tribune (1872-1963); May 22, 1928; ProQuest Historical Newspapers Chicago Tribune (1849 - 1986)
pg. 32

ALAN DALE DIES SUDDENLY; WON FAME AS CRITIC

(Picture on back page.)

New York. May 21.—(AP)—Alan Dale, dramatic critic for the New York American, died suddenly tonight on a railway train between Plymouth and Birmingham, England, word received here by relatives announced. He sailed 10 days ago for a vacation abroad.

Dale, whose real name was Alfred J. Cohen, was born in Birmingham, England, May 14, 1861.

Educated in English schools, he engaged in journalism in New York as dramatic critic for the Evening World from 1887 to 1895, and in the same capacity for the New York Journal from 1895 to 1915. Subsequently he became dramatic critic for the New York American. He was the author of several novels and books of criticism and of the play "The Madonna of the Future," produced in 1918.

[W. H. Vander Weyde Photo.]
NOTED CRITIC DIES.
Alan Dale (Alfred J. Cohen) stricken on English railway train. *(Story on page 32.)*

Reproduced with permission of the copyright owner. Further reproduction prohibited without permission.

1 Quoted in *The Oxford Companion to the American Theater*, ed. Gerald Bordman (Oxford: Oxford UP, 1984), 114–15.
2 "Emily Stevens as Cubistic Madonna," *New York Times* 28 Jan. 1918.
3 "Police Complain of 'Madonna of the Future,'" *New York Times* 14 Mar. 1918.

"A Storm of 'Relentless Fury'": The Critical Reception of *A Marriage Below Zero*

> The sins of Sodom and Gomorrah have been used for the first time by the novelist, and the result is horrible, but readable. —From a review of *A Marriage Below Zero, Sacramento Daily Record-Union*[1]

That Cohen chose the publishing house of G.W. Dillingham for the publication of his novel may have stemmed from the speed with which he hoped to produce and disseminate a novel whose topicality made it a commercially smart venture. Yet with its price of fifty cents, *A Marriage Below Zero* was hardly inexpensive. The novel was widely reviewed and promoted, with an advertisement in the *St. Paul Daily Globe* promoting the book as by "one of the most popular authors."[2] No doubt because Cohen worked for a Pulitzer newspaper, the novel received three positive notices in the Pulitzer-owned *New York World*, where it was praised for its intensely topical interest and real-world correspondences (see Appendices A1–A3). "Stranger unions have been known in this city than that treated in 'A Marriage Below Zero,' but it is reserved for the novelist to tell what perhaps the writer of facts would not dare to do," observed one of these reviews. "That a careful search of the divorce records would reveal many cases like the peculiar story told in this novel is an undoubted fact. Whether it would be necessary or even desirable to make them known is questionable" (p. 193). Elsewhere the *New York World* praised Cohen for the "greatest delicacy" (p. 196) with which he handled his material. The notice in the *Sacramento Daily Record-Union* cannily grasped the novel's pioneering treatment of male same-sex erotics—surely one reason that the book was "selling like hotcakes" (see Appendix A5, p. 197). The *New York Daily Graphic* declared the novel "extremely moral" in dealing with its "curious" theme and quoted at length from the scene in which Elsie walked in on her husband and Jack (see Appendix A4, p. 197). In an advertisement, G.W. Dillingham cited a *Cincinnati Enquirer* notice that deemed the novel a "very bright and pleasing" work that undertook in a "delightful way" the "social evil question." I have been unable to locate this review, although that newspaper elsewhere did cite Cohen's novel in an article on cases of same-sex love (see Appendix A10).

---

1 See Appendix A5.
2 Advertisement for Dickinson's Books, *St. Paul Daily Globe* 21 Mar. 1890.

These reviews aside, the critical reception was damning. The most outraged notice appeared in *Belford's Magazine*, which decried the "monstrous forms of human vice" depicted in the novel, complaining that "[t]here are some deformities with which art cannot deal, and some social possibilities which are beyond the province of fiction and belong only to the surgeon's table and the dissecting knife." The *Belford's* reviewer took comfort in the idea that "[f]ortunately, the majority of persons, masculine and feminine, who may read this book will not comprehend its meaning"—a curious judgment given the wholly unambiguous nature of the novel's theme (see Appendix A6, p. 197). More sophisticated reviewers questioned the book's originality, with a review in the *Los Angeles Times* accusing Cohen of penning a "clumsy and vulgar paraphrase of that nasty French novel" by Adolphe Belot (1829–90), a work also cited in the *New York World* review of 25 March 1889 (see Appendices A3 and A7, p. 198). Belot's novel, *Mademoiselle Giraud, My Wife* (published in France in 1869 and translated into English in 1891) was a first-person fictional account of a young man's discovery that his wife had a female lover. Thanks to Cohen's "infamous" novel, the *Los Angeles Times* opined, "novelists of passion" were now "under a cloud." Lest readers not guess that the novel was pseudonymously written, the paper informed them that its "author calls himself Allan [sic] Dale but is really a recently imported London Jew named Cohn [sic]" (see Appendix A7, p. 198).

In a preface to his subsequent novel *An Eerie He and She* (1889), Cohen bemoaned the "storm that burst with relentless fury over my unprotected head" on the publication of *A Marriage Below Zero* (see Appendix C8, p. 247), a point he reiterated in the introduction to his series of sketches of famous actresses, *Familiar Chats with Queens of the Stage* (1890), where he observed that his novel had been "ruthlessly savaged by most of the literary critics."[1] Yet in advertising *An Eerie He and She*, G.W. Dillingham promoted the book as "By the author of 'A Marriage Below Zero,'" claiming that the earlier novel "was selling faster today than at any time since its publication."[2] In subsequent years critics praised the book. In 1907 the journal *Current Literature* referred to

---

1 Alan Dale, *Familiar Chats with Queens of the Stage* (New York: G.W. Dillingham, 1890), 35.
2 *The American Bookseller* 17 Sept. 1889: 413.

the "talented author of 'A Marriage Below Zero.'"[1] Nor did Cohen's career as a novelist and theater critic appear to suffer from his authorship of *A Marriage Below Zero*. The *Savannah Courier* speculated that the novel had made its author nearly $5,000—an extraordinary sum at the time—and concluded that the "writers of the Zola style of literature received more than their reward," a peevish suggestion that naturalistic writers such as the French novelist Émile Zola (1840–1902) and, by implication, Alan Dale had been overcompensated financially for their fictional focus on shocking social problems.[2] There was talk in the press of an adaptation for the stage, an irresistible possibility for a man as saturated in the theater as Cohen but an unlikely development given that New York theatrical productions were far more vulnerable to public outcries and local censorship than works of fiction.[3]

In the new century, critics disparaged Cohen's novel as aesthetically impoverished and as a setback in the enlightened depiction of same-sex passion. In a 1906 letter cataloguing various key texts dealing with homosexuality, the American writer Edward Prime-Stevenson (1858–1942) anathematized Cohen's work as a "feeble and crude story with a vulgar title,"[4] a judgment he reiterated two years later in his study *The Intersexes* (1908), where he described the novel as "lacking in any artistic development" (and characterized Arthur in sexological terms as a "uranian, apparently a passivist, who cannot shake off his

---

1 "The Moral Trend of the American Drama," *Current Literature* (Nov. 1907): 551.

2 "Literary Fellows," *Savannah Courier* 19 Sept. 1889: 4. This linking of Zola to Alan Dale is curious given that *A Marriage Below Zero*, with its concentration on a middle-class drawing-room milieu, would seem to have little in common with Zola's fiction, with its absorption in the gritty social conditions of prostitutes, laborers, and other working-class characters.

3 Not until the future film comedienne Mae West's 1927 play "The Drag: A Homosexual Comedy in Three Acts" would the subject of male homosexuality be addressed on the New York stage. West's play ran for several weeks before closing amid controversy.

4 Letter to Paul Elmore Moore (10 Mar. 1906), quoted in Edward Prime-Stevenson, *Imre*, ed. James J. Gifford (Peterborough, ON: Broadview P, 2003), 137–38.

sexual bondage to an older and coarser man").[1] Stevenson's dismissal undoubtedly stemmed from his pro-homosexual allegiances. His novel *Imre* (1906), set in Budapest and described by its author as a "little psychological romance" focusing on two men, was one of the first novels dealing with homoerotic relations to allow its male couple a happy ending, a striking contrast to the deadly denouement of *A Marriage Below Zero*, a resolution in the plot that clearly offended Stevenson. For most influentially, Cohen's novel established a longstanding tradition in which works of fiction addressing romantic and sexual relations between men inevitably ended in murder, suicide, or another form of death. This doleful pattern lasted well into the twentieth century with such notable novels as *The City and the Pillar* (1948), by Gore Vidal (1925–2012), and into the twenty-first century in the afterlife of fictional works such as Annie Proulx's (1935–) short story, "Brokeback Mountain" (1997), which was adapted for film in 2005.

From Fictions of Classical Devotion to Cautionary Tales of Vice

Cohen's approach to the subject of male same-sex eros was only one of numerous ways in which erotic and emotional affiliations between men were represented in late-nineteenth-century writing. Other literary genres taking up same-sex eros were far more elliptical, as they explored same-sex erotics in an unconsciously structured, coded, or semi-coded fashion. There was, for example, the male adventure tale in which men bonded in settings in which women were either necessarily absent or peripheral to the story. That literary sub-genre included works such as Sir Henry Hall Caine's novel *The Deemster* (1887), which focused on a "brotherly passion for which language has yet no name,"[2] and Conrad's *Heart of Darkness* (1899), in which several women have marginal status in a narrative dominated by the male duo of Marlow and Kurtz. Richard Burton's suggestion in the 1895 "Terminal Note" to his translation of *The Book of a Thousand Nights and One Night*, widely known today as

---

1 Edward Prime-Stevenson, *The Intersexes: A History of Simulsexualism as a Problem of Social Life* (privately printed, 1908), 383.
2 Sir Henry Hall Caine, *The Deemster* (Auckland: Floating P, 2014), 98.

The Arabian Nights, that "pederasty" was pervasive in what he deemed the "Sotadic Zone" (a reference to the Greek-Egyptian poet Sotades, author of homoerotic poetry), while perhaps laughably anecdotal, presented a relatively modern conception of same-sex desire as ulturally and geographically relative: "Within the Sotadic Zone the Vice is popular and endemic, held at the worst to be a mere peccadillo," Burton observed, "whilst the races to the north and south of the limits here defined practise it only sporadically amid the opprobrium of their fellows who, as a rule, are physically incapable of performing the operation and look upon it with the liveliest disgust" (see Appendix C3, p. 220).

Other turn-of-the century writers looked to Classical and Renaissance times in order to affirm more positively the sexual relations between males. No two figures were more important in articulating, albeit in highly coded terms, the exalted nature of male–male affection in Classical and Renaissance terms than John Addington Symonds and Walter Pater (1839–94). Partly as a mode of defense in the wake of the new criminal and medical establishment, the Aestheticist and Decadent movements associated with these writers had come to propagate oblique, idealized conceptions of homoerotic life and sexual identity, sometimes expressed as a belief in a visionary elevated realm of male friendship and beauty, as in Kains Jackson's notion of a "New Chivalry." Pater set the tone for a richly archaic understanding of exalted homosocial experience in his novel *Marius the Epicurean* (1885), in which the eponymous Roman hero forges friendships with other male youths. Pater's "Conclusion" to his study *The Renaissance* (1873) became notorious for its seeming endorsement of hedonistic pleasure and pure sensation, especially scandalous given that Pater taught suggestible male students in his role as a professor at Oxford (see Appendix C1). This backward-looking credo and euphemistic nomenclature, redolent of superior Classical and Renaissance cultures, rubbed against the new—and ultimately widely successful—medical and legal terminology, evident in the prevalence in Robert Louis Stevenson's novella *Strange Case of Dr. Jekyll and Mr. Hyde* (1886) of doctors and lawyers, all bachelor members of "Clubland" in a supernatural tale of its main protagonist's double life.

In 1923, Virginia Woolf, reviewing Fitzpatrick's biography of Lady Henry in the *Times Literary Supplement*, concluded that the sources of Isabel's marital dilemma were multiple but not merely personal:

The Victorian age was to blame; her mother was to blame; Lord Henry was to blame; even the saintly Mr. Watts was forced by fate to take part in the general conspiracy against her.... Between them each natural desire of a lively and courageous nature was stunted, until we feel that the old Chinese custom of fitting the foot to the shoe was charitable compared with the mid-Victorian practice of fitting the woman to the system.[1]

For Woolf, Lady Henry's domestic crisis had to be construed through the trenchant lens of feminist critique, for the scandal for her was paradigmatically related to a Victorian "system" involving not only duplicitous husbands and deficient matriarchs but also "saintly" and complicit confidantes. Interestingly, in her review Woolf left unmentioned her own relation to Lady Henry (Isabel was Woolf's first cousin once removed and until Isabel's death a Bloomsbury neighbor). Woolf was equally oblique about the specifics of the Somerset scandal, referring to the "famous catastrophe" befalling Lady Henry and noting that Gladstone had refused to invite her to his home because of the nature of her accusations against her husband, the so-called crime "that was only mentioned in the Bible." It is unlikely that Woolf would have read *A Marriage Below Zero*, although one can speculate that as an innovator of literary modernism, with its detailed calibration of hidden, interior subjective states, she would have recoiled from the novel's melodramatic confrontations and emotional excesses. For based on Woolf's silky obliquity in leaving inexplicit the dire circumstances that ensnared Isabel, it is clear that modernist evasions, eschewing outrageous plots, served to cloak Victorian sensations—even ones as "hot" as "marriages below zero."

---

1 Virginia Woolf, "The Chinese Shoe," in *The Essays of Virginia Woolf: Volume III, 1919–1924*, ed. Andrew McNeillie (New York: Harcourt Brace Jovanovich, 1989), 390.

Same-Sex Scandal in Nineteenth-Century Britain: A Brief Chronology

Scandals involving homosexual male activity occurred with some frequency in nineteenth-century Britain, whereas there were few such cases in the United States, although case law in America generally followed English legal custom. Much less frequent were scandals involving same-sex activity involving women.

1811   In Scòtland, the House of Lords declares, regarding a charge of cunnilingus between two women, that "the crime here alleged has no existence."

1818   British law allowing for men convicted of sodomy to be put in a public pillory is overturned.

1822   Percy Jocelyn, the Bishop of Clogher, is arrested after being caught with a guardsman in the White Lion Tavern in the Haymarket.

1825   Arrest of twenty-five men in an upstairs room at the Barley Mow Tavern in the Strand, seven of whom are convicted of indecent assault.

1828   A series of decisions in the British Parliament limited the definition of the offense of sodomy, imposing a greater burden of proof on the prosecution, but was offset by a new version of the statute enacted as part of the reform of the criminal law by Sir Robert Peel, prescribing that penetration alone (without emission of seed) sufficed to establish the crime. In parliamentary debate the word "buggery" is foresworn in favor of what Sir Robert Peel terms "the crime *inter Christianos non nominandum*" (Latin: the crime not to be named among Christians).

1829   Spike in police arrests for homosexual activity in the City of London in the area between St. Paul's, Bishopsgate, the Thames, and Finsbury Square.

1835   27 November: London execution of James Pratt and John Smith, the last men in England executed for sodomy, after they were witnessed by a landlord and his wife having sex in another man's lodgings. The novelist

Charles Dickens visited the two men at Newgate Prison while they were awaiting sentencing, a visit he wrote about in "A Visit to Newgate" (1836), where he noted that the "nature of [their] offence rendered it necessary to separate them, even from their companions in guilt." An appeal was denied. "It is the only crime where there is no injury done to any individual and in consequence it requires a very small expense to commit it in so private a manner and to take such precautions as shall render conviction impossible," declared the Home Secretary, Lord John Russell, in asking that the men be spared death. "It is also the only capital crime that is committed by rich men but owing to the circumstances I have mentioned they are never convicted."

1836   Cessation of death penalty for buggery, a crime that included homosexual acts.

1841   Lord John Russell attempts to remove the term "unnatural offenses" from a list of capital crimes but he is forced to withdraw his proposal due to lack of support in Parliament.

1850   The newspaper *The Yokel's Preceptor* writes of widespread homosexuality in the theatrical profession.

1861   The death penalty for "buggery" (by which was meant anal intercourse) is formally abolished in England and Wales.

1869   The Austrian human rights activist Karl-Maria Kertbeny coins the terms "homosexual" (to replace terms such as "sodomite" and "pederast") and "heterosexual," nomenclature that eventually finds widespread usage in Britain and America.

1870   Arrest of Ernest Boulton and Frederick Park, also known as Fanny and Stella, for "conspiring and inciting persons to commit an unnatural offense," a reference to their habit of dressing in female attire. In a trial that fascinated the British public, they are acquitted for lack of evidence.

1877   Lady Isabel Somerset petitions the court for separation from her husband and sole custody of her son owing to her discovery that her husband, Henry, a prominent member of the British government, has a series of male lovers. The court decides in her favor while allowing her husband parental visitation rights.

1881	Publication of 250 privately printed copies of *The Sins of the Cities of the Plain; or the Recollections of a Mary-Ann*, by "Jack Saul," the purported memoirs of a male prostitute in England, who observes that "the extent to which pederasty is carried on in London between gentlemen and young fellows is little dreamed of by the outside public."
1885	Passage of the Labouchère Amendment by the British Parliament, which criminalizes "acts of gross indecency" between men.
1889–90	Arrest and prosecution of several men in the Cleveland Street case, which targeted a West End London male brothel and its well-heeled male clientele.
1889	Publication of *The Criminal* by Havelock Ellis, a noted sexual theorist who argued that criminality is not a trait in all individuals but is the product of a certain type of individual, an idea that implied a congenital basis for homosexuality.
1890	Publication of Oscar Wilde's novel *The Picture of Dorian Gray* in America in the Philadelphia-based magazine *Lippincott's*, a work that receives some positive reviews in America but is received with largely hostile reviews when published a year later in Britain.
1891	Mabel Scott unsuccessfully sues her husband for cruelty, claiming that her husband, Earl Russell, had been sent down from Oxford for an affair with his math tutor.
	In a poem, Oscar Wilde's lover Alfred Lord Douglas refers to "the love that dare not speak its name" to describe male same-sex desire.
1895	Oscar Wilde convicted of "gross indecency" and sentenced to hard labor at Reading Gaol.
1905	German-language publication of Sigmund Freud's *Three Essays on the Theory of Sexuality*, which argued that "perversions" and "sexual aberrations" were common features of human sexuality, an argument that proved widely influential as a fundamental psychoanalytic concept.

Alfred J. Cohen: A Brief Chronology

1861	14 May: Born in Birmingham, England.
1870–77	Attends King Edward's School, Birmingham.
1880s	Works as a stenographer for Leander Richardson, London-based journalist for the *New York Dramatic Times*.
1885	Publishes *Jonathan's Home* in London.
1886–87	Lives in Paris.
1887	Arrives in America and soon joins the staff of the *New York Evening World*.
1889	Publishes *A Marriage Below Zero* in America; publishes *An Eerie He and She*.
1890	Publishes *Familiar Chats with Queens of the Stage* and *An Old Maid Kindled*.
1891	Publishes *Miss Innocence*.
1892	Publishes *Conscience on Ice*.
1893	Publishes *My Footlight Husband*.
1894	Publishes *A Moral Busybody*.
1895	Becomes the theater critic at the Hearst-owned *New York World Journal* (in 1901 renamed the *New York American*).
1899	Publishes *His Own Image*.
1902	Publishes *A Girl Who Wrote*.
1914	May: Leaves his position as theater critic at the *New York World Journal*.
1918	Cohen's play *The Madonna of the Future* opens at New York's Broadhurst Theater on Broadway and runs for several weeks.
1928	21 May: Dies on train en route from Plymouth to Birmingham, England.

A Note on the Text

This edition of *A Marriage Below Zero* reproduces the original 1889 edition of the novel published by G.W. Dillingham Publishers in New York.

A MARRIAGE BELOW ZERO

I seek no sympathies, nor need;
The thorns which I have reaped are of the tree
I planted,—they have torn me,—and I bleed:
I should have known what fruit would spring from such
   a seed. —Byron[1]

Soft love, spontaneous tree, its parted root
Must from two hearts with equal vigour shoot;
While each delighted and delighting gives
The pleasing ecstasy which each receives:
Cherish'd with hope, and fed with joy it grows;
Its cheerful buds their opening bloom disclose,
And round the happy soil diffusive odour flows.
If angry fate that mutual care denies,
The fading plant bewails its due supplies;
Wild with despair, or sick with grief, it dies. —Prior[2]

INTRODUCTION

I suppose I am rather frivolous. I believe in the voice of the majority, to a certain extent; and it has announced my giddiness and superficiality so frequently, that there is nothing left for me to do but succumb to this view as pleasantly as possible. I never listen to the minority in any of the social questions with which I

---

1 From *Childe Harold's Pilgrimage* (IV.10) by George Gordon, Lord Byron (1788–1824), English Romantic poet. The poem launched Byron's career and inaugurated the figure of the Byronic hero. Although it was known only to a small coterie during his lifetime, Byron had numerous affairs with both men and women. The poet had originally written a stanza for inclusion in *Childe Harold* that reflected on the fate of William Beckford (1760–1844). Like Byron, Beckford was a wealthy, celebrated writer with aristocratic connections. He had been ostracized by English society for many years because of his rumored homosexuality, a fate referenced in Byron's evocation "Gainst Nature's voice seduced to deed accurst," a line cut from *Childe Harold*. Cohen may have been alluding to Byron's sexuality by including this quotation at the beginning of his novel—or he may simply have been drawing on the speaker's self-punishing words as a way to invoke his heroine's woeful decision to marry Arthur Ravener.
2 From the poem "Solomon on the Vanity of the World" (1718) by Matthew Prior (1664–1721), English poet and diplomat.

am confronted. It would therefore be inconsistent to pay much attention to its estimate of myself.

Butterfly-like I flutter about in society, living in the all-sufficient present, reckless of the future, and absolutely declining to recollect the past.

I have a mother who loves me a great deal more than she did some time ago, when I seemed to tacitly insist that she should grow old decently and gracefully. Now I do my best to assist her in her vigorous struggle for perpetual youth, and she is thankful to me; she appreciates my efforts. Ah! it is good to be appreciated, sometimes.

"I really don't know what I should do without you, Elsie," she says, in an occasional outburst of good nature. "You are such a comfort to me; you make me feel as though I were your sister. Sometimes I think I am."

So you see that her affection for me is by no means maternal. I call her "mother" from force of habit, though, accustomed as I am to the word, it often sounds rather ludicrous in my ears.

Conventionality forbids me to use her Christian name. People have always had pronounced prejudices in favor of what they call filial respect, and a quarrel with conventionality is generally fatal, as I have learned. So we trot around to receptions, and kettledrums,[1] and dinners and dances as mother and daughter. I would willingly pass for the former if it were possible to do so, but it is out of the question, unfortunately for dear mamma.

I shall never leave my mother. We shall continue our trot about the social world, until one of us is obliged to give in. I hope I shall be the first to fall, because, like the little boy in the song, I could not play alone. I am convinced that my mother also hopes that she will be the bereaved one. She enjoys life so much, that I cannot blame her.

My demise would necessitate her withdrawal from society for a year or so, but Madame Pauline, in Regent Street, really furnishes such delightful mourning, that, as Mrs. Snooksley Smith said to me the other day: "it is positively a pleasant change to wear it." Mr. Snooksley Smith had been gathered to his fathers a few months previously, so that I know she spoke from experience, poor lonely widow.

I wear a wedding ring. It is concealed beneath a scintillating

---

1 An afternoon tea party. In Victorian England, large gatherings were often described as "drums" and the kettledrum associated the afternoon gathering with the tea kettle.

cluster of diamonds which I have purposely placed on the third finger of my left hand, but it is there. I hate it. It is in the way. If I thought I should ever marry again, I would make it a point of insisting that the lucky man should despise those little golden badges as much as I do.

I must wear mine until I die, I suppose. You see everybody knows that I am Mrs. Ravener; all my friends seem to take an ill-natured delight in emphatically using my married name. I may be as frivolous as I choose, as recklessly flippant as I possibly can, but my wedding ring must remain. It does not upbraid me for my conduct. Not a bit of it. I have a perfect right to do everything in my power to forget it. I would fling my ring to the bottom of the Thames, and still maintain my unquestioned right to do so, but,—ah! there is always one of those detestable little conjunctions in the way.

I hope I am making you wonder what all this means, dear reader, because I intend tearing myself away from mamma for a little and devoting some time to you. You say you would not like to inconvenience mamma? Oh, you need not hesitate. I shall tell her that I need a little rest, and shall interpret her surprised "What nonsense, Elsie!" into a motherly injunction to take it. She is still a little afraid of me, you see. She remembers that, like Mr. Bunthorne,[1] I am very terrible when I am thwarted. Though nothing in my behavior nowadays indicates that I have the faintest suspicion of a will of my own, mamma knows better. Perhaps in the solitude of her chamber she wishes that dear Elsie were the sweet little gushing nonentity she appears to be. In time I may make her forget that I have ever been anything else. Perhaps as she grows old (if she ever does) her memory may be dulled. It is just possible that she may pass away in the fond conviction that her only daughter has never crossed her will. Who shall say that I am not charitable?

I am going to write the story of my married life. I intend to

---

1 Bunthorne is a central character in *Patience; or, Bunthorne's Bride*, a comic operetta by Arthur Sullivan (1842–1900) and W.S. Gilbert (1836–1911), which opened in April 1881 in London. Through the character of the poet Bunthorne, the wildly popular operetta satirizes the aesthetic movement of the 1870s and 1880s in England. The aesthetic movement emphasized aesthetics over moral, social, and scientific themes in literature and art. It has been argued that the character of Bunthorne was modeled on the writer and playwright Oscar Wilde (1854–1900), who in 1895 was infamously accused of "gross indecency" for homosexual relations.

open old wounds by confession which, it is popularly said, is good for the soul. The task may do me good. A little taste of bitter recollection can but enhance the value of the sweet vapidity of my present life. I can pause while I am writing, if I feel at all overwhelmed by the flood of reminiscence, which will pour in upon me by the gates which I voluntarily open, to congratulate myself that it is all over forever.

Like the little girl who used to get out of her nice warm bed, and make her sister call out, "There are mice on the floor," so that she might have the pleasure of rushing back again and huddling up under the clothes in an ecstacy of comfort, I will recall the past, in order that I may enjoy the present all the more.

Perhaps that present palls upon me sometimes, though no one guesses it, and I hardly suspect it myself. Possibly it needs all the contrast with the past that I can give it, to render it endurable. I say "possibly" you know. I wish to be consistently frivolous.

You will be able to remember these remarks when you have read the record of the events which I am about to chronicle, and when you close the book, say with a sigh of relief: "Well, in spite of all, she is living happily ever afterwards."

CHAPTER I.

No, I shall not weary you with a long account of my childhood, and all that sort of thing. When I read a story, I always skip the pages devoted to a description of the juvenile days of the hero or heroine. They are generally insufferably uninteresting, or interesting only to the writer, and I can find no excuse for selfishness, with such a weapon as a pen in one's hand.

My mother was left a widow when I was a baby. There is a mournful sound about that piece of intelligence, which is absolutely deceptive. In reality it was a most satisfactory outcome of what I was always told was an extremely unhappy marriage. I heard that my father was a charming man, well read, intellectual, courteous and refined. His death was a happy release for both. Poor papa could not tolerate the shallowness of his spouse's hopes and aspirations; while mamma looked upon her husband as an encumbrance, and an obstacle in the way of her social ambition. A husband is very often unnecessary when you are once in the swim of society. When he has given you the protection of his honorable name, and endowed you liberally with the goods of this world, why, the most delicate thing he can then do, is to cease reminding you of these facts, by taking himself off. At least that is the way a great many people look at the matter, I am told.

I was a year old when papa died. What I was there for, I cannot imagine. There was absolutely no reason for my existence. My mother despised children from the bottom of her heart—or, I might more aptly say, the place where her heart was supposed to be. But I thrived on my bottle. I grew disgracefully fat, and outrageously healthy, and it soon became apparent that there would be no difficulty in rearing me. The only person who could have felt any satisfaction at this was my nurse, who, without me to take care of, would have lost a good situation.

I have promised to say little about my childhood, and I will respect my promise.

I was packed off very young to an extremely aristocratic school, where for years dear mamma left me to myself, pursuing her own sweet course in the labyrinthine mazes of society. She paid my bills regularly, and they were pretty big ones, for nothing that could make me subsequently interesting among mamma's dear friends, was neglected. I was to go into society very young. I think she wanted a little excitement, and imagined that she might get some entertainment from a nice, accomplished daughter. Everybody was aware of the fact that she had one, you see, and also cruelly remembered her real age; so why not use the girl to as much advantage as possible? So, I presume she reasoned.

I was "finished"[1] in the most approved manner. I was taught to play the piano with the most provoking persistence, and made day and night hideous with nay frenzied interpretations of things in variations, of pyrotechnical morceaux, and of drawing-room "selections."[2]

I sang songs with *roulades*[3] which would have frightened

---

1 Reference to the norm of sending young women from the upper classes—those considered part of society—to finishing schools. Such schools primarily taught etiquette, conversation, and musical performance.

2 As part of a finishing education young women were expected to perform piano and sing. "Variation" refers to the musical form of theme and variation, in which a fundamental theme is varied. "Morceaux" refers here to a short musical composition. "Drawing-room selection" is a satirical reference to the selections of popular pieces of music played during drawing-room gatherings.

3 Musical term for a quick passage of notes, in particular one sung to one syllable.

Patti,[1] and effective little *chansons*,[2] with plenty of tra-la-la and tremulo[3] about them. Creatures on whom the education I received would be likely to take effect, ought to be caged up, as dangerous to the community, in my opinion. I spoke villainous French, in order that I might vulgarly interlard my sentences with an occasional Gallic expression. I have done so above. You have Mme. Bobichon, instigated by mamma, to thank for it. A long haired, beery German was going the rounds of the drawing-rooms at this time (I ought to say *salons*, I suppose), and talking the gullible Londoners into the belief that he was a musical prodigy. I was taught German, I presume, in order that I might be able to tell him, in his own language, how much I adored him. I was very accomplished, in a word—desperately so. I will say this, however: I despised my education. I could see through its superficiality even then.

I enjoyed my school days thoroughly. I liked the society of the merry, laughing, giddy girls I met. Towards the end of my "finishing" period, I went home for a holiday, and the return to school was simply delightful. I dreaded the idea of leaving it for a home which I knew I should detest, and for a mother in whom I had not the faintest interest. At seventeen, however, I was taken into the bosom of my family, and the happiest period of my life came to an abrupt end.

I remained quietly at home for three months before I became that silliest of human beings, a blushing *debutante*.[4] (She doesn't blush long, poor thing.) I had one dear friend whom I regarded as a sister. Letty Bishop had left school two years before I emerged, so that when I was ready to burst upon the social world, she was already a full-fledged society girl.

I shall always remember the ball mamma gave to introduce me to the world. It was a great event for me, an absolute and utter revelation. I rejoiced at the idea of meeting my old school friends, and of resuming the pleasant relations we had enjoyed, without restriction. I was also particularly anxious to become acquainted with members of the male sex, of whom I had heard

---

1 Adelina Patti (1843–1919) was a leading coloratura soprano who was particularly celebrated for the purity of her voice and her *bel canto* technique.
2 French: songs.
3 A vibrating effect used by singers to convey emotion.
4 A young lady from the upper or aristocratic classes who, having reached maturity, would be introduced to society at a formal ball.

so much from my friend. I knew none, except John, the butler, who I cannot say impressed me very favorably.

I supposed that men were nice, sensible, jolly beings, immeasurably superior to girls, and with so many more privileges. They could marry whom and when they chose—I thought it, at least—and had unlimited power over creation in general. I hoped in my heart of hearts that I should soon be chosen, and that some young man would carry me away from mamma to a life which would be more endurable.

As I just said, that ball was an utter revelation to me. I was going to rush at the dear girls I knew, gushingly glad to meet them again after such a long separation, and burningly anxious to take them off to indulge in those nice long talks we had at school.

But when I saw them in my mother's house I hardly recognized them. Could it be possible that these affected, fragile creations, were really the same girls who, only a few months ago, had surreptitiously purchased indigestible cakes, openly read sentimental novels,[1] and enthusiastically sworn eternal friendship the one for the other? Why, they had no eyes for anything female now; all their attentions seemed turned in the direction of the men.

They greeted me with chilling politeness, and turned from me with ill-concealed haste to salute members of the other sex. Of course I had no doubt that they were as eager to meet men as I was. Still, I was not prepared to be treated in this way.

If the behavior of my feminine friends surprised me, I was completely astounded, before the evening was over, at that of the other sex. Why, it was impossible to talk sensibly to these men. They made silly speeches, and showered compliments upon me in a manner that simply caused me consternation and hurt my self respect. I could not imagine what they meant by being so personal. It would have only been after years of familiar intercourse that a girl would have ventured to talk to me as did these men, whom I had never seen before, and with the utmost assurance. It seemed to me that when strangers gave utterance to such ridiculous remarks, they were guilty of nothing less than impertinence.

When they were not unpleasantly self-satisfied, they were absurdly bashful. No girl is ever so contemptuously ill at ease as a bashful man, for whom I have never been able to feel any compassion.

---

1 A genre of fiction developed in England in the eighteenth century in which strong emotional responses were elicited in characters and readers.

One of our young hereditary legislators[1] asked me to dance, and willing to put him at his ease, for his arms seemed to embarrass him, and his blushes amounted to a positive infirmity, I consented. He seemed to me to be a foolish young peacock, one of those men who Carlyle says attain their maximum of detestability at twenty-five, and ought to be put in a glass case until that period, after which they are supposed to improve.[2] He danced well. I have since learned that most social peacocks do. The poetry of motion seems to accompany lack of brains. When once my lord had disposed of his arm around my waist, he was another being, oh, so much improved!

When the dance was over, he led me into the refreshment room, and brought me an ice. I needed it. I had danced boisterously because I was young enough to enjoy the exercise for itself alone. I could have passed a much pleasanter time, however, had my partner been my one friend and *confidante*, Letty Bishop, than I had done with the gawky arms of young my lord encircling my waist.

"What a delightful waltz," sighed my lord, as he watched me greedily eating my ice. He was no longer embarrassed, my efforts had been successful.

"Yes," I replied, "I love dancing, and I think you waltz nearly as well as even Miss Bishop, that pretty girl sitting over there."

I pointed to a chair where Letty was reclining, surrounded by, I believe I counted seventeen young men. I thought I had paid him a great compliment. I had enjoyed my dance, and felt in a better humor. My lord did not seem at all elated, however. He became silent, and eyed me sentimentally.

"Why don't you have an ice?" I asked, presently, feeling annoyed at his stupidity. "This pineapple is very good—there are real pieces of fruit in it."

"Ah, Miss Bouverie," said he, "I am not in an ice humor."

"Ha, Ha! what a good pun!" I laughed flippantly, wishing he would remove his eyes. "You ought to keep me in countenance,[3] though. I always think people look so gluttonous eating by themselves."

---

1 A member of the House of Lords, the upper chamber of the British Parliament.
2 Thomas Carlyle (1795–1881) wrote in *Sartor Resartus* (1836) "that it were a real increase in human happiness, could all young men from the age of nineteen be covered under barrels, or rendered otherwise invisible; and there left to follow their lawful studies and callings, till they emerged, sadder and wiser, at the age of twenty-five."
3 Appearing to advantage; maintaining her bearing.

My lord took a chair and an ice at the same time, and sat down beside me. He spoke very little, which I ascribed to the fact that he was enjoying his ice. When he had finished, he asked me if I had any more dances to give him. I looked at my programme. I had none. My lord scowled.

"Miss Bouverie," he said, "you are the only girl here I care about dancing with. All these belles of sixteen seasons weary me," languidly, "and you give me only one meagre waltz."

"I think you are very rude to my guests," I answered, vexed. "They are nearly all young girls, and most of them are nice ones, too. I would as soon dance with you as with anybody, but as this is my mother's party, I believe I am not allowed to choose. I must take everybody who asks me, I suppose. Not that it matters much, however," I added indifferently. "I can't see that a partner makes much difference as long as he dances well. One has no time to talk."

My lord looked surprised. "You are too young," he said, with what I considered unpardonable frankness. Then in a low tone, "Miss Bouverie, I am so glad you are now 'out.' I shan't refuse any more invitations. I've been sending refusals to everybody lately, you know."

Lucky people, I thought. I rose in disgust, and left him. I felt sick at heart. I had been dancing all the evening, and all my partners annoyed me. They appeared to imagine that I was a doll, and condescended to play with me. Was that the way men always treated girls, I asked myself? A long time has elapsed since that evening, but though I have since learned that a man who never says a pretty thing, is an abnormal being who will ultimately sink into obscurity, I wonder that it should be so.

I was completely disappointed. Even Letty Bishop seemed to view me with less interest, while the men were around. She had known me longer than she had known them, and surely I ought to have been considered first.

I felt that I could never like the other sex if it were composed exclusively of creatures like those with whom I had danced, under the most favorable circumstances too, namely, in my mother's house. From what I had seen, I judged that in the social world, women must be the sworn enemies of women, and men the everlasting foes of men. Girls I had heard declare themselves to be eternal friends, never spoke to each other during the evening, and I failed to notice a man address a word to one of his own sex, which would indicate any friendly interest in it.

I wept bitterly as I cast aside my fine feathers that night. My self-respect was wounded. Men had treated me as though I were a silly toy, and I had expected so much from them, and had thought they would be even more companionable than women.

Companionable! Great goodness!

You will probably have arrived at the conclusion by this time, dear readers, that I was a fool. If, however, I possessed no peculiarities, I should not venture to be sitting here. Indeed, I suppose I should be a respectable British matron, with half-a-dozen sturdy children, and—let me see, it is ten o'clock—I might now be ordering a boiled leg of mutton with caper sauce for my little olive-branches' dinner.

CHAPTER II.

Miss Bishop lived in that terribly respectable quarter of London known as Colville Gardens,[1] where the rows of houses look as though they are pining to be allowed a little architectural license, or an escape of some kind from the exhausting restrictions of the prudery in which they have been designed.

Letty was a strange girl, a curious combination of extreme frivolity, shrewd common sense and warm-heartedness. I liked her, because she was the first girl who had ever shown me any kindness. She would listen to my ideas of things with the utmost good temper, point out where she thought I was mistaken, and allow me the luxury of differing from her; which you will admit is a favor usually hard to obtain from friends. Letty Bishop's father was by no means rich. He had been left a widower many years before, and to Letty was assigned the duty of tending his latter years. This she did with a devotion which I admired. I might have emulated her example, but my mother would have shuddered at, and repudiated, the idea of "latter years."

After my miserable failure as a "blushing *debutante*" I was not long in seeking Letty's society. Early the next morning I was in Colville Gardens. I found Letty in the breakfast-room, reading a parliamentary debate in one of the morning papers, so that she could discuss it with her father when he returned from his office. She was attired in the wrapper which women affect nowadays. She threw down her paper when she saw me, and advancing toward me, gave me an effusive kiss on each cheek.

---

1   A *cul-de-sac* in Kensington, London. It was developed for the well-to-do in the early 1870s as a series of one-family dwellings with identical architecture.

"So glad to see you, dear," she said, "I expected you would be round this morning. Elsie, let me congratulate you on your great success. I'm really proud of you."

I looked what I felt—surprised. That I had been successful, was something I had never contemplated. "I don't know what you mean, Letty," I murmured. "I never spent such a mournfully wretched evening in my life. But," I added, "put on your things and let us go for a nice walk, and I will tell you all about it."

"Now you know, dear," said Letty, sinking into her comfortable chair, "that if there is one thing on the face of this earth which I cordially detest, it is a 'nice walk.' It makes one look so dreadfully healthy, and I abhor dairymaid beauty. No, dear, if you have anything to tell me, say it here, in this cosy room. I'm all ears."

This was not strictly true; Miss Bishop's ears were of the style which our imaginative novelists liken to "dainty pink shells." But I knew what she meant, and was not in a particularly humorous mood, so I took off my things and sat down. "Letty," I said, quietly, "tell me why I was a success."

I felt and looked rather dejected, but she did not appear to notice this.

"Why you were a success," she replied energetically, "because you had more partners than you wanted; because you looked lovely in that dear little white silk dress; because all the men noticed you and asked numerous questions about you, and be-cause—well, my dear, I can't give any more reasons; they are obvious. You must know them as well as I do."

I was disappointed. "Tell me, Letty," I asked, "was this a representative party? Was it an average affair?"

"Far above the average, my dear," was Letty's prompt re-sponse. "There was at least a man to every two girls, which is unusual, there being generally about seventeen times as many women as men. Then the men were really very nice. Mrs. Bouverie deserves great credit for her selection. The wallflowers were composed of those who deserved to be wallflowers, which is worth noting. The supper was excellent, the floor good, the music admirable, and the arrangements perfect."

Miss Bishop folded her hands after these dogmatic utterances, and half closing her eyes looked at me through her heavy eyelashes. I fidgetted and was uncomfortable.

"If the selection of men were really good," I said thoughtfully and grammatically, "I never want to see a bad selection. Letty, every one of my partners made fun of me. What I have done

I don't know, but a man must think very little of a girl to be constantly telling her that her cheeks are like roses, her eyes like stars, her lips—Ah; I sicken when I think of it. Do you mean to say that men talk like that to girls whom they really like and respect?" I was half crying.

Letty rose and kissed me. "You are an innocent little thing," she said, with plaintive condescension, "and my dear,"—quite cheerfully—"I am afraid you are going to have plenty of trouble. Why, I assure you, that a man who doesn't say pretty things to girls is looked upon as a man who can't say them—that is, a boor. Men who talk sense—and there are very, very few of them,—are considered egotistical nuisances. Once I had a partner who had traveled considerably, and he would insist upon describing his travels. He used to carry me off to the Red Sea, lead me gently to the desert of Sahara, or row me tenderly over the lakes of Switzerland. He was very wearisome. I hated him. Yes, Elsie, dear," she went on, seeming positively to enjoy my look of disgust, "I would sooner any day hear something about my pretty eyes and my peach-like cheeks, than a graphic description of the Saharan desert, in a ball-room."

My best friend was leaving me alone and a feeling of desolation came over me. "Can't men talk with girls as they would with men?" I asked. "It seems to me that they must take us for very inferior beings. Men surely don't pay each other idiotic compliments, do they?"

Letty grew serious, and a faint blush deepened the "peach-like" color to which she had already referred. "What men say to one another," she remarked, "I am afraid our ears would hardly tolerate. When my brother Ralph was at home—before he went to China—we always used to have the house full of young fellows. I used frequently to come upon them, when they were laughing heartily, and evidently enjoying themselves. I wanted to laugh as well, but they invariably stopped when they saw me, as though I were a wet blanket. Once or twice I asked them to tell me what was amusing them. The youngest of the party blushed, while the oldest adroitly changed the subject. I presume," said Letty, with charming resignation, "that they were afraid of shocking me. I didn't think so then, but I do now. Men like their little jokes, but—I am afraid we shouldn't."

"I wish mamma would let society alone," I pouted sullenly, feeling thoroughly ill-tempered. "I know I shall be forced to flutter about drawing-rooms until one of these men wants my star-like eyes and my satin complexion for his own. I don't look forward to much happiness. I'd sooner be a governess, or a shorthand writer, or—or—anything." I ended in a burst of indignation.

Miss Bishop laughed, and then became thoughtful. "Elsie," she said presently, "have you ever met Arthur Ravener and Captain Jack Dillington?"

"No," I said shortly, "and I'm not particularly anxious to do so."

"Arthur Ravener and Captain Jack Dillington," pursued Letty, disdaining to notice my petulance, "are known in society as Damon and Pythias.[1] They are inseparable. Such a case of friendship I have never seen. I half expected they would be at your mother's party, but I presume they were not invited. I have never met one without the other. They always enter a ball-room together and leave together. Of course they can't dance with each other, but I'm sure they regret that fact. They are together between the dances, conversing with as much zest as though they had not met for a month. Girls don't like them because they talk downright, painful sense. Men seem to despise them. You might appreciate them, however," with a smile.

---

1 In Greek mythology, the legend of Damon and Pythias is one of loyalty and friendship. According to legend, Pythias was accused of plotting against the ruler, Dionysius I, and was sentenced to die. On the condition that Damon took his place and would be executed if Pythias did not return, Pythias was allowed to travel home to say goodbye. Being delayed by pirates, Pythias did not return on time. At the moment of Damon's imminent execution, Pythias returned, which so impressed Dionysius that he pardoned Pythias. In nineteenth-century literature the term "Damon and Pythias" signified true friendship. In Theodore Winthrop's (1828–61) novel *Cecil Dreeme* (1862)—a work that prefigures some of the concerns of Cohen's novel—a young man laments the end of a friendship with the handsome youth Cecil by declaring, "Every moment it came to me more distinctly that Cecil Dreeme and I could never be Damon and Pythias again. Ignorantly I had loved my friend as one loves a woman only" (Theodore Winthrop, *Cecil Dreeme* [Boston: Ticknor and Fields, 1862], 353). By century's end, however, the term suggested a baleful alliance. In Stevenson's *Strange Case of Dr. Jekyll and Mr. Hyde* (1886), set in a late-Victorian Clubland in which bachelors predominate, a character remarks of Dr. Jekyll, "He began to go wrong, wrong in mind ... Such unscientific balderdash ... would have estranged Damon and Pythias" (Robert Louis Stevenson, *Strange Case of Dr. Jekyll and Mr. Hyde*, ed. Martin Danahay, 3rd ed. [Peterborough, ON: Broadview P, 2015], 38).

"I'm sure I should," I said, enthusiastically. "Men who are capable of feeling deep friendship cannot be fools. I should like to know them, Letty. As long as I have to be a society butterfly, I may as well make myself as comfortable as I can under the circumstances."

"You're a strange girl," remarked Letty, with a sigh, "but," reflectively, "I suppose you can't help it. The next opportunity I have I will introduce you to Arthur Ravener. I can promise you he will pay you no compliments. He'll talk books or politics or—anything unseasonable."

"Or Captain Jack Dillington?" I suggested.

"They rarely speak of one another," said Miss Bishop. "Why, I don't know. Some people call them mysteries, because they can't understand them; but—you shall judge for yourself."

"Thank you, Letty," I said, gratefully, and I brought my visit to a close.

Perhaps as I walked home slowly, I may have indulged in a little complacent recognition of my own superiority. I had a soul above social shallowness, I told myself, and it was hardly likely that I should ever be happy in my home surroundings. I know now that it is one of the laws of nature that a budding woman should rejoice in the admiration of the other sex, should court its favor, and should be plunged into dire misery if she find it not. I must have been a peculiar girl, I suppose. Peculiarities do not always bring undiluted happiness to their owners. I paid dearly for mine, and the debt is not yet liquidated.

CHAPTER III.

Four weeks later, after a weary round of festivities (so called), I was sitting discontentedly in Lady Burlington's tawdry drawing-room, wondering why it was that the time passed so slowly. Miss Angelina Fotheringay was singing "*Voi che sapete,*"[1] with a hideous Italian accent, and in a gratingly harsh voice. When she began I was anxious to see how she would conduct herself with regard to the high notes in the song, and was prepared to respect her if she would calmly and delicately evade them. Such a proceeding, however, was evidently far from her intentions. She went over them neck and crop, landing in the midst of a heart-rending

---

1 Aria from *The Marriage of Figaro* (1786), with music by Wolfgang Amadeus Mozart (1756–91) and libretto by Lorenzo Da Ponte (1749–1838).

shriek, but placidly pursuing her course uninjured. My nerves were shocked. I had an ear for music and was therefore clearly out of place.

I wonder why girls will sing Italian and French songs which they cannot pronounce, when there are so many pretty English ballads which are within their scope. French people laugh at our rendering of their songs, and make most unflattering allusions to our efforts. They have a right to make these allusions. You will very rarely, if ever, hear a Frenchwoman attack an English song. She prefers a field in which she knows she will be at home.

"Thanks, so much, dear," I heard Lady Burlington bleat as the songstress concluded amid a volley of applause. I applauded, too, because I was glad the song was at an end.

"I know I am dreadfully importunate," continued my hostess, "but won't you give us one more song? It is such a treat to hear you. Do, dear," pursued Lady Burlington, as Angelina became coy. "There's that pretty little thing you sing so sweetly, let me see—what is it? Ah, I remember 'Angels ever bright and fair.'"[1]

"Angels ever bright and fair," a pretty little thing! Ye gods!

Miss Fotheringay sat down at the piano again, and having hooked a vapid-looking youth to turn over the pages for her; proceeded to request those unhappy angels to take, oh, take her to their care. She concluded with an operatic flourish, and then without being asked favored the company with a little something in variations, of which I shall never know the name.

I felt positively ill, and when Lady Burlington requested me to play, pettishly declined. As I have already said I had a stock of drawing-room pieces which my fashionable professor had selected; but I hated them. I was thoroughly cross, and longed for something or somebody to distract my mind.

No sooner had I expressed this longing to myself than I noticed two young men enter the drawing-room. They attracted my attention at once. The younger was a tall, slightly built man, about twenty-five years of age. His features were so regular, and his complexion so perfect, that if you had shaven off the small golden moustache which adorned his upper lip, and dressed him in my garments, I felt that he would have done them much more credit than I could ever hope to do. He was extremely pretty. His

---

1 A line from Georg Friedrich Handel's (1685–1759) dramatic oratorio "Theodora" (1850). This may be intended ironically, since the piece concerns the Christian martyr Theodora, a suggestion that Elsie is herself a kind of martyr.

clothes were faultless, his light hair was carefully brushed, and his appearance altogether irreproachable.

I cannot say as much for his companion, who must have been some ten years his senior. This gentleman had a puffy face, with thick red lips, and beady black eyes, something like those of a canary, but not as clear. He had the most unpleasant looking mouth I have ever seen, and as he wore no moustache whatever, it was very visible.

The two new arrivals sat down together during the progress of a song. Then they made their greetings in a quietly dignified manner, and were soon separated in the crowd. I noticed that the younger man looked continually after his friend when the latter went his way. I was still wondering who the two gentlemen were, when I saw Letty Bishop energetically steering her way in my direction, followed closely by the younger.

"Ah, I've been looking for you, Elsie," she said impulsively, regardless of etiquette. "I want to introduce you to Mr. Arthur Ravener. My friend, Miss Bouverie, Mr. Ravener."

Mr. Ravener took the vacant seat beside me, and on closer inspection I found his complexion quite as perfect and his features quite as regular as they had seemed when there was distance between us.

"You do not appear to be enjoying yourself, Miss Bouverie," he said in soft, musical tones.

"I am not indeed," I answered, vexed that he had been able to read my feelings so easily. "I think musical evenings are detestable."

"Query: Is this a musical evening?" Mr. Ravener sank his voice to a whisper, and I laughed outright. The ice was broken.

We entered upon a conversation which was thoroughly delightful, to me at any rate. I found that Arthur Ravener was fond of music, and understood it thoroughly. He asked who were my favorite composers. I told him that I had never been allowed to have any favorites. I had been dosed with Brinley Richards, Sydney Smith and Kuhe,[1] and the effect had been extremely injurious. I liked to hear classical music. It did not weary

---

1 Brinley Richards (1817–85) was a Welsh composer; Sydney Smith (1839–89) was an English pianist and composer whose approximately 400 compositions and transcriptions were wildly popular in recitals and drawing-room salons; Wilhelm Kuhe (1823–1912) was a German composer and pianist whose fantasias and etudes were widely played in Victorian salons.

me in the least; in fact, if I had been properly educated, I might have proved a fairly competent musician.

He was drawing me out, actually. I had not said as much since I left school to any new acquaintance. Here I was talking to a man with as much ease as though he were one of my beloved feminine school-friends. Mr. Ravener listened to me very attentively. He interposed soft "Oh, indeeds," and "Ah's" in a very pleasant manner, and appeared to be interested. He was very serious and extremely deferential. His face showed none of the changes that steal involuntarily over the features of most men when they speak to young girls. He talked to me as unconcernedly as though I were a man. I became as confidential as though he were a woman. I said presently, "if you are so fond of music, how is it you come to evenings like this?"

"May I address the same question to you?" he asked.

"Oh, that's another thing," I replied. "Girls can't do as they like, you know. They have to follow in the paths their fathers and mothers make for them. But I should have thought it would have been different with men."

"It is not, however," said Mr. Ravener, quietly, and I suppose he thought that settled it, as he dropped the subject. I noticed that he seemed to be eagerly searching for some one in the crowd, and at last I saw his eyes rest upon his unprepossessing friend.

"Are you afraid your friend is not enjoying himself?" I asked, rather cheekily I admit.

He reddened slightly. "Captain Dillington always enjoys himself," he said quietly. "He is very happy in society."

I remembered Letty's story of Damon and Pythias, and longed to know something of these two young men, one of whom at least was different from the ordinary drawing-room specimen. Arthur Ravener was certainly attractive, and I felt I was going to be interested in him, so I must be excused if I showed too much curiosity.

"How rarely you find two really sincere friends," I remarked, rather sentimentally. "The present time seems to be wonderfully unsuited to such a tie."

"That is true"—very laconically.

"I think there is nothing so beautiful as friendship," I went on, with persistence.

"You have heard of Damon and Pythias," he said quickly, reading me like a book. I blushed deeply and was then furiously angry with myself. "I don't mind," he went on. "Make all the fun of us you like."

"Mr. Ravener," I protested, "I assure you that when I heard of the friendship existing between you and Captain Dillington, I became interested in you." (A pretty little declaration to make.) "I don't see where any fun comes in. I am tired of the stupid men I meet at such gatherings as these. They have not enough feeling about their composition to allow them to make friends. Far from feeling amused at Damon and Pythias, I am deeply interested in them."

Arthur Ravener looked pleased. I went on gushing like the school-girl I was. "I can think a great deal better of a young man who is capable of being sincerely attached to a companion, than I can of those foolish chatterboxes over there, who are forever telling me I have pretty eyes, pretty hair and a pretty figure, as though I had not been intimately acquainted with myself for the last seventeen years. Don't think I laugh at you, Mr. Ravener, I am very much interested." Then, so ingenuously that it could hardly be considered rude, "I should like to hear all about Captain Dillington, and how you came to know him?"

"There surely can be nothing to tell," he said in strained tones. "What is the friendship between two young men that you should deem it worth discussing?"

"It is worth discussing," I impulsively asserted. "What are we going to talk about? You are not going to tell me about my sylph-like[1] form, or compare my charms with those of my less fortunate friends?"

"No," he replied gravely, "you will find that is not my style when you know me better. I trust we shall know each other better, Miss Bouverie," he remarked quietly.

"Yes." I blushed in my prettiest manner, and cast my eyes down. I was determined to impress Arthur Ravener favorably. I looked extremely well when my long fringed lids could be seen advantageously. Picture my disgust and annoyance when, looking up again, I found I was alone, and just in time to see Arthur Ravener vanishing from the room with Captain Dillington. Even my acquiescence in his wish for our better acquaintance had not been sufficiently interesting to keep him at my side.

He was gone. "Well," I said to myself, "the claims of friendship are great. He is not very polite, but let him go"—which was extremely kind of me, as he had already gone.

Later in the evening I saw the two young men again. Arthur Ravener did not approach me, but bowed in an astonishingly

---

1 A sylph is an imaginary spirit of the air.

friendly manner, and I, anxious not to seem piqued, returned the nod, accompanied by a smile.

I was subsequently made acquainted with Captain Dillington, for whom, after I had been in his society five minutes, I felt an overwhelming dislike. I cannot say what it was that induced the impression, but Captain Dillington reminded me of a toad, from his beady little eyes, to his sleek, smooth shaven face. He was conspicuously and effusively polite, which I always consider an unpleasant feature in any man's behavior. Though he paid me no compliments, I was uneasy in his society; again I say I do not know why. We discussed various subjects; he in his oily, complacent manner, I in my superficial, gushing way. I was delighted when he left me, but I could not recover my previous serenity.

It was now the hour when departures were expected with resignation; in fact, Lady Burlington was yawning most openly—if I were in a flippant mood, I should consider that a tolerably decent pun—and I could see the poor thing thought she had entertained us sufficiently.

"Good-night, dear Lady Burlington," I said affectionately, with a smile which mamma would have given six years of her life to see; "I have spent a delightful evening."

May I be forgiven that sin, and the thousands of others of a like nature which I have committed, rebelling as I have rebelled against their absurdity. May all who sin in a like manner be forgiven. May only society that knows these words are mostly sins, and that yet accepts them, be unforgiven! That is what I wish.

"How did you like them?" asked Letty Bishop, as I stood in the hall being cloaked, while I silently vowed to myself that I would tell no more lies to my hostesses.

"Who's them?" I inquired ungrammatically and peevishly, for I was tired.

"Arthur Ravener and Captain Dillington."

"I don't know," I answered. "Mr. Ravener was away from me before I could make up my mind whether I liked him or not. I forgive him freely."

"Ah!" said Letty, with such detestable unction that, friend though I was, I could have enjoyed boxing her ears, "he doesn't pay you compliments. I expect the amiability was all on your side."

I made no answer, but with a hasty "goodnight," I jumped into the carriage which was awaiting me and was borne homewards.

CHAPTER IV.

Arthur Ravener called to "see mamma" a few days later, at least that was the nominal object of his visit, I believe. There is a great deal of humbug about us Londoners. In America young men when they are slightly smitten call upon a girl openly and without beating about the bush; here they ask to see the papas, and the mammas, and the brothers, and the duennas,[1] and everybody but the person they really want.

The idea of any young man deliberately calling to see mamma was so ludicrous, that when I heard of it I laughed. I knew he had come to see me, and I should have thought all the more of him if he had admitted the fact like a man. I was studying hard when I heard him go into the library. I was not puzzling over mathematics, or physics, but was extremely engrossed in a cook-book. I had made a tart, the crust of which was so hideously and irrepressibly solid, that when I had tried to insert a knife in it, the contents of the plate had flown ceilingwards, and cook had looked at me sardonically happy. I hated the woman for that look. I went into the library with a little dab of jam on my cheek, and I was too lazy to worry about it. It was a big room, filled with exquisitely bound books. Dear mamma was very anxious that every volume should be beautifully leather-covered. The contents of the covers were a secondary consideration. It was the correct thing to have a library. It was a good place into which to usher people.

"I thought I would just run in to see if you had recovered from your fatigue of the other night," he said, after we had exchanged salutations.

"Is that why you wished to see mamma?" I asked demurely.

"Of course," he answered. "Mrs. Bouverie might prefer to give me the information herself."

"She couldn't," I declared rather boisterously, "for the simple reason that she never knew that I was fatigued. As a matter of fact I was not. I was bored. The only pleasant part of the evening was furnished by you. There is a compliment for you, before you have been in the house five minutes."

I was very lively indeed, but the arrival of mamma dampened my ardor. She sailed into the room, and seemed extremely pleased to see Mr. Ravener. She liked young men, and always treated them graciously. She did not stay long, however, but

---

1 A female chaperone for a young woman.

begged to be excused. Some girls might have considered this a delicate and motherly piece of consideration. I did not. I had nothing to say to Arthur Ravener or any other young man that might not have been published in the daily papers if the editors had seen fit to inflict it upon their readers. He took one arm chair and I sat opposite. I did not feel at all called upon to talk about the weather and other pleasantly conventional topics. Mr. Ravener had certainly made a most favorable impression upon my maidenly heart.

"You are all over jam, Miss Bouverie," he remarked, as I sat down.

"Don't remind me of my troubles," said I, "I have been cooking very unsuccessfully, and I feel miserable. By the bye, pardon my rudeness in forgetting to ask after the health of Captain Dillington."

There had been a smile on his face as I began my speech. It froze at once—as they say in the novels. A pained blush spread itself slowly over his face. "Captain Dillington," he said deliberately, "is well. Why are you so interested in him?"

"Only because you are," I replied flippantly. "It is the mutual attachment of you two young men that interests me. I think I told you so before, Mr. Ravener."

There was silence for a long time. It was not an eloquent silence. I employed a few leisure moments in removing the jam from my face. He bit his small moustache, as young men often do, more I believe to show that they have one to bite, than because they like it.

"Miss Bouverie," said Arthur Ravener, "you say you were interested in me because you found that I did not pay you silly compliments, and talk nonsense. Now don't think me impertinent, if I tell you that I rejoice in the fact that I have met somebody who does not care for such nonsense. Perhaps you will like it better when you are older"—regretfully.

"Never," said I. All the jam was now removed, and though I felt sticky, no one could guess that fact.

"Do you think a young man and woman ought to converse as though they were brother and sister—platonically, I mean?"

"Mr. Ravener," said I, pettishly, "I do not intend to talk metaphysics with you. I have ideas of my own. I like a man, if I have to meet him often, to talk sense."

"Suppose you fell in love?"—tentatively.

"Yes," said I, trying hard to blush a little and failing in a most abject manner. "You are rather impertinent, Mr. Ravener, but no matter. If I ever fell in love, I should see no necessity for discussing it with my 'loved one.' I should not like him any better if he deared and darlinged me. I think I should despise him. I know some people must be demonstrative. Letty Bishop kisses her father about sixteen times in the course of an evening. I suppose she likes it, but it always seems to me very unnecessary. I cannot imagine myself kissing mamma, even if—even if—" I hesitated.

"Even if what?" he asked, unpardonably interested.

"Never mind," sharply. "I was going to reveal family matters to a stranger. You are a stranger, you know. I was going to say—don't think me awful—that I cannot imagine myself kissing mamma even if she did not powder."

He looked rather shocked at my frankness, and I respected him for it. He did not smile, and I went back to my theme. "I could not be demonstrative," I declared. "It seems to me so dreadfully coarse. I flatter myself that I am extremely matter-of-fact."

"I thought so," he said, "and so did—" He stopped in some slight confusion, and reddened in that most provoking manner that people have.

"So did who?" I asked.

"I was merely going to say—"

"Mr. Ravener," I said deliberately. "I want to know who else thought as you did about me."

I suppose he saw I was somewhat determined. "Captain Dillington," he answered in a low tone.

I was thoroughly displeased, and most unreasonably so. Only a few moments previously there was I declaring that the intense friendship of these two young men was something I admired. Now I felt vexed because these boon companions should discuss a girl in whom one of them confessed that he was interested. Men are right when they say one should never expect logic from a woman. I place myself at the head of the unreasonable list.

"You are vexed?" he asked, really troubled.

"Not a bit," promptly. Women cannot reason, but no one can beat them at fibbing. (Fibbing is a polite word for it.)

He seemed relieved. "Do you know, Miss Bouverie," he said as he rose to go, "I can talk to you, as I can to no other girl. That is a positive fact. I don't feel that the instant I leave you, you will run to some feminine bosom and dissect me."

"I shouldn't care enough about you to do that," I said rudely. Could anything have been more impolite? If he could have done anything to increase the good impression he had made upon me, he did it then by simply laughing in a hearty, boyish manner, without an atom of vexation apparent. I had used words of the same purport to partners at some of the hateful parties I had attended, and had been greeted with "Cruel Miss Bouverie"; "Oh, Miss Bouverie, you do not mean it"; "You treat me very badly, Miss Bouverie."

How they annoyed me, those men. I must confess that Arthur Ravener was rapidly becoming more than interesting. Frankness is one of my characteristics.

CHAPTER V.

I firmly believe that if I had told mamma that the Grand Mogul was coming to dinner, and that the Mikado of Japan[1] intended dropping in during the evening in a friendly way, she would simply have remarked, "I am pleased to hear it; we must entertain them." Arthur Ravener's frequent appearance at our house caused not the least surprise, and interested her but slightly. "He is a nice young fellow, Elsie," she said on one occasion. "He is very attentive to you, of course, but there is something about him I don't quite understand. He is cold and undemonstrative, and yet I can tell that he likes you. He seems to have something on his mind."

"Well, that is better than not possessing a mind to have anything on," I retorted in my unpleasantly pert way, "as is the case with the usual nonentities of society."

"Elsie," said my mother, "I dislike to hear a young girl like yourself belittle the people you are accustomed to meet. You may be far superior to them, but—excuse me—I doubt it."

I was snubbed and subsided.

One afternoon as I was walking down Oxford Street, I saw Arthur Ravener and Captain Dillington approaching. Only the latter noticed me at first. He nudged Arthur and, with an indescribably ugly smile on his face, said something to him. I longed to know what it was, womanlike, because I instinctively felt it was not for my ears. Arthur reddened in a most uncomfortable way, and Captain Dillington laughed. I felt annoyed. I resolved that they should stop and speak to me, though I am sure they had no intention of so doing. Accordingly when they raised their hats, by a dainty little feminine manoeuvre, I contrived to make them stop. Captain Dillington greeted me boldly. Arthur Ravener seemed tongue-tied.

---

1 Grand Mogul: European term for the ruler of the Mughal Empire of India; Mikado: archaic term for the Emperor of Japan.

"Why do you never come to see us, Captain Dillington?" I asked in my airy way, as they turned and walked back with me.

"Would you care to have us both, Miss Bouverie?"

"I don't see why not. There is plenty of room for you."

"I wonder if you will always be as accommodating, Miss Bouverie?" There was something so insolent in his tone, that I became scarlet in the face. I cannot explain what there was offensive in his speech. You who read it will say that I made a mountain out of a molehill. It impressed Arthur Ravener as it impressed me.

"Take care, Dillington," I heard him say in a low voice, as I turned towards a shop window to cool down.

"If you care to come, Captain Dillington," I said haughtily, "we shall be pleased. If you do not care to come—" I shrugged my shoulders; that is very expressive.

The Captain looked alarmed. "I assure you, Miss Bouverie," he said, "you misunderstood me. I should be delighted to call. I am not at all bashful. I feel convinced that we shall meet a great deal"—he made a marked pause—"later."

I cannot describe the look on Arthur Ravener's face. I feel that novelists would call it "the look of the hunted antelope brought to bay." I have no doubt their simile is a good one, though I have never seen an antelope hunted or otherwise.

"Captain Dillington pays very few visits," said Arthur Ravener, lamely. "He sees very little society, indeed."

"Except yours," remarked the Captain.

"Except mine," echoed Arthur, slowly. "But, Captain," appealingly, "I should like you to call one day this week upon Mrs. Bouverie; I think you could manage it if you tried, couldn't you?"

Captain Dillington nodded, and I, not at all anxious to prolong the scene, skipped into a shop with a hasty "good afternoon."

I confess I was puzzled. What Arthur Ravener could see to admire in Captain Dillington it was utterly impossible for me to divine. That the tie which held them together was strong and binding, I could not for a moment doubt. I have always heard that dissimilar spirits form friendships of long duration, but I could not realize that this would hold good in the case of Arthur Ravener and Captain Dillington, one an apparently frank young man who could only just have "begun to live," the other a repulsive being, with no particularly redeeming feature.

I had already seen them often together, and I knew Arthur Ravener was a different man when removed from his friend. It was not true that Captain Dillington saw but little society. He accompanied Arthur on all occasions. In fact, I had never met the one without the other, except at home. Captain Dillington was the chaperon, or at least I looked upon him in that light. However, excuses will never stand analysis.

"What are you doing in here, Elsie?"

I turned round, and beheld Letty Bishop laden with parcels.

"I came in here to look at some—" I began to stammer hopelessly. I never could fib successfully when taken by surprise, which shows that I was an amateur in the art.

Miss Bishop opened the door and looked down the street. Of course she saw the retreating forms of Damon and Pythias, as she called them.

"No, dear," she said calmly, "you came in here to look at nothing at all. You wanted to avoid a certain couple I see fading in the distance. Are you going home, Elsie?"

Yes, I was going home. I admitted the fact. We stepped out into the noise of Oxford Street.

"Elsie," said Letty, suddenly, "I want to talk to you seriously on a subject upon which—pardon me, my dear—I am afraid your mother will have but little to say. You and I have always been great friends, have we not, dear?"

I hate any one to be affecting, especially in the street. I had an awful idea that there was pathos in Miss Bishop's voice, but I made a vow that nothing should induce me to weep and redden my nose, no matter how harrowing she became.

"Yes," I said, "we've been great friends, Letty, and as neither of us intend shuffling off just yet, I vote that we go on being friends, and say nothing about it."

"You can be as flippant as you like," said Miss Bishop severely, "but I am going to talk to you just the same. You remember, Elsie, at the beginning of the season, how miserable you were at all the festivities, and how you dreaded the silly men, as you called them, whom you were obliged to meet. I told you of Damon and Pythias. I introduced you to Arthur Ravener."

"Well?"—impatiently.

"I never imagined that the introduction would lead to anything."

"No?" I was really boiling over with rage, but I tried to conceal that fact.

"No. But it has. People are coupling your name with that of Arthur Ravener. No, don't interrupt me. If I did not care for you, I should say nothing. Look here, Elsie. I am quite certain that you will never be happy, if you do anything rashly. Arthur

Ravener is very unpopular. The men won't look at him. I was speaking to my cousin Ned about him the other day, since I have noticed how you encouraged him."

"I—"

"—and Ned told me to warn any friend of mine against him. Why? I asked. He would give me no reason, but, my dear, Ned is a conservative old fellow, and you so rarely hear him say a bad word against anybody, that if he does make an attack it carries weight with it. Personally, I like Ravener; but, my dear, I cannot help listening to what people say. Why I heard the remark the other day that the only reason Ravener and Dillington went into society at all, was to borrow its cloak of respectability."

"Perhaps you think they are highway robbers in disguise, or forgers, or playful assassins?"

"I think nothing, my dear. I only tell you what people say. I do that merely because it was I who introduced you. I had no more idea that you and Arthur Ravener would ever care for one another—"

"Did I say I cared for Arthur Ravener?"

"No, but you do, and my prophetic soul tells me that you will throw yourself away upon him."

"Don't listen to what people say, my child," I remarked loftily, "and you will be a great deal happier. Since you have been talking I have come to the conclusion that I like Arthur Ravener immensely. When I marry it will not be for the sake of my lovely society friends—but for my own. You have done your duty, my dear. You have warned me against a young man of whom you know positively nothing. Thanks. If I can return the compliment at any time, command me."

Then, thinking I could not improve upon this cutting rejoinder, I tripped away.

CHAPTER VI.

No one who has followed me thus far can accuse me of having tried to make myself attractive to my readers. My later experiences have taught me that girls who despise what are generally acknowledged to be the pleasures of girlhood, will get but little sympathy in this world. Perhaps that is as it should be. I must have been eccentric.

I remember that I once heard a young man who had been dancing with a corsetless maiden, a believer in the laws of health, declare that such girls ought not to be allowed in a ball-room. To be accepted by society, you must follow the laws it prescribes. The right to be eccentric must be earned—and it takes time to earn it. What right had a chit like myself to declare that I found the young men whom I was called upon to meet, undesirable and uninteresting? Who put such ideas into my head? I cannot lay the blame upon anybody. The ideas were there. Topsy-like, I suspect "they growed."[1]

The subject I now have to deal with is my engagement. I had grown to like Arthur Ravener very much. I thought we had a great deal in common. I never felt that a woman was a silly chattering doll when I was with him. He would talk upon any subject with me, and never once in all our intercourse did he pay me a single compliment. He never showed that he admired me. All he ever said was that he liked talking to a sensible girl who looked upon the world very much as he did himself.

One evening as I was sitting alone at a detestable "musicale and dance," and wondering as usual why girls wasted their best years in training themselves to shine at such entertainments, I noticed Arthur Ravener and Captain Dillington enter the room. The former looked anxiously around—for me, of course, I knew that; the latter remained standing at the door, where he could see all that was going on. The reception accorded Damon and Pythias was always polite, but never cordial. The men seemed to avoid Captain Dillington, and he usually tacked himself to the skirts of some plump old matron, who talked of nothing more exciting than servants and other domestic relaxations. I imagine that Arthur Ravener must have pursued a similar course before he met me—but then my imagination always did go a long way.

"How do you do, Miss Bouverie?" Arthur Ravener in evening dress was extremely comely, but I could have found it in my heart to wish that he were not so pretty.

"I am so glad you have come, Mr. Ravener, to raise me from the Slough of Despond.[2] I was going gradually down—down—down."

---

1 Topsy is a mischievous girl in the American novelist Harriet Beecher Stowe's (1811–96) anti-slavery novel *Uncle Tom's Cabin* (1852). Another character, Miss Ophelia, asks her, "'Do you know who made you?' 'Nobody as I knows on,' said the child, with a short laugh.... 'I spect I grow'd. Don't think nobody never made me'" (Harriet Beecher Stowe, *Uncle Tom's Cabin* [Boston: John P. Jewett & Co., 1852], 37–38).

2 A deep bog in *The Pilgrim's Progress* (1678), an allegory by the English Christian writer and preacher John Bunyan (1628–88). In the allegory, the pilgrim sinks under the weight of his sins and his guilt.

He smiled. I wondered if the little curl in his moustache were natural, or, if not, how he managed to bring it to such perfection. He did not seem to be in a talkative humor, so I felt called upon to make a little conversation. I looked around the room. Of course I knew I could say it was very warm. That is always a safe remark of an evening. It would also not have been out of the way to suggest that there were a great many present.

Ah, there was a good subject for conversation in the young couple opposite, a bride and bridegroom, a couple three months old—matrimonially old, I mean. They were evidently very much enamored and they sickened me. It was very rude of me to take them all in; but they had no idea I was staring at them, so it was all right. I saw him take up her dance programme, and scan the names with a frown, she all the time glancing at him with pride and admiration. Then he whispered something in her ear, taking care to brush it with his moustache, and she put one dainty gloved finger on his lip. He sat down beside her and for five minutes they talked so earnestly that I am quite convinced they forgot the fact that they were "in society." I am ashamed to say I listened to them. It was not an edifying conversation. He declared that an evening spent away from her was a terrible ordeal. She asserted that it was a good thing to dance with other men, as the contrast between them and her own dear husband showed her how immeasurably superior he was.

And all this time I forgot I was to amuse my companion. I looked at him. He was listening to the bride and bridegroom also. Shame upon us both.

"Does that interest you?" he asked.

"It disgusts me," I answered emphatically.

"Ah!"—I fancied he had awaited my answer a little anxiously. He looked satisfied.

"I do not believe in such demonstrative devotion," I went on. "There is nothing beautiful in it to me."

"No," he said. "It will never last. In two years it will take a very great effort on her part to keep him at her side. She will by that time probably think the effort not worth making."

I was silent. Perhaps at that moment something told me that my ideas were morbid. It is possible that quick as a flash of lightning my womanhood asserted itself. I say it is possible, and that is all.

"Elsie."

It was the first time he had uttered my Christian name. There was nothing at all tender in the way he pronounced it. I blushed slightly and looked a little conscious. Of course I could make no answer. I sat silent and eyed my gloves (which were rather soiled, by the bye, and not worth eyeing).

"Elsie," he said, "you criticise the conversation of that young couple opposite. But put yourself in her place. Would you prefer your husband to sit calmly by your side, and talk,—perhaps as you and I have talked so often,—quietly, undemonstratively, and sensibly. Would you be satisfied to marry a man who absolutely declined to be the conventional lover, writing ballads to your eyebrows, and extolling your virtues, real and imaginary, while the love fever lasted?"

His face was very pale, and his hands nervously clutched the side of my chair, as he leaned slightly towards me.

"Yes, I would be satisfied," I said.

At that moment I felt acutely happy. Of course I knew to what he was coming. I always laugh when I read novels in which the heroines "look up with large surprised eyes," or "innocently wonder" what a proposing lover means. A girl always knows when a man is asking her to marry him. If he expressed himself in Chinese or Hindostanee she would understand him just as well.

I felt I could be happy with Arthur Ravener. He was entirely different to any other man I had met, and the difference seemed to me, then, to be in his favor.

"Elsie," he said, in very agitated tones, "you have remarked very often that you despised these demonstrative beings. When we first met, you told me frequently that I was different—that you found pleasure in my company. I have seen your face brighten when I approached, and, Elsie, I am emboldened by these signs of your esteem, to ask you to be my wife."

I put my hand quietly in his. You, readers, who have perhaps disapproved of my flippancy, will be astonished to hear that for the moment it left me completely. I was deeply moved by Arthur Ravener's proposal. I was delighted. I really believe I felt as an engaged girl ought to feel,—full of admiration for the man who had honored her, and keenly alive to the fact that this world was after all a good place in which to be.

I looked at Arthur. His face was livid. Its startling pallor gave me a shock. I forgot everything for the moment in my anxiety for his present welfare.

"You are ill?" I said.

He looked at me in surprise.

"No," he replied in a low tone. "I am well. Should I not be

well"—with a great effort and a strained smile—"when you have just accepted my—my suit?"

Have you ever experienced the unpleasant sensation of knowing that somebody was staring at you, and been impelled to look in their direction? Of course you have. So you will not be surprised if I tell you that I turned from Arthur Ravener and glanced toward the door. Captain Dillington had been staring at me. He looked confused, I am glad to say, when I returned his stare with interest. In fact he turned immediately away, and began an animated conversation with one of his favorite plump matrons.

"Arthur," I said, impulsively, "I know you and Captain Dillington are such great friends that I want to ask you if he likes me?"

There was no coquetry veiled in this question. I sincerely wished to know how I stood (to use a commercial expression) with the bosom friend of my affianced husband.

Arthur Ravener positively started at my question. For a few seconds he seemed unable to answer.

"I—I am sure he does," he stammered at last. "Yes, Elsie, Captain Dillington does like you. I—I am sure of it. Set your mind at rest."

"Pooh!" said I, inelegantly, feeling that Richard[1] was himself again. "My mind is quite at rest. I'm not going to marry you both, you know"—a remark that was neither pretty nor funny, but vulgar. My carriage had been announced and Arthur was fastening my "*sortie de bal*"[2] around me. In the hall stood Captain Dillington. He bowed and then extended his hand to me.

"May I congratulate you, Miss Bouverie?" he asked.

"You may," I answered blushingly. Then it occurred to me that it was rather strange Captain Dillington should know anything about my engagement. Arthur had not left my side since I had accepted him as my future husband. Then I reflected that Arthur and the Captain were great friends; that the Captain probably knew that Arthur intended asking me to be his wife; that he had seen us in earnest conversation, noticed my "happy expression," and put two and two together—an arithmetical process practiced by many. Still, I was not quite satisfied, although I decided that it would be better to appear so.

"I trust we shall see a great deal of each other"—after a pause—"later."

---

1 As in 1889 original text. Cohen momentarily erred in referring to Arthur as "Richard."

2 French: departure from the ball. Here, a woman's evening cloak.

He had made this identical speech the other day, I remembered.

"I hope so," said I. I would try and like him for Arthur's sake, though I was perfectly convinced I should not succeed. The hall door was open. Arthur came down the steps with me. He was still pale.

"Good-night, Arthur," I said, extending my hand.

"Good-night."

His fingers scarcely closed around mine. I had shaken hands with him a dozen times during our acquaintance, and had always told him he ought to take lessons in the art. But his salutation had never been so coldly inexpressive as to-night it seemed to me. I shivered slightly, then drew myself into the obscurity of the carriage and rolled home.

CHAPTER VII.

Arthur was very anxious that our engagement should be a short one. My mother would have been perfectly satisfied to have escorted me to the altar on the day following our betrothal, if fashion had established any precedent for such a course. But no, she could not remember any respectable folks marrying after an engagement of less than three months.

"People might talk," she said, and I knew that settled it. There was no more awful possibility. An earthquake would have been pleasant, and a conflagration merely an episode in comparison.

"I don't see why Arthur is in such a hurry," she went on. "Really, you have given him no cause for jealousy; your conduct is always irreproachable. In fact if I were a man I should run a mile to avoid you. I have often thought that your manners must be far from attractive to the other sex."

"Thanks, mother."

"I am sure I am very pleased that it is all going to end so happily, but I cannot consent to your marriage in less than three months. No such case can I remember, except, of course, that of Lady Stitzleton's daughter, which is too shocking for me to discuss with you. Tell Arthur he must wait for three months. I can't for the life of me understand his hurry. You will excuse me for saying it, Elsie, but I confess he does not seem to be particularly—"

"Tender, do you mean, mother?"

"*Épris*[1] is an excellent word to use in this case," said my parent. "If you cannot understand it, however, you can substitute tender. Of course I know that it is very bad form to make any demonstrations in society, but when alone, a little effusiveness is entirely pardonable. You and Arthur were in the library together for a few minutes the other night—perfectly proper of course. As I happened to pass the room, I looked in, prompted of course by my motherly interest. You were at one end of the room, he at the other, and I—"

"Never mind," I said hastily, reddening with vexation. "It shall be as you say—three months."

I stalked from the room thoroughly annoyed. I did not dare to ask myself the cause of my ill temper. Demonstrations of affection I had frequently declared disgusted me, and I had engaged myself to a man who confessed that he thought as I did. I had no reason to complain of Arthur. His behavior toward me had not changed in the slightest since our engagement. He had not attempted to avail himself of the privileges which books on etiquette[2] (I had glanced through them) accord to engaged couples. He had never kissed me, nor hinted at the slightest inclination to do so.

I loved Arthur Ravener, I was proud of the prospect of becoming his wife; but—lest my future history be considered inconsistent with that which I have already related—I will frankly admit, at the risk of being called a contemptible humbug, that I should not have objected in the least if Arthur had been just a trifle less glacial. I admit that now; I made no such admission at the time. I only felt a little discontented, and mentally changed the subject when there was any probability of my discovering the reason of my dissatisfaction.

The news of our engagement soon spread. Shall I be considered egotistical if I say that the men who had previously—so it seemed to me—looked down upon Arthur Ravener, now appeared anxious to know him, and apologetically anxious, too? They had evidently more respect for Elsie Bouverie's affianced husband, than for Captain Dillington's bosom friend. It was rather inexplicable to me, but I was pleased nevertheless.

Arthur was a constant visitor at our house. He never brought

---

1 French: enamored.
2 Victorian society was a highly regulated environment in terms of courtship rituals. Books such as *The Habits of Good Society: A Handbook for Ladies and Gentlemen* (1869) and *A Guide to the Manners, Etiquette, and Deportment of the Most Refined Society* (1879) were widely read as guides to correct deportment.

Captain Dillington with him. Indeed he always seemed to be so embarrassed when I asked him to do so, that I at last desisted. It was no desire to know the Captain better that prompted me to invite him to join us. He repelled me as no one either before or since has done. But I knew he was my future husband's boon companion, so was perfectly willing to sink my prejudices. I also thought as there was nobody but a blind old bat of a housekeeper in the flat which they had furnished, and in which they lived, that Captain Dillington must feel rather lonely when Arthur was away. Arthur was a very thoughtful young man. He never stayed very late at our house. Although he did not say so, I was convinced that he did not care to leave his friend alone too long. Such consideration for another pleased me. Had I not every right to reason, by analogy, that when I was his wife, he would show me the same devotion?

I thoroughly dreaded the day when I had to tell Letty Bishop of my engagement. I felt that she would be a wet blanket of the most distressing type, and—somehow or other—I wanted to steer as clear of wet blankets as possible. I was agreeably surprised to find that Letty gave my "news" very little attention, for the simple reason that she had similar information to impart. Yes, Letty was engaged. I had known her betrothed for some time, and had included him in the ranks of the men I despised. He was a butterfly. He admired every girl he met, or seemed to do so. However, if Letty was satisfied with him, why, so was I. I was glad to listen to all she had to say about him, as by doing so, I gave her no opportunity to make unpleasant remarks concerning Arthur Ravener. She hoped I would be happy, and laughingly begged me not to hold her responsible for the match. She talked a great deal of nonsense about her Reginald, and I could not get interested. They were evidently a conventionally gushing couple.

"Arthur," said I, that night, adopting my favorite would-be jaunty air, "what will become of Captain Dillington while we are on our honeymoon; there are such a number of places I want to visit, and I'm not going to be hurried." Arthur reddened painfully, and then averted his face. "I was thinking, Elsie," he said with a sickly smile, "that we would abolish that old-fashioned notion of honeymooning, and go immediately after the wedding to your house in Kew."

My mother had presented me with a delightful little villa near Kew Gardens,[1] and it was settled that we were to live there during

---

1 London's Royal Botanical Gardens.

the first year of our wedded life at any rate. But I could not believe that we were to domesticate ourselves on our wedding day.

"You—are joking, Arthur," I said weakly.

"I don't see why," shuffling uneasily on his chair. "I think traveling is an abomination, and, really, you know, honeymoons are not fashionable. Are you—are you" (very anxiously) "very desirous of going out of town?"

"I don't care particularly," I said with magnanimity. "I took it for granted that we should make a trip. I would have preferred it; but, of course, if you would sooner not—"

"What is that, Elsie?"

Enter my maternal parent at an inopportune moment, as usual. She saw we were engaged in discussion and I felt she was anxious to assist us.

"Arthur does not want to take a wedding trip, mother," I said, "and I was telling him that I had been reckoning upon one."

"It is out of fashion, Mrs. Bouverie," remarked Mr. Ravener, looking with appealing eyes at the arbitrator. "I am sure you will agree with me that it is. No one is better acquainted with the usages of society than you are" (deferentially).

Oh, the hypocrite! I knew she would succumb to that, and so did he. If it had not been for that disgustingly polite speech, I felt that she would have decided in favor of the trip, as she had already confided to my care a fist of commissions which I was to execute for her in Paris.

"You are right, Arthur," she said, promptly. "Honeymoons are becoming obsolete in the best society. There is something extremely *bourgeois*[1] about them to my mind." There was not the faintest remembrance of the commissions in her tone. Her foible had been touched. Arthur was triumphant, but he looked rather doubtfully at me. He evidently did not want me to think that he was positively averse to a honeymoon.

"Where do you propose going after the wedding?" asked mamma.

"To Tavistock Villa, Kew," was his rejoinder.

"Of course you will not receive for several months?"

"Oh, no—no—," impatiently, "we shall remain in retirement, and see none but—but the immediate family, and—and intimate friends."

---

1 Originally a French term for the middle merchant class, used disparagingly in this sense to distinguish between the working class and the upper class or aristocracy.

Well, I must let Arthur settle such matters, I thought. After all, perhaps he was right. Honeymoons must have distinctly unpleasant features. Traveling was a nuisance, and with the best of intentions, and the largest purse, it was impossible to obtain home comforts at continental hotels, I had heard. When I told Letty Bishop that we had decided to abolish the honeymoon, she opened her eyes in surprise. Was such a thing possible? Surely Arthur Ravener was even more eccentric than she had originally supposed, and she had given him credit for a considerable portion of eccentricity. What! Settle down to common-place matrimony, and receive the butcher, the baker and the greengrocer in the first week of married life! What could he mean?

"Don't be absurd, Letty," I said fretfully, in reply to this outburst. "It was my idea and not his." (There was a whopper, but I felt I must do something desperate.) "I dislike traveling, and I am convinced that we should quarrel before we reached Paris. And then, my dear," faintly, "I should not care for my husband to see me—seasick." (That was an inspiration.)

"Well, Elsie, I suppose you know best what you like. It looks queer, though. Honeymoons may not be fashionable in the very, very highest society; but, my dear, you don't belong to the very, very highest society."

"Don't dare to say that to my mother," I cried, "or she would kill you in her frenzied indignation."

I tried to believe that I was satisfied, but I was not. With all my superiority, I was disappointed.

CHAPTER VIII.

My marriage was not a particularly interesting event from an anecdotal standpoint. My mother was far too precisely conventional to allow anything to interfere in the slightest with the rule laid down by that terrible tyrant in petticoats, Mrs. Grundy.[1]

I was rather surprised that Arthur cared for the amount of publicity which I saw would attend the event, but he positively gloried in it. He seemed anxious to have his marriage recorded in the four corners of the globe. The feminine newspaper correspondents, who called to ask for the particulars of Miss

---

1 Mrs. Grundy is a name for a conventional, priggish person, based on a minor character in Thomas Morton's play *Speed the Plough* (1798). A similarly straitlaced figure with the name of Mrs. Grundy appears in Samuel Butler's novel *Erewhon* (1872).

Bouverie's bridal dress, Miss Bouverie's trousseau,[1] and Miss Bouverie herself, I had strict injunctions from my betrothed to satisfy as far as possible.

My wedding morning was one in which novelists delight—plenty of sun, and a delightfully invigorating atmosphere. I was as happy as a bird. The prospect of freedom from the hateful society chains, which I felt would in a few years deprive me of my much prized liberty, added to the love which I felt for Arthur Ravener, were the causes of my bliss.

I was a dainty little bride in my white robes, but I still had the horrible feeling that I was not nearly as pretty as Arthur. The flush on his cheek, his full red lips, long eyelashes, and splendid complexion far surpassed my efforts in those directions. He was more noticed in the church than I was—by which you will perceive that my excitement did not prevent my powers of observation from having full play. Perhaps it was his beauty after all that gained for him the contempt of men. The sterner sex have their weaknesses, and we do not monopolize,—as they are so fond of asserting,—all the petty envy and spite in this world.

I saw all my old friends in the church. My "belongings" certainly out-numbered Arthur's. Two hideous old maiden aunts, one dilapidated uncle, and three lachrymose cousins constituted his force of relatives. I feel it is awful of me to allude in such terms to people who could now claim relationship with myself, but I do not intend to conceal anything from my readers.

A drowsy old minister, so well known that I suppose he thought that any exertion on his part was unnecessary, made us man and wife, and kept his gaze rivetted all the time on the bridesmaids, who imagined they were not paying proper attention on that account, and seemed at a loss to know what to do to get rid of his eyes.

How I should have enjoyed the wedding if it had been somebody else's. Letty and I, in a corner of the church, could have picked everybody to pieces and amused ourselves generally. I can even imagine what I should have said about myself, and I know I should have sworn that Arthur was rouged. My bridesmaids I should have revelled in criticising, because I thoroughly disliked every one of them. My mother had selected them, and I had nothing to do in the matter but submit.

Arthur seemed to be in a dream, from which he only awoke

---

1 A bride's collection of clothes, house linens, and other personal and domestic belongings.

when the reverend gentleman put those extremely leading questions to him. His voice was hoarse as he answered. His hand trembled as he placed the wedding ring on my finger. His fingers were icily cold. Only once did he look at me. I fancied then that there was just a faint tinge of compassion in the glance. I met it with a proud smile. Ah! he little knew what a lucky girl I thought myself.

After the ceremony came a reception and breakfast, at which everybody I had ever seen seemed to be present. In the evening there was to be a ball, at which, of course, we were not to be present. I was glad for once to follow fashion's dictates. Early in the afternoon Arthur and I said good-bye to a few hundred people, and stepping into the carriage which was waiting for us, set out for Tavistock Villa.

★★★★★

As we rolled away from the metropolis towards our country home, I tried hard to direct my thoughts into those channels through which I felt they ought to flow. Here was I, a bride of a few hours, leaving home without a regret and without a reflection of "childhood's associations," the new life, and other pathetic subjects over which nineteenth century brides are popularly supposed to become sentimental. I must put it all down to the flippancy of my nature.

Arthur made no attempt to break the silence. If I was an unusual bride, certainly he was the most utterly unconventional bridegroom it was possible to imagine. His eyes were fixed dreamily upon two little fleecy clouds which were floating about artlessly above us. He could not have looked more hopelessly subdued if he had been sitting in a funeral coach, and going to bury a friend. I suppose my glance aroused him.

"Are you enjoying this ride, Elsie?" he asked, kindly.

"Yes," I answered, noting his effort to amuse me, and feeling grateful to him for it. "I suppose," I said, laughing, "that all these people would be staring at us if they knew we were bride and bridegroom. They take us for brother and sister, undoubtedly."

"Or an old married couple," he added, smiling.

"I wonder if we ever shall be old commonplace people," I went on happily. "Imagine us fifty years from now, Arthur—you a nice reminiscent old man with white hair (you see I decline to think of you as cross and crotchety), sitting on one side of the fire, and I, a talkative old body, having outlived every weakness but that furnished by the tongue, which no woman could outlive if she were a female Methuselah."[1]

Arthur laughed, and seemed for the first time since I had known him to be perfectly at his ease. I put my hand ("my little gloved hand," as my friends the novelists would say) on his arm. He might have squeezed it if he had chosen. I am quite sure I should not have objected, except perhaps by a little maidenly coyness, which does not amount to very much. Arthur, however, took no notice whatever of my innocent little hand. Indeed, by a movement he made as if to look out of the carriage window, he contrived to shake it off. This I did not notice at the time, but as I have since become accustomed to think and brood over every little incident of those days, I have remembered it.

After that we talked merrily for the remainder of the ride. I was determined that I would start my married life with mirth. Men hate miserable, doleful women. Nine out of ten of them would sooner have an ugly wife who laughed than a pretty one who cried. Now I resolved that Arthur Ravener should have a wife who was both pretty and jolly. So I was as lively as I could be.

Tavistock Villa came into sight all too soon. It was a pretty red brick house, which I shall not attempt to describe. I am an utter failure from an architectural standpoint, and only know two things in that line: that some houses are Gothic[2] and some are not. The house had been the gift of my mother, and it had been furnished by my husband. We went in.

I was loud in my admiration of his taste as soon as we had passed the front door. Every article of furniture seemed to have been selected with excellent judgment. I will not weary my readers with a description of tables and chairs and carpets, which have nothing to do with my story.

"Here are your rooms, Elsie," said Arthur, opening the door of an exquisite little boudoir, "and you can be as completely alone here as though you were Robinson Crusoe on the desert island."

"I shall not want to be alone very often, dear," I said, gushingly.

"I have a couple of rooms on the other side of the house fitted up for myself, to smoke and write in," he went on, rather hesitat-

---

1   The oldest person mentioned in the Old Testament. He is reported to have died at the age of 969.

2   Refers to an architectural style that flourished in Europe during the Middle Ages.

ingly, paying no attention to my pretty little speech. "You see I do a little literary work, and I—I—do not want to be disturbed."

"You shall not be disturbed, Arthur," I said, dutifully. "Let me go and inspect your rooms, please."

He looked annoyed. "They are in great disorder, Elsie," he said, "and I don't think you had better venture into them."

"I feel a wifely interest in them, dear," I pleaded with a smile.

"Not now," he said hastily.

"I believe you're a Bluebeard,[1] Arthur, and that the bodies of a dozen preceding Mrs. Ravener's lie festering in that room. I shall wait until you go out, like the last and surviving Mrs. Bluebeard did, and then make a voyage of exploration."

"You will not be repaid for your trouble," he said, smiling. But he was vexed. I could see it.

"I don't see why your rooms are at one side of the house and mine at the other, Arthur," I said. "It's very unsociable, I am sure."

"Nonsense," was my husband's testy response. "Every man ought to have a den of his own, in which he can smoke, or read, or write."

"I know it," was my prompt rejoinder, "but, though it is an odious thing to say, I could have permitted you to smoke in my boudoir."

"You are not your mother's daughter," he said, laughing rather uneasily.

Arthur then introduced me to a young French girl, whom he had engaged as my maid. Marie was certainly a pretty woman, not a bit Gallic to look at. She had honest gray eyes, an excellent complexion, and brown hair. I liked her appearance and thanked Arthur for his thoughtfulness. Since I had entered Tavistock Villa I had seen nothing but evidences of his earnest desire to make my life there pleasant. When we had finished inspecting our new home, or rather, when I had come to the end of my gushing superlatives, and his services as guide were no longer required,

---

1 French literary folktale written by Charles Perrault (1628–1703), published in Paris in 1697. *Bluebeard* tells the tale of an evil nobleman who systematically kills all of his wives and hides the corpses in his basement. Having married a new young wife, Bluebeard informs her that she has access to all rooms in the castle except the basement room. While Bluebeard is away the wife enters the room and upon her gruesome discovery drops her key, leaving Bluebeard to discover her transgression. Upon this discovery he attempts to kill her but she is saved by her brothers.

we decided to take a stroll through the pretty Kew roads, and return in time for dinner. He led the way and I followed. Down the dusty, charming little lanes we went, talking all the time, and laughing frequently. I had never known Arthur so entertaining as he was that afternoon. He told me stories of his school days, of his dead father and mother, of his musical studies, and of all his old friends. I was not obliged to catechize him. He talked freely and seemed to enjoy it.

That was a delightful afternoon. I shall always remember it. I can see the delicious little town as I saw it before it became hateful to me. I can recollect my first impressions of the sunny thoroughfares, the lovely gardens, and the comfortable, unpretentious houses.

It was dark when we turned back. I was rather tired. The day had been somewhat fatiguing. It is rather an unusual event in one's life to be married. Arthur might have offered me his arm, I thought. But he made no attempt to do so as I walked by his side. We found dinner awaiting us. It was a very elaborate meal, with I don't know how many courses. I seemed to have come to the end of my good spirits. I did not feel inclined to talk, and as Arthur appeared to be wrapped in his own thoughts (not agreeable ones, either, if I can judge from his face) silence prevailed. It seemed strange to be sitting there at dinner with him. I felt rather sorry that he had objected to the honeymoon; I really began to wonder, now that I had seen Kew, how we could possibly amuse ourselves there for any length of time. I wondered more for his sake than for my own, as I know that to men variety is always charming.

"Elsie," said Arthur, breaking the silence at last, "do you think, dear, that you could get along without me this evening. You have Marie—and—and I must run up to town?"

My husband was very intently regarding the walnuts on his plate as he asked this question—very intently indeed.

"Of course, Arthur," I replied, quickly, "if you must leave me, go by all means. I would not like to interfere with any of your business arrangements, or—"

"You are a good little woman," he said, but he did not look into my face and thank me for what I really considered a sacrifice. I thought it was rather strange that he should be obliged to go up to London so soon. Surely he could have transacted any business he might have had before we started, though as Arthur was "a gentleman" (in the language of the directory) I was at a loss to imagine what business could call him away, and surely the poorest commercial drudge took a holiday and devoted the first week at least of his married life, exclusively to his wife. However, there might be a hundred reasons for his departure, and I had no doubt that when I had earned the right to know what they were, he would permit me to do so.

"I may be rather late, Elsie," he said hastily, "but do not worry." He left the room a few moments later, and returned overcoated and ready to start.

"Amuse yourself, Elsie," he said. "Do anything you like, and try not to be homesick. Good-bye, dear."

He was leaving without kissing me. Though I had protested so often that I would not tolerate a demonstrative husband, Arthur's conduct seemed so strange, that a feeling of resentment came over me. I did not look up.

"Good-bye, Elsie," repeated my husband, uneasily approaching me. "What is the matter?"

"Nothing."

"Well, good-bye."

"Good-bye."

He started for the door, and the next instant I was after him. "Arthur," I cried impulsively, "you shall not go from me in that way, even if you intend being away only half-an-hour. Kiss me."

He bent forward and touched my lips with his, so coldly and undemonstratively, that I shrank back, and looked at him in surprise. I felt chilled. "Come back early," I said, returning to the room hastily, anxious to be away from him. I decided that I would go to my boudoir, so calling Marie to keep me company, we went upstairs to that cosy little apartment.

I had a long evening before me and the prospect was not a lively one. I could not feel at home in Tavistock Villa, which a few hours ago I had never even seen. It seemed to me that Arthur ought to have stayed with me, no matter what sacrifice he made. I knew very little about brides and bridegrooms beyond what I had read in novels, nine-tenths of which either ended with a couples' engagement, or began, in early married life.

I went to the drawing-room and tried the piano, but somehow I could derive no amusement from it. I glanced at a couple of books, but their unreality disgusted me. The heroine in one of them was sentimental to idiocy, with a flower-like face and violet eyes, while the principal character in the other was a hoyden with whom I could find no sympathy. I went back to my boudoir. It was delightfully comfortable. I installed myself in an easy-chair, made Marie sit opposite, poor girl, and then closed my eyes.

"Is it that Madame is recently married?" asked Marie presently, more, I felt convinced, to break a silence that was becoming oppressive than from any real interest in me or my belongings.

"Did you not know that we were married this morning, Marie?" I demanded rather sharply.

"*Comment!*"[1] She was interested now to such an extent that the exclamation she uttered was in her own language. "You were married this morning—to-day?"—with incredulity.

"Certainly," said I. "When my husband engaged you did he not tell you that he was about to be married?"

"No, Madame," replied Marie. "When I called regarding the advertisement he told me I was to be maid to his wife. In consequence I thought you were long married. But, Madame, pardon me, if you were married to-day, why is it that Monsieur leaves you so soon alone?"

"Why not?" I was furious with her and would have given a sovereign[2] for the privilege of administering a sharp slap. I could not answer her question. I knew of no answer. It was evident, however, from her unfeigned surprise that Arthur had done a very unusual thing when he left me alone on my wedding-day. My instinct told me that he was entirely in the wrong. Marie, however, had confirmed this hardly admitted view. She sat with her mouth slightly open, staring at me in such unpleasant surprise that I was forced to turn my face away.

"You are very rude, Marie," I said at last, desperately angry at the girl's stupidly apparent astonishment. "Don't you know that it is the height of impoliteness to stare at anybody like that? I am surprised at you, a Frenchwoman, behaving in such a manner."

It did me good to manifest a little surprise on my own account. I saw no reason why she should be permitted to monopolize it all.

"Madame will excuse me," said the girl quickly. "I am not yet entirely used to English customs. It seemed so droll to me that a bridegroom should leave his bride—Madame will pardon me."

I rose and paced up and down the room. What a fool I was to worry myself about such trifles. Arthur had shown nothing but the most delicate consideration for me up to the present, and yet because he asked my permission to absent himself for a few hours on our wedding-day, I worked myself up into a state of nervous excitement on the ground that the proceeding happened to be a little unusual. Pshaw! what nonsense. Had we not a whole life-

---

1 French: how!
2 A British gold coin worth one pound sterling, now minted only for commemorative purposes.

time to spend together? How could I be so ridiculous? "Ha! Ha! Ha!" I burst out laughing. Poor Marie must have experienced another surprise concerning English customs. She looked up, her gray eyes round as saucers. "Is Madame ill?"

"Fiddlesticks!" I exclaimed, with unpardonable inelegance. "Let us come into the drawing-room, and I will teach you how we waltz over here."

Alas! with all the efforts I made, the time dragged horribly. It was now midnight, and there had been nothing to break the monotony of the evening. I wondered what they were doing at home. Dancing, of course, for my sake. The ball was now at its height, and my mother was in a state of dignified ecstasy. Marie sat in a low armchair, yawning. She tried to yawn gracefully, I am sure, but it was quite impossible.

"Go to bed, Marie," I said, peremptorily, at one o'clock.

"I will wait with Madame," was the reply.

And again we sat down to the contemplation of each other's charms. How lonely it was! We made a round of the house and saw that everything had been properly secured for the night, simply because I felt so nervous that I could not sit there inactive. I will not attempt to describe all the weird noises we heard, because everybody who has sat up in the early hours of the morning knows exactly what they are. At three o'clock I started violently. I think I must have been asleep. The striking of the clock in the hall aroused me.

"Marie," I said a few minutes later, "I am going to bed. My husband will not be back to-night, that is very sure. I will wait no longer. Good-night."

To my surprise Marie kissed me. I remember hoping that she did not intend to do so every night. I hated affectionate people as I have already said often enough. I was almost dead with fatigue. I went to my room, undressed quickly, and was soon in a deep, dreamless sleep, from which I awoke when my watch told me it was ten o'clock, and the sun was dancing merrily over the daintily carpeted floor.

CHAPTER IX.

I felt thoroughly good-natured, and was determined to be as smilingly gracious as I possibly could when I met my eccentric husband. Of course I should not even allude to his most unaccountable behavior, but I had no doubt at all that he would be utterly repentant, and that his remorse would even go so far as to melt the ice of his manners.

I selected one of the nattiest little morning dresses that my trousseau contained. It was one of those charmingly devised costumes that would render the most hideous woman acceptable. Now, I was not hideous by any means, and when I took a final look at myself before descending, I had never appeared more comely, I thought. In spite of my early morning vigil, the roses bloomed becomingly on my cheeks, and my eyes sparkled with health.

Down the broad staircase I sailed. I was Mrs. Arthur Ravener now, so it would not do to "trip." Matrons sail.[1] That term has a very dignified sound in my ears. Before entering the breakfast-room, I peeped coyly in. Yes, there sat my husband, deep in a newspaper. He had already begun breakfast, and must have poured out his coffee, and buttered his toast with his own manly fingers. I walked in.

"Good-morning, Arthur," I said, coquettishly, taking my seat at the head of the table. Perhaps I had better confess that I felt a little nervous.

"You are late, Elsie," remarked my husband, laying down his paper. "I thought I would take the initiative and begin breakfast. I hope you do not think it impolite on my part?"

"Not a bit, I shall soon catch you up. I'm as hungry as a hunter. This Kew air seems to be invigorating."

In reality I had no appetite at all. The thought of breakfast sickened me, but I was determined, with all the perversity of my sex, that he should not know it.

"I am glad of that, Elsie," said Arthur, smiling at me kindly. He rose, poured me out a cup of coffee, buttered a slice of toast for me, helped me to some cold partridge, and went back to his seat. He had looked just a trifle uneasy, I fancied, when I entered, but he had now completely recovered. The awful idea occurred to me that he would make no comments whatever on his absence last night. As I had always heard that between husband and wife there should be complete confidence, I resolved that I would do violence to my feelings and broach the subject, as a matter of principle, if for no other reason I did not want abject apologies, but I was not going to be treated with such sublime disrespect.

"Will you have half my newspaper, Elsie?" asked Arthur, as I sat silently devouring my partridge, with all my good temper rapidly vanishing.

---

1 Here used to make a distinction between the walk of the young woman and the slower, more dignified walking of a married woman.

"Thank you." He handed me a couple of sheets.

"They have given a splendid account of the wedding," he said, "and I suppose that all England knows about it now."

"Why are you so anxious for all England to be informed that you are a Benedict?"[1] I enquired scornfully.

He reddened and made no reply. I glanced carelessly through the half column of silly gush, learned that I had made a very interesting bride, and noticed some very flattering allusions to my husband. "After the reception," I read aloud, "the bride and bridegroom left for Kew, where they will spend the honeymoon in their handsome home, Tavistock Villa." "They might have added," I said, laying down the paper and trying to speak indifferently, "that the bridegroom returned to London early in the evening, and was back in Kew again in time for breakfast."

I leaned forward in my chair to enjoy the effect of my sarcasm.

"Don't be foolish, Elsie," said my husband, from behind his newspaper, "I told you I was obliged to go up to London, and I know you are too sensible a little woman to stand in my way in a case like that."

"Stand in your way!" My cheeks were the color of peonies. I was horribly indignant.

"Elsie," said Arthur, "I don't want you to be vexed. You are very young, and—and—well, I am older. There was really no cause for you to worry last night. This house is as safe as a—a bank. Kew is a very quiet, respectable sort of place, and such things as burglars are almost unknown. I—I—was going to telegraph you that I was unable to return, but—but—"

"But what?"—sharply.

"I was afraid a telegram might alarm you. Now, Elsie, there is not a soul who knows anything about this—this—this affair, and I would not talk about it."

"Talk about it?" I exclaimed in angry surprise. "With whom?"

"W-with anybody. With your mother, for example."

"Oh, no," I laughed satirically. "It would not interest her. I am not a gossip, Arthur. Our affairs can interest nobody but ourselves."

"You are a thoroughly sensible girl, Elsie," said Arthur, with what sounded like a little sigh of relief. "Now, hurry with your

---

1 A newly married man who was formerly an avowed bachelor, like the character of Benedict in Shakespeare's *Much Ado About Nothing* (c. 1598–99).

breakfast, dear, and I'll take you for a nice long drive, and we'll have luncheon out."

That restored my drooping spirits more than anything else could have done. I forgot all about my grievances. After all they were not very formidable. If I never had anything more to contend with during my life, I might think myself fortunate.

It was a glorious day and I was determined to enjoy myself. Arthur had a neat little phaeton[1] waiting at the door, and into it we stepped. Arthur took the whip, and off we went at a delightful rate. How keenly invigorating the air was! I thought of Letty Bishop and remembered how she hated such drives. The bane of her life was a red nose, and she would have had an extremely conspicuous one had she been with us today. After a delicious drive of a couple of hours, we "put up" at a little hotel, and Arthur ordered a most tempting luncheon. What a blessing an appetite is! We were both hungry. The last vestige of my woes vanished as I found myself opposite to a plate of succulent natives.[2] My good spirits must have been contagious. Arthur caught them, and was his own amiable, amusing self. He talked and laughed and told some excellent stories. I had never found myself with so agreeable a companion—and to think that he was my husband! What a senseless girl I had been to worry. I promised myself that for the future I would indulge in no more idiocy.

"Just think, Arthur," I said, as he dallied with some cheese (dallying with cheese is my own idea) and I made a combination of almonds and raisins, "Marie imagined we were old married people. You never told her that we were just married—you sly boy."

"Did you?" It was really very strange why Arthur should get so uncomfortable at my little innocent remarks.

"Of course I did. I don't propose to sail under false colors, as an antiquated dowager."

"What did Marie say?" with eagerness.

"She was very, very surprised. She thought you were so droll to go off to the City as you did. I was angry with her, and she said she was not accustomed to English habits." I spoke cheerfully; I had quite forgiven him.

My husband did not look pleased. "I do wish you would not chatter about me and my business, Elsie," he said with marked

---

1 A light four-wheeled carriage with one or two seats facing forward and drawn by a pair of horses.
2 British oysters.

vexation. "If Marie makes any more impertinent remarks, send her away."

I said nothing. Arthur was an oddity—*voilà tout*,[1] as my mother loved to remark. I must give way to him in a proper, wifely manner. I was resolved that "amiability, amiability, always amiability," should be my motto. So I cracked him three most inviting filberts and laid them as a peace offering on his plate.

"By-the-bye, Elsie," said my husband presently, as we were thinking about departing, "Captain Dillington is coming to dinner tonight."

If he had given me a sound box on the ears I could not have been more disagreeably surprised. I lost all idea of keeping to the text of my motto. What did he mean by asking this man to our house, the day following our marriage? Why, my mother had told me that as we were not going on a wedding trip, we must live in retirement for a month. I had Fashion on my side, thank goodness.

"To-night!" I exclaimed aghast.

"Why not?"

"It is not usual, Arthur. Why c-can't we have a nice l-little dinner alone?"

"Nonsense. It is perfectly proper to ask one's parents and most intimate friends to the house, I am sure. Elsie, I cannot put Captain Dillington off. You—you do not want me to do so."

He appealed to me. What could I say? I felt that an untruth would be the only thing that would please him. If I told the truth it would be to the effect that I hated Captain Dillington at all times, and my hatred was, if possible, intensified, just now.

"No, no," I said, choking down a little sob, "don't put him off. When d-did you invite him, Arthur?"

"When?"

"Yes, when?"

"Last night."

"Oh, you saw him last night. D-did you meet him accidentally?"

"Elsie!" exclaimed Arthur fretfully, "don't catechize me. What makes you so cross? I want to amuse you. I am doing all I can to prevent you feeling in the least homesick. I am very, very anxious for you to be happy, and you look miserable because I ask my greatest friend to the house. Why you yourself said that our great friendship was a source of admiration to you. It first attracted your attention."

---

1 French: that is all.

He spoke the truth. I had said all that and more. Of course I meant it. I did admire sincere friendship—but surely there was a limit to all things. His affection for Captain Dillington certainly need not interfere with his love for me. I was his wife after all. I would not argue, however. Captain Dillington was to come to dinner. So be it. I would reserve a careful analysis of my statements for a future occasion.

"I am foolish, Arthur," I said, rising. "Come, let us go home, and see that at any rate Captain Dillington will have something to eat."

He took my hand and pressed it lightly. His eyes looked into mine with gratitude clearly expressed in their depths. Yes, my self-sacrifice had its reward. I jumped at the crumbs he threw to me, and swallowed them ravenously. I could have digested more with perfect facility. We went back to Tavistock Villa. The drive home, however, was not very pleasant. The atmosphere seemed to be less invigorating. There were clouds in the sky. The horses were tired, and the dust, which the wheels of the phaeton sent up in columns, almost blinded me.

There were but few arrangements to make for the accommodation of our guest. I made myself charming in a dress of pale blue silk, and went down to the drawing-room. Captain Dillington was already there. He and Arthur stood with their backs to the door as I appeared. They were in earnest conversation, and did not even hear me enter.

"Good evening, Captain Dillington," I said affably, extending my hand.

"Ah, Mrs. Ravener—delighted I am sure." There was horrible unction in his greeting. Was I so blinded by prejudice that everything this man did simply nauseated my soul?

"I do sincerely hope that I am not intruding," he went on blandly. "I told Arthur—"

"Not at all," I said in the tones which a refrigerator would use if it could speak. "How are things in London?"

"You were there but yesterday," with a smile, as though he were determined that I should not forget this. "There is positively nothing new—positively nothing."

The announcement of dinner was a welcome sound in my ears. How heartily I wished before commencing it that it was over. It was not a very trying ordeal, however. My husband and Captain Dillington talked on a variety of subjects, and I did not feel it at all necessary, under the circumstances, to include myself in the conversation. I did not absolutely wish Captain Dillington to feel that his presence was unpleasant, but I likewise did not wish him to congratulate himself on the fact that it was pleasant.

After dinner I rose, and, leaving them to their own resources, went into the drawing-room. I played some of my beautiful *"morceaux de salon,"*[1] not because I liked them, but because it passed away the time and made a noise. I was not happy enough to indulge in any of the dainty little pieces in which I generally delighted when alone.

It was ten o'clock before they joined me. Captain Dillington congratulated me upon my "exquisite touch" and said a few conventional things, after which the two men sat down to a game of chess.

What a wearisome parody of amusement chess is, in my opinion; I suppose I am not intellectual enough to appreciate it. I remember I once tried to learn it, but I never could remember how to move the pawns, and always called out "check" at the most ridiculously inopportune moments.

I sat in a low rocking chair and yawned desperately. I made no pretense of occupying myself with fancy work,[2] which I despised most cordially.

I took up the *Times* and tried to get interested in the agony column.[3] I wondered what it was that A. B. would hear of to his advantage if he communicated with Mr. Snipper of Lincoln's Inn Fields.[4] I tried to imagine what a weight of woe would be lifted from the heart of Lottie L. when she read that all would be forgiven if she would only return to Jack D.

"You are tired, Elsie," said Arthur at last, pausing in an interesting move as I yawned in an ultra-outrageous manner.

"Very," I said.

Then he forgot that I was there.

At midnight they were still hard at it. My eyelids were closing with fatigue. I was raging inwardly (which ought to have kept me awake, but it did not).

At one o'clock I could stand it no longer. I rose from my chair and went towards the door.

"Good-night," I said, looking straight in front of me. If they replied, I did not hear them. I fled to my room.

---

1   A selection of short compositions picked for the drawing-room recital.

2   Ornamental needlework.

3   The advice column in a newspaper.

4   Until 1895 private property but today the largest public square in London. Throughout the nineteenth century the area was popular with affluent barristers, probably owing to the area's proximity to the Inns of Court, where barristers had their professional associations.

CHAPTER X.

I could not sleep. I tried my hardest to woo the old humbug Morpheus,[1] who is always on hand when not wanted, but fails to respond to urgent appeals. I was as wide awake as I had been in the early morning, with the sole difference that I was now feverish and oppressed. I rang the bell that communicated with Marie's room. She responded to the call, looking horribly sleepy and unlovely, poor girl.

"Marie," I said, "I cannot sleep, Would you mind sitting with me until morning? I don't know what is the matter with me, but I am too wide awake even to doze."

I threw open the window of my room and let the cool night breezes blow through my refractory tresses. It was a glorious moonlight night, and as I looked at the pretty little gardens in the lovely blue-white illumination, I felt less ill at ease.

"Madame will take cold," Marie ventured to remark.

"Madame is not so fragile as she looks," was my reply. A crunching sound below made me start and look down. Surely I could not be mistaken. My husband and Captain Dillington were in the garden, slowly walking up and down, arm-in-arm. They were smoking placidly, and conversing in low, earnest tones, between puffs. I sent Marie to bed with a promptitude which must have caused her considerable astonishment. Truly by this time her ideas of English customs must have been of the Munchausen order.[2] I did not know Arthur was so fond of nocturnal rambles. How glad I should have been had he asked me to join him. Perhaps he supposed that I was a delicate little reared-in-the-lap-of-luxury maiden, and felt that my wifely duties consisted in looking pretty and sitting at the head of the dinner-table. What a mistake he made!

I could see the two men distinctly, though they could not detect me behind the pretty plants that adorned my windows. I could hear them talking, though it was impossible to distinguish what they said while they were at a distance. They were approaching me, however, and as they came nearer their words fell distinctly on my ears. "She is a dear little thing, Dill," said Arthur nervously.

---

1   The god of dreams in Greek mythology.

2   Karl Friedrich Hieronymus Münchhausen (1720–97) was a German nobleman and famous inventor of tall tales. His book *The Surprising Adventures of Baron Munchhausen* was published anonymously in London in 1785 and was later discovered to be authored by Rudolf Erich Raspe (1736–94).

"What of that?" came quickly from the lips of the Captain.

"She deserves a better husband. I am beginning—"

"Don't begin then," angrily, "your wife is a mere child. Give her a comfortable home, handsome dresses, and the thousand little comforts that women love, and she will be your devoted admirer for many years to come. Don't let her read trashy books, and when you go into society, monopolize her yourself."

"Perhaps you are right, Dill," sighed Arthur, "you always are, old man, but—poor Elsie!"

I could hear no more. They were already far away, and I had strained my ears—if that be possible—to understand this much of their conversation. I am not sentimental, as I think I have already proved. It may have been the strange influences of the hour that unnerved me. The tears coursed slowly down my cheeks. The garden was blotted from my sight.

The conversation between my husband and Captain Dillington had been couched in the language to which I had been accustomed all my life, and yet I could not have understood its meaning less, if it had been spoken in Greek. Why did I deserve a better husband? Arthur was as good as I was, I loyally believed. He might have a few eccentricities, but I had more faults. For each of his eccentricities I had two faults. I was flippant, childish, emotional. Perhaps, too, I myself was eccentric. Letty Bishop had always said so; my mother had ever declared it. It was Arthur who merited a better wife, not I who deserved a better husband. He had been rather inattentive to me during these early days of our married life. The only reason could be that I was not sufficiently attractive to him. I had not yet studied him enough to conform to his views. It surely was a wife's duty to conform to her husband's views, and not a husband's obligation to regulate himself to his wife's ideas. You see what a dutiful little lady I was inclined to be.

I kept my eyes fixed upon the garden, and longed for an opportunity to go to Arthur and settle any little difficulties before they widened into an impassable gulf.

The opportunity came. With joy I saw Captain Dillington leave Arthur, throw aside his cigarette, and go into the house. I presumed that he intended to continue as our guest. I had made no preparation for him, however.

I dressed quicker than I had ever done before in my life, and throwing a long cloak over me, rushed down the stairs, pell mell, forgetting my previous views upon the matronly "sail." It was very dark in the hall. The lights had been diminished to a glimmer. I stumbled on my way to the door, and should have fallen if some one had not come to my aid.

"Mrs. Ravener!" exclaimed Captain Dillington—for he it was—in great surprise, "what are you doing about at this hour?"

"Have I not as much right to be about, as you call it, as you and my husband?"

He made no answer. I could not see his face.

"You were not going out, surely, Mrs. Ravener?" he asked, a few seconds later.

"I was going out, and I am going out," said I with beautiful redundancy.

"You will take cold," he suggested, quickly; "the night air is very chilly, you know."

"Good-night, Captain Dillington,"—preparing to join Arthur. "I presume you intend remaining with us. You do not think of going up to town at this hour?" Sweetly hospitable, but I could not help it.

"Oh, no."

"*Au revoir*, then."

"Let me take you to your husband, Mrs. Ravener; you may stumble again, you know."

"Thank you, Captain Dillington, I can find my way."

"Let me accompany you; I am in no hurry to retire."

"No," I said sharply. "I should make no more ceremony with you than you do with me, if I wanted you. I wish to see Arthur, alone—alone, Captain Dillington."

"As you wish." He shrugged his shoulders, and with his unctuous smile, left me. I went forthwith into the gardens.

Arthur had taken possession of a rustic seat. His delicate profile was clearly defined in the moonlight. He was evidently deep in thought—and I suppose he had no idea that his reflections were about to be interrupted. I walked quickly across the damp, dewy grass, and before he knew it, I was seated beside him.

"Arthur."

He started violently, and almost jumped from his seat.

"Elsie!" he exclaimed. "You here, and at this time. Why did you come? You will take a severe cold. You should not have ventured out."

"Would you mind very much if I did take a severe cold?"

"How can you be so foolish, Elsie?" he asked testily. "Of course, I should mind. Have I not charge of your future life? What is putting such strange ideas into your head, dear?"

"Arthur," I said slowly, "I was at my open window just now,

and I heard you talking with Captain Dillington. Oh, I did not distinguish much of what you said," I went on, as I noticed he looked disconcerted. "You declared that I deserved a better husband, and Captain Dillington thought that I was a mere child, and that as long as I had a comfortable home, I should be happy. Am I a mere child, Arthur?"

"Are you?" he asked slowly, not meeting my eyes. "If you are, Elsie—and I believe it now, as I believed it when I first met you—try and remain so. Elsie, dear, be innocent and good as you now are as long as you can, for your own sake, and—" there were tears in his eyes—"for mine. If you only knew, dear, how anxious I am that your life should be a happy one—that through no fault of mine you should suffer—" he was agitated as I had never seen any man before. "Why did you come out to me here, Elsie. Why—why did you come?" this in feverish, excited tones.

"Because I love you, Arthur," I exclaimed vehemently, throwing my arms around his neck, all my theories as to the absurdity of demonstrative behavior gone to the winds.

"Don't, Elsie," he said, unclasping my arms.

"I will," I said, "I am your wife; you have no right to repulse me. Arthur," noticing with surprise his look of alarm, "you prefer Captain Dillington's company to mine. You selected him for your midnight stroll. You—you—you think n-n-nothing of me. Oh, Arthur, you are unkind, cruel, heartless."

I burst into a passion of tears, which were as much a surprise to me as they were to Arthur. It must have been years since I had wept, and now I was succumbing to a regular storm. I became hysterical. I remember feeling that I was making a fool of myself, and trying to laugh with the most ridiculous result.

"I may be a child," I sobbed, "but I don't want to be slighted; you—you are slighting me. You—do not care for me. You do not,—no—no—you do not. You hate me, I know it. You—wish—you were n-not married. Let me go home. I—I don't want to go, but—if—y-you think it would be better—Why don't you speak? Speak, Arthur, speak."

By this time I was beside myself, I was wrought up to a state of extreme excitement. Arthur said nothing. He took my hands quickly in his. I looked at him; his face was ghastly in its whiteness. His lips were as bloodless as his cheeks. His fingers were icy. I shrank back from him. My excitement disappeared as rapidly as it had come. I sat beside him limp and subdued.

"Elsie," said Arthur, presently, in a broken voice. "I—I must be an awful wretch."

He put his hand before his eyes; I could see the tears trickling through his slender, white fingers. My heart reproached me. Why, oh, why was I born emotional? A plague upon emotional women, one and all, say I.

"You are not—you are not," I murmured, "I am to blame after all. Don't mind what I said, dear. It is this scene, and this—this hour which have affected me. I—I could not sleep—I—"

Arthur again took my hands in his. In his eyes, as he fixed them upon my face, I saw "a something" that sent a thrill of ecstatic bliss through my heart. He leaned forward, and pressed a kiss—warm and tender—upon my lips—the first he had ever voluntarily given me. I looked up.

A cold shudder ran through my frame, a feeling of intense disgust seemed to permeate my soul. Before us stood Captain Dillington, coldly statuesque and hatefully conspicuous. Arthur dropped my hands. The flush upon his face, which I could see in the moonlight, faded. His eyes still fixed upon mine—he had not looked at the captain—grew coldly and studiously friendly as ever. The change was startling.

"I trust you do not object to my cigar, Mrs. Ravener?" asked the intruder politely.

I would rather have inhaled the smoke of ten thousand cigars lighted at one time, than listened to one word from the repulsive lips of this man.

I could not answer him. "Good-night, Arthur," I said, and rising sped across the lawn to the house, and regained my chamber. I slept.

CHAPTER XI.

For eight days Captain Dillington remained with us, a most unwelcome guest as far as I was concerned. He knew it, too, I suppose. I was too young to be able to dissemble. I disliked the man so thoroughly, that I made the fact only too apparent.

My interview with Arthur in the garden, however, had eased my mind considerably. I felt now that I could soon win my way to his heart, if I could only succeed in gaining his confidence. This, I reflected, must not be forced, but carefully and studiously worked for.

Captain Dillington's visit was a source of horrible discomfort to me. To be sure, while he was in the city during the daytime, Arthur took me for a "constitutional,"[1] but after dinner I was left entirely to my own resources and those of my faithful Marie, whom I was now beginning to appreciate more than I could have thought possible. The men sat down to their detestable game of chess, and long after midnight, at which time I left them, Marie informed me that they remained at the table. When I met them at breakfast, they were polite, amiable, talkative; they seemed to think that as long as they were satisfied, all was well.

How delighted I was when Captain Dillington at last informed me that he must return to London. I was so happy that I believe I favored him with a radiant smile, and oh, deceit! oh, hypocrisy!—hoped he would come again. I imagine he fully understood the frame of mind which induced the utterance of such a flagrantly improbable wish. I fancied I saw him bite his lips, though he merely bowed and thanked me.

"Arthur," I said, clasping my hands, while a flush of pleasure mantled my cheeks as Captain Dillington, with his valise and smile disappeared from our sight, "he has gone—at last."

Now, generally speaking, a fact that is so self-evident as the one which I had just mentioned, would need no further comment. Of course he had gone. We had seen him go. But under the circumstances it seemed to me that Arthur might have said something. He stood with his eyes fixed upon the ground, making little circles in the smooth gravel with the point of his shoe.

"Arthur, dear," I continued, laying my hand with its conspicuous gold circletted finger on his arm, "I am so glad."

My husband did not look up. "What is your objection to Captain Dillington?" he asked. "I am sure he always treated you kindly—and no one could have been more polite."

"I am jealous of him, Arthur."

I got no further in my playful remark. "How dare you talk such nonsense?" he asked, passionately, turning upon me furiously and positively glaring at me. "Women are all the same, inconsistent, foolish, unstable as water. They do not know their own minds from one moment to another. I was wrong to believe you when you declared that you would never discountenance our friendship—that you admired it—that—pshaw! what a fool I was! Great heavens! that I should have been so deceived."

"Stop!" I exclaimed, my voice ringing out so loudly that it

---

1 A walk taken for the improvement of one's constitution.

astonished me, though I was too indignant and alarmed to pay any attention to it. "You have no right to talk in that manner to me, and I will not permit it. Captain Dillington's presence in this house was an affront to me, and he knows it if you do not. I still say I admire friendship, but when it causes a man to treat his wife with complete indifference and as a necessary incumbrance in his house, I retract and declare that I despise it—despise it from the bottom of my heart."

I turned my back upon him in silent disgust—silent, because in my bitter indignation I could say no more. Heaven knows that these angry words were called forth by himself, I would willingly have forgiven the first week of neglect and indifference, if with Captain Dillington's departure, he had shown the least sympathy for me. But to champion the cause of that intruder and disregard mine—I was no saint. He had slapped one cheek, but I would take good care that he should not slap the other.

"Have I treated you with neglect?" The anger was gone from his voice. I had frightened it away.

"Have you?" I asked scornfully. "You have treated me with such marked coldness, that even my maid, Marie, has been gossiping with the other servants about it."

Ah, I had made a mistake. I knew it the moment the words were out of my mouth.

"She has, has she?" he exclaimed in a towering rage. "She shall leave the house to-night. I will not pay a pack of drones to gossip about me. She shall go, and this minute, too."

"She shall not. If she leaves your house" (I was beside myself with rage and excitement, and was hardly accountable for what I said) "I will go too."

"Elsie!" There was actual fear in his voice. He looked so handsome as these varied emotions stirred him, that—alas! that I should say it—I felt that my indignation could not last much longer. As he uttered my name, he looked at me earnestly, and with a pained, wearied gaze. I began to feel sorry for him. Despise me, readers, and mentally declare that you would have acted far differently.

Women so often start in as plaintiffs and end as defendants in their controversies with the other sex.

"I mean it," I managed to say in a low voice.

"You would ruin my reputation," he began in a grieved tone. Unpardonably selfish as the remark was, it made just the impression upon me that he probably intended it should do.

"How can you say it?" I asked. "Arthur, listen to me. I love you, and I begin to think that I love you too well. If I did not care for you, I should be glad when you absented yourself from me, but—but—as it is—it—breaks m-my heart."

I was going to give way. I felt quite sure of that.

"Don't, Elsie," said Arthur, hastily. "Don't. I cannot stand scenes. I want you to be happy. I would not for the world see you in such distress, but—"

"But, what—"

"Nothing. Elsie, let us go for a long walk and drop these painful subjects." Painful subjects! He said it, I assure you.

"No," I said, sadly. I would not make myself cheap. He did not want me, I felt sure. I must try another policy.

"What are you going to do to pass away the morning?"

"Oh, I have a wealth of amusement," I said, smiling through my tears. "Do—do not trouble any more about me. You probably have some w-writing to do. Do not let me disturb you. Goodbye," and I ran away to my room.

Yes, I must try another policy. Perhaps I was letting him see too plainly that his neglect caused me pain. It might be that, like some men of whom I have since heard, he disliked to know that a woman was running after him. If I treated him as he treated me, perhaps I might teach him a little respect. Men do not like weak, clinging beings—at least some of them don't, and perhaps my husband belonged to that class. At any rate I would change my policy. Why do I say "change my policy?" I had none before. I was simply acting as my heart told me to act. Now I would follow the course prescribed by my reason. I could lose nothing by so doing, and I might gain my husband's love.

I congratulated myself that I had refused to accompany him on that walk. I was really dying to go, but I would deny myself the pleasure for the sake of possible results. He had not insisted—it would have been no use if he had—I told myself. Perhaps he was annoyed at my refusal. I sincerely hoped that he was. I trusted that he was even seriously angry and would resent my non-compliance with his request.

I must confess that the afternoon passed away most tediously for me. I called in Marie, and made her talk herself tired. I tried to be amused at her chatter, but I found it insufferably uninteresting. She would tell me all about Paris, and her own dull life in that city. The poor girl was the daughter of an honest little

Rue du Temple *fabricant*,[1] and her history was not exciting. If she had only been the daughter of a dishonest little *fabricant*, she would have been far more entertaining, I thought. I felt that she was supplying me with conversational gruel, and I was in a condition of mind when I wanted curry. As the hour for dinner drew nigh, I dressed myself carefully. Everything I could do to make myself look pretty—I did. I was determined that Arthur should admire me.

I recovered my spirits sufficiently to be able to "sail" downstairs, and as I reached the dining-room, the flush of excitement came to my cheeks. I wondered how it would all end. Arthur was not in the dining-room, so I threw myself into an armchair to await him. I was rather impatient. I suppose it was natural that I should be. I took up a newspaper and tried to read. I did not have to try very long.

"Mrs. Ravener." It was James, the butler. I suppose he was not sure that I was in the chair, as I was covered with newspaper.

"Yes, James."

"Master told me to give you this note."

I snatched it from the man's hands, and read it hastily. "Dear Elsie," it ran, "I have just received a telegram that calls me up to town immediately. Do not wait dinner for me, and pray do not be angry. Your affectionate husband, Arthur Ravener."

Oh, this was cruel. I waved my hand to James to dismiss him, and then flung myself upon the sofa in an agony of weeping. For twenty minutes I gave my grief full play, and then, when anger came peeping in, I let it enter and take possession of my soul. I rang the bell. James, with suspicious promptness answered the call.

"James, did any telegram come here for your master this afternoon?"

"Not to my knowledge, madame."

"Are you sure?"

"Quite."

"Go ask the servants, and find out if anybody brought a telegram for Mr. Ravener to the house to-day."

He soon returned. "No one has received any telegram. If one

---

1   Rue du Temple is a street in the Marais district of Paris, France, which throughout the mid-nineteenth century was home to the more affluent of the merchant classes. *Fabricant*: French for a manufacturer. Here used to disparage the merchant and manufacturing classes.

had come to the house," he added with the officiousness of his class, "I should have known it."

"You may go."

My blood was boiling. I would not be set aside. Perhaps Arthur Ravener thought I was a milk-and-water maiden.[1] He made a great mistake. "I gave him the option between peace and war," I said to myself, "and he has chosen war. So be it."

I tried to be lively, but it was a failure. I was changed. I was no longer a flippant girl, but a jealous woman. Does any one know what a jealous woman really is? I think not. Perhaps a volcano always on the eve of eruption is about the best simile I can suggest.

CHAPTER XII.

I am not going to weary my readers by describing in detail the ensuing days of my married life. I adopted the new policy I had mapped out. I became apparently indifferent to my husband's presence, uninterested in his nightly outgoings and his matutinal incomings, while at the same time I treated him with studied politeness and friendly affability. We talked and laughed at the dinner-table. We discussed politics—I made it a point of disagreeing with him, for the sake of permitting him to try and win me over to his way of thinking. Of course I let him finally convince me, and then declared how foolish I must have been ever to have thought otherwise. Then we talked books—I in my superficial way, he in his earnest, well read manner. I knew the names of the authors of nearly all the popular works of the day; I was one of those airy beings who examine the covers of books, dip into catalogues, and taste literature, as it were, from the outside.

He was really so entertaining that at times I forgot I was only playing a part. I could not help thinking that he would have enjoyed the conversation just as much if it had taken place with somebody else. I suppose I seemed rather bright—some women as shallow as I was often manage to appear so. I do not believe he appreciated this brightness because it belonged to his wife, but merely—bah; I hate analysis. After all, what I believed on this subject is neither here nor there.

I made not the slightest impression upon Arthur Ravener. A month had flown by since I had stood in my dollish finery at the

---

1 A woman with milk and water in her veins rather than good red blood; i.e., subservient or submissive.

hymeneal altar. Our walks had been dropped. That was one of the effects of my policy. He seemed perfectly satisfied. He had evidently thought that these "constitutionals" were necessary for my happiness. If I chose to discontinue them—well, then, they were not necessary for my happiness. It was very simple after all.

At breakfast, at luncheon, and at dinner, here I was—there he was. He was as platonically kind as any man could be. He always made enquiries as to my health, my wishes, my plans. I had but to suggest a thing, and I had his acquiescence almost before I had made the suggestion. And all this time, I was eating my heart out for love of this iceberg.

Women must be contemptible things. If I were a man I suppose I could not give utterance to such an ungallant remark, but no one can find fault with me when my sex is taken into consideration, and I am quite sure I shall find plenty of sisters to agree with me.

The old adage about the woman, the dog and the hickory tree, which nicely explains that the more you beat 'em the better they'll be, seems to me wonderfully true. Why should I care for this man? I was very young, of course, but I knew perfectly well that this utter neglect was simply outrageous. I remembered my horror at the compliments and pretty speeches with which my partners in the ball-rooms of my friends had overwhelmed me. I had hated them for their silly, tinsel-bound sentiments; their ill expressed admiration. I still did so. I should have been just as disgusted if I had heard them at the present time. But there was a happy medium to all things.

Between the conspicuously ridiculous adulation of comparative strangers, and the brotherly indifference of the man I had married, there must be a middle path of warm yet not necessarily demonstrative affection. I thought of the bride and bridegroom whom Arthur and I had criticised one night. "It disgusts me," I recollected saying, when Arthur had asked me if their conversation, to which we had listened, interested me. Well, I had no cause for such disgust in my own home. Arthur's indifference seemed to be unaffected by any policy I might adopt. I even tried to make him jealous. There was a bashful youth, who wore glasses and a perpetual smile, living close to Tavistock Villa, with an adoring mamma and two prim sisters, to whom Hector[1] was as the apple of their eye. He had frequently cast admiringly modest

---

1 In Homer's epic poem *The Iliad* (c. ninth/eighth centuries BCE), the Trojan prince Hector is a great hero of the Trojan War.

glances in my direction when he had stumbled across Marie and me in our daily walks.

"*Il a l'air joliment bête,*"[1] Marie said to me once in the loud security of the French language as we passed the gallant youth. He must have thought the remark was a flattering one, because he looked even more seraphically pleasant than usual. Dasy was his surname. He lacked the *i* which would have given him some claim upon the dainty characteristics of that little flower.

Mr. Dasy amused me. The delectable idea occurred to me to use him. I would cultivate his society. I would make Arthur desperately jealous. I had always heard that those bashful, rose-colored youths were the most dangerous, and if I had heard it, surely my husband had. Who could possibly introduce us? Of course I could smile at him and encourage him that way, but I was not inclined to have recourse to the methods of an unscrupulous flirt, when I was very far from being one. How I wished that flirting came as naturally to me as it did to some women.

I could call on Mamma Dasy if I liked. Neighborly courtesy would surely sanction that, but I felt I could not do it. I had an awful idea that this mamma might patronize me. I had a hideous presentiment that she would come and see us and wonder why we were not more affectionate. I could tell by her face that she was one of those women who think it the duty of a young married couple to do a little billing and cooing pro bono publico.[2] I could not possibly introduce prying eyes into my strange household. I think I should have dreaded any eyes at all, at that time. I was growing morbid. Even Marie was too many for me occasionally.

Fortune favored me. One afternoon, feeling more wretched than usual, and knowing that my husband was safely shut up in his sanctum and that I should not see him until dinner time, I took up a book and strolled towards the gardens. I selected a shady spot, opened my volume, and was soon engrossed in its contents.

When I looked up I found that I was not alone. There, sure enough, as large as life, and equally ugly, sat the Misses Dasy— sister Euphemia[3] and sister Sophronia. They were knitting. If they had been reading I should have looked up in surprise; if they had been drawing, my hair would have stood on end; if they had

---

1 French: He seems pretty foolish.
2 Latin: for the public good.
3 A Christian saint martyred for her faith at Chalcedon, c. 304–307 CE.

been indulging in small talk, it would have seemed indecent;—but they were knitting. It looked so natural. They belonged to the knitting class of females. As I said, I looked up. I smiled. Sister Sophronia smiled. Sister Euphemia smiled. We all smiled.

"How strange we do not meet more frequently, Mrs. Ravener," quoth sister Euphemia. "Hector says he often comes across you and your maid." "Yes," chirped sister Sophronia, "we wondered why we so rarely met you."

I thanked the stars—mentally, of course—that I had not been inflicted before. Now, however, I was rather glad to see them, as by them I might find access to dear Hector. So I told no fib when I remarked that I was charmed, though I am afraid that I should not have permitted a fib or two to stand in my way if they could have done me any good.

"Mr. Ravener does not believe in country walks, I suppose," remarked Euphemia presently, "like most men," she added.

Hateful sister Euphemia! I am convinced that her acquaintance with men must have been limited to dear Hector, and—as Portia[1] says—God made him, so let him pass as a man.

"Hush, Euphemia," said Sophronia in an audible aside, and in a virtuous tone. She could not have made any remark less calculated to please me. It was evident they had been discussing us.

"My husband is a literary man and writes all day long," said I, with one of the serenest, most child-like and fancy-picture smiles I had ever conjured up. "I dislike to disturb him, you know. Men are such queer things, are they not?"

"Yes," laughed Sophronia girlishly.

"Indeed they are," simpered Euphemia, dropping a stitch as a punishment for her giddiness.

"Is your brother a literary man?" I asked boldly.

"Oh, no," said Sophronia, scornfully, "dear Hector is nicely established in the hop business—malt and hops, you know." (Evidently imagining that I might think he was a dancing master.) "He is taking a holiday just now. He has been working so hard. Dear Hector!"

"He admires you, Mrs. Ravener," quoth Euphemia. "He says you have a face like a woman in—in—some painting, I can't remember the name."

Great goodness! Perhaps he referred to one of the paintings given away with a pound of tea. She was so vague, that fond sister.

---

1 The heroine of William Shakespeare's play *The Merchant of Venice* (c. 1596–98).

"Mr. Dasy compliments me," I said artlessly. "Do you know I think he is a very interesting looking young man. Hector you said his name was? Ah, it is not a misnomer." I sighed just a little. I felt they always told Hector everything. I was convinced that my utterances would be repeated unembellished. We chatted on pleasantly for half an hour. I made myself as nice as I possibly could, and I think I succeeded in impressing them favorably. I reserved my master-stroke for my departure.

"Good-bye, dear Miss Sophronia—good-bye, dear Miss Euphemia," I said gushingly, as I rose to go. "I am so delighted to have met you. You must call upon me" (I had to say it). "I have enjoyed this afternoon hugely. The gardens are certainly charming. I really think I shall come every day this week, beginning with to-morrow—" this with a little affected chirrup which might signify that I did not really mean it.

Ah, they would tell Hector, and he would accompany them to-morrow. For a beginner in the fashionable art of diplomacy, I was not so bad after all. They looked admiringly after me as I went, and I felt that they would gaze in my direction long after I could see them.

I was formally introduced to Mr. Dasy the following day. The modest hop merchant was completely overwhelmed. He grew purple in the face at everything I said for the first quarter of an hour, which means that his countenance was tinged with that royal hue during the entire fifteen minutes, for he allowed me to do all the talking. I did not flirt. I tried to do so, but could not succeed. I spoke sensibly, flattered Mr. Dasy a little—if that does not give discredit to my statement that I spoke sensibly—and simply allowed him to see that I liked talking to him. Hector certainly was not given to flattery.

He told me all about hops, the magnificent prospects for next year, how last year's crop had been anything but a good one; how terribly small the profits were in these times of cut-throat competition, and similar edifying facts. His talk was hoppy in the extreme. I felt that if only I could have talked malt the combination would have lulled us into beery intoxication.

For a week I cultivated the society of Hector Dasy. I should have been bored to death if I had not kept my object in view. I walked him up and down the Branston Road, in front of the windows of Tavistock Villa. I knew Arthur saw us at least twice, but he said nothing at all.

He was just as amiably indifferent when I met him at dinner; he spoke just as entertainingly; not by the faintest indication on his part, was I hurting him. Branston Road only possessed about half a dozen extremely detached houses, so I was not at all afraid of the neighbors. If the thoroughfare, however, had been densely lined with tenements, I do not think it would have made the least difference in my course of action.

At last I resolved upon a final stroke. If it did not succeed I would drop Mr. Dasy, perfectly convinced that I could never make Arthur jealous. It was rather a risky thing to do. I asked Hector Dasy to bring me a book that I particularly wanted, and kept him during the entire afternoon, my willing slave. Before this, I told James to give Mr. Ravener's letters into my possession and to inform his master, as soon as he came in, that I had them. I did this merely in order that Arthur should be forced to enter the drawing-room and see how nicely Hector Dasy and I agreed.

Never had any afternoon passed so slowly for me. The presence of this young man annoyed me intensely and all the more because in order to keep him, I was forced to talk prettily and incessantly. Mr. Dasy was something of a coxcomb[1] with all his bashfulness. I saw with alarm that he really imagined I liked him. I wondered what he would have said if I had told him the true facts of the case. Just before six o'clock, which was my husband's time for returning from town, when he passed the day there, I completed my Macchiavellianism.[2] I had purchased a quantity of wool, which I wanted wound. I was determined that Mr. Dasy should hold it for me. I made him kneel on the rug before me, and at six o'clock I was winding for dear life, and he was smiling beatifically.

Ah! I heard Arthur's step at last. I could always recognize it. James was telling him that I had his letters. James had told. He was coming in my direction. The door opened. He entered.

Now for my *rôle*.[3] "Arthur," I said with affected hesitation, "let me introduce you to my friend, Mr. Dasy—Mr. Dasy, my husband, Mr. Ravener."

I watched Arthur's face. I did not dare to look at poor Mr. Dasy. My husband's countenance showed positively no change.

---

1 A fop.

2 Application of the principles of statecraft and politics described by the Italian Renaissance philosopher and diplomat Niccolò Machiavelli (1469–1527), particularly in *The Prince* (1532). The term implies behavior defined by cunning, intrigue, ruthlessness, and duplicity.

3 French: part or role.

"I am glad to meet you, Mr. Dasy," he began, "I see you are making yourself useful. Isn't it rather too much to ask visitors to assist in such a laborious operation as wool winding, Elsie?" he said, smiling at me in all good fellowship, perfectly satisfied as though Hector had been Marie or—not to libel my French maid by comparison—a dummy from a tailor's shop.

"Mr. Dasy has been here idling away the afternoon," I said as lightly as I could, "and I thought I would utilize his services."

"Delighted, I'm sure," put in poor Hector, who had been looking for his tongue and had only just found it.

"You have my letters, have you not, Elsie?" asked Arthur, coming at once to business.

"Yes," I said coldly, "I took them because I thought they—er—looked—er—important," lamely.

Hector Dasy soon found an opportunity to go. Of course he knew I had a husband, but I presume he had not reckoned upon an introduction while wool-winding. Poor Hector! I felt a little guilty, or should have done if I had given myself the time.

"Dasy seems a nice young fellow, Elsie," said Arthur coolly, at dinner that night. "His family have lived in Kew for years. Eminently respectable. Old Dasy left them well off. I am glad you have discovered congenial society among our neighbors, Elsie," looking at me in such a friendly, disinterested fashion that I shuddered. "You are mistress here, dear, and you can ask as many people to Tavistock Villa as you like. I shall never interfere."

Of that I now felt certain. Well, my plot had been an utter and a dismal failure. All my time had been spent for nothing. I had cultivated this non-entity with an object in view. The nonenity was there in all his cultivation, and the object had disappeared. I could never make my husband jealous.

What could I do? Tavistock Villa was becoming disgusting to me. I could not endure its atmosphere much longer. I would go up to London to-morrow, make a confidant of my mother—a thing I had never yet done—and hear what she thought about the situation.

CHAPTER XIII.

You, my fair young readers, will imagine that nothing could be easier than to go to your mother, and tell her—well, anything on earth. That is because you have the right kind of a mother. I had the wrong kind. I am well aware that such a sentiment is not pretty from anybody's lips, but as you already know, I am one of those candid beings who conceal nothing, even when concealment might be beneficial.

There had never been any confidence between my mother and me. She had always considered me uninteresting, and I—well, I could never realize that she really existed out of society. Her ambition never extended beyond the "set" in which she moved; her ideas were suggested invariably by those immediately above her in rank; worldliness reigned rampant within her.

I had been glad to leave her house, and rejoiced to escape from society's prospective thraldom. And now I was going to consult my mother on a question of vital importance. I was about to appeal to the very worldliness which I condemned, to assist me in my dilemma.

I had no difficulty in leaving Tavistock Villa for London. I do not suppose that if I had set out for Timbuctoo,[1] any very unconquerable obstacles would have presented themselves.

My journey to town was without incident; my arrival at Grosvenor Square,[2] stupid. The butler was far too well bred to express any surprise when he beheld me; the maids whom I met *en route* to my mother's morning-room, were too well drilled in fashionable idiocy to look either pleased or interested when I burst upon them.

My mother had only just risen. She had been at an ultra-swell reception the night before, and was to be present at another that evening, so that the interval between the two was to be spent in a lounge-chair with a novel and a few newspapers—those that chronicled in detail the events of society.

She pressed a farcical kiss upon my brow, said she was charmed to see me—though she wasn't—wondered why I had come in such an informal manner and so disgracefully soon, hoped dear Arthur was well, and—well, would I not sit down, and take off my cloak?

I unbosomed myself without any delay. I did not attempt to shield Arthur's neglect. I felt that he deserved everything I could say—and more. I did not tell my mother that I was miserable, because my ideas of misery and happiness did not coincide with

---

1   Used in several languages to refer to a faraway, exotic place, Timbuktu is a city in what is present-day Mali, Africa.

2   A large garden in the exclusive Mayfair district of London. While today it is a public park, it would at this time have been exclusively for use by the occupants of the houses surrounding the garden.

hers. I simply laid the situation before her, and asked her superior knowledge of the world what it all meant.

Her languor disappeared as I proceeded; she even sat up straight in her lounge-chair, and when I came to an end she deliberately closed her novel—a tacit recognition of the fact that I was more entertaining than her author.

"Well, my dear," she said blandly, when I paused, "this story is strange indeed, but—but singularly interesting."

"Interesting?" I asked, horrified.

"Yes, my dear, certainly interesting. Though I always thought Arthur Ravener a peculiar young man—you remember when I saw you two in the library that day—I never supposed that he suffered from anything but bashfulness. Bashfulness, though a grievous fault in these enlightened days when young men are supposed to have overcome any little gaucheries[1] long before they attain their majority, is not an unsurmountable objection. You see what I mean? I always thought—you know, Elsie, I do a great deal of thinking in my quiet way—that you and he would settle down into a commonplace, everyday couple. Not for one instant did any idea to the contrary enter my head."

She was gratified. I could see it. With disgust in my soul, and no very filial reverence written upon my unpleasantly mobile features, I was obliged to realize the fact that this society mother was entertained by the story of her daughter's marital misfortunes.

"It was only the other day," she went on, "that I heard that Lady Erminow's daughter who was recently married to that young scapegrace Erickson—you remember her, Elsie, that pretty golden-haired girl—was living so unhappily with her husband. He is a slave to alcohol, my dear. Nothing could be worse than that. It is the lowest, most degrading passion. Lady Erminow has my heartfelt sympathy. By-the-bye, Elsie, Arthur, you omitted to tell me—is he abstemious?"

"Yes—as far as I know," I answered, bitterly.

"I thought it," said my mother, triumphantly. "The cause of his neglect must be found elsewhere. Do not worry yourself at all, Elsie."

"What do you mean?" I asked excitedly. "Do you think you know why he neglects me?"

My mother looked at me with intense scorn. "Of course I do. Do you suppose I have lived so long in the world without being

---

1 French: awkward, embarrassing, or unsophisticated manners.

able to diagnose this simple case of domestic infelicity. My dear Elsie, another girl of your age would not need aid in this matter. The case is absolutely transparent. Husband indifferent, always away from home, uninterested in wife—why, my dear child, it is all as plain as a pikestaff."[1]

I listened eagerly. If I only understood the situation I had no doubt but that I could grapple with it. How glad I felt that I had come. If I knew the malady, surely I could find the remedy.

"One thing—before I proceed, Elsie," continued my mother, now so interested that her novel fell to the ground unheeded. "Your case would not be considered at all strange in society, and rest assured, dear, that you would not suffer in the least. Society is a kind friend—my best,—as I have told you so often. Still for the present I do not think I would ventilate my grievances, if I were you—"

"What do you mean?" I interrupted indignantly.

"Hear me, Elsie, and do not be so impulsive, please. As I was saying, for the present I would not ventilate my grievances, as in such a very young married couple, they might—remember I say 'might'—cause a little comment. If you had been married twelve months, or even six—yes, I think six," she added, reflectively, "I would not caution you thus. You see—"

"Nothing," I exclaimed, angrily, "you explain nothing."

"If you do not understand the case," continued my mother, looking rather keenly at me, "perhaps it would be better for your interests—and mine, for I am your mother, Elsie—that you should not do so. Live quietly for a few months more, and then—"

"I will not!" I cried, rising energetically from my seat. "I will not endure such a home, unless there be some very excellent reason why I should do so. I love my husband—I may as well tell you that; but when I see myself neglected in such a shameful way, through nothing that I have done, I will not submit blindly to it. Tell me what the cause of this trouble is, if you know, and I will try to remedy it. If I can do so, and can gain Arthur's love, no one will be happier than I. If I cannot, I will leave him, before the—the—whole affair k-kills me."

I burst into tears.

"You are unreasonably excited," said my mother, sternly, "or you would not dare to talk to me of leaving your husband. Why, girl, your position would be gone—and mine too. You talk of

---

1 Completely obvious.

suffering through no fault of your own, but you seem extremely willing to let me suffer through no fault of mine. If you left your husband, I might as well close my establishment. All London would talk, and I—I pride myself upon furnishing no food for idle and detrimental gossip."

She rose from her seat and walked up and down the room, thoroughly and selfishly roused.

"Why will you not take my advice?" she asked. "Go home and stay there quietly for a few months. Then I will tell you what to do."

"I will not!" I exclaimed passionately.

My mother reflected. She saw that I was determined. I was. As I sat in that room I resolved that if I could not discover the cause of my husband's coldness—and discovering, vanquish it—I would leave my married life forever.

"If you will not," said my mother, after a good two minutes of complete silence, and in a wisely calculating tone, "something must be done. Of course, Elsie, there's a woman in the case."

A woman in the case! What woman? What did my mother mean?

"The expression is not a pretty one," resumed my parent, taking my surprise for ladylike wonder at the construction of her phrase. "But it means everything. You know, Elsie, that the French in every catastrophe that happens, declare that 'cherchez la femme'[1] will explain everything."

"I do not understand you," I said in a dazed way. "Why there is not a soul in our house but the servants and my maid, Marie."

"Perhaps not," said Mrs. Bouverie. "But there are plenty of souls out of your house, my dear, and—according to your story— that is where your husband spends the greater part of his time. His neglect of you is only too clear. He is interested in some other woman, and with her he spends his time. Have I made myself clear?"

She had. I started up, surprised at my own obtuseness and burning to settle this question once and forever. But—no, I could not understand fully.

"If he is interested in some other woman," I asked helplessly, "why did he marry me? He asked me to be his wife. Nobody forced him to do it. I didn't suggest it."

My mother laughed harshly. "I suppose not," she said. "Perhaps he wanted you to be his wife on account of the superior

1 French: look for the woman.

social advantages a married man enjoys. Perhaps as a married man his liaison could be carried on more favorably. Perhaps—there are a hundred suggestions I could make. Don't let us forget the fact, also, that you were dowered handsomely."

"Nonsense; he did not want my money, be quite sure of that. Mother," I said, putting on my cloak and buttoning it all wrong, "you are right, there is a woman in the case, and I was blind not to have seen it."

"No doubt your husband's friend, the Captain, is the go-between. That might explain his intimacy with your husband, might it not?"

Of course it might.

"Yes," I said. "What would you advise me to do?"

"I suppose you ask that," said mamma, severely, "in order that you may do something else. You are too obstinate, too self-willed to ask advice. Still," seeing that I looked threatening—I must have done so for I am sure I felt it—"perhaps I had better make a suggestion or two. Go home to your husband and tax him with his infidelity; you will easily see by his manner if the shot strikes home. Don't be impulsive and—ridiculous—as you generally are. Try a little diplomacy. If your husband denies everything—come to me, and I'll help you with a detective or two."

"I will," I said promptly.

"And now, go, Elsie," sinking wearily into her chair, "I declare you have fatigued me. I shall never be able to get through the reception—all this on top of my fatigues of last night."

She waved me away. I did not offer her my brow to freeze. I could not.

Her words rang in my ears all the way home. "A woman in the case." Yes, of course there must be. What a bat I must have been not to have suspected it before. I was eccentric. There was no doubt about it. I ought to have waited a few years before I had married, and gained a little experience in the world. But no! If the price of such experience was the forfeit of my self-respect, I did not want it.

A woman in the case! Who could she be? I wondered if she were more attractive than I was. What a fool I had been to imagine that he would notice me, as I strutted before my glass in the silly pride of a peacock! He was all the time thinking of some one else. I wondered why I could not picture this "some one else." I seemed utterly unable to realize the fact that Arthur Ravener could love another woman.

However, my future should soon be decided. I was excited, earnest, and eager to begin my self-imposed task.

CHAPTER XIV.

The strength of my resolution to arrive at a definite comprehension of the situation in which I found myself, acted in a sort of sedative manner upon my unstrung nerves. Though I raged during the ride from Grosvenor Square to Kew, at the end of my journey I was calm; desperately calm.

I dressed for dinner with just as much care as usual, and though I did not "frivol" before the glass,[1] and think what an attractive little lady I was, I omitted nothing in my *toilette* that could render me more comely.

I found Arthur in the dining-room when I entered that gloomy apartment, and we greeted each other in just the same friendly, platonic manner that had ever marked our demeanor towards one another. We sat opposite to one another at the long table, and I prepared myself for my usual hour of small talk upon the theatres, the latest pictures, the political situation, and a variety of other topics.

I could feel no interest in anything, however. Horrible visions of Arthur, my husband, *tête-à-tête* with another woman, would fill my brain to the exclusion of everything else; disgust at my husband's deceit; contempt for my own inability to please him; wonder as to how it would all end, and a bewildering attempt to remember everything I had planned to say, played havoc with my conversational powers.

Yes, I was outrageously jealous—blindly, hatefully jealous, with the jealousy which Sardou loves to imagine and Bernhardt[2] to portray, and though I was by no means dramatically inclined, I felt that my situation was unusual. I tried to prolong the meal. I was determined to "have it out," as the saying is, and yet I dreaded the process, because I felt that Arthur must be guilty. I knew I should feel sorry for him. He was one of those few men who could make you pity him at the same time that he cut your throat, and I was one of those many women in whom unnatural compassion exists in all its power.

---

1 Spend a foolish (or frivolous) amount of time before the mirror.

2 Victorien Sardou (1831–1908), French playwright who, along with Eugène Scribe (1791–1861), was celebrated for developing the well-made play, a genre of popular theater depending on a tight plot and a dramatic climax that often involves the revelation of a secret past; Sarah Bernhardt (1844–1923), French actress who won international recognition for her dramatic style of acting, and one of the world's most famous actresses throughout the nineteenth century.

Dinner was over. I could not prolong it any further if I tried. He had risen from the table. He was about to leave me—"Arthur." I swallowed a lump. My voice sounded choked.

"Elsie," he said, turning at once, and coming back to me. He stood and looked in my face with the cool, un-ardent friendship which I hated to see there. "What is it?"

He waited patiently while I gulped again and strove to be cool.

"May I speak to you, Arthur?"

He laughed.

"Why, Elsie, have you not been speaking to me for the last hour. I always like to hear you, dear. You are one of the most thoroughly sensible little women I have ever met. I—"

"Don't!" I cried, with a gesture of disgust. "Spare me. I do not want to discuss the newspapers, or talk pretty nothings, I wish to speak with you—quietly, you know—on a—a serious matter, con-connected only with ours-selves. Will you come into my sitting-room. Don't—be —afraid. I—I—will not k-keep you l-long."

My teeth chattered in my head with nervousness. I felt cold. My husband looked more uncomfortable than I did. He fidgetted with his feet. His lips twitched slightly. Oh, he knew what was coming as well as I did.

"Will you come?" I repeated as he stood mute and uneasy before me.

"Of course," with an effort, "if you wish it."

If I wished it? I bore him off to my sitting-room. He had never entered the apartment before with me, except when he first introduced me to it. I closed the door. He waited until I took an arm-chair by the window. Then he quietly sat down at the other end of the room and picked up a book. His evident fear that I was about to become demonstrative, while it cut me to the quick, was not without its ridiculous side.

"Ha! Ha!" I laughed hysterically, "you need not be afraid. I won't kiss you. I've not brought you here to tell you how I love you; that would not be original enough to please you—or me. Ha! Ha! Ha!"

I threw myself back in my chair and laughed until the tears rolled down my face. I felt the acutest anguish—and still I laughed. My heart was harrowed by this man's neglect and contempt—and still I laughed. I could not help it. I suppose it was a physiological peculiarity.

Finally I covered my face in my hands and sobbed convulsively.

"Elsie," cried Arthur in the greatest alarm, "you are ill. What is the matter? I" (rising) "will go for Dr. White."

He wanted to get out of the room. If he did, I should see him no more that day. He reckoned without his host.

"I want no doctor," I declared, rising and standing with my back to the door, all hysteria vanished. "If I do, James shall go, and you can remain here with me. I—I know you will like that."

Again I laughed long and passionately. I was becoming exhausted by this most exhausting emotion. Great goodness! I must make an effort. Here the minutes were slipping quickly by and I had not accomplished a thing. My rival was yet unknown to me.

"Excuse me, Arthur," I said quietly, after a long pause in which he paced the floor uneasily, "your experience with women," I looked him keenly in the face, "will tell you that I—I—am—am—out of sorts."

"What do you mean, Elsie?"

No one could have better feigned surprise I told myself. Arthur Ravener must be an accomplished actor. There was the genuine astonishment, caused by a revelation, upon his face.

"You know what I mean," I answered.

"I do not. I swear it."

"You do," I cried, trying unsuccessfully not to ruin my cause by bitter denunciation. "You do"—more quietly. I walked over to him, grasped his arm, and looked into his face. "Now," I said, "tell me honestly, and as a man, that you do not know what I mean."

He shook me off. He was growing angry. "I will tell you nothing," he said, not glancing at me, "until you have explained yourself."

"Very well. Listen. When a young girl marries a man who a few hours after the wedding leaves her alone in a strange house; who makes a lame excuse for his action and subsequently increases his offense against respect and affection by permitting her to pass her time in absolute solitude; who for love substitutes the coldest and most indifferent friendship; who spends a large part of his time in town, leaving her in the country, and attempts no sort of explanation—when he does all this, what is she to suspect?"

He had been growing paler while I put the questions, but as I concluded he started up in undisguised fear—yes, it was fear.

"Suspect?" he asked, hoarsely. "What right have you to suspect anything? All shame upon the education of girls to-day, if a child like you dares to suspect."

He was as white as a sheet and unreasonably angry.

"You are an excellent diplomat," I said satirically. "You knew too well what a child I was when you married me. The extent of my knowledge of good and evil had been very well gauged by you. I have suspected nothing, and you know it. But, thank Heaven, my blindness has been cured. I can see it all now."

"You have been gossiping," he exclaimed, glaring at me.

"I have done nothing of the kind. I have been neglected and humiliated. I knew no reason why this state of things should exist, so—I asked my mother's advice."

The shot struck home. Arthur Ravener gasped for breath. He seemed absolutely unable to speak.

"You—asked—your—mother's—advice," he managed to articulate, presently. "And—what—did—she—tell—you?"

"She told me this, and I confront you with it: that there was undeniable proof in your neglect that you cared nothing for me, except as a sort of respectable cloak, but that there must be another woman whom you loved, and whom you visited when you were not at Tavistock Villa."

"Ah!"

If I had not known that such a thing must be impossible I should have imagined that Arthur's exclamation was one of relief. The expression of his face changed at once from one of intense alarm to comparative composure. He took a seat, leaned his elbows on his knees, covered his face with his hand, and remained silent.

"Why do you not speak?" I asked impatiently.

"Listen, Elsie," drawing closer to me. "I will be brief. Years ago I vowed I would never marry; you may think that was a boyish resolve. It was not; I thoroughly meant it, as a man. The reason was that women were too exacting, though a house without a women in it was and still is to me a terribly lonely, uninteresting place. I resolved never to marry. I met you. As you say very justly, I studied you carefully. I came to the conclusion that you were unlike other girls—that we would live quietly and happily together as friends—you going your way and I going mine. I say I firmly believed that this could be done when I married you. I esteemed you greatly, and, Elsie," he paused for a moment, "my esteem has been increased tenfold. Lately, however, it has seemed to me that our life was becoming distasteful to you. At first I thought nothing of the symptoms, but I was unable to think thus lightly of them, later. Elsie," his voice quivering with emotion, "suppose we have made a great mistake?"

For a few moments I was bewildered. His argument was made in such a pathetic tone, that I felt unnatural compassion for him at the expense of my own womanliness would ruin the situation, if I were not on my guard.

"I do not understand you," I said. "You have not answered my mother's suggestions. If—if you love another woman, make a clean breast of it to me—your wife, and oh, Arthur," melting in spite of myself, "I—I will try to—to forgive you the wrong you have done me."

I seized his hand in a frenzy of grief. If only he would tell me all, everything could be remedied, I felt sure.

"Who is the woman?" I asked boldly.

He made no answer.

"Tell me who she is and all shall be set right."

He smiled at me pitifully. "She does not exist," he said. "Elsie, you are the only woman in the world to me."

I recoiled from him in disgust. "You are equivocating," I said sternly. "Be frank while there is still time."

"I am frank," he said in a choked voice.

"Swear that you are telling me the truth."

"I swear it."

I arose. The numbness of despair was upon me. My suffering was deadened, my nerves were lulled into temporary quietude. There was nothing further needed. He had lied to me. I knew that. I had been so blind, that the light shed upon me by my mother's revelation seemed twenty times more powerful to me than if it had not come upon me so suddenly.

"Thank you," I said, opening the door. "Let me apologize for having detained you so long. Good-night."

He had nothing more to say. He passed out of the room, without one glance in my direction.

CHAPTER XV.

The months dragged themselves slowly away as though they hated to go, but would infinitely prefer to remain and gloat over my misery. I could not make up my mind to confer with my mother again. Although she had told me she would aid me, I seemed unable to pluck up the courage to know the worst.

My life at Tavistock Villa was unchanged. My relations with my husband were colder than ever. Though never once did he allude to the subject of the conversation recorded in the last chapter, I could see that it had made an impression upon him. He looked at me wistfully; our conversation was strained; a horrible form had stepped in between us, assuming shape as definitely as did the geni in the Arabian Nights[1] story, from a mere shadow.

You would think that his course of action would have been changed. Not a bit of it. We met as before at breakfast and at dinner, after which he would leave the house. He never attempted any explanation, and I, always on the eve of desperate measures, maintained an equally guarded silence.

Of course I was in Grosvenor Square frequently during those wretched days, but as I did not allude to my misfortunes, my mother, selfishly afraid of a scandal which might endanger her eminently respectable position in the society which she loved a great deal better than she did her soul, made no effort to ascertain the situation of affairs.

I suppose my husband and I might have lived together pleasantly. There are women in this world—I have met a few of them—who have occupied similar positions with a smile on their faces. I could not do it. I was not a humbug, I was sorry to say. If only young girls were forced to study the elements of humbuggery as a part of an academic curriculum, what a quantity of subsequent suffering some of them would be spared! The study might be absolutely necessary to only a few, but it would be of benefit to all.

My cup of anguish was full when I met Letty Bishop—married and wonderfully happy. Dear me! How she loved that husband of hers. I compared her affection for dear Reginald to mine for Arthur Ravener, and then stopped. Her husband returned her love with interest. There never was a better mated couple.

I met them at my mother's house one evening. Arthur was with me for the sake of appearances, I suppose. How he ever managed to tear himself away from HER I could not imagine. I did not ask him for any information on the subject.

"What a happy couple!" I said with a sigh. I could not help the remark. Arthur was beside me. I was sitting, like an antique,

---

1   *One Thousand and One Nights*, known in English as *Arabian Nights* from its first English-language publication in 1706, is a collection of Middle Eastern and South Asian folktales. In 1885, the British writer and explorer Sir Richard Burton (1821–90) published the first unexpurgated version of this work, for which he wrote an accompanying "Terminal Essay" that explored unusual and exotic sexual practices supposedly located in what he called the "Sotadic Zone" (see Appendix C3).

faded wallflower in the drawing-room, while the others talked and chatted and laughed and gossiped at the other end of the room. He followed my eyes and saw Reginald talking in a whisper to Letty, while a pink-faced maiden executed a *morceau* on the piano.

"They are very impolite to talk while Miss Lancaster is playing," he said coldly.

"They have so much to say," I suggested.

"Doubtless."

"We shall never be troubled with such a burning desire to speak," I went on scornfully.

"That is your fault. I am always willing to talk with you. I enjoy talking with you, Elsie. You are unhappy, and it grieves me sorely to know it—because—because—I am helpless. Our marriage was a—a—mistake. You will not make the best of it. You are eating your heart away with worry. I would give all I possess to have it otherwise."

"You must imagine," I said sternly, "that I am either a lunatic or an idiot, otherwise you would not talk to me so senselessly."

"I imagine nothing of the kind."

"Then you did when you married me?"

"I did not. I thought, as we said so often, that you were in earnest when you declared you would be satisfied with quiet friendship instead of impetuous passion—"

"Then, as you imagine you were mistaken, you propose allowing matters to remain as they are."

"I do not see what else to do. Elsie, why need we quarrel? I esteem you. I admire you, I am sorry—"

"Thank you very much," I said bitterly. "You are very kind. You do me a great honor. You esteem me. You admire me. Oh, that is charming of you. Could you not have esteemed me and admired me without this nonsense?" pointing to my wedding ring. I would have flung it from the open window before us, only I, too, had appearances to keep up.

He made no answer, and I left him, going over to my friend Letty, and permitting her to pour her rhapsodies into my ears. She enjoyed the process immensely, and—well, I could just stand it, and that is about all.

Before I left my mother's house my mind was made up. I would dilly-dally no longer. I would accept my mother's aid, and settle matters finally. I was, as Arthur said, eating out my heart, and it would be better to act while there was still something left of it. I would see my mother on the following morning, and before I returned to Kew I would know that my "case" was in hands that would dispose of it satisfactorily.

I did not sleep at all that night, but with the ever faithful Marie by my side "killed time" as best I could. Marie was a good girl, but like most of her class, officious. She thought it quite correct to openly sympathize with me, and declare that *monsieur* treated his wife shamefully. This irritated me, and, if anything, made me still more fretfully anxious.

I was in Grosvenor Square early the following morning, and burst into my mother's room while she was putting a little suspicion of something rosy upon her face.

"Good gracious me, Elsie!" she exclaimed in amazed vexation, as I threw myself into a chair, "you should indeed cultivate a little repose. You really alarm me with your impulsive movements."

I made no answer. I was not in a humor for repartee of any kind. I waited as quietly as I could while mamma hurried a little china dish containing red out of sight, fondly imagining, I suppose, that I had not seen it. Then she sat down with a hectic flush on one side of her face.

"Domestic troubles, of course," she said, satirically.

"Of course," I replied, with equal satire.

"Well?"

"You said you would help me when I needed your services. I need them now," I replied.

My mother meditated. I could see that she was unwilling to assist me. She dreaded anything happening which might give the matter publicity. In a word, she was afraid of me, and I admit, not without reason.

"I do not like interfering between man and wife," she began tentatively.

But I was equal to the occasion. The avalanche had started on its course, and nothing could now stop it.

"Very well," I said with palpably assumed indifference, "if you will not aid me in a matter concerning my happiness, I shall leave my husband at once."

As I said, my indifference was palpably assumed, but my mother was one of those who cannot see a pin's point below the surface. The random shot took effect.

"You will do nothing of the kind," she said, severely. "I beg of you, Elsie, to do nothing rash. You will bring my gray hairs with sorrow to the grave," tearfully.

She had employed that expression ever since I could remember, and its dramatic force was impaired by old age. When I used to spoil my frocks at school, when I said rude things, when I insulted my governess, or when I overdrew my weekly allowance—errors with which she was always made acquainted—I was ever threatened with bringing her gray hairs in sorrow to the grave.

She walked to her *secretaire*,[1] and sat down. Then, taking a sheet of note paper with a crest and monogram of enormous proportions, she scribbled a few lines in a bold, back-hand. Folding the sheet, she placed it in a heavily monogrammed envelope, which she left open as she handed it to me. It was addressed to Octavius Rickaby, Esq., Holborn Viaduct.

"Go there," she said, shortly.

"Who is Octavius Rickaby?" I asked feebly. My mother smiled contemptuously. "Of course you wouldn't know," she said. "Mr. Rickaby is a very clever private detective—or rather the head of an admirably conducted private detective office. He conducts a great many society cases"—sinking her voice to a whisper—"in fact I could name several of my friends whom he has helped. Of course, Elsie, if you make a fool of yourself, and fail to put him in possession of every detail of your case—every detail, mind—you must not be surprised if he fails. If you make a confidant of him, he will be of very material assistance, in fact your husband will not be able to wink unless you know it. He is reasonable, and, my dear, he is perfectly upright. He will never trouble you after you have settled his bill."

My heart sank within me. The word detective had an awful significance in my mind. In fact, I think I would as soon have invoked the aid of Mephistopheles.[2] Detectives always suggested murders and abductions and burglaries to me. A great many people will doubtless sympathize with this feeling.

My mother was "eyeing" me. "You do not intend to consult Mr. Rickaby, I see plainly," she said. "You will be sorry for it one of these days."

She might be right. After all, a detective might be of great service, and something must be done. "I will see Mr. Rickaby, and at once," I declared, rising with determination. "I am much obliged to you, mother. I am sorry to have disturbed you," I said, really becoming cheerful as I resolved upon immediate action; "I know I am an awful nuisance. Now go on with your dressing." I meant painting, but accuracy at times is detestable.

---

1 French: a desk with a cabinet for papers and a writing shelf.
2 The devil.

I drove at once to Mr. Rickaby's office in Holborn Viaduct, and was soon in front of a large glass door with the words "Octavius Rickaby" in gleaming black letters staring me in the face. I did not dare to stop and think for one moment. I walked straight in, just as my excitement, born of my eagerness to act, was wearing away like the effect of a much abused drug. I found myself in a neat little office, comfortably furnished, and not at all murderous or penny-dreadful[1] looking. A polite young clerk, in a blue tie and a jovial face, which he seemed perpetually endeavoring to harmonize with the solemnity of his position, received me.

"Please take my card and this letter to Mr. Rickaby," I said, trying to appear as indifferent as though it were part of the daily routine of my life to consult with private detectives.

Of course I expected to be kept waiting. I ignorantly classed detectives with doctors and lawyers and editors, who are always "very busy just now," or if they are not, they pretend to be for the sake of appearances. I was agreeably surprised when Mr. Rickaby said he would see me at once. No, there could be no humbug about that man.

The great Octavius was stout and rubicund—another favorable point with me. No one could have looked less mysterious, and more matter of fact. I believe I half expected to enter his presence with an "open sesame,"[2] and to behold two or three imps of darkness skipping about with a caldron between them. He rose as I entered, placed a chair for me, and leaned back in his own cosy, cushioned seat.

"Tell me everything, Mrs. Ravener," said Mr. Rickaby suavely, "no one comes to see me unless he has something to tell. Consider me your doctor or your lawyer. Explain your case, and I will diagnose it."

He said all this in rather a fragmentary manner, expecting me to begin, and uttering each new sentence as he noticed that I remained silent.

He encouraged me by his patience and well-bred demeanor. I told him my story,—at least as much as I could of it. I omitted

---

1 British serial pulp publications popular in the nineteenth century that featured lurid and morbid crime stories and cost a penny.

2 "Open sesame" (from the French Sésame, ouvre-toi) is a magical term in the story of "Ali Baba and the Forty Thieves" in One Thousand and One Nights. The uttering of the phrase prompts the opening of the mouth of a cave in which forty thieves have hidden a treasure.

the fact that Arthur left me a few hours after our wedding. Mr. Rickaby remained silent for some moments after I had finished. Then he asked me if I had taxed Arthur with neglect. I told him I had done so in a very vigorous manner.

"You suspect that you have a rival?" he asked, looking at me keenly.

"What am I to think?"

"Have you ever discovered any letters or papers in your husband's possession that would lead you to such a belief?"

"I have not tried to discover any," I said.

"Will you do so?"

I promised that I would, but begged him not to wait for any possible discoveries on my part before he began proceedings in the matter.

"You have not told me everything, Mrs. Ravener." Mr. Rickaby said this with such an air of certainty that I was dumfounded. He had not removed his eyes from my face during the progress of my story, or during the time he had interrogated me.

"I have told you all—all I—I can tell you," I said in a low tone, averting my head. Still those eagle eyes were rivetted upon me. They seemed to burn into my soul. I was disconcerted and rose hastily.

"Do not stare at me so," I said angrily, walking to the window.

"I beg your pardon, Mrs. Ravener," he remarked quietly, "I am sorry to annoy you. Sit down." I sat down. "You know," playing musingly with a paper knife, "I often have customers who tell me all they can—like you," he said, "so I have to adopt other means to learn the information withheld. I read it in their faces."

"Then—?" I began furiously.

"You need not trouble to tell me any more," he said quietly. "It is not necessary."

I cannot describe my sensations. They were too painful to be recognizable in pen and ink. My face burned and my lips were parched. I was almost sorry I had come. But the worst was over, and I must bring this loathsome interview to an end.

"Do you think that—that," I hated to use the horrible expression that I had heard from my mother's lips—"there is a woman in—in the case?"

"It is possible," he said indefinitely.

"Possible!" I echoed in surprise. "What do you mean?"

"Mrs. Ravener," said Mr. Rickaby, "I will not express an opinion; I have no right to do so. I will possess myself of all the information I can. I will find out where your husband goes."

"You will?" I exclaimed joyfully. "Then, Mr. Rickaby, if you will do that you can leave the rest to me. Just find out for me where he goes, and I will then see what it will be best for me to do. Leave me to discover who the woman is. I—I should like to know—exclusively."

I told the truth. I did not want even a detective to possess himself of all my husband's secrets. To my surprise Mr. Rickaby seemed relieved.

"You will do this," I asked, "without going any farther?"

"Most willingly," he replied, "I will obey your instructions to the letter. It is to my interest to do so." That satisfied me.

CHAPTER XVI.

I returned quietly home—that is to say, I was quiet when I reached Tavistock Villa. The interval between my departure from the office of Mr. Octavius Rickaby and my arrival in Kew was spent in the tedious process of schooling myself to be what I was not, and never could be—cold and stony. I felt that everything depended upon the systematic manner in which I conducted my investigation. If I gave the reins to my impulsiveness, I knew I should ruin my case.

My case! How I hated the sound of the words. The love I had brought to my wedded life had resolved itself into a subject for detectives; the husband, whom a few months back I had sworn at the altar to love and honor and obey, had become a suspect, whose conduct must be investigated; the promise of wedded felicity had degenerated into the certainty of—a case.

I might desist even now in my attempt to understand my situation. If I did so I could live comfortably, even luxuriously to the end of my days. I was rich, and could consequently make as many friends as I chose; I was intelligent—passably so—and could interest myself in the current events of the day. I was young—ah! that was it. Why was I young? Alas! I needed love, sympathy and respect. I was womanly in spite of my eccentricities, which were those of an ignorant, obstinate girl. What woman, young and impulsive, would consent to accept a situation such as that which had been thrust upon me—or into which I had voluntarily stepped, if you will,—for I do not attempt to defend myself?

No, I would not suffer such humiliation. "Let this be the last of my scruples," I said to myself as I dressed for dinner. "Let me know exactly what stands between me and my husband's love. It may possibly be removed, and then—." I loved Arthur desperately. If I could only have hated him, how much better would it have been for me—and for him.

"Madame is feverish," said Marie, suddenly, as she watched me in my efforts to beautify myself with those fine feathers which are correctly supposed to make fine birds.

Her words gave me a shock. I looked in the glass. Yes, I was feverish. My cheeks were burning. There was a hectic red upon each. Evidently I had not succeeded in schooling myself into composure.

"What can I do, Marie?" I asked helplessly. "I do not want to have red cheeks."

Marie looked rather surprised, but her French experience thus appealed to, did me excellent service. At the end of ten minutes the color of my countenance was beautifully normal. The hectic spots had disappeared, at least from sight.

I went down to the dining room to eat my hateful dinner with Arthur. He was in a hopelessly conventional good humor. I succeeded—admirably, I thought—in emulating his complacence. To show the effect of my determination to keep from my husband any suspicion of my thoughts and actions, I chatted pleasantly upon a variety of subjects—the hackneyed aggressiveness of Lord Randolph Churchill; the new comic opera at the Savoy; the coming concert at St. James' Hall; Lady Toadyby's costume at the Queen's drawing-room; the accounts of Sardou's new play in Paris, with Bernhardt in the title role and—yes! I did it—the latest divorce case, minus the details, of course.[1]

I read everything, understood nearly all that I read, focussed it in my mind, and you see was prepared to present it in good evening dress as an accessory to the dinner of my lord and master. I consider I did bravely. I had never done better. Arthur looked up thoroughly pleased. He little knew that beneath my coat—the coat that Marie put upon my cheeks—two scarlet spots were burning, and that my soul sickened of Lord

1 Lord Randolph Churchill (1849–95) was a Conservative member of the British Parliament and the father of Prime Minister Winston Churchill (1874–1965). The Savoy Theatre in London was built to house the popular comic operettas of Gilbert and Sullivan, which came to be known as Savoy operas. St. James's Hall was London's main concert hall from its opening in 1858 to the opening of the Queen's Hall in 1900. The Queen's drawing-room was an event at which young girls of the aristocracy were presented to the court. Lady Toadyby is an invented name punning on the term toady, short for toad-eater and signifying a sycophant.

Randolph Churchill, the Savoy Theatre, St. James' Hall, Lady Toadyby and all the rest of it.

Dinner was over—thank goodness!

"Are you going out to-night, Arthur?" I asked carelessly.

"Yes, Elsie, I—I—think so. Why?"

I had long ceased to interest myself in his actions as far as he could see. He had, therefore, a right to feel rather surprised when I questioned him on the subject now.

"Nothing," I answered vaguely.

"Can I do anything for you?"

"Oh, no, thank you." I was so amiable that he was more taken aback. "I must be careful," I said to myself.

As I vouchsafed no further remark, he left me, and half an hour afterwards I heard the front door close behind him.

Now, then, if I could only aid Detective Rickaby in any way. I had several long hours before me, with nothing more inviting than a novel which had been recommended to me by dear Miss Euphemia Dasy, and which I knew I should hate, with which to distract myself.

I went at once to Arthur's study, at least as far as the door, which I found locked. I shook it rather severely, in the silly hope that it would yield to such inducements. The chivalrous and interesting James happened to pass me at the time. He cast a look of intense surprise in my direction.

"You can't get in," he said with a grin.

"So I perceive," I remarked with affected resignation, walking slowly away as James departed for the lower regions. I slipped on a big straw hat, ran into the garden, and surveyed the prospect of effecting an entrance into my husband's sanctum from that point. It was not so hopeless. The room had a large window, not more than three feet from the ground, opening into the garden. The window was shrouded with thick curtains, so that it was impossible to see from the garden into the room.

With supreme satisfaction I noticed that the window was unlocked. My course was not left long undecided. It may not have been a particularly ladylike, but it was a vigorous one. I sprang upon the window sill, stood up, and very soon saw the glass obstacle raised sufficiently to permit my entrance into the apartment.

Arthur's sanctum was a rather large room, divided by heavy plush portieres[1] into two. That in which I now stood was fit-

---

1 From French: curtains.

ted up comfortably as a writing room. There was an oak desk; one of those delightful leather-cushioned reading chairs which adjust themselves so amiably to the various positions of the most exacting body; a teeming book-case, a music canterbury filled with music, and other useful articles of furniture. There were some charming pictures upon the wall and, in a word, the apartment was evidently that of a man of refinement. Bitterly, I acknowledged that fact to myself, and thus began a little logical process of reasoning which rendered me all the more miserable. Arthur was a man of refinement—he must be; there could be no use denying it; he appreciated what was refined, and despised the vulgar and the common—his room showed that. He did not appreciate me—therefore I could not be refined; he despised me—therefore I was vulgar and common. The fallacy of this reasoning is of course very evident, but it was not evident to me at that time. Can you wonder at it?

I had sunk into this reading chair, and was evidently forgetting the real object of my intrusion. I had not come here to meditate. Heaven knows, I had ample time and opportunities for that pastime elsewhere.

I pushed back the plush portieres, and stood in the back portion of Arthur's sanctum. It was fitted up as a bedroom. There was a large brass bedstead, a wash-stand, closets for clothes. So, when my husband did not spend the night out—and I had imagined he always did so—this was where he slept. It was rather a curious notion—but I had come to the conclusion that Arthur was rather a curious man. I wondered why he had objected to my visiting his sanctum. Surely he must have been aware that I would have preferred knowing he was in the house than supposing him out of it. Then a number of odious ideas came rushing into my head to bewilder me with the hideous probability that they were facts.

Could I discover no evidence against him without the aid of detectives? I went into the first half of the room, and tried the oak desk. The keys were in it—thank goodness! My lord had evidently grown careless, in the belief that he had an obedient little fool of a wife who would never dare to disobey his slightest behest. Ah! he made a mistake. I remembered my wedding day, and my mild, dutiful pleading to be allowed to inspect my husband's rooms. "They are in great disorder, Elsie," he had said. "You had better not venture into them." And my laughing rejoinder had been, "I believe you're a Bluebeard, Arthur, and that the bodies of a dozen preceding Mrs. Raveners lie festering in that room." I opened the oak desk. It was filled with neatly arranged papers. I examined them all carefully. Alas; they were fearfully uninteresting. Old letters from his parents—I did not read them; literary efforts with the "returned with thanks," marked in tell-tale prominence; bills paid and unpaid, and similar documents of an equally useless description, as far as I was concerned. I went through them all with trembling fingers, dreading and hoping to find some incriminating papers. I was just about to leave the desk, when it suddenly occurred to me that I had missed opening one of the little drawers. I returned to my task, opened the drawer, and came across a little file of receipted bills. I had discovered so many already that I saw no use in examining them. Something prompted me however to glance at them.

They were monthly rent receipts. I read: "Received from Mr. Arthur Ravener the sum of twelve pounds for one month's rent in advance, for the furnished house, No. 121 Lancaster Road, Notting Hill,[1] London, W., due 1st inst. Received payment, B. J. Smith."

How could that interest me? Arthur had probably lived in Lancaster Road, Notting Hill, at one period of his existence. I saw no reason why he should not have done so.

My eyes fell upon the date of the uppermost receipt. The papers dropped from my hands. I started back in terror.

The last twelve pounds acknowledged by Mr. B. J. Smith had been paid for the use of No. 121 Lancaster Road, during this month—this very month of May. Arthur had a perfect right to those premises at the present moment. He might be there now.

Oh! I saw it all now clearly before me. Tavistock Villa was the home of Arthur's neglected, despised wife; No. 121 Lancaster Road, Notting Hill, was the abode of his mistress. He loved her so well, that he could sacrifice his reputation for her. Perhaps he brought her occasionally to the room in which I now stood. To no other part of the house did he dare to take her. Over Tavistock Villa his hated wife reigned; her supremacy must not be called into question. Even then I felt a spasm of pity for Arthur. He was kind to me after all. He consulted my wishes, he gratified them, he was good and brotherly. And how difficult such a course of action must have been to him, when he daily and hourly had the

---

1 Neighborhood in London. Notting Hill was developed through the mid-nineteenth century as a wealthy suburb of London and attracted, if not the very wealthiest, the upper class and well-to-do upper middle class.

image of a dearly beloved one in his mind. I loved Arthur dearly; I could not have shown the amount of endurance to another man that Arthur manifested to me. As I said, I felt a spasm of pity for Arthur. The spasm was soon over, and in its place a fury of bitterness swept over me. Who was the wretch who could take a husband so shamelessly from his wife? How did she dare to do such a thing? Had she so little knowledge of her own sex as to suppose that she would remain undiscovered very long? Did she not dread that discovery, or tremble at the inevitable meeting with an insulted and indignant wife?

I suddenly remembered where I was—in his room, and possibly in hers. I made haste to leave it. I was anxious to start for Notting Hill that moment, while the fever of animosity was burning so fiercely within me.

The cool night air calmed me somewhat. I reflected upon the inadvisability of such a hasty course. I had put my case in the hands of an able detective. I had better wait at least until I heard from him. He had asked me to try and discover any letters or papers in my husband's possession, that would lead me to the belief that I had a rival. I had been successful, I thought. Mr. Rickaby had promised to let me know where my husband went each night. I would wait until I heard from him.

I did not have to wait long. Two days later a gentleman called to see me. He would not disclose his business to James. He must see Mrs. Ravener. It was a special agent of Mr. Rickaby's private detective bureau. He had come to inform me that he had tracked my husband for two nights to—I almost laughed as he gave the address—No. 121 Lancaster Road, Notting Hill, W.

"I will go there myself," I said mentally, "I will see him in the house. I will see her—and then—" well, subsequent events should take care of themselves.

CHAPTER XVII.

It was a dark, dismal sort of an evening. A small provoking rain was falling, the trees dripped incessantly, and the mud in the Kew thoroughfares was horribly and consistently thick. I sat at the window of Tavistock Villa, watching the men returning from the city to their quiet, suburban homes. I wondered if they were glad to free themselves from the much maligned atmosphere of London for this invigorating air, or if they would have preferred the metropolis, with all its unhealthy faults, to the sedate and monotonous wholesomeness of Kew.

I would sooner live ten years in the city than fifty years in the country. I hate the balmy atmosphere of rurality; I loathe the suburban surroundings. Give me the city with its life, its motion, its meaning, its excitement. I could not sympathize with rural man.

> "Fixed like a plant on his peculiar spot,
> To draw nutrition, propagate—and rot."[1]

We had just dined. In a few moments I should doubtless see my husband set out for the city, and I had made up my mind that after having given him a good hour's start, I would follow him. I had matured no plans. The only thing I had decided upon doing was gaining admittance to No. 121 Lancaster Road, and then suddenly confronting the guilty couple. I would not permit any one to announce me. If Arthur in his unhallowed household kept servants, I would dispense with their aid. I would confound my husband and his paramour; I would glory in his trembling confusion, and gloat over the irremediable, hopeless guilt in which I had surprised him.

I was a jealous woman, goaded to action. There is nothing more dangerous in the animal kingdom.

I did not have to wait long for my husband's departure. I saw him hurry out into the wet, uncomfortable night, with a protecting umbrella above his head. He had merely uttered a conventional "good-night" to me, when he left the dining-room. I believe he now imagined that I had settled down into the placid daily enactment of the role of an injured wife. I had fretted at first, protested, even rebelled, but now it was all over; the uselessness of such revolt had become apparent. I am convinced that those were his ideas.

I rang the bell for Marie. "Bring me my long cloak, hat and veil," I ordered; "I am going up to London at once."

"At once!" echoed Marie in surprise, "this wet night?"

"Yes," I replied impatiently, "if any one should call, you can say I have gone—Oh, anywhere."

"To Madame, your mother—to Grosvenor Square?"

"Exactly," I replied, happily untruthful. No one would call, but it was best to be on the safe side.

I covered my face with a dark veil, the hackneyed device of

---

1   From Alexander Pope (1688–1744), *An Essay on Man* (1734), Epistle II.

the mysterious woman. I did this because I was afraid I might be recognized on my way to London. I did not want tongues to wag, at least until I gave them an unqualified right to do so. I was dressed long before it was advisable to start, and threw myself into an armchair in the drawing-room, waiting for the minutes to pass. I was wonderfully calm, and rejoiced at that fact. Angry people generally get the worst of it in this world. Quiet wrath does more effective work than an ebullition of fury.

Half an hour later I was in the damp night air, ploughing my way through the mud. I had decided that I would go to Notting Hill by the democratic Underground Railway.[1] So I walked as quickly as I could to the Kew station, which was not far from Tavistock Villa. I had not very long to wait for the arrival of the train. It soon came roaring into the station. I ensconced myself comfortably in a first-class carriage, and threw myself lazily back in its blue cushioned seat.

I was not alone. Two young men sat opposite to me, and to my dismay I recognized Archie Lucknow and Melville Potterby, two detestable society whipper-snappers, whose hideous mission on earth, it seemed to me, was to persecute the gentler sex with attention. Thank goodness they did not recognize me through my veil. I had no particular anxiety to be seen on the road to London at eight o'clock at night, and alone.

"I can't help thinking, dear boy," Mr. Lucknow was saying in a low tone, "how deucedly uncharitable you are. Now you brand young Honeyworth with a mark of Cain,[2] in sheer willfulness. You have no evidence to substantiate what you say. It is cruel, positively it is, my dear boy. I am not a very straight-laced fellow, as you know, Potterby, but hang it all, if I care to hear this kind of thing."

"It is true, nevertheless," said Mr. Potterby, imperturbably. "No evidence is necessary. Eyes are evidence in this case."

"Well, we will drop the subject. You see how mistaken you were in the case of Arthur Ravener. You had branded him—everybody, had, in fact. His name was on the lips of all fellows. He was shunned. What happened? He married; tongues ceased wagging, and now there is not a fellow in the crowd that maligned him, who would not be glad to apologize for his brutality."

---

1 The London Underground, the world's oldest underground railway, opened in 1863. The Kew Garden Station opened in 1869.
2 The mark put upon Cain when he killed his brother Abel; i.e., a mark of infamy.

Mr. Lucknow came to a pause. Oh! if they would continue talking! If they could only imagine how vitally interesting to me their conversation was! Perhaps it was just as well they could not imagine this, however.

"I would not apologize to Arthur Ravener," said Mr. Potterby in the same low tones, which, however, were distinctly audible to me.

"Then you are not the fellow I thought you"—very severely.

"Sorry, my dear boy, but can't help it. Before I apologize to Ravener, I'd like to know Mrs. Ravener's side of the story. People may have ceased talking. Ravener's marriage was always, in my opinion, brought about solely with that object in view. And he married a very young girl, as ignorant as a new-born babe."

"She was a silly little fool," said Mr. Lucknow, rather savagely.

I had snubbed him with great persistency, so I could not complain at his vehemence.

"Yes, and you know—" What Mr. Lucknow knew I could not learn, as Mr. Potterby's voice sank into a whisper which was hopelessly beyond my scope. They said no more. What I had heard simply whetted the edge of my curiosity. I wondered what Arthur had done, before I knew him, to cause gossip. It seemed to me that a quiet, refined young man, such as I previously supposed him to be, could not have given any very serious offence.

Perhaps, however, it was this very *liaison*, which I was now bent upon breaking, that had set his friends talking. That must be it. This horrible woman had been his bane. People had discovered her existence, and of course no young man in this enlightened century would recognize Arthur's unsavory life. I supposed that although the youths of to-day were silly and tedious they were at least strictly moral.

"Notting Hill."

Here I was at my destination. I alighted hurriedly, not daring to look at my fellow travelers, and was soon in the street. Now for No. 121 Lancaster Road.

I had no idea where it was, but a kindly policeman informed me that it was not more than seven minutes' walk from the station. He spoke the truth. Lancaster Road was so easy to find that even I could make no mistake about it.

When I had reached the thoroughfare, and commenced my search for No. 121, all the semi-jauntiness which I had called to my assistance, left me. The thought of my mission, and indignation at the causes of it, filled my mind. I began to dread my task.

Lancaster Road seemed to be deserted at this early hour. It

was only nine o'clock. Not a solitary person had I passed yet. The big gray houses towered gloomily on each side of me. Bright lights shone from the windows, probably illuminating those happy homes which are in no city more plentiful than in London.

I was counting the numbers, my heart palpitating as I slowly approached that at which I should stop. I felt half inclined to go back at this eleventh hour, and live as I had been living these past few months, contentedly. No! content was no longer possible for me. I could not meet my husband again until I had seen my rival; and until he knew that I had seen her.

I stopped in front of a small gray house involuntarily. I seemed to feel instinctively, even before I had looked, that it was No. 121, and I was right. There were the three figures that to me made so sinister a combination, engraved on a little brass plate on the door. Then I took a leisurely view of the house in which Arthur chose to live, apart from his wife. It was a little, two story, gray-stone house, old fashioned, and rather unusual in its appearance. There was a tiny green grass plot in front, separated from the road by an iron railing, in which was a small, unlatched gate. It would have been a very ordinary looking house in a provincial city, but it was not at all suggestive of London. I looked at it with genuine curiosity, which for a moment swallowed up my anger. It was a very inexpensive place, but, love—guilty and illegitimate, but still love—dwelt there. Arthur preferred that simple little house, with one to whom he could give his heart, than the costly beauty of Tavistock Villa, with the wife whom he despised.

I brushed away the tears that rose unbidden to my eyes, with angry hands. This was no place for sentimental regret. I was here to act, and act I would.

There seemed to be only one room in the house which was lighted, and that was situated to the left of the front door. A light, reddened by warm, thick curtains, shone from its windows. Darkness reigned everywhere else. There was no light even in the hall. The glass above the front door looked black.

How was I to gain admittance? If I rang the rusty looking front door bell it would probably alarm them both. They were doubtless prepared in case of surprise of that kind, and such a course would certainly place me at a disadvantage. It was not likely that they kept servants, who might in the future prove unfortunate witnesses against them.

What could I do? I pushed open the gate and walked towards the stone steps leading to the front door. A thin iron grating separated me from the basement entrance. I touched it, and I could feel the gritty rust on my fingers. This basement entrance was in all likelihood never used now. I shook the grating slightly. Imagine my surprise, my joy, when it yielded without any difficulty to my gentle persuasion, and stood open. I entered immediately, only too pleased to be shut out from the sight of any passer-by, or of any policeman, to whom my position would have appeared rather strange.

I shut the iron gate behind me, descended two steps, and walked into the kitchen. It was in utter darkness. Not an object in front of me could I see. I groped my way about, feeling distinctly uneasy. Whether this kitchen were ever used, or whether it were in ruins I could not tell. I would have given a sovereign for a match—for one moment's light.

I presumed that this house was built like most houses, so I did not despair of finding my way upstairs. I could not discover the door leading to the basement hall, nor that by which I had entered. I grew frightened. The awful idea dawned upon me that I might have to stay where I was until daylight. I almost shrieked as I stumbled against some resisting object. It was nothing more alarming than a chair. I sat down and tried to quiet myself. My heart was throbbing wildly, and I could feel violent pulsations in my temples. They might hear me upstairs. The noise I made might alarm them. They would leave the house. I should be its sole tenant, and—

I started up. I would not terrify myself by such thoughts. By a mighty effort I collected myself as it were, and began my ridiculous hunt for the door with more deliberation. I was rewarded by success.

I had gained the stairs. I walked slowly upwards, found the door at the top of the stairs open—what should I have done had it been locked?—and stood in the hall. Now I could see the door of the room for which I was bound. The hall was in absolute darkness, but faint streaks of light, which would have been unnoticed under less obscure circumstances, revealed to me the whereabouts of the guilty couple. It was impossible now that they could escape me. I must see them. As this certainty forced itself upon me, my excitement became all the more intense.

I did not dare to move from behind the hall door where I had retreated, I surveyed the situation. Six or eight steps would take me to the room where I could discover all. The door would in all probability be unlocked. From whom had they to fear intrusion? They were safely secluded—or they fancied they were—in their own castle. I had only to suddenly open the door and face them.

My courage began to fail me. My position was an unenviable one. I wondered how matters would be three hours from now—if everything would be settled; if I should have discovered all. Then I carefully lacerated my feelings by reviewing events connected with my unhappy marriage. I pictured my absurd scruples. I had heard that evening that I was a silly little fool. That was the truth. I was silly, I was unworthy—

Without concluding my self-condemnation, I rushed from my hiding-place to the door of the room whence came the light. Without hesitating one moment I turned the handle, and giving a mighty push, which was absolutely unnecessary, I entered.

The sudden light coming upon my eyes, accustomed for the last half hour to utter darkness, blinded me. I could see nothing. Then two figures abruptly moving stood out before me in the glare. My dazzled inability lasted but a few seconds. Then before me I saw my husband, pale as death, trembling, his eyes wide with amazement, advancing towards me. I waved him off, standing with my back to the door. The room was a small one. At the other end of it was his companion.

The amazement of Arthur was not as great as that which must have been visible on my own face, as I beheld, ghastly in his pallor, but still boldly defiant—Captain Jack Dillington.

I burst into hysterical laughter.

CHAPTER XVIII.

Captain Dillington and my husband seemed unable to utter a word. My laughter did not last long. Quick as a flash of lightning came the thought to me that I was in a very ridiculous situation. After having shown my hand in a most hopeless manner, I had discovered my husband *tête-à-tête*[1] with—the abandoned woman I had pictured, the wanton destroyer of my domestic happiness I had imagined? No, with his bosom friend—the friend who long before I had come upon the scene had played the role of Damon to Arthur's Pythias.

Of course, as I stood before them, my hysterical laughter silenced, my breast heaving with emotion, and the fever spot burning on each cheek, they knew why I was there, what I suspected. But was it merely my sudden arrival that was responsible for the death-like pallor of my husband's face? Why did Captain

---

1 A private gathering of two, here used to imply an affair.

Dillington assume such a palpably defiant air, if there were no reason why he should defy me?

Such thoughts coursed through my mind much quicker than they can flow from my pen. After all had I shown my hand? Yes and no. I remembered that my mother had suggested Captain Dillington as the medium by which my husband communicated with his paramour. Why not assume that, in default of anything more substantial? That Captain Dillington was in some way responsible for my husband's despicable conduct, I was now as convinced as that I saw him before me. He had some influence over Arthur Ravener, the weaker vessel. This idea gained complete supremacy over me. It was then with Captain Dillington that I would deal—this deadly friend whom I would hold responsible.

I stood before the door, as I said, and simply stared at the two men, after my laughter had been subdued. Arthur grasped the back of a chair, and stood looking at me, as though he were obliged to look. Captain Dillington took a seat with a mighty show of composure, and awaited developments.

Arthur was the first to speak, and he did so gaspingly, "Why—why—d-did you c-come here, Elsie?" he asked.

"Why—why—did I come here?" I repeated mockingly.

"It is quite natural that your wife should be here, Arthur," said the Captain in his most elaborate manner. "She had suspicions—most natural, my dear fellow. She was jealous. You have no right to complain. Jealousy, as I look upon it, is merely an outcome of love. Is that not so, Mrs. Ravener?" (turning to me) "You—pardon my curiosity—thought that you would find a—a—well—a lady with your husband?"

The leer with which he accompanied these remarks was too indescribably repulsive to analyze. I determined to contain myself as much as possible.

"It is with no lady that I have business here," I said, with a miserable attempt at loftiness. "It is with you, Captain Dillington, and with no other."

I watched the effect of these words, shot at random. It was undeniable. Captain Dillington gasped. The blood left his cheeks and his lips. He was taken utterly aback. I had evidently started in the right direction. He must be the go between, but as I had seen no woman, it was not necessary that I should mention one.

"You are surprised, Captain Dillington?" I demanded quietly, though I was trembling with agitation.

"I—I simply do not understand you."

"Do you understand me, Arthur?" I asked, turning to my husband.

"I—I will not listen to your suspicions," began my husband, with such a weak attempt at resistance that it sounded more like an entreaty. "Elsie, you have no right here. You—you betray w-want of confidence in—in me. I will not stay—"

"You will!" I cried, placing my back to the door. "You shall not leave this room. Don't dare to try it," I continued, losing all my calmness, as a tide of anger swept over me, overwhelming caution. "Captain Dillington, if you attempt to stir from the room" (he had made a step forward) "I will open the window and rouse the neighbors. I don't mind scandal, perhaps, as much as you and he do. I can explain my presence here. You cannot."

"This is your husband's house," said Captain Dillington, angrily. "He has invited me here. I have nothing to explain. While I was a guest at your house, it was easy to see that I was not welcome. Your husband saw it. I saw it. So as we have always been great friends, he chose to invite me where there was no danger of my being insulted. That explains my presence here, I think."

"No, it does not. That does not explain your presence here, and you know it. You know it too, Arthur Ravener," I cried, turning to the helplessly distressed object all in a heap on the back of a chair. "Do you think, Captain Dillington, that I will continue to tolerate the conduct of this man, who left me on my wedding day, and who kept you, a hated guest—yes, you are right, a hated, detested, loathed guest—in our house, when it should have been sacred to ourselves? Do you think that because I am young and ignorant—no, I am no longer ignorant—that I will bear with this? You know very little of women if you can suppose it. You probably thought you were dealing with a helpless fool. Let me tell you that you have been watched by detectives for the past week, at my instigation, and that I know all."

It was a desperate game of bluff, but it met with triumphant success. As I paused for want of breath, I saw that Captain Dillington was literally unable to speak.

He had warmed himself into anger a few moments before, but in the shock of this great surprise, it had died away. My husband had averted his face, and was looking at the wall with very great persistence. So far the field was my own. I had worked myself into a great passion, and these hits had not been premeditated.

"I will live no longer as I have been doing," I went on, "I have discovered enough. I have hoped against hope. I have dreaded this hour. But it has come, and I will not fear it. I have told you that I do not mind scandal, and I shall not hesitate to apply to the Divorce Court."

Captain Dillington pressed his hand to his heart. My husband came towards me, and took my hand.

"Elsie," he said, "do not—do not, for the love of Heaven speak like this. You cannot mean what you say. You cannot, you would not do it?"

"I would," I exclaimed, furiously, "I would do it. You have tried my patience. I have no interest in you any more. I gave you all, and you have treated me with contempt. I will not live with you any longer. I will not—I could not. The thought of your infamy would rise up before me at all times. I will be free, and you shall, you must be free, too."

I burst into tears, I could not help it. After all, I had done bravely, and I was not made of stone. I had ceased to wonder who was the woman in the case. I had succeeded in confounding the two men so well without her aid, that I felt comparatively satisfied. In fact I did not want to know who she was.

Captain Dillington recovered himself some what when he saw my tears. "Mrs. Ravener forgets that in a divorce suit a great many things must be proved. You say you have had us watched by detectives. May I ask if they have discovered the identity of the co-respondent?"

The coolness with which he spoke almost amused me. I laughed amidst my sobs. "I—I have all the evidence I need," I managed to say. "Suppose," with an attempt at mirth, "I—I should make you co-respondent, Captain Dillington?"

He smiled, but it was with a great effort, I could see.

"Very good, very good," he said, with manifest uneasiness.

"Do not—do not talk like that, Elsie," said Arthur, imploringly. "You will not bring this—this scandal upon us all. You—you did love me, Elsie. I do not believe that I have quite killed your love. You would not ruin me like this. You would not bring disgrace upon your family." He broke down, sobbing.

"The disgrace," I said sternly, feeling contempt for these pitiful arguments, "is brought by you, sir. My character is spotless, as you well know. I have given you every opportunity to avoid scandal, but you failed to suppose that I could do anything but submit to your heartless neglect. You have aroused me. It has taken you twelve months to do it. If you had married a girl who had mixed more with the world, she would not have lived with you one week. I had peculiarities, however, and you thought they would give you an opportunity to carry out your wretched plans without interruption; that is why you married me. I was warned against you—you need not start—but I disregarded the warning, and I have dearly paid for my folly. My punishment has been great, but it shall end from to-day. To-morrow I will leave Tavistock Villa, and I never want to see it again."

I began to button my cloak and gloves. I had said enough. I would now leave them to do exactly what they chose. I had no more interest in my husband, I told myself.

"You are going, Mrs. Ravener?" queried Captain Dillington in a mocking tone, his jeering exuberance once more asserting itself.

"I am going," I said.

Arthur seized his hat, and sprang towards the door. "I will go with you, Elsie," he said in a pleading tone.

"You will not," I exclaimed. "You shall not enter the house—with me, at any rate."

"He has a perfect right to do so," remarked Captain Dillington. "It is his home; you are his wife."

"And you—?" I asked pointedly. My jest about the co-respondent in the case had annoyed him so much before, that I thought I would administer another stab with the same weapon.

He turned away hastily for a moment. "I am his friend," he then said, "and"—boldly—"I am not ashamed of it. We were at college together, and our intimacy has been continued since those days. I will aid Arthur Ravener whenever I can; I will do anything for him. He is my bosom friend, and I am ready to say so before anybody. Now, are you satisfied?"

He snapped his fingers defiantly, but I was not going to allow myself to be beaten. My game of bluff had been successful. Perhaps he was trying the same tactics. He should not succeed.

"As far as you are concerned—perfectly," I said.

I opened the door. Arthur followed me.

"If you persist in coming," I said, "of course you must do so. After all, it does not make much difference; your apartments do not clash with mine."

He winced, but said nothing. He cast a glance, uneasy, suspicious, wretched, at Captain Dillington, and then left the room with me. He opened the front door, and we stepped out into the night air. Captain Dillington remained where we left him. Not another word did he utter.

"Shall I call a cab?" asked Arthur, nervously.

"If you choose," I said carelessly. "You insist upon accompanying me, so that I cannot help myself. Oblige me, however, by not troubling to talk. I have nothing to say. I don't want any explanation. That house," pointing to No. 121 Lancaster Road, "speaks for itself."

He hailed a passing four-wheeler, and we were soon rolling homewards. I buried my face in the cushions, and resolutely declined to think of my grievance during the long, weary ride home. Arthur made no attempt to speak. He stared, in a dazed way, out of the side windows, though he could not have seen much; and so we reached Tavistock Villa.

CHAPTER XIX.

There is one malady dear to the heart of modem novel-writers. It is helpful, pleasantly dangerous, and yet to be vanquished. Of course I allude to brain fever.[1] Once get your hero into some scrape from which there is no outlet, and you are forced to call upon brain fever for help. He lies dangerously ill for weeks, months; makes several delirious confessions; arises once more the ghost of his former self, and in the meantime, what? All difficulties have been smoothed away, and the eager interest of the unsuspecting reader has been relieved of its keen edge. Brain fever is a boon to the novel writer, and like all cheap boons it has been woefully abused.

Brain fever, however, is not nearly as frequent in real life as it is in novels. It is fiction's way out of a climax.

I have jotted down these thoughts because I remember they occurred to me during the days which followed the events described in the preceding chapter, when time hung heavily on my hands, and I could settle to nothing.

When we reached Tavistock Villa on that important night, Arthur retired to the rooms he had fitted up for himself, and I went silently to my own apartments. We attempted no explanations. We had no word to say. There was not even an uttered "good-night."

Next morning my husband sent for me, and I went at once to his room. He told me he had not slept all night, except for a few minutes at a time, when he had been awakened by alarming dreams. His face was flushed and his eyes moved constantly. It was easy to see that he was ill.

"Elsie," he said, "if people should call to-day, t-tell them that I—I am indisposed—th-that I cannot see them. You will do this?"

---

1 The name for a condition in which it was thought that part of the brain became infected or inflamed.

"No one shall disturb you," I promised. "We will have a doctor, presently, for I am afraid you are indeed indisposed."

"Do not send for a doctor," he said, excitedly, "I do not need one. I do not, indeed, Elsie, I assure you."

"You are mistaken," I said, coldly. "I insist upon sending for Dr. White. Perhaps you will allow me to have my own way for once."

He looked at me reproachfully. I felt guilty—as though I were hitting a man when he was down. Dr. White came. He said that Arthur must have been subjected to some long-continued mental anxiety, and that he needed careful nursing. I was not to be unnecessarily alarmed if at times he had hallucinations, such as imagining himself surrounded by enemies, or suspecting that people were plotting to do him harm. His nervous system was run down.

"Your husband has not been living as quietly as he might have done, I infer, Mrs. Ravener?" Dr. White asked rather hesitatingly.

I crimsoned. How could I tell this man that my husband's pursuits were unknown to me? He noticed my confusion.

"Dr. White," I said at last, deliberately, resolved to tell as much as I could, "I see no use in concealment. A medical man must receive strange confidences. The truth is that I know little more about my husband's life than you do. All I can tell you is that during the last year he has spent most of his time out of the house."

"Exactly," with significance. "I thought as much," with sapient consideration; then, "Well, Mrs. Ravener, if you will take my advice, you will forgive everything, and make no allusion whatever to the past. What your husband needs is complete rest and change, and a few months' devotion to him on your part will restore him to you. My dear young lady, this is not an unusual case—"

I started up. "Not unusual?" I interrupted. Then I reflected that all he knew of the case, and all that I intended he should know, might not be unusual.

"Not unusual," he said. "Young men of fortune like your husband, marrying at an early age, cannot break suddenly from old associations, from bachelor friends, from—ah! how do I know? That is why I always say to friends who I hear are about to wed: 'Reflect well, my boy. A wife is exacting. She will call you to account for yourself. All your gay[1] doings must be renounced.

---

1   Frivolous, lewd, or hedonistic, but almost certainly not homosexual, as the latter was a connotation that originated in the United States in the early 1920s.

A woman gives herself up to you. You must reciprocate.' You love your husband?" he asked, suddenly jerking his voice from an anecdotal crooning to a professional tone.

"Yes," I said in a low voice.

"Then, Mrs. Ravener, it is a case of plain sailing. Try to forget your injuries. Leave this country as soon as you conveniently can, and take your husband with you. What would you think of a trip across the Atlantic to America? It would be the making of you both. If," stammering, "as y-you suspect, and—as—I—suspect, Mr. Ravener—er—has—er—ties—er—here, which he should not have—er—what better means of breaking them could you possibly discover?"

He was right, the scheme was an excellent one. All this time I had been giving way to my indignant anger at my husband's cruel treatment, but I had never thought of attempting to remove him from temptation. Here was I planning separation, divorce and other scandalously revengeful proceedings, when, in reality, perhaps all my husband wanted was a change. He was weak, and he was under the influence of a man with an iron will, I felt sure. Perhaps I might be a little too submissive, but Arthur was my husband and I loved him.

"Dr. White," I said, rising and taking the old man's hand, "I—I thank you, your suggestion is a kind one—so kind and good that—that—it would not have occurred to me."

I buried my face in my hands. Yes, I was too vindictive. Even this morning, when I had seen Arthur feverish and oppressed, I could not forget the past few months. I thought only of my own wrongs. Who knew but that Arthur was as much sinned against as sinning? In this world too much charity is impossible.

"Mrs. Ravener," said Dr. White, pretending not to see my tears, "I have left a prescription on the little table in your husband's room. See that it is made up. I will look in again. You have nothing to be alarmed about. Your husband will recover, and—my dear—I hope that you will both, like the good people in the fairy tales, live happily ever after. Now, now—no tears," he said, placing his hand on my bowed head. "Be as cheerful as you possibly can. I always say that my prescriptions should be diluted with cheerfulness. Ah! it is a wonderful thing."

While he was talking, I rose and dried my eyes. By the time he had finished, I could smile at him. He was satisfied and left me. As he went from the room, James entered with a card. "The gentleman is waiting," he said, with a quick look in my face.

The card was that of Captain Dillington. I tore it up savagely, forgetful of the servant's presence, and flung the pieces into the empty fireplace.

"Tell Captain Dillington," I said, "that Mr. Ravener is ill this morning and cannot be seen. If he calls again, tell him the same thing. James," approaching him, "do me a favor—it will indeed be a great one. Never permit Captain Dillington to set his foot within this house again. You will do this?"

"Yes, ma'am," he said, pleased at being asked to confer a favor, "I will. The Captain tried to brush past me this morning, but I heard the master tell you not to let people see him. I was in the room at the time, you know. So I just pushed the Captain back. He gives me a terrible look, but looks don't hurt any one. 'I'll take your card,' says I, and when he sees that I mean it he hands me one."

"You have done well," I said.

I was determined that Captain Dillington should see Arthur no more. Exactly what was the understanding between them, I did not know, but that the elder man was partly accountable for the delinquencies of the younger, I was perfectly persuaded. At any rate I would be on the safe side. I would refuse Captain Dillington admittance every time he applied for it, without consulting Arthur.

During the next few days I was constantly in my husband's room. As Dr. White led me to expect, he had hallucinations. He seemed to fancy that someone was pursuing him, but it was impossible to shape his incoherent utterances into any intelligible form. They lasted but for a short time, and left him weak, but entirely rational.

"Arthur," I said on one of these occasions, "I have a proposition to make to you. We have never taken any journey together"—I was going to refer to the lacking honeymoon, but determined to avoid any allusion to the past—"and I should like to go away very much. Suppose we were to take a trip to America?" I watched his face. His eyes fell. He turned away his head.

"It is very far," he said vaguely.

"Yes," I assented cheerfully, "that is why I am so anxious to take the trip. I think a little sail on the herring-pond[1] would do us good," I continued, with an abortive attempt to be funny. "Dr. White said you needed a change."

"When would you want to go?" he asked uneasily.

"Any time, dear," I said. Then, as if the idea had come to me

---

1 The Atlantic Ocean.

suddenly, "I think it would be best to start at once. Suppose that as soon as you are able to go out, your first ride be to Liverpool?" He was embarrassed. "I will think it over," he said weakly. He never alluded to my threats of divorce. He seemed to have forgotten all about them. Since he had been ill, I had been kind, and as much like my former self as I possibly could.

Two days passed. Arthur's health was improving rapidly. We could start now at any time he chose to name, but he seemed in no hurry to refer to our American trip.

On the third day, when I tried to enter Arthur's room, I found the door locked. I was alarmed and knocked until my knuckles complained very painfully. I stopped suddenly, arrested by a noise I heard in the room. It could only have been the opening or shutting of the window, but it sounded strangely to me. I knocked again. Arthur hastened to the door and opened it. His face was red, and he seemed agitated. I looked at him in surprise.

"Why did you lock the door?" I asked, not sharply but curiously.

"Why not?" he said with a nervous laugh, "is there any law against it, Elsie?"

"None that I know of," I said, still rather uneasy in my mind. "Were you out in the garden, Arthur?"

"I? No."

"I thought I heard the window open?"

"My dear Elsie," he said, "why should I go into the garden by the window? You forget I am not strong enough yet to jump. If I wanted a walk, I should suggest an airing in a proper way." Arthur's manner was by no means reassuring.

"Then the window was not open?" I asked carelessly.

He hesitated a moment. "No," he replied, "it was not."

The matter was certainly not worth pursuing any further. I could have sworn that I had heard the window shut, but then perhaps my imagination, stimulated by a locked door, may have led me into error.

That night Arthur informed me he would accompany me to America any time I chose. I was delighted, and thought of nothing but the probable success of our journey away from scenes fraught with so many painful associations.

CHAPTER XX.

Once away from Kew, and my old spirits reasserted themselves. As we rolled away from Euston to Liverpool's only and original

Lime Street, I was as happy as—I was going to say—a newly made bride, but, alas, that hackneyed simile has no meaning for me. Every old corn field we passed delighted me; I made Arthur buy me illustrated papers and fruit at every station, and nearly caused him to miss the train at one halting place because in my insatiable desire for chocolate I sent him forth to the refreshment room.

Arthur was at first inclined to be subdued, as I suppose it was proper he should be, but I soon thwarted his intentions. I was determined that we would both of us forget the past, and start out afresh. I would be as engaging as a maiden yet to be wooed, and he,—well, he should woo me. I was resolved that I would not be wifely. I would consider that we were simply on good terms, and I was going to try hard to make him love me. Pshaw! A fig for the fact that I was really his wife. He would be glad to remember that by and by, I told myself.

So I broke every bit of ice I saw, and long before we had reached Lime Street, he was laughing at my idiotic behavior. We made a couple of fools of ourselves.

I wonder why English people who take railway journeys feel that they must eat as soon as the train starts. It has always caused me a great deal of amusement. On this particular occasion, a phlethoric old matron waited until she had waved her chubby hand at about fifty fond relations on the platform, allowed a tear or two to course portentously down her cheeks, and then sought consolation in her hamper. For the next thirty minutes she was busily engaged in dissecting a chicken. Ugh! how greasy she was at the end of that time. I was rude enough to stare at her, and I presume the poor old soul thought I coveted her chicken. She offered me some. At first I thought of accepting it and going halves with Arthur, but I caught his imploring glance and decided to be abstemious.

Of course we traveled with the usual ruddy-faced[1] Briton, who before he was fifteen minutes out was caught peeping into a little spirit flask. They always amuse me—those exploring tipplers who seem anxious to impress you with the idea that they are merely making a scientific test. I have a detestation for red noses, both male and female, which of course means that I very frequently have one in cold weather—or at least used to do so, until I discovered that perfect French jewel, Marie, my maid.

1　Red-faced, here used to denote a lower-class and/or alcoholic person.

Dear readers, you will never know what comfort is until you have a Gallic "assistant." Of course they are expensive luxuries, but you can economize elsewhere.

My pen runs on. As I think of that delightful trip, coming as it did when life seemed darkest, all my happiness comes back to me, and I write now as I felt then.

As I was not desirous of parading myself, limp and seasick, before a select and fashionable audience, we decided not to patronize a Cunarder,[1] even though it be so rapid. I was not so burningly anxious to be in America. I did not care where I was, so rejoiced was I to be away from London. So we ensconced ourselves meekly on one of the Inman steamers,[2] which was quite good enough for me.

It seemed unnatural, going away without anyone to see us off, especially as nearly every one on board cried farewell to somebody on the tender. I felt hard-hearted because I "sailed away from my native land," without a tear. I tried to be affected, but I couldn't. I wished that I had given the polite little fellow, who had carried my valise for me, half-a-crown extra to cry when the steamer started, and wave his hand to me.

"You are as bad I am, Arthur," I said, as we stood at the rail and watched the tender taking its farewell-sayers back to the dock. "There's not a solitary tear trickling down your countenance. I'm really vexed with myself, but they won't trickle. I can't help it."

"I am glad of it, Elsie," said Arthur, fervently. I knew he was thinking that they had trickled sufficiently during the past few sad weeks.

"I am not," I persisted in declaring. "It is unseemly to go about with all one's unshed tears while everybody else is lavishly distributing them in all directions."

No sooner had the tender disappeared from sight, and our own anchor had been lifted (isn't that deliciously nautical? I flatter myself it is extremely creditable), than I saw sixteen people—I counted them—rush up to the Captain and ask him if it were

---

1 A British-American steamship operated by the Cunard Line. For many years through the mid-nineteenth century, the Cunard Line had a reputation for being the fastest and most fashionable way to cross the Atlantic Ocean.

2 Inman Lines operated from 1850–93 (when it was incorporated into American Line) as one of the most popular ways to cross the Atlantic.

going to be "rough." Poor man! I suppose he is overwhelmed in this manner at every trip.

He thought it was going to be one of the finest voyages he had ever made, he said, and the sixteen timid ones went their way rejoicing.

It is the correct thing, nowadays, to be eternally and consistently *blasé*,[1] as my dear mother would say, especially on one's travels. To speak of my transatlantic trip of course makes it at once apparent that I have never been to America before. I admit it, and must also confess that my voyage interested me immensely, and all the more because my expected seasickness was never realized.

To have seen us all in the saloon on the first night was in itself an entertainment. We were all very stiff, and suspicious, and unfriendly, being mostly English, and took our places at the table under protest as it were. We were soon supplied with passenger lists, and before attempting to nourish our bodies we fed our curiosity by wondering "who was who," and trying to "locate" the different passengers.

There were at least a score whose identity we soon discovered. They belonged to that class which an American on board declared to be composed of "chronic kickers—gentlemen who, if they went to Heaven, would vow their halos didn't fit." They found that their names had been spelled wrong, and complained loudly:

"I made a point of spelling S-m-y-t-h-e and here they have me down as Smith."

"I call it disgusting. They've made me John P. Bodley, when I distinctly remember telling them my name was J. Porterhouse Bodley."

"Oh, Mamma, they've never mentioned Jane. I wanted them to put 'and maid.' How annoying!"

"Why, Eliza! They've actually got us 'J. Rogers, wife and family,' in one line, instead of mentioning each of our names, as I asked them to do."

And so they made themselves known.

The first meal was the only one of which many of the passengers approved. They had made up their minds to be seasick, and seasick they were. One young woman announced that she had been under medical treatment for three days before starting, and that her doctor had advised her after the

---

1 French: seeming unimpressed or bored.

first meal to go to bed during the rest of the voyage. That such a man should be allowed to practice!

Arthur and I sat at the Captain's table, close by the Captain, which I am told was a great honor. That dignitary seemed to wish us to think so, at any rate. He was full of graceful condescension at first, and three courses had sped quickly away before he favored us with our first nautical story. Of course everyone at the table was convulsed with laughter. It put us all in a good temper, and led us to look upon one another with less suspicion.

After dinner Arthur and I walked up and down deck, talking gaily of our plans. Not a sentimental word passed from my lips; no one could have been more affectionate and sisterly than I was. I firmly believe that he understood and appreciated my efforts. He looked at me gratefully from time to time. That friendliness which had been so oppressive in his manner to me formerly, was not so apparent.

I pictured our return to England, the past forgotten like an ugly dream; the future full of promise; the present given up utterly to the love which though late might overwhelm us with its long delayed delight. As I painted the glowing probabilities on my susceptible mind-canvas, I could not school my voice to the mild, platonic utterances which I felt I must affect. Words of love rose to my lips; I trembled at my own emotion.

"Are you not glad to be—to be here?" I asked him as quietly as I could.

He paused for one moment. Then in a low tone—"Yes," he said.

He was sincere. But there was none of the passion in his voice that I—unhappy girl!—could not keep from mine. He gave me affection in return for love. Well, at any rate, he seemed to be thawing. I had every reason to rejoice.

As I said before, I was not seasick. When we arrived at Queenstown,[1] I recognized the fact that I had slept soundly, and arose in the best of spirits. I found my husband on deck, watching the men carrying the mail-bags on board. He also had slept well, he informed me.

It was a superb day, a bright sky overhead, a lovely green opaque sea around us, while the pretty coast of Ireland, as seen from Queenstown's snug little harbor, completed a most fascinating picture. We were both of us in excellent spirits, and chatted

---

1   Cobh, a city on the southeast coast of Ireland, was named
    Queenstown from 1844–1922. It was a major transatlantic Irish
    port and the last port prior to crossing the Atlantic.

lightly on every subject but that of ourselves. We laughed at the queer old creatures who clambered up the sides of the big ship and cajoled us into purchasing murderous looking blackthorns, bog-oak ornaments of the most funereal type, and other quaintly Hibernian wares.[1] How charming Ireland is—from a distance!

As we left Queenstown, people seemed to have made themselves at home on board, and to have resigned themselves to something more than a week of irrevocable sea. Men who had made their first appearance clad in the height of fashion, were hardly to be known in their hideous comfortable sea-garments. Traveling caps replaced the shining *chapeau-de-soie*;[2] loose warm ulsters, the daintily fitting overcoats; while time-honored trousers were called into a brief resurrection. The ladies donned their plainest, most unbecoming attire. Any one who had a grudge against any particular dress, wore it. There is little coquetry in attire on shipboard. Woman, from a pictorial point of view at any rate, is at her worst. Perhaps for the first time in her life, she is caught napping, so far as her attire is concerned.

A great number of the feminine passengers installed themselves with graceful invalidism on steamer chairs rug-enveloped. They were so determined to be ill that I should really have sympathized with their disappointment had Neptune[3] declined to affect them as they expected to be affected.

We were soon one big family, united in the common desire of reaching port speedily and safely. I had so many acquaintances before a week was ended, that my days were entirely taken up with them. We had our little scandal society on board, and discussed at afternoon tea those who were not at the table. Womanhood always finds its level, and womanhood is not womanhood without gossip.

The queer things I was told about America on that ship! One portly damsel took me to one side and informed me in a mysterious whisper that clothes were terribly expensive in America, but that I could purchase undergarments for next to nothing. Another American told me that New York houses were so much more civilized than London dwellings, because they all had stoops. What a stoop was, I had no idea. After a time it occurred

---

1 A blackthorn is a walking stick made from the blackthorn shrub; bog oak ornaments are made from oak found in peat bogs; Hibernian means of or belonging to Ireland.

2 French: a silk hat worn by gentlemen.

3 The Roman god of water and the sea.

to me that the houses must be trying to follow the example of the leaning tower of Pisa. That stooped. I received information on all sides, and as my mind was pleasantly blank in regard to the country discovered by Christopher Columbus, I was pounced upon by everybody who wanted to talk.

My husband rarely left my side. He never entered the smoking-room, and kept distinctly aloof from the other men. We were hardly ever alone. With the exception of a half-hour's stroll on deck each evening after dinner, my husband and I never enjoyed a *solitude à deux.*[1] Those brief half hours were devoted to general conversation. We never referred to the troublous period that had preceded our voyage.

I was rather glad that my time was so much occupied by my friend-passengers. I was able to acknowledge very soon the fact that my husband found increasing pleasure in my society. Our after dinner walks, I could see, were very pleasant to him, and at the end of a week conversation grew less general.

One evening he was unusually silent, and I made no effort to talk. We sat looking at the foamy milk-path that marked the course of the ship. I soon felt that his eyes were fastened on my face. I did not speak. My policy was not to attempt to force results in any way.

"Elsie," he said, presently, "some time ago I remember saying to you that perhaps our marriage was a mistake." I started. He went on: "I now believe that it was not. Elsie, no other woman would have been as patient as you have been, or made the sacrifice you have made in—in—really expatriating yourself for my sake. I—I—am very grateful, dear."

"You have nothing to be grateful for," I said, gravely. Then lightly throwing off the sentimental mood to which I would have loved to give sway, "I don't consider this expatriation, this is merely a pleasant voyage, and it is even more delightful than I anticipated."

"It is delightful," he said, seriously.

I imagine our fellow-passengers considered that we were rather eccentric. The men seemed to look down upon Arthur—or at least I thought so. What looked to me like contemptuous glances were cast by them at my husband when he was sitting in the midst of the medley of feminine passengers, who had evidently "taken a fancy" to me. Arthur seemed indifferent to these manifestations, if he noticed them at all. But they aroused in me

---

1 French: the solitude of two, i.e., private time together.

a feeling of violent indignation. I could have gone up to these whippersnappers and told them that I believed my husband to be better than they were; but perhaps it was lucky I did not adopt this course.

I was quite ready and eager to forgive Arthur everything. I had resolved that not a single allusion to my unknown rival should ever cross my lips, unless, of course, my husband showed himself to be subsequently unworthy of my love, which I did not believe he would do. I had not the faintest curiosity to know who the woman was. In fact I was glad I was absolutely ignorant on the subject. As soon as I felt convinced that our happiness was assured, I had promised myself that I would try to understand the influence which Captain Dillington possessed over my husband, and then gently to withdraw him from it. It was bad. I was quite certain of that.

And so, more happily than I had imagined even in my most sanguine moments, our voyage across the Atlantic was accomplished. We said good-bye to the friends we had made on board as sorrowfully as though we had known them for a lifetime, and prepared to join the busy throng in the American metropolis.

CHAPTER XXI.

We went to a quiet hotel, "on" Broadway, but far from the noise and bewildering traffic of that turbulent thoroughfare. It was a comfortable, unostentatious little house, not startlingly impressive, like some of the caravansaries miles above us, nor gloomily monotonous like the so-called family hotels where women who are too disgracefully lazy to attend to household duties, and men who are too idiotically weak-willed to protest against this, abide in stupid sloth.

We had a dainty little suite of three rooms. There was a small, prettily furnished parlor, from one side of which Arthur's room opened, while from the other side my own chamber could be entered. It was a tiny, kitchenless flat, and—as the colored handmaiden who attended to our wants, expressed it—it was "just as cute as could be."

No more complete diversion from the painful events of the past could have been desired than this visit to New York, where everything was new to us; where suggestion from associations was out of the question; where we were unlikely to meet a soul whom we knew; where even the English newspapers, when they reached us, were ten days old, and consequently uninteresting, and where no social claims could form an excuse for separation.

The programme of our first few days in America was as follows: Breakfast at ten o'clock in that dear little parlor, which, I reflected, was gradually becoming all that separated us the one from the other; a glance though the American newspapers, so that no one could accuse us of living entirely out of the world; a drive, either through that magnificent park,[1] which does not boast what I have always willfully considered an intolerable nuisance, a "Rotten Row,"[2] upon what New Yorkers call "the road"; then dinner in the big dining-room. After dinner we retired to our own little parlor and I read from some popular novel to my husband. I did not weary him with instructive books, because I thought he needed recreation, and because I hate instructive books myself. I recollect how I used to have Smiles' "Self-Help,"[3] thrust upon me by an enterprising governess, because she said it was "the most instructive, and at the same time the most amusing book," she could find.

I read to Arthur some good modern novels. When I saw that the dose was sufficient, I desisted, quickly closed my book, kissed him, and departed into my room.

And this treatment, I flattered myself, was most efficacious. I do not believe I gave a thought to my unknown rival during all those pleasant, happy days. I am sure I should have known it if I had. I loved my husband so dearly in this voluntary exile, that I was quick to notice his every look and expression, to account for them, to understand them.

He was gratified. Slowly but surely I was able to recognize in his manner a change from the wooed to the wooer. Alas! that a woman should ever be forced to woo a man. Still, when that man is her own husband, there are extenuating circumstances to be placed to her credit, as I think you will readily agree. My attentions did not weary him. Once or twice I grew tired of reading aloud, and he noticed it before I did. Then quietly but firmly he took the book from my unwilling hands, closed it, and laid

---

1 Central Park, New York City.
2 Rotten Row (from "Route de Roi"), a broad equestrian track in Hyde Park, London. Unlike Hyde Park, Central Park was designed with separate circulation systems for pedestrians, horse-back riders, and pleasure vehicles.
3 Samuel Smiles (1812–1904), *Self-Help; With Illustrations of Character and Conduct*, published in 1859 and widely read in Victorian England.

it gently on the sofa. The slight but embarrassing pause which followed that action was broken by comments he made upon the story in question, that led to an amiable discussion of its merits, its probabilities, its characters. I gave my views with my usual flippant recklessness, and at last had the delight of knowing that I entertained him.

I believe I have called my married life unhappy. Ah! why should I say that, with the memory of those few sunny days vividly before me? Nothing can take that memory away from me. Those days were mine; I had worked for them laboriously, and they came simply as the reward of labor. I earned them. They were not the fullest joy that could have been given me, but they were inexpressibly dear, and as I think of them my eyes moisten and my lips tremble.

At the dinner-table, one night, we heard a very spirited discussion upon the merits of a sensational preacher, who was attracting large audiences—yes, "audiences" is the correct word—to his church, and exciting a good deal of newspaper comment at the same time. The majority of those who took part in the discussion were inclined to the opinion that the reverend gentleman was far too secular in his pulpit addresses; while the minority contended that he struck bravely at the root of crying evils from the very best place where it was possible for a man to strike at them. What was a pulpit for, said they, if not to redress evils by ventilating them? They, for their part, did not care to listen to the old-fashioned sermons that pleased generations past. The sermons might not be orthodox in the accepted meaning of the word, but they were interesting, clever and virile.

"Let us go to-morrow and hear this much-talked-about gentleman, Arthur," I said to my husband as we returned to our parlor after dinner. "We can then pass upon his merits or de-merits in our own particularly learned way. What say you?"

He laughed.

"We will go, Elsie," he said. "You shall pass upon his merits or de-merits as usual, and I will simply curb your impetuosity in whatever direction you may argue—also, as usual."

So the following morning, which happened to be Sunday, instead of casting our eyes through the voluminous newspapers, we disposed ourselves to thoughts of church, a novelty to both of us, I am sorry, though obliged, to confess.

This home of sensationalism was a very modern-looking building—as, of course, was appropriate. I was surprised when I found that it was a church, so extremely secular was its appearance.

It was situated a long way from our hotel, but in what street I cannot remember, though I am quite sure it was above Fortieth Street and below Fiftieth.

Crowds of people were entering the building as we reached it—exquisitely dressed women, black clad respectable looking men, and comely children in all their Sunday finery. I was told that this was a distinctly American congregation. It was certainly a most refined and intelligent looking gathering of men and women.

We took our seats in a pew, from which we had an excellent view of the presiding minister. He was a tall, thin, dignified, quiet looking man. At the first glance one might have expected an orthodox, prosy, soporific sermon, but a more careful inspection of the man revealed a pair of keen, bead-like eyes, which seemed to "take in" every man or woman present in a most unusual manner; tightly compressed lips, and fingers that spasmodically clutched the book they held.

"He doesn't look sensational," I whispered conclusively to my husband.

"He looks very sensational," was the reply.

The preliminary service was a short one, and at the close of a hymn, exquisitely sung, suddenly looking up I saw the minister in the pulpit ready to begin. He made none of those prefatory announcements which are death to the artistic impressiveness of a sermon. Standing in his pulpit, he waited till the last deliciously tuneful strain of the choir had died away, and then gave out his text, clearly and deliberately. Before he had reached the end of the text, he had rivetted my attention, and during the entire sermon I listened to him spell-bound, unconscious of my surroundings.

This was the text:

> "Then the Lord rained upon Sodom and upon Gomorrah brimstone and fire from the Lord out of Heaven;
>
> "And he overthrew those cities, and all the plain, and all the inhabitants of the cities, and that which grew upon the ground.
>
> "And he (Abraham) looked towards Sodom and Gomorrah, and toward all the land of the plain, and beheld, and lo, the smoke of the country went up as the smoke of a furnace."[1]

---

1 Genesis 19:24–25, 28.

He spoke of the optimists who flatter themselves that the sins of the earlier ages are unknown to-day; who believe that civilization has dealt out death to the evils that corrupted a younger world. He tried to show that optimism was the natural sequence of ignorance; that all sin was the result of human weakness, inherited, or by some physiological freak, innate; that there was not a solitary vice recorded in the times gone by that did not exist to-day, magnified and multiplied. Sin could take no new shape, and no one could assert after a careful study of humanity, that it had forgotten any of its old forms. Men were the same now as they were when we first heard of them. Their lives, shortened slightly perhaps by civilization, were identical; their death, as inevitable; their physical sufferings synonymous; their joys similar.

He alluded to those who knew of the existence of hateful sins, and who from misplaced scruple, failed to mention them.

"Do not call me illogical," he said, "I do not believe that sin could be abolished by all the sermons in the world. But at least it should be diligently pointed out that it may not gather increased victims. Its spread can be avoided; its contagion diminished. Men will sin as long as the world exists; but many sin voluntarily, won over by those with whom vice is natural."

The pessimism of the sermon frightened me. With him there was no hope of eradicating evil; merely of lessening its influence upon those with whom it was forced to come in contact. It was a very deep, obtuse lecture—too deep for me, I am afraid. I did not understand it thoroughly, though its gist was perfectly clear to me. The methods of the man would have attracted attention anywhere, but I never want to hear another such sermon. I do not believe it could do good. People do not want to be thrilled on Sunday. They need to be comforted and taught to hope for the best. As his last words were uttered, and the congregation, which had listened breathlessly, eagerly, to every word, watched the speaker descend from his pulpit, I looked for the first time since the beginning of the discourse at my husband.

His face was as white as death. His eyes, widely open, were staring fixedly at the pulpit, which was now empty, as though he expected further utterances. His hands hung limp and nerveless at his side.

I touched his arm. He started violently, and turned a face from which every expression of good-fellowship, trust and hope seemed to have fled.

"Arthur," I said, seriously alarmed, "what is the matter? Are you ill? Don't—don't look at me like that."

He tried to smile.

"I wonder if he has delivered that lecture before," he said huskily.

His strange tone surprised me—accustomed as I was, by this time, to surprise.

"Probably not," I said. "Popular preachers, as a rule, do not deliver old sermons, I should think,—for their own sakes."

"Let us go home," he said. "I can't sit through the rest of the service."

As we were going out Arthur asked one of the ushers anxiously if the Doctor were going to speak again that night. The usher smiled.

"No," he said. "One lecture is all he can manage. He exhausts himself. He's as weak as a rat after one of his talks."

My ideas upon the weakness of rats being decidedly limited, I could only infer from the context that it was extreme. We passed out into the street.

"I did not want to hear him again," said Arthur presently, as we walked homewards, "but if he had spoken to-night I feel I must have gone. What an awful sermon!"

"It was indeed," I assented, "we are surely not such hopeless cases as that man wants to make out."

"Do you think so?" he asked.

I looked at him, wondering.

"I am sure of it," I said, with the beautiful certainty of one who never studies any question except upon the surface.

"You are a dear little girl," he said suddenly, with what I considered absolute irrelevance, "and I would believe you rather than—than him. Let us go home and talk. Do you know, dear, I am beginning to feel so happy in your society—No, no" (hastily), "not as I used to be, Elsie. You are doing so much good. I bless the day when we left London."

I looked up at him gladly; could any words have been sweeter than these to me? I doubt it.

CHAPTER XXII.

We dined with the multitude that afternoon, and I was glad of it. Arthur was feverishly uneasy. He seemed unable to forget the sermon he had heard in the morning, though why it should have affected him so painfully, I could not exactly understand. Of course I supposed he felt remorse for that part of his life—of our lives—which had brought us to this far off country, and exiled us on its hospitable shores.

Women are not uncharitable, say what you will. I was anxious that my husband should suffer no more for those misdeeds which, it seemed to me, had been so thoroughly left to the past. I wanted him to forget them. I was trying to forget them myself. I flattered myself that my most sanguine hopes would be realized, and that we should return to England as warmly devoted a couple as readers could ever hope to consign to "living happily" ever after.

I was on "pins and needles" lest the subject of the popular preacher should be broached at the dinner-table. There was one old bore present, whom I had seen at the church, and as I knew he was a person with a distinct desire to talk upon the least provocation, I dreaded any opportunity occurring for an outbreak on his part. No one else appeared to have attended divine service that morning, thank goodness! The conversation was beautifully secular, referring to the stage, for the most part.

I had hard work to keep the guests to that subject, but I succeeded. I asked fifty idiotic questions, in the answers to which I had not the faintest interest, beyond the fact that they took up considerable time. I caught the eye of the bore, as I mentally christened him, angrily fixed upon me. He was waiting his opportunity to talk preacher. I knew that. I was determined to prevent his attacking the subject, and I was successful. When I felt a pause coming, I had another question ready to fling broadcast at any one who chose to answer it. I was unfailing in my efforts.

When we finally rose from the table, I cast a look of triumph at the poor old fellow opposite to me. He was biting his stubbly moustache to hide his mortification. He had not been allowed to put in a word edgeways, and he was keenly miserable.

"Was I not thirsty for information, Arthur?" I asked my husband, as he settled himself in our mutual parlor to read the paper, a task with which our church-going had interfered.

"Horribly so," he said, laughing. He seemed to have somewhat recovered himself, though his face was still flushed, and I could see that his hands shook slightly as he held the paper. "What induced you to talk so much, Elsie?"

Oh, men are obtuse beings! He had no idea that my conversational efforts were merely made to spare him pain.

"I had nothing else to do," I answered flippantly. "And I

thought my voice sounded well to-day; then, you know, it was Sunday, and I wanted to give them all a treat. Do you see?"

He laughed again. "Elsie," he said, "sometimes I wonder, after listening to your speeches, how it is that you really have depth after all. People who never heard anything but your small talk would think you were good for nothing else."

"Do you think that?" I asked, trying not to appear anxious.

"No, Elsie. Indeed I do not." He glanced at me lovingly. There was a look in his eyes that I had never seen there before. I dropped mine in embarrassment. "I am only thankful—yes, thankful from the bottom of my heart—that you can still be the same little girl as before, after—after what you have endured, since our—our marriage. No, Elsie—" as I made a gesture of disapproval—"there is no reason why we should not discuss the past now, because—because—"

"Because?" I asked breathlessly.

"Because it is losing its interest for me, I am sure," he said in a low tone.

I felt convinced that he spoke the truth. I was confident that no rival supplanted me now, and I saw no harm in congratulating myself already upon the success of my plan. That evening I was in an unusually hilarious mood. I saw success before me in large shining letters. Imperceptibly my manner changed, from that of the love-sick girl, yearning for one kind word from the man upon whom she has lavished all her affection, to the half arrogant self-consciousness of the woman who knows her power. The fool that I was! Great heavens! That such a thing as feminine coquetry should ever be spoken of as charming!

I talked so much nonsense, chatted away so incessantly, and put such a decided veto upon any serious conversation, that Arthur looked at me reproachfully. Surely I had won the right to be gay, I told myself. It had not been often that I had been able to indulge in any frivolity.

"One would think you were on wires to-night, Elsie," said Arthur, in a tone of gentle protest, as after having fluttered all around the room, I sat down beside him.

He took my hand. It was the first time he had ever voluntarily done so. Months ago I would have given years of my life for that little endearment. My heart beat violently as his burning fingers closed over mine; but the devilish spirit of feminine coquetry possessed me; I withdrew my hand abruptly.

"Don't!" I said, rather pettishly.

There was an embarrassing pause; at least it must have

been embarrassing for him. I can only think that I was out of my mind that night.

"I suppose when I get back to England," I went on quickly, "that I shall have to set to work and write my impressions of America. Dear me! how extensive they are. Their range is so wide, reaching from this hotel to Central Park, and from Central Park to this hotel. You shall do the editing for me, if you will, and I shall begin as soon as we reach London. Do you consent, Arthur?"

"I cannot think yet of returning to London," he said, almost inaudibly. "I—I—do not want to think of it."

"But you must," I remarked, fanning myself with the newspaper which I had taken from him and folded into a convenient shape. "I am sure neither of us intend to become naturalized Americans, so I don't see why we should remain much longer. I like New York—that is impression No. 1—don't you?"

"I love New York," he said fervently.

"Like the actors and actresses who are interviewed in the newspapers. They all of them seem to love America before they have seen it. I suppose they hope to go home with lots of dollars in their pockets, and want to impress the Americans favorably by liking their country. Don't you think that is a fact, dear?"

I waited for a reply as anxiously as if the question had been one of vital importance.

"Very probably," was the absent rejoinder.

I took up a book and tried to settle down to reading. The letters danced before my eyes, and I flung the book aside with a laugh. I unfolded Arthur's newspaper and gazed stupidly at the advertisements. A dentist offered to extract teeth free of charge, if only the extractee would consent to wear the false article. He had for sale "elegant full gum sets," "gold combination sets," and "platina lined, porcelain enamelled sets." Of course they were all fearfully cheap. I noted that Mr. John Smith had a two-year-old colt to offer the public for a consideration. It was brown, and had no spots, though it possessed the luxury of a half brother with a record of 2.23; warranted sound. I smiled at the tailor who declared he would make any man a "nobby" suit of clothes for a mere song, and pitied the poor lady who wanted a loan to finish a new house. Poor thing! Why did she begin it, without sufficient money to see the building, to its bitter end? I was genuinely interested.

The little clock upon the mantlepiece struck eleven o'clock. How late it was getting! I folded up the newspaper, and sat bolt upright in my chair. I looked at Arthur. His eyes, which seemed to shine like five coals, were fixed upon mine. I crimsoned, for no reason that I can think of.

"It is getting late," I said in a low tone, looking helplessly at the clock.

"Yes."

"We have cooped ourselves up too much to-day," I said, at random. "I wonder why we did not go out this afternoon; the weather was beautiful, and we—we—"

I could not finish the sentence, simply because I did not know what I was going to say when I began it. I sat uneasily listening to the ticking of the clock. It irritated me, and sounded loud as the tramp of soldiers, in the uncomfortable silence that prevailed.

"To-morrow, Arthur," I said, with an effort at levity, as I rose to go, "I shall make you take me for a long walk, as I think it will do us both good. Exercise, you know, is always desirable, and—and—good-night."

I gave him my hand. He took it and, rising, drew me towards him, holding me fondly, firmly in his arms. Bending forward he murmured hoarsely, "Why need we say good-night?"

For one moment I lay quiescent upon his bosom. The next, though my pulses throbbed painfully, and I could feel the hot, feverish blood burning through my veins, I withdrew myself from his clasp, and ran precipitately into my room.

I remained breathless behind the closed door, waiting for him to speak, or at least to let me know that I had not offended him by my abruptness. I waited in vain for five minutes; then I opened my door. He had retired to his room. Looking up at the glass ventilator, I saw that he had put his light out.

In an agony of mortification I retired to my chamber, and throwing myself upon the bed, I cried out against the coquetry inherent in the best of my sex. I had reason to cry out against it.

CHAPTER XXIII.

My sleep that night was fitful and troubled, and I arose the next morning with a sense of oppression quite unusual with me. Hitherto, when I had retired at night a pessimist, the morning sun invariably brought with it relief, which I believe it is its pleasant mission to do, and I awoke an optimist. But as I dressed on this particular day, I felt uneasy, and anxious without any apparent cause, I told myself.

What had happened to justify this state of mind, I asked?

Certainly my wedded life had never looked so promising as it did now. I had won my husband's love, most surely. Could a caprice or two on my part extinguish the flame which I had fanned so long and so diligently? Pshaw! The idea was ridiculous. I was out of sorts. I would not give way to my gloomy thoughts. I would exercise my will, and be happy in spite of myself. That night Arthur and I were to accompany a charming English couple, whose acquaintance we had made at the hotel, to the opera. It was an appointment dating from a week ago, and I remembered it with regret. I would have preferred passing the evening alone with my husband. However, I reflected that I could not offend these people, who were of that genial, whole-souled class, whose acquaintance is a privilege, and whose friendship is nothing less than a boon. After all, a future of unoccupied evenings was before me. Arthur and I undoubtedly had time even to grow tired of one another, I thought, and I smiled at the idea.

At that moment an ebony head-waiter knocked at the door and brought in our breakfast, and two minutes later my husband emerged from his chamber, looking bright and pleasant. At all events, I said to myself, if there were any presentiments in the atmosphere, they had all fallen to my share.

"What a lovely day," remarked Arthur, with daring originality as we took our seats at the cosy little round table, and I began to pour out the coffee.

"Yes," I assented, handing him his cup. "After breakfast we are to go for a nice long walk on Broadway to look at the people, and after dinner we are engaged to Mr. and Mrs. Donaldson for the opera."

"You have the programme carefully mapped out," he said, laughing. "Have you been thinking about it long?"

"All night," I said, thoughtlessly.

He looked at me for a moment. My words had no significance however, other than their literal meaning.

"What do they sing at the opera to-night?" he asked, carelessly.

"Lohengrin."[1]

"I hate Wagner."

"Then you have no right to say so," I assented vigorously, as I dropped an extra piece of sugar into my cup. "If you dare

---

1 Romantic opera by German composer Richard Wagner (1813–83) first performed in 1850. The most commonly heard part of the opera is the bridal chorus.

to tell Mr. and Mrs. Donaldson such a thing, the same hotel will never hold us."

He laughed. He was evidently happy this morning. We chatted pleasantly until breakfast was a thing of the past. Then, after having dismissed the morning papers, as was our custom, we started out from the hotel for our walk.

I felt better. My husband's good-humor was contagious. It affected me, and I can assure you I was not unwilling to be affected. It was a lovely sunshiny spring day, and Broadway was at its best. It was thronged. Dainty women tripped in and out of the big, well-stocked shops; the beautifully dressed children attracted my attention, and filled me with admiration of juvenile Americans; dapper little men walked quickly by, always, in a hurry on general principles. There was a blue sky overhead. Winter had been successfully vanquished and humanity seemed anxious to celebrate its defeat.

I hummed the one song my mother used to make me sing "before company," when I was at home, and its refrain:

"The merry, merry sun, the mer-ry sun
The merry, merry sun for me-e-e-e."[1]

Then there was a high note at which I had always quaked, and occasionally lowered, much to the anguish of my maternal parent, who liked a good, tuneful shriek, laboring under the impression that it indicated a cultivated voice.

Arthur and I did not talk much, as we were both too intent looking about us to enjoy conversation. The most delightful thing about this walk was that we were not perpetually stopped by a friendly "How d'ye do?" "Fine day," or similar every-day greetings. In London we should have been thus annoyed every five minutes if we had selected Regent Street or Oxford Street, the Broadways of the English metropolis. We were absolutely unnoticed, and it was unspeakably pleasant. I began to think that after all there were worse places than New York in which to make a home.

We were now approaching Madison Square,[2] and I looked

---

1 Lines from the song "I Love the Merry Sunshine" by Stephen Glover (1813–70).

2 Location in New York City formed by the intersection of Fifth Avenue, Broadway, and 23rd Street and dominated by Madison Square Park, which opened to the public in 1847. By the 1870s, the neighborhood had become an aristocratic and upper-class enclave dominated by brownstone townhouses and mansions.

around with interest at the lively scene; at the big buildings; the people hurrying about in every direction; the tinkling tram-cars on all sides; the large, lumbering "four-wheelers" jolting over the uneven pavements; the nurses and perambulators just visible on the square; Fifth Avenue stretching far away; the curious, uncomfortable looking omnibusses; and the quaint, Swiss-chalet-like structure marking a station on the elevated railway, to be seen traversing the wide thoroughfare on the left. I was fascinated. We crossed the street and found ourselves in front of an enormous, ponderous, gray hotel.[1] A large portico stretched from the entrance to this building, and afforded a standing place for a score or so of men, apparently bent upon ogling passers-by, who unfortunately could not avoid passing them.

I hate a congregation of men, anywhere, so I walked quickly past this group and stopped before I reached the corner to allow Arthur to come up with me. I turned. He was not by my side. He was standing in front of the portico gazing into the lobby. As I waited, he approached me, and I was startled as I looked at his face.

It was livid, and he was trembling violently.

"I am ill, Elsie," he said, quickly. "I must be ill. Perhaps it is my heart. I—I think so. Let us go home."

He looked ill indeed. I told myself that it must be heart trouble, as a few moments before he had been perfectly well, and there was nothing else I could think of to affect him in that manner. We returned to the hotel, and I insisted upon sending for a doctor. Arthur rebelled, but I would not give way. The Doctor declared that there was nothing at all the matter with Arthur's heart. It was sound. He thought his system was out of order generally, and wrote out a prescription. In fact he did what most doctors do, in the usual pompous, would-be impressive way.

"I am going to send down word to Mrs. Donaldson," I said, half an hour later, "that we cannot accompany her to the Opera to-night. I can't say I'm particularly sorry," I added, carelessly.

Arthur started up quickly from the sofa upon which he had been reclining. "You must go," he declared, "there is no reason why you should not do so. Do not offend these people, Elsie. We have found them very pleasant acquaintances, and I believe they are only going to accommodate us."

I looked at him in amazement. His eagerness was almost pain-

---

1 The Fifth Avenue Hotel, the most luxurious and elegant hotel in New York City.

ful to see; there was a bright red spot upon each cheek, and his eyes shone fiercely. His gentle, sympathetic manner of the past few days seemed to have disappeared.

"If you insist upon my going," I said, to humor him, "I will go; but I would sooner stay at home with you."

"Nonsense." He spoke so roughly that the tears started to my eyes. He saw this and looked remorseful.

"I will follow you, Elsie, if I can," he said. "Perhaps I m-may join you during the evening, though—"

He got no farther. He was ill, I thought, and possibly an evening alone would do him good. I had given him no opportunities to miss me since we had been in America. I had found so much pleasure in his society, that I was determined to enjoy it. Did I not know, clearly enough, that he loved me, at last? Had I not been able to recognize that fact with sufficient distinctness? Of course I had. He wanted me to go to the opera, and I would go and amuse myself. I should be able to think of him waiting for me at home, and growing perhaps miserably lonely in my absence. He would possibly tell me when I returned that he could not spare me again, and then how thoroughly happy I should feel! Perhaps, after all, Arthur's indisposition was for the best. I felt that it might be, and my spirits, which had been rapidly sinking since my return from our walk, rose with considerable energy.

We dined in the big dining-room, Arthur declaring that he was not ill enough to be treated as an invalid, and after that meal I robed myself in gorgeous apparel. Arthur walked up and down the parlor, and through my closed door I could hear his quick uneven footsteps. I was soon ready, and my husband wrapped me up in my *sortie de bal*.

"Good-night, dear," I said briskly.

"Good-night."

"Are you not going to kiss me?" I asked, reproachfully, as he took my hand, and let it drop rather coldly, evidently inclined to make this do duty as a farewell salutation.

He bent over me in silence, and pressed his lips to my upturned face. The kiss chilled me. It reminded me of the first he had ever given me, and I shuddered slightly. For one moment a great feeling of disappointment came over me; the next brought with it the remembrance of last night, and my anxiety was swept away as by a consuming flame.

I ran lightly down stairs and joined the genial Donaldsons. They were waiting for me in the parlors. When I saw Mrs. Donaldson, I really felt pleased that my husband was absent. She was *décolletée*[1] in a way that made my cheeks burn. The strip of satin that, for politeness' sake she called a bodice, was so bewilderingly narrow, that one had to look for it carefully, in order to find it. She was a nice little woman, this Mrs. Donaldson. I liked what I knew of her, but I had no desire to know quite as much as her attire revealed.

"How charming you look," she said as I entered the room, and turned my eyes away from her chubby beauty, "and what a bright color you have in your cheeks. One might almost suspect rouge," she added, laughing.

The bright color was all on her account. I have no doubt it looked very pleasing, but I knew it would not remain. I was one of those unfortunate girls who rarely look rosy unless they are blushing or suffering from indigestion.

Mr. Donaldson was delighted with his wife. To him she was a perpetual source of pleasing astonishment. He saw nothing improper in her costume—or rather want of costume—and I am quite convinced that if she had set forth for the Opera, attired in a sweet smile and a tunic, he would have been satisfied. I reflected that there would probably be other women as outrageously clad as my friend, and reconciled myself in this manner to being seen with her.

I was right. In the vast Opera House[2] the display of feminine undress was so startling, that it took my breath away. It was ten times worse than anything I had ever seen in London. I had been told that New York was, in many respects, an exaggeration of London, and I felt I could believe it.

"Lohengrin," as I had already said, was the opera; not that it mattered much. The occupants of the boxes paid very little attention to what was going on upon the stage. They talked and laughed and recognized one another; opera-glassed the other side of the house, and commented upon each new arrival within range of their vision. It was a lively scene, at any rate.

Mr. and Mrs. Donaldson pretended to be very fond of Wagner, and I believe they imagined that they were. Being strangers in the city they had few friends to recognize, and were tolerably interested in the opera. Mrs. Donaldson's costume proved to be positively prudish. There were others that were so much more astonishing, that I felt quite sorry for her. She had started out

---

1 French: wearing a dress with a low-cut neckline.
2 The first Metropolitan Opera House was located at 1411 Broadway between 39th and 40th Streets.

prepared to astonish the natives, and lo! it was the natives who were astonishing her.

I treasured up a few descriptions with which to regale Arthur when I went home. I imagined I heard his hearty laugh, and that phrase of his, "Your speeches always amuse me so, Elsie."

Dear old man! How pleasant the future looked, stretched out before us! What happiness there seemed to be held in store for us by coming years.

I looked at Mrs. Donaldson. She was yawning desperately, and seemed vexed to be caught in the act.

"It is not a good performance, by any means," she said to justify herself. I agreed with her. I was anxious to go home. Arthur had not joined us, and I had heard all the Wagner I wanted for this evening. I tried to delicately insinuate to Mrs. Donaldson that it would be advisable to leave early and avoid the crush. She would not hear of this, however, and favored me with such a Medusa-like[1] stare, that I was silenced most effectually.

The opera was over at last, and slowly and solemnly we wound our way down the broad, reel carpeted staircase. A carriage was awaiting us and we were soon rolling hotelward. On the whole I was rather glad I had accompanied the Donaldsons. The scene at the Opera House had amused me somewhat, and I had plenty to say to Arthur, which was in itself a boon. As my husband was not sentimental, and I was determined to be as prosaic as possible, a few novelties to be added to our conversational stock would not be amiss. I wondered if the evening had seemed very long to him. I felt he would not like to admit that it had, but I was resolved that my object should be to force him to make that confession. I pictured him seated in the arm-chair reading and waiting for me—especially waiting.

I said good-night to the Donaldsons as soon as we arrived at the hotel, and resisted their invitation to supper. Supper indeed! Going quietly upstairs I coyly knocked at the parlor door, and then drawing back into the shadow, waited for it to be opened. There was no answer. In my coyness, I supposed I had not made myself heard, so with decidedly more energy, I knocked again.

It was long past midnight. Arthur must have fallen asleep, I reflected. He was tired, and such a vigil was by no means encouraging. So I turned the knob of the door and walked in.

The gas was burning brightly; there was an untidy gathering

---

1 In Greek mythology, Medusa was a monster whose gaze turned her onlooker to stone.

of newspapers upon the sofa, and the room had all the appearance of an extremely occupied apartment. Arthur was not there, however. With a little sob of utter disappointment, I told myself that he had not waited up for me. Oh! how unkind of him, when he knew how much I should have appreciated that little act of attention! In his place, I would have remained awake all night. Pshaw! What peculiar creatures men were, I thought. Their ideas were so absolutely opposed to ours that it was wonderful such a thing as a matrimonial partnership could ever exist for any length of time. Then I stopped in my mental deliberations to remember that I had left Arthur avowedly indisposed. How could I tell that he had not been taken worse during the evening? Surely it was my duty to ascertain the facts of the case. I felt a qualm of remorse as I saw how ready I was to place my husband in the wrong.

I went to the door of his bed-room and knocked. There was no answer.

Becoming seriously alarmed, I knocked again; this time loudly, with the same result. Then, resolved to stand upon no ceremony, I opened the door and walked into his room. It was in complete darkness. A cold apprehension of trouble seized me, and I shivered violently. I went to the table where I knew he kept his matches, and with trembling fingers drew one from the box. I dreaded to light it. I struck the match, however, and closed my eyes for a second. When I had summoned up courage to look around me, I saw that the room was empty. The bed had not been occupied, and my husband's coats had disappeared from their hooks in the closet, as I could see through its open door. My knees shook, and I almost fell, as I saw that his trunk and valise had also gone.

For a moment I was too dazed to realize what all this meant. I sat down upon the bed, and held my hands to my forehead, which was throbbing so vigorously that it almost deadened the recognition of any other fact. Arthur had gone and taken his trunk with him. He had left me without a word of explanation. I sprang up, rushed from the room, and startled down stairs to see the hotel clerk and ask him if my husband had left any message with him. I dreaded to face the man at such an hour, and then I suddenly remembered that the clerk who had been on duty before midnight had undoubtedly been succeeded by this time.

I ran back to my rooms. The perspiration was dripping from my forehead and the glimpse I caught of my ghastly face in the looking-glass, which hung above the mantelpiece, frightened me. Ah! there was an envelope in the frame of this looking-glass, which was evidently meant to attract my attention. I made a bound forward and seized it. It was addressed simply to "Elsie."

A cry escaped my lips as I saw this. He had left me, and this was his explanation. The letters on the envelope became enveloped in a blurred mist, and I could see nothing. I steadied myself by grasping the mantelpiece with one hand, while I pressed the other, holding the letter, against my heart. I must have stood thus for a minute; then, with a feeling of astonishment at my own helplessness, I broke upon the envelope and read this, written in a trembling, hurried hand, mis-spelt and blotted:

"ELSIE:
"No one will ever know how I have tried to obliterate the memory of a sinful past, and make you the husband, which—noble girl that you are—you deserve. I have long recognized the fact that the old miserable ideas which we have discussed so often, and which led to our marriage, were impossible. I say I have tried to become a good, manly husband to you. I thought I had succeeded until this morning, and so did you, poor girl, but it seems we were both mistaken. I am a wretch. Forget me. Return to England with the Donaldsons next week. I shall come to you no more. After this final step, it would of course be impossible. I make no excuses for myself. I am not worth any, and no one recognizes that fact more than,
"ARTHUR RAVENER."

The room seemed to be revolving. An awful giddiness overwhelmed me, and I fell heavily to the floor.

CHAPTER XXIV.

I do not know how I passed that awful night. I have a dim recollection of sitting up in hopeless dejection, on the sofa, conscious only of my intense longing for daylight. I could do nothing while darkness reigned; in fact I was absolutely helpless. I could only hope that the darkness which rendered me powerless to act, would have the same effect upon my husband. I could understand nothing. I seemed to be dazed. Not an idea of the truth dawned upon me. Our relations had been so pleasant; I was just about to attain the object of my visit to America, when, in the most inexplicable manner, my husband had left me. As I look back now I wonder how I could have been so dense. It appears to me now that the veriest blockhead could have grasped the situation.

At seven o'clock I sent for the hotel clerk, and asked him if he could tell me anything about my husband's departure from the hotel. In his suave, horribly superior manner, he informed me that he had not been on duty, and the "gentleman" who had been in charge of the desk before midnight, would not be "around" again until noon. I was in despair. I told this fat, oily official that it was really a matter of life and death with me. If he would only send for the clerk who had last seen my husband, I would pay liberally for the trouble I gave. This, and this alone, seemed to invest the case with interest for him. He promised to send for the day clerk, and in a short time I found him in my room. He could tell me very little. At about nine o'clock Mr. Ravener had ordered a carriage, and had taken a small trunk and a valise with him. He had not said where he was going, or anything concerning his return.

I begged the clerk to send for the man who had driven Mr. Ravener from the hotel. He looked with gentle surprise at my distress, as though it were extremely incomprehensible to him. Arthur had left with the few lines he had written me, money to the amount of five hundred pounds, and I tipped the clerk recklessly. He was thereupon much impressed with my case, and promised to do all he could to help me.

The driver was a big, burly fellow, with a red nose, and a florid, bull-dog face. My heart sank when I saw him. Heaven help all who have to depend upon so sottish[1] a class of people for important information. He had great trouble in remembering the fact that he had taken anybody from the hotel at nine o'clock the evening before.

"Think! think! man," I cried frantically. "If you will remember everything, and tell me what I want to know, I'll give you this."

I held up a ten-dollar bill before him, and his eyes flashed with eager desire through the heavy, drunken film that covered them, as he saw the money. He sat down, stopped chewing the tobacco which he had been masticating vigorously and attempted to think, with a brutish effort. Then he referred to a little book that he carried in his pocket, and in a few minutes

---

1 A class of people marked by excessive drinking.

a ray of something distantly related to intelligence lighted up his features.

"The gen'lman told me ter take him to the big marble building on the corner o' Twen'y-third Street and Broadway,"[1] said he stolidly. "He said he guessed it was an hotel, and I said I guessed he meant the Fifth Avenue. When we got there, a man come to the carriage and helped him out. I guess the man was expectin' him. No, I didn't hear what they says. A porter come up and took the gen'lman's baggage. He give me a five dollar bill, and told me not to wait. That's all I know, mum."

"What kind of a man met Mr. Ravener at the hotel?" I exclaimed, gasping, with a terrible fear upon me.

"I dunno, mum," was the answer. "A ordinary, every-day gen'lman, he seemed to me. He was rather stout, I think, but I didn't pay no partickler attention to him, mum. I ain't in the habit of lookin' at every man I meet so as I can give a description of him afterwards, mum."

"Was Mr. Ravener's baggage taken upstairs?" I asked, trying to speak calmly.

"I dunno, mum. Ye see when I got my fare I just skipped. T'wasn't no good my waitin' around."

"All right—now go," I said hurriedly. "Here's the money."

I wanted to be alone. I dismissed the hotel clerk, and began to dress quickly. I would go to the Fifth Avenue Hotel at once. I should doubtless find Arthur there. I absolutely declined to think at all until I could solve the case. I would not torture my mind by imagining this, and suspecting that. I would, if possible, deal with facts only. I had no difficulty in keeping my mind a blank. I was bewildered by the magnitude of the misfortune that had fallen upon me in a strange country. I was soon ready to start, and ordering a carriage, I told the driver to take me to the Fifth Avenue Hotel, and wait for me there.

No sooner had I arrived at the hotel, than quick as a flash of lightning, a great deal of what had been inexplicable lay solved before me. This was the big building that Arthur and I had passed the preceding day. I remembered the crowd of men standing under the porch, and the annoyance I felt at being ogled. I had walked alone to the corner of the street, and, turning, had beheld Arthur gazing in at the lobby. His livid face had filled me with alarm, and he had declared that he was ill. That night he had

---

1   The location of Madison Square Park, a commercially vibrant area of Manhattan throughout the nineteenth century.

been driven to this hotel. The reason was too clear for even a blind fool like myself to fail to understand. He had seen some one in the lobby—some one whom he had not expected to see. I could not doubt who it was—no, I could not doubt it, though I would have given all I possessed to be able to do so.

I walked into the hotel, elbowing my way through a crowd of wide-staring men, and went at once to the clerk. I asked him if a young man named Arthur Ravener had arrived at the hotel the previous night. He referred to his register, but could find no such name. I told him he must be mistaken; but this had the effect of rendering him mute. I forgot that an American hotel clerk could not possibly, under any circumstances, be mistaken. I then informed him that I had just spoken with the driver who had conducted Mr. Ravener, with his baggage, to the hotel, and left him there. He was surprised, but he had not been "on duty" at that time. He suggested that I speak to Mr. Price, the detective of the hotel, who was always in the lobby, and whose keen eyes saw everybody who came in and who went out.

I found this detective courteous, well-informed, and remarkably intelligent. I explained my case to him.

"Last night," he said, "shortly after nine o'clock, a carriage drove up to the hotel. It contained a young man, and I noticed that his face was deathly white. In fact, it was this circumstance that interested me at first. This ghastly hue could not have been normal with any living being. Before he had time to leave the carriage, a fellow, of whom I will speak presently, rushed out and opened the door. He called to a porter, and after having dismissed the carriage, ordered that the trunk and valise which the gentleman with the white face brought, be sent to the dock of the Guion[1] line of steamers, with his own."

I uttered an exclamation of horror, and the detective stopped in alarm. "Go on," I cried.

"The two then went upstairs. The young man seemed to be much excited. He could hardly reply to the glib remarks of his companion. He appeared to be in a dream. I suspected that there was something strange about this, Madame," said Mr. Price, safely, "but I did not see on what ground I could interfere. The gentleman who met your—your—husband?—arrived from England about three days ago. He brought a big black trunk, labelled conspicuously 'J. D.,' while he registered under the name

---

1 Steamship company operating the Liverpool-Queenstown-New York City route from 1866–94.

of Frank Clarke. A leather pocket-book was found in the hotel the other day. It contained a large sum of money. Mr. Clarke claimed it, and declared that it belonged to him, although the name on the cards which were in it was—"

"What?" I asked breathlessly, although I knew full well.

Mr. Price drew a slip of paper from his pocket. "The name was Jack Dillington," he said. "Captain Jack Dillington. I was very suspicious when he claimed this pocket-book. He was able to tell me exactly its contents. He explained that the cards belonged to a friend, and I had to believe him."

"Although you saw his trunk marked 'J. D.'?" I asked impatiently.

"Yes," replied the detective. "I had my suspicions, but what could I do? A man can travel under any name he likes; we may suspect that he is doing so for some improper purpose, but unless he does something which justifies our suspicions, I am afraid we could not make out a case. Mr. Clarke, or Dillington, behaved himself properly. I was not asked to watch him. I could not suppose that he—he—"

"Was running away with a woman's husband," I said, wearily. Fate seemed to be against me. I felt it was useless to struggle.

"Exactly," he assented, looking at me keenly.

"I am much obliged to you for having told me all that you know," I said, in the same tired way. He bowed, and I went out to my carriage. I told the driver to take me to the Guion line dock.

It was not much use, though I thought I might as well drain my cup of misery to the dregs. I saw it all. Arthur had told Captain Dillington of our proposed trip to America. I remembered the day when I had gone to his room and found the door locked. I called to mind the sudden shutting of the window which I had unmistakably heard. Captain Dillington had probably consented to this departure, and the fool whom I had married had not suspected that he would be followed. Consequently, when by mere chance Arthur had seen Dillington in the lobby of the Fifth Avenue Hotel, he had been astounded. The horrible influence which this man exerted over the weaker vessel must have been all-powerful. It had in one moment knocked away the barriers which in weeks of perseverance I had raised. I had been right in one respect. It was only by removing him from this man, whom I felt to be his evil genius, that I could have hoped to win my husband.

For the first time I began to doubt if there were a "woman in the case," after all. But the doubt brought no relief to my mind. I almost wished that I could have known that my husband was on his way to some woman who loved him well, even if unwisely. As it was, I could only suppose that the Captain's evil influence was exerted over Arthur for some object that I could not guess at, though I felt sure it must be wicked, and to be feared.

At the Guion dock, I learned that the Alaska had sailed for Liverpool at six o'clock that morning. I had no difficulty in ascertaining that two gentlemen had driven up about ten minutes before the vessel sailed. One of them was stout; the other slight and with a pale face.

I almost laughed at the completeness with which one piece of evidence fitted into the other.

I drove back to my hotel. I was alone in a strange country, but it was not that fact which annoyed me. No one would run away with me, I was sorry to say. I thought of the future, and it seemed so black that I could not look into it.

I resolved to make one more effort to save my husband from a fate which I did not understand. I saw that a Cunard steamer was sailing the next day—the fast Etruria. I could reach Liverpool before the Alaska.

I had no sooner seen this than one last ray of hope roused me to energy. I packed up my few goods, and the next day I was speeding across the ocean.

I have little more to say. I arrived in Liverpool, as I thought I should do, a day before the Alaska. I put up at the Adelphi Hotel, and gave orders that as soon as the Alaska was sighted I should be notified. I went down to the dock in due course. I watched the crowd of cabin passengers alight from the tender, but my husband and his accomplice were not to be found. Later, I learned that several passengers had landed at Queenstown, and I could not doubt but that they had been among them. They had probably suspected that I might follow on a fast Cunarder, and had rightly thought that I should not stop at Queenstown.

Well, they had won the battle, and if two men could find any glory in having vanquished one weak woman, let them find and keep it, I said to myself bitterly.

I was defeated and heart-broken. I returned to the house in Kew, "wound up" my affairs there—as they say in the mercantile world—and went abroad, in seclusion.

CHAPTER XXV.

A grave scandal was agitating the never very placid surface of Parisian society, and causing an immense sensation in the

French metropolis. Men of high standing were involved, and names that had hitherto stood in lofty superiority, were mentioned in connection with one of the most disgraceful revelations that Paris had known in many years. The newspapers might possibly have ignored the affair as much as possible on account of the nauseating nature of the details, but this course could not be pursued. The names of the malefactors were too well known and too prominent. The people demanded that the details be made public, and when the reputable journals maintained a silence upon the matter, they transferred their allegiance to one or two disreputable papers that dealt with scandal without gloves. It was evident that the case must be ventilated, and bowing to the inevitable, each journal took it up.

Everybody knows that the French papers are none too nice, so it will be readily understood that happenings bad enough for them to endeavor to suppress must indeed have been bad.

The London papers devoted a great deal of space to the scandal; in fact they seemed to gloat over it, and when it was subsequently hinted that the contagion had spread to the English metropolis, Londoners grew more and more interested each day.

"We know of no spectacle so ridiculous as the British public in one of its periodical fits of morality," says Macaulay. "In general, elopements, divorces, and family quarrels pass with little notice. We read the scandal, talk about it for a day, and forget it. But once in six or seven years, our virtue becomes outrageous."[1]

It seemed as though this "once in six or seven years" had come.

I was in London at the time of which I write, brought from the seclusion into which I had withdrawn, by business connected prosaically with my financial affairs, and requiring my presence. For two years I had been trying to live down the memory of the events that had wrecked my life. I had not seen my husband since the night I had left him to go to the opera. We were still bound by the ties of matrimony. My friends had suggested divorce, but I dreaded the publicity of the courts, and, after all, why should I suffer it? The tie that bound me was not irksome, since he, to whom I was bound, left me to my own resources.

One afternoon, shortly after my arrival in London, I picked up the *Daily Telegraph*, more in idleness than in curiosity. Of

---

1 Thomas Babington Macaulay (1800–59) in *Edinburgh Review*, June 1831.

course I had heard about the scandal which seemed to be dragging London and Paris into a cesspool of vice. The journal in question was particularly sensational on the day in question. In spite of myself, I was compelled to read. I had not gone far, before I was startled into painful interest. One of the ringleaders of the evil-doers had been arrested at Newhaven, where he had just landed from Dieppe and Paris.[1] He had made a full confession, and the London police had seized upon it with avidity. He declared that there were many Londoners in Paris at the present time, who were deeply involved in the matter. The principal of these, he said, was a man who was passing under the assumed name of Delacroix. He was an Englishman whose real name was Dillington.

I uttered a cry as this name, fraught with such bitter recollections for me, was thus brought to my attention. For two years, I had neither heard nor seen it, and now, in cold type, it stood before me. I could not doubt that the Dillington mentioned, was the one who had been instrumental in destroying my happiness. The article went on to say that he was staying at present at a little hostelry known as the Hotel Vaupin, in the Rue Geoffroy-Marie.[2]

I rose with an impulse of overwhelming force upon me. Dillington at the Hotel Vaupin; my husband must be there too. Yes, he was still my husband in the eyes of God and man, and he must be saved while there was yet time. The thought of his danger swept away for the moment all memories of the bitter wrongs I had suffered at his hands. They faded from my mind as though they had not existed. I saw him only as he was that night when he had asked me why I need leave him, and I, impelled by a fatal feminine coquetry, had rushed away, leaving his passionate question unanswered. Perhaps I might have saved him then if—no, it would not bear thinking about. I would go to his assistance at once, flinging all conventionalities to the winds.

I hastily packed a small valise, ordered a hansom, and one hour after I had become acquainted with the *Telegraph* article, I was

---

1   Newhaven in the south of England was the main port for ferry service to and from Dieppe, France. From Dieppe, railways connected to Paris.
2   Street in the north part of the 9th Arrondissement of Paris on the right bank of the Seine. It borders the 18th Arrondissement and Montmartre, and contains part of the traditional red light district, Le Pigalle.

on my way to the Charing Cross Station.[1] I was not afraid of meeting anybody, as I had been on a former journey, also taken in the interests of my miserable marriage. I did not care who saw me, and yet, as though to contradict this mental avowal, I gave a sigh of relief as I found the railway carriage, which took me to Folkestone,[2] unoccupied.

I arrived in Paris early the following morning, before the sleepy officials at the Gare du Nord,[3] seemed to have shaken off their slumbers. I had no time to think of putting up at any hotel; speed was a question of life and death with me; so summoning a *fiacre*,[4] I had my valise put inside, and told the driver to take me to the Hotel Vaupin. He had never heard of it, he said. I started, surprised that a man like Captain Dillington, whose ideas I had always thought were of the most extravagant, could be found at an hotel unknown to a station cab driver. I told the man that the Vaupin was in the Rue Geoffroy-Marie, and then it was his turn to stare. I urged him to hurry, and he did so, seemingly under protest. Down the interminable Rue de Lafayette we went. It had just begun its day's life, and the last of the *chiffoniers*[5] was seen vanishing as though he could not stand the glare of the morning. Soon we turned into the Rue de Trevise; then, crossing the Rue Richer, we entered the Rue Geoffroy-Marie.

It is a narrow, dirty little street, in the centre of the commerce of Paris. The Hotel Vaupin had a conspicuous gilt sign in front of it; the driver drew up, and opening the door of the carriage, assisted me to alight. I told him to wait for me, as I had no idea of remaining in the semi-squalor of this locality very long. He eyed me suspiciously, and said he would wait, but he would like to be paid for the trip we had already made. Angry, even at this delay, I paid him, and passed at once into the hotel.

The proprietor was a big, burly, flaxen-haired fellow, phleg-

---

1   Railway station in London.
2   Town in southern England from which the South Eastern Railway company connected to Boulogne, France.
3   Railway station in France serving northern France and northern international connections including the UK.
4   A French cab, a small four-wheeled carriage for hire.
5   Misspelt French: rag-pickers, a term for people who rummage through urban refuse in order to collect material for salvage. Cohen may have been thinking of Charles Baudelaire's (1821–67) recently published *Les Fleurs du mal* (1888), which included a poem, "Le Vin de chiffonniers," in which Parisian rag-pickers are featured prominently.

matic, yet still a Frenchman. He came to the door to meet me. I hesitated for a moment, and then asked: "Is M. Delacroix in?"

He looked at me keenly, and did not answer at once. "Does Madame not know?" he asked, haltingly.

"Know what?" I demanded, with a sinking heart.

"M. Delacroix was arrested this morning," said the proprietor, "at my hotel, too—alas! that I should tell it. He is charged with being involved in these—in these scandals, and—"

He went on in an affably recitative manner, but I heard no more. What a fool I had been to imagine that the French authorities would ignore the confession that I had read in the *Telegraph*. They had acted upon it at once. It had probably been known to them before the *Telegraph* had gone to press.

"Was M. Delacroix alone at this hotel?" I asked breathlessly. The proprietor seemed to be taken aback at my excitement—for a moment only, however.

"M. Delacroix came to this house some weeks ago," he said. "He was accompanied by a young gentleman, *un charmant garçon*,[1] who occupied a room adjoining his, and—"

"Go on," I cried, frantically.

"He is still here."

"Ah!" This exclamation escaped me; I could not help giving it utterance. "I will go up to his room," I said, trying to quiet my throbbing pulses. I felt that I could not move. Now that I knew Arthur was here, I hated to see him; to confess, by this interview, that I understood his unhappy life. I made a mighty effort, however, and was ready, when the proprietor told me that the apartment was the first room to the right, on the second floor, to seek it.

I slowly ascended the uneven, miserably carpeted staircase. Not a soul did I meet. If there were any other occupants than Arthur in the hotel, they kept themselves out of sight. I stopped in front of room No. 18. It was the first to the right on the second floor. I knocked at the door, but received no answer. I listened, but nobody seemed to be behind the thin, cracked door to which a lock and key offered but slight security. I repeated my knocks without the least success, and, at last, I retraced my steps, found the proprietor, and told him that he must be mistaken; that the young Englishman must be out.

"No, he is not out," said the man vigorously. "I have stood here all day. I wished to warn him," hesitatingly, "for—for I liked

---

1 French: a charming young man.

him. He has not left his room. I can swear to that. Come with me; I think I can make him hear."

Oppressed by the awful character of the events in which I seemed myself to be involved, I followed him, and again ascended the creaking staircase. The proprietor's emphatic knock was as unsuccessful as mine. He waited for a minute or two, and then opening the door of the room next to No. 18, which he told me had been occupied by M. Delacroix, he entered that apartment. He tried a door inside, connecting the two rooms. It was locked.

There was a strange look upon his face as he came out. "I will break open the door," he said.

The task was not a hard one. An application of his big shoulder to the frail portal; a not very powerful push, and the lock gave way. We stood inside the room. It was darkened. The proprietor went to the window and drew up the shabby blinds. As much light as the close proximity of another house would allow struggled into the room. It was in complete disorder. The bed had not been slept in. The floor was littered with books, newspapers and clothes.

I turned, and in an old chintz-covered armchair by the fireplace, saw my husband. His face was white, his head was bent slightly forward. He looked as though he had fallen asleep in an uncomfortable position.

"Arthur," I cried, springing forward with a loud cry; but the proprietor, who had been standing by the chair for a minute, came forward and pulled me towards the door.

"He is dead," he said simply.

Dead!

In a dazed way I walked up to the chair and coldly glanced at the face, which, white and expressionless, looked to me unlike that which I had known as my husband's. The proprietor quietly went from the room and left me alone with Arthur. On the mantel-piece my staring eyes saw a small bottle, on which a label marked "laudanum"[1] stood out with fearful clearness. Then I realized it all. With an agonized cry I flung myself into the unresisting arms of my husband. I kissed his cold, dead lips, his face, and the open, unseeing eyes, as I would have kissed him in life, had he willed it so. Ah! he could not ward me off now. He was mine, and I would cherish him forever.

Suddenly I sprang back, a horrible feeling of repulsion creep-

---

1   Tincture of opium, used widely in the nineteenth century for a
    myriad of ailments.

ing over me. Just above Arthur's head, on the wall, I saw two portraits, placed together in a single frame. One represented my husband, happy and smiling; the other showed the hateful features of Captain Dillington. My grief gave place to a violent, overpowering sense of anger. Tearing the frame from the wall, I threw it roughly to the floor. The glass broke with a crisp, short noise; but with my feet I crushed it into atoms. Then stooping down, I picked up the photographs, and tore them into smallest pieces. In the same frenzied manner, I went to the window, opened it, and gathering up the bits of glass—regardless of the fact that they cut my hands until the blood flowed freely—I flung them with the torn photographs from the window, and looked from it until I saw them scatter in all directions. Then turning away, and without another look at the dead form in the chair, I left the room and the hotel.

THE END.

Appendix A: Contemporary Reviews

1. From *The New York World* (26 February 1889) (unsigned review)

Book Note. "A Marriage Below Zero" is the title of the novel just finished by Alan Dale. It is dramatic and original, and fully in keeping with the author's other productions. It will be published by Dillingham, successor to G.W. Carleton & Sons. Alan Dale's "Brother Jonathan," printed in London, is much like Max O'Rell's "Jonathan and His Country" [sic] but as Dale's book appeared a year in advance of the other he can not be accused of plagiarism.[1] Alan Dale's dramatic criticisms have attracted universal attention, and "A Marriage Below Zero" is looked forward to with much interest.

2. From *The New York World* (22 March 1889) (unsigned review)

A copy of a new novel, entitled "A Marriage Below Zero," by Alan Dale, published by G.W. Dillingham, has just been received at this office. The book will probably be on the newsstands by this time. Stranger unions have been known in this city than that treated in "A Marriage Below Zero," but it is reserved for the novelist to tell what perhaps the writer of facts would not dare to do. That a careful search of the divorce records would reveal many cases like the peculiar story told in this novel is an undoubted fact. Whether it would be necessary or even desirable to make them known is questionable.

Elsie, the heroine of "A Marriage Below Zero," is an ingenuous schoolgirl, who, when introduced into society, finds its inanities unendurable. She despises the silly speeches of the men, the heartless nothingness of the women. In Arthur Ravener she meets the man of her choice. She hears that he

---

1 The reference is to Alan Dale's novel *Jonathan Home* (1885), which the newspaper compares to *Jonathan and His Continent: Rambles through American Society* (1889), a book of observations about the United States by Max O'Rell, the pen name of Léon Paul Blouet (1847–1903), a popular French journalist who lectured widely in America.

has a warm friendship for a school friend, who is known as Capt. Dillington, and she feels that a man capable of sincere friendship is worth knowing.

Arthur Ravener appears to be interested in Elsie, and she encourages him. A marriage takes place and the couple retire to a little country house in Kew, near London. Elsie soon discovers that she has a rival absolutely unknown to her. The presence of Capt. Dillington in her house annoys her extremely. He makes his appearance the day after the marriage and remains! The friendship she thought so beautiful frightens her. Her husband's neglect becomes so marked that she appeals to her mother to aid her in discovering her rival.

The identity of this person is the story of "A Marriage Below Zero." It may safely be said that the identity is startling and absolutely unconventional. The book ends in a very unexpected way, and the last chapter is highly dramatic.

3. From *The New York World* (25 March 1889) (unsigned review)

The category of novels which leave one hardly any doubt as to whether it were not better far that they had never been written has been augmented by "A Marriage Below Zero." Mr. Alan Dale is the author of this book, a writer favorably known to the readers of New York papers by breezy, spirited, dramatic criticisms and several short stories.

The first difficulty the critics will encounter in Alan Dale's novel is as to what it is all about. If he discovers this, as he probably may before the work is finished, his next thought will be that the work commends itself to the censorship of Anthony Comstock, esq., as the only critic qualified to deal with it.[1]

It is a contribution to the Catulle Mendès school of literature and will have to be clubbed in with the "Mlle. de Meaupin" of Gautier; "Mlle. Giraux, ma *femme*" of Belot; "The Annals of a Quiet Watering Place," by "Nora Wardell";

---

1 Anthony Comstock (1844–1915) was an American social-purity crusader who founded the New York Society for the Suppression of Vice.

"The Princess Daphine," by an anonymous writer, and a few others of that class.[1]

Alan Dale is evidently indebted to Belot for the idea of his story, and two or three of the leading episodes are closely fashioned on that porme [sic] excretion. This malarial cycle of novels which fasten on the morbid relations of epicene human beings make "Nana," "La Terre" and Zola's novels in general seem like the balmy exhalations of spring blossoms by comparison.[2] The Almighty criticized this sort of thing by the decidedly drastic conflagration which befell Sodom and Gomorrah, to which Alan Dale refers in his pages.

There are certain phases of humanity so bad that the public moralists and daily press shrink from the denunciation of them. This therometrical novel has espoused one of these purulent plague spots as its theme.

On a road in Summer a curious spectacle is sometimes offered to the observant wayfarer. He will decry two small black beetles laboriously propelling a sphere over the ground. One of these "tumble-bugs" usually has his back to the little ball of manure (he is evidently the more respectable bug of the two) and gushes it along with his hind feet. This is what is done

---

1   These are misspelt or garbled references to various nineteenth-century authors and texts with variously illicit sexual themes.
    Théophile Gautier (1811–72), Catulle Mendès (1841–1909), and Adolphe Belot (1829–90) were French writers associated with the Aesthetic and Decadent movements. Gautier's novel *Mademoiselle de Maupin* (1835) concerns a man and a woman who both fall in love with a woman disguised as a boy. Its preface contains one of the earliest defenses of aestheticism. Belot's novel *Madamoiselle Giraud, Ma Femme* (1870), cited by several reviewers of *A Marriage Below Zero* as a likely source, is narrated by a young man who discovers his wife has a female lover (see Introduction, p. 39). With the reference to "Wardell," the writer may have been thinking of Frances Cowley Burnand (1836–1917), author of "Annals of a Quiet Watering Place" (1891) and a writer who was associated with *Punch* magazine and was known for satirizing the Aesthetic movement in writings such as "The Colonel," a work reviled by Oscar Wilde. *The Princess Daphne* (1885) is novel by the English writer Edward Heron-Allen (1861–1943) that deals with psychic vampirism.

2   The French novelist Émile Zola (1840–1902) was the author of numerous naturalistic novels. *Nana* (1880) concerns prostitution and *La Terre* (1888) deals with the decline of a rural French family.

in this story. Capt. Dillington, a robust, ruddy, meaty man (?), and Arthur Ravener, a smooth-faced, rosy, pretty fellow (?), are two epicenes who amuse themselves with a sphere of ordure.

Conformably to that dictate of Horace, which says:
> "Non tamen intus
> digna geri promes in scaenam."[1]

The author does not permit his tumble-bugs to roll their ball of dung before the public. He only covertly insinuates that they do roll it behind the scene, not without some escape of the odor.

Alan Dale has handled the unpleasant themes with the greatest delicacy and the conduct of his story may be interesting to readers as ignorant and innocent as Mrs. Ravener.

Alan Dale is the pseudonym of a young man, but it is quite in keeping with the perversion of sex upon which the book is based that the story be told by a young woman. There are several passages in the book which are strong, and the novel could be enjoyed if its *motif* were rigidly excluded from the mind. But Mr. Dale does not write *pueris virginibusque*.[2]

4. From *The New York Daily Graphic* (5 April 1889) (unsigned notice)

From G.W. Dillingham comes a novel by that well-known man about town and flaneur who writes under the name of Allen Dale. It is called "A Marriage Below Zero" and is a very curious story. It is written in the first person professedly by the wife in this same marriage. It deals with a remarkably indecent story in a remarkably decent way. There is nothing to be said against the morals of the story; it is extremely moral in its teachings, and its

---

1 Latin: One should not put on the stage anything that should be kept unseen [i.e., behind the scenes]. From Horace's treatise on poetics, *Ars Poetica*, published in 18 BCE. Horace is arguing that some actions on the stage are so horrible and incredible as to defeat the dramatist's purpose and he offers some quite visceral literary examples: "Let not Medea slaughter her boys in front of the people, nor let Atreus cook up human guts out in the open, nor let Procne be turned into a bird, nor Cadmus into a snake. Whatever you disclose to me in such a way, disbelieving, I despise."

2 Latin: for boys and girls.

strange theme told with quite notable skill in avoiding the disgusting and revolting. Here to part of one of the most remarkable scenes: [The notice then quotes at length from the chapter in which Elsie walks in on her husband and Jack.]

5. From *Sacramento Daily Record-Union* (20 April 1889) (unsigned notice)

Alan Dale, the dramatic critic of the *Evening World*, has written a book called "A Marriage Below Zero," which has set Gotham a-talking. The sins of Sodom and Gomorrah have been used for the first time by the novelist, and the result is horrible, but readable. Alan Dale's name is Alfred J. Cohen, a clever young Englishman who has resided in New York for five years. The book is selling like hotcakes.

6. From *Belford's Magazine* (June 1889) (unsigned review)

In producing this book the writer, who wisely conceals his identity under an evident pseudonym, has touched the very lowest stratum of indecency. Not one word may be said in palliation of the work; it makes no pretense of teaching any lesson; it points no moral; it utters no warning. It is simply and avowedly a literary orgie, a saturnalia in which the most monstrous forms of human vice exhibit themselves shamelessly. No, the hideousness of sin was not here depicted for the purpose of reformation or cure. The author's intention was to make a sensation. Lacking the talent to write a pure, honest, manly book, and aware of his inability to awaken the interest of the public by legitimate means, he resolved to startle it into attention through disgust and loathing. He chose the vilest of themes, a vice which upright men wish to disbelieve in and all men with healthy minds shudder at, and upon it built a dull and disagreeable story. It is a case of pure vanity, a morbid craving for notice and a determination to be talked about at all hazards, not different, though a thousand times more reprehensible from the motive which causes a Frenchman to throw himself from the Vendome column in order to get his name in the papers.

Fortunately, the majority of persons, masculine and feminine, who may read this book will not comprehend its meaning, and to such it will appear only intensely stupid and obscure. There are some deformities with which art cannot deal, and some social possibilities which are beyond the province of fiction and belong only to the surgeon's table and the dissecting knife. In human nature there is a capability of moral hideousness which the most worldly-wise cannot reflect upon without a shudder. But these forms of disease, for they are nothing more, are infrequently manifested, and the writer of fiction who drags them into the light of day and descants upon their monstrosities deserves the severest and most unqualified reprobation.

The erotic in fiction has at least the poor excuse that it is the dark side of an instinct which in proper development is one of the beautiful things of life. But in "A Marriage Below Zero" there is nothing erotic, nothing so decent or dignified as the most unlicensed passion. Perverted animalism of an unnamable sort forms its plot and incident. The story is supposed to be told by an innocent young woman who, however, in the course of it shows herself to be far more knowing than most men. We conclude as we began by saying there is not one good or worthy point, not one excuse for existence, not a touch of true, pure, or honorable feeling in the whole of this scandalous offspring of a morbid imagination, and we believe that it will speedily sink into the oblivion it so richly merits.

7. From Countess Annie De Montaigu, "Hot and Sticky: A Budget of Midsummer Chat from New York," *Los Angeles Times* (11 August 1889)

The novelists of passion are rather quiet. They are under a cloud now on account of the infamous volume, "A Marriage Below Zero," which was the culminating point of that sort of literature. The author calls himself Allan [sic] Dale, but is in reality a recently imported London Jew named Cohn [sic].[1] He gained no credit for his work, for as soon as it was issued it was recognized as a clumsy and vulgar paraphrase of that nasty French novel, "Mlle. Giraud, Ma Femme." The result of all this was to cast discredit upon the less open believers in obscenity, and to throw them into the background for a time. They are indomitable, however, and will "bob up serenely" in the autumn as if nothing had happened. According to latest advices Amélie Rives-

---

1   In a personal jab, the reviewer goes on to express alarm over the excessive number of "Hebrews" immigrating to New York City.

Chanler, Laura Daintry, Laura Jean Libby, Winona Gilman and Gertrude Atherton have each and all a story ready for the press, in which frailty and naughtiness are exploited to the very quick.[1]

8. From "Professional Reform," *The San Francisco News Dealer* (September 1890)

The arrest of Mr. Farrelly, manager of the American News Company, for selling immoral books, was an outrage.[2]

Britton, it appears, is desirous of rivaling the notoriety of Comstock; he is the paid agent of a new society of cranks, organized, it would seem, mainly for the purpose of putting Comstock's society in the shade.[3] An unbridled Comstock going it alone was bad enough, but a free-footed Britton is distinctly worse.

Among the immoral books for handling which the manager of the News Company was arrested and placed under bail pend-

---

1 Popular American poet and novelist Amélie Rives (1863–1945; pseudonym of Princess Amélie Rives Chanler Troubetzkoy) was the author of the best-selling melodramatic novel *The Quick or the Dead?* (1888). Laura Daintry (dates unknown) was the American author of the novels *Eros* (1888) and *Fedor* (1889). Laura Jean Libbey (1864–1924) was a widely read writer of what were known as "dime-store romances." Gertrude Atherton (1857–1948) was a prominent and prolific American author of feminist leanings, in her time often compared to Henry James (1843–1916) and Edith Wharton (1862–1937), who in an 1899 article in *The Bookman* derided Oscar Wilde as a representative of "the decadence, the loss of virility that must follow over-civilization." There is no record of a writer by the name of Winona Gilman. Given that the list includes writers of daring material, the author may have had in mind Charlotte Perkins Gilman (1860–1935), the well-known author of such works as "The Yellow Wallpaper" (1892), a story that dealt with a woman whose constricted marriage leads to her mental breakdown.

2 In August 1890, Patrick Farrelly (c. 1837–1904) and several of his employees at the American News Company were arrested for distributing obscene books in New York City, some of them published by G.W. Dillingham, the publisher of *A Marriage Below Zero*. They were later acquitted by a grand jury.

3 Along with Anthony Comstock (1844–1915), Detective J.A. Britton was a member of the New York Society for the Prevention of Vice, an organization launched in 1873 that was devoted in part to the censoring of literary works it deemed immoral. It was disbanded in 1950.

ing trial, were Tolstoi's "Kreutzer Sonata," Dumas' "L'Affaire Clemenceau," and Balzac's "The Devil's Daughter."

Of course it cannot be expected that a literal-minded, notoriety-seeking paid agent like Britton can discriminate between good and bad books, or that he can know what constitutes immoral literature and what does not.

To his limited understanding Rabelais and Edgar Saltus, Balzac and "Alan Dale" Cohen, Byron and Oscar Wilde are one and the same—morally, artistically and otherwise.[1]

He sees nothing but a naked woman in the Greek Slave and an indecent exposure in Lady Godiva. He combines the moral gauge of Peeping Tom of Coventry with the insensibility of Peter Prim.

> A primrose by the river's brim
> A yellow primrose was to him,
> And it was nothing more.[2]

Britton cannot conceive that Tolstoi and Balzac are rigid moralists and towering teachers. To inculcate the lessons that they drew from observation and experience of humanity, they have adopted the same methods—but with infinitely greater skill, accuracy and success—that are employed by the shining lights of the pulpit. There is not the slightest doubt that even some of Britton's clerical instigators use illustrations of bad examples to enforce their arguments.

The moralist who seeks to hide and pretends to ignore the existence of evil is a fraud and a fool; the moralist who exposes its disastrous effects, and does not hesitate to cut into the root of social wickedness, is wise, and comes to exert the beneficial influence for which he is striving.

We neither ask, nor have we the right to expect, that such a mind as Britton's should recognize the art value of the works of Tolstoi and Balzac, for it is not to be supposed that a man who sets up for a puritanical censor either could or should reach the altitude of the literary critic. But the self-respect of a liberal community demands that the functionary who proposes to regulate their mental diet for them shall be gifted with the modicum

---

1 Cohen is being linked to various writers whose literary works were received as scandalous for their erotically charged material.
2 An excerpt from "Peter Bell" (composed in 1798), a poem by William Wordsworth (1770–1850).

of intelligence requisite to discriminate between gold and dross, purity and foulness, sane literature and rotten rubbish.

If this delectable creature—described by the *Herald* as "a kind of spawn from Comstock"—is sincere in his desire to rid the bookstalls of pernicious material, why does he not arrest the publishers of such filth as "A Marriage Below Zero," "The Picture of Dorian Gray"; such crime-breeding sheets as the so-called police papers; and such receptacles of scantily veiled obscenity as one or two of our "society" journals?

Procedure instituted against such enemies of good morals would have the sympathy and support of all decent men in the community.

But no; with the brutal stupidity that is the trade-mark of all hired "reformers," Britton turns his sanctimonious back on the real offense and the real offenders, invades the domain of the kings of literature, and uses the machinery of the law to oppress an entirely innocent citizen.

The arrest has brought no actual indignity upon Mr. Farrelly. The only person, thus far, who has suffered the reproach of outraged public opinion is Britton himself. And it is likely that he will regret eventually the means he has taken to secure cheap notoriety as a guardian of public morals.

With such an agent insidiously working in our midst, it would occasion little surprise if the members of the Bible Society were individually indicted for disseminating the impolite words in which the Old Testament is peculiarly rich; if the statuary in the Metropolitan Museum was soon attired in ulsters and Quaker gowns, and the nude picture plentifully bedecked with fig-leaves; if the ballet at the Madison Square Garden were made to dance in *princesse* gowns; or if Shakespeare were banished from the boards.

These things are not impossible while Britton is at large and the law gives him authority to prosecute and to persecute.

9. From *The Los Angeles Herald* (21 February 1891) (unsigned article)

The Erotic in Literature

Literature with love taken out would be as bald as the front row in a theatre.... Don Juan is erotic. So is Ernest Maltravers. Saltus and Ross have made so imperfect an impression on our mind that at the moment we are unable to recall the names of many of their books.[1] Take Marriage Below Zero as a specimen. That is meant to deal with subjects erotic. Sexual passion as existing in the human soul is the subject. But while both off shoots deal with this concrete subject in some of its phases, these writers approach the topic with very different methods, and with very variant forms of inspiration. Sexual love leading up to its full fruition is the theme. Don Juan is free indeed, so is Ernest Maltravers. But in all their broad, free treatment of their Anacreontic material how idealized they always are! They are always absolutely free from all coarseness, all grossness, all vulgarity and all filth. Love is there. All heights and depths of human passion are sounded and laid bare to the eye of the mind. Passion glows at a white heat, and is gratified until it is satiated in the poem and in the novel; but in all the delirium of the passion lust is kept in the background, and love is the pure priestess who presides at all the mysteries of the relations of human nature.

10. From *The Cincinnati Enquirer* (5 March 1891) (unsigned article)

[Although not exactly a review of *A Marriage Below Zero*, this article is remarkable for its linking of the events of the novel with perceived instances of men—and, prominently here, women— demonstrating same-sex preferences. Drawing on gossip and innuendo, this article may not have been the newspaper's only reference to Cohen's novel; an advertisement from the novel's publisher quoted the newspaper as praising the novel as a "very bright and pleasing" book, a notice that I have been unable to locate.]

Another Theory: Some Instances When Men Have Loved Each Other and Women Likewise

There is a theory that has been advanced other than that of hypnotic influences.

---

1   *Don Juan* (1819) is a popular poem by the British poet Lord Byron (1788–1824); *Ernest Maltravers* (1837) is a novel by the Victorian writer Edward Bulwer-Lytton (1803–73), the eponymous hero of which is an aristocratic youth who falls in love with a working-class woman; Francis Saltus Saltus (1849–89), American poet of Decadent verse; it is unclear who the Ross referenced here is.

Were the two unfortunate men lovers?[1] Such instances of men living together and foreswearing men's company and society are numerous and well authenticated.

About a year ago there appeared a novel entitled "A Marriage Below Zero."

It did not have a large circulation, and the critics said little about it. Yet it dealt in cold facts, fancily-dressed up of matters well known to the medical men and scientists but not to the general public. The plot in brief is of two men in London society who were inseparable companions. Gentlemen avoided them. One was stout and strong, the other effeminate and delicate.

As the story goes the delicate one loved and married an elegant lady, yet nothing he could do could wipe out the malign influence of his old companion. Their married life was unhappy. They came to America to get out of the reach of this evil influence. The stout man followed them over and the couple attended a church where the divine discoursed upon unnatural crimes, quoting from the Scripture numerous citations to prove the existence of such offenses, which were prevalent in the nations of the East. That night the husband was lured back to England by his evil genius, thence to France, where his wife found him dead in bed in an obscure hotel.

Has the case of a marriage below zero been repeated in real life and is truth stranger than fiction? Was this friendship something more than mere Platonic? Of women's friendship for each other history is full.

There are living in Xenia, Ohio in Greene County two maiden sisters who are millionaires.

They are two Miss Roberts, whose father is credited with amassing a fortune in traffic with the Indians. They swore early in life to live for each other, never to wed men. They have so lived for nearly half a century and will continue to do so until death claims them.[2]

In January 1884 a remarkable case was reported in the *Enquirer*

---

1   Here and elsewhere the article would seem to be referring to the widely covered Russell–Scott trial in England, which had begun in November 1890 with a wife's charge of sodomy against her husband (see Introduction, p. 17).

2   Emesetta and Diana Roberts were two sisters who lived on their family's estate in Xenia, Ohio, located in Greene County, until their deaths in 1900 and 1914 respectively. Although descendants of affluent landowners, there is no evidence that the two women were millionaires, as the article suggests.

from Wincester, Virginia. Lydia Rebecca Payne, having worn woman's clothing for thirty years, suddenly sheds the feminine attire, puts on men's clothing, and gets married. She was styled Becky and donned a man's hat, and was known to the community as a very strong masculine sort of a woman. She could wield an ax and do all sorts of farm work. A Miss Hinton came to be one of the family. She was assigned to a room with Becky.

Friendship ripened into love, and Becky started after a license. She was advised to consult a physician. She did so and was pronounced a man, and wedded Miss Hunter under the name of Ernest Macguire Payne. The affair created a great deal of comment at the time and will be recalled by readers of the *Enquirer*.[1]

In 1870 there was a middle-aged couple [who] started a small farm in King's County, New York. They lived in apparent harmony for about two years, when a violent quarrel broke out and it was discovered that they were a pair of maiden ladies who had sworn to live together. The supposed quarrel was caused by jealousy.

11. From the *Los Angeles Times* (3 December 1891) (unsigned article)

The developments in the scandalous divorce trial in London between Countess Russell and Earl Russell remind one strongly of an erotic novel published in this country within the last year under the title, "A Marriage Below Zero" that recounts the

---

1 In early 1884, Lydia Rebecca Payne arrived at the Frederick County, Virginia, courthouse to request a license to marry her close friend Sarah Hinton. This was refused on the grounds that two women could not marry. According to contemporary newspaper accounts, Payne returned shortly after, this time with a short haircut and wearing male attire and again petitioned for a license to marry Hinton. No Virginia marriage record exists for the couple. However, a Berkeley County, West Virginia, marriage license book dated 24 January 1884 indicates that a license was issued for Lydia R. Payne and Sarah M. Hinton. Payne returned to the Frederick County courthouse in March 1884 with a petition to legally change her name to Lawrence Register Payne, drawing on testimony from Dr. W.P. McGuire. The court granted the change of name, evidently based on McGuire's medical expertise. See Vince Brooks, "'The Mystic Chords of Memory': The Payne Family of Frederick County," http://www.virginiamemory.com/blogs/out_of_the_box/2015/10/28/the-mystic-chords-of-memory/.

experience of a young wife who was robbed of her husband's affections by an evil-minded man, with the shadow of a dark and nameless crime making up the background. Many people who read that book probably thought it was a hypothetical or an impossible case; but the exposure of the inner workings of the Russell household shows that it is not entirely impossible, even in the *crème de la crème* of English aristocracy. The report reads like a chapter on the last days of Sodom and Gomorrah. Earl Russell is pictured as "a weak-eyed youngish-looking man, with hair of a red tinge and what is known in slang parlance as a 'washed out' appearance generally." During the recital by the Countess of a story which damns him before the civilized world as lower than the brutes, the Earl frequently buried his face in his hands to hide his laughter. What a sickening comment on the degeneracy of a once noble line—the grandson of Lord John Russell brought to such a pass! It must be something of this sort which Lord Tennyson refers to in his Locksley Hall when he says:

Cursed be the sickly forms that err from nature's rule!
Cursed by the gold that gilds the straitened forehead of
a fool.[1]

---

1 From "Locksley Hall," an 1842 dramatic monologue by Alfred, Lord Tennyson (1809–92) concerning a rejected suitor's return to his childhood home, Locksley Hall.

Appendix B: Two Nineteenth-Century Historical and Literary Instances of Same-Sex Coupledom

1. Charles Dickens, "A Visit to Newgate," *Sketches by Boz* (London: John Macrone, 1836)

[In his essay "A Visit to Newgate," the novelist Charles Dickens (1812–70) described his visit to the press-room of the condemned ward of Newgate Prison. There Dickens saw James Pratt (1805–35) and John Smith (1795–1835), the last two men in Britain sentenced to death for the crime of sodomy, awaiting execution. They had been arrested the year before after a landlord and his wife claimed to have witnessed them though a keyhole having sex in a London boarding house in the room of William Bonill. The landlord broke down the door and confronted the two men. Although Bonill was not at home at the time, he had returned to his quarters with a jug of ale shortly after the two men were detained and himself was charged. Another man observed by Dickens at Newgate was Joseph Swann, who had been convicted of extortion. All three men were kept in separate quarters from other condemned men in Newgate because of the sodomitical nature of their offences, although Swann distanced himself from Pratt and Smith because he was a blackmailer of "sodomites" rather than a sodomite himself. Pratt and Smith were hanged outside Newgate before a crowd on 27 November 1835. (Swann was spared execution and was transported to Australia, as was Bonill.)]

In the press-room below, were three men, the nature of whose offence rendered it necessary to separate them, even from their companions in guilt. It is a long, sombre room, with two windows sunk into the stone wall, and here the wretched men are pinioned on the morning of their execution, before moving towards the scaffold. The fate of one of these prisoners [Swann] was uncertain; some mitigatory circumstances having come to light since his trial, which had been humanely represented in the proper quarter. The other two [Pratt and Smith] had nothing to expect from the mercy of the crown; their doom was sealed; no plea could be urged in extenuation of their crime, and they well knew that for them there was no hope in this world. "The two short ones," the turnkey whispered, "were dead men."

The man to whom we have alluded as entertaining some hopes of escape [i.e., Swann], was lounging, at the greatest distance he could place between himself and his companions, in the window nearest to the door. He was probably aware of our approach, and had assumed an air of courageous indifference; his face was purposely averted towards the window, and he stirred not an inch while we were present. The other two men were at the upper end of the room. One of them, who was imperfectly seen in the dim light, had his back towards us, and was stooping over the fire, with his right arm on the mantel-piece, and his head sunk upon it. The other [probably Pratt] was leaning on the sill of the farthest window. The light fell full upon him, and communicated to his pale, haggard face, and disordered hair, an appearance which, at that distance, was ghastly. His cheek rested upon his hand; and, with his face a little raised, and his eyes wildly staring before him, he seemed to be unconsciously intent on counting the chinks in the opposite wall. We passed this room again afterwards. The first man [Swann] was pacing up and down the court with a firm military step—he had been a soldier in the foot-guards—and a cloth cap jauntily thrown on one side of his head. He bowed respectfully to our conductor, and the salute was returned. The other two still remained in the positions we have described, and were as motionless as statues.

2. From Leo Tolstoy, *Anna Karenina* (1877; trans. Constance Garnett, 1901), rev. Leonard J. Kent and Nina Berberova (New York: Random House, 1965)

[Leo Tolstoy (1828–1910) was a novelist whose most widely-known works are *War and Peace* (1869) and *Anna Karenina* (1877). In this scene from Chapter 19 of *Anna Karenina*, Anna's lover Count Vronsky is breakfasting at the officers' mess hall of his army unit when he encounters "the inseparables," a pair of officers who are clearly homosexual and who tease Vronsky, who is visibly annoyed by them. (In Russian, the term "inseparables" is slang for a homosexual pair.) In his essay on Tolstoy's novel in *Lectures on Russian Literature* (1981), Vladimir Nabokov maintains that these two officers represent the "first homosexuals in modern literature."[1] The novel's presentation of same-sex erotics as structured—and perhaps shaped—through a pair of men of like sexual affinities is similar to the depiction of homosexuality in *A Marriage Below Zero*. (Tolstoy's novel was first translated into English in 1887 in a translation by Nathan Haskell Dole and published in America.) The scene is remarkable in its suggestion that men of clear homosexual leanings were tolerated in the army in nineteenth-century Russia.]

From the billiard room next door came the sound of balls knocking, of talk and laughter. Two officers appeared at the entrance-door: one, a young fellow, with a feeble, delicate face, who had lately joined the regiment from the Corps of Pages; the other, a plump, elderly officer, with a bracelet on his wrist, and little eyes, lost in fat.

Vronsky glanced at them, frowned, and looking down at his book as though he had not noticed them, he proceeded to eat and read at the same time.

"What? Fortifying yourself for your work?" said the plump officer, sitting down beside him.

"As you see," responded Vronsky, knitting his brows, wiping his mouth, and not looking at the officer.

"So you're not afraid of getting fat?" said the latter, turning a chair round for the young officer.

"What?" said Vronsky angrily, making a wry face of disgust, and showing his even teeth.

"You're not afraid of getting fat?"

"Waiter, sherry!" said Vronsky, without replying, and moving the book to the other side of him, he went on reading.

The plump officer took up the list of wines and turned to the young officer.

"You choose what we're to drink," he said, handing him the card, and looking at him.

"Rhine wine, please," said the young officer, stealing a timid glance at Vronsky, and trying to pull his scarcely visible mustache. Seeing that Vronsky did not turn round, the young officer got up.

"Let's go into the billiard room," he said.

The plump officer rose submissively, and they moved towards the door.

---

1   Vladimir Nabokov, *Lectures on Russian Literature* (New York: Harcourt Brace Jovanovich, 1981), 173.

At that moment there walked into the room the tall and well-built Captain Yashvin. Nodding with an air of lofty contempt to the two officers, he went up to Vronsky.

"Ah! here he is!" he cried, bringing his big hand down heavily on his epaulet. Vronsky looked round angrily, but his face lighted up immediately with his characteristic expression of genial and manly serenity.

"That's it, Alexey," said the captain, in his loud baritone. "You must just eat a mouthful, now, and drink only one tiny glass."

"Oh, I'm not hungry."

"There go the inseparables," Yashvin dropped, glancing sarcastically at the two officers who were at that instant leaving the room.

Appendix C: Modes of Homosexual Exploration and Advocacy in Nineteenth-Century Britain

1. From Walter Pater, "Conclusion," *Studies in the History of the Renaissance* (London: Macmillan, 1873)

[Walter Pater (1839–94) was an English literary and art critic who taught at Oxford University for many years. Considered one of the key founders of the British Aestheticist movement, he exalted the Italian Renaissance as a cultural high point of Western civilization that implicitly provided a model for Victorian artistic and social values. His work *Studies in the History of the Renaissance* (1873) included influential studies of Leonardo da Vinci (1452–1519), Michelangelo (1475–1564), and Giorgione (1478–1510). But the book was controversial for its "Conclusion." Pater's writings won followers such as Oscar Wilde (1854–1900), who studied under Pater at Oxford, but *The Renaissance* (by which short title it has come to be known) was denigrated by Victorian writers for its supposed hedonism. The novelist George Eliot (1819–80) described the volume as "quite poisonous in its false principles and false conceptions of life."[1]]

To regard all things and principles of things as inconstant modes or fashions has more and more become the tendency of modern thought. Let us begin with that which is without—our physical life. Fix upon it in one of its more exquisite intervals, the moment, for instance, of delicious recoil from the flood of water in summer heat. What is the whole physical life in that moment but a combination of natural elements to which science gives their names? But those elements, phosphorus and lime and delicate fibres, are present not in the human body alone: we detect them in places most remote from it. Our physical life is a perpetual motion of them—the passage of the blood, the waste and repair-

---

1 George Eliot, letter to John Blackwood, 5 Nov. 1873, quoted in Denis Donoghue, *Walter Pater: Lover of Strange Souls* (New York: Alfred Knopf, 1995), 58.

ing of the brain under every ray of light and sound—processes which science reduces to simpler and more elementary forces. Like the elements of which we are composed, the action of these forces extends beyond us: it rusts iron and ripens corn. Far out on every side of us those elements are broadcast, driven in many currents; and birth and gesture and death and the springing of violets from the grave are but a few out of ten thousand resultant combinations. That clear, perpetual outline of face and limb is but an image of ours, under which we group them—a design in a web, the actual threads of which pass out beyond it. This at least of flame-like our life has, that it is but the concurrence, renewed from moment to moment, of forces parting sooner or later on their ways.

Or if we begin with the inward world of thought and feeling, the whirlpool is still more rapid, the flame more eager and devouring. There it is no longer the gradual darkening of the eye, the gradual fading of colour from the wall—movements of the shore-side, where the water flows down indeed, though in apparent rest—but the race of the midstream, a drift of momentary acts of sight and passion and thought. At first sight experience seems to bury us under a flood of external objects, pressing upon us with a sharp and importunate reality, calling us out of ourselves in a thousand forms of action. But when reflection begins to play upon these objects they are dissipated under its influence; the cohesive force seems suspended like some trick of magic; each object is loosed into a group of impressions—colour, odour, texture—in the mind of the observer. And if we continue to dwell in thought on this world, not of objects in the solidity with which language invests them, but of impressions, unstable, flickering, inconsistent, which burn and are extinguished with our consciousness of them, it contracts still further: the whole scope of observation is dwarfed into the narrow chamber of the individual mind. Experience, already reduced to a group of impressions, is ringed round for each one of us by that thick wall of personality through which no real voice has ever pierced on its way to us, or from us to that which we can only conjecture to be without. Every one of those impressions is the impression of the individual in his isolation, each mind keeping as a solitary prisoner its own dream of a world. Analysis goes a step further still, and assures us that those impressions of the individual mind to which, for each one of us, experience dwindles down, are in perpetual flight; that each of them is limited by time, and that as time is infinitely divisible, each of them is infinitely divisible also; all that is actual in it being a single moment, gone while we try to apprehend it, of which it may ever be more truly said that it has ceased to be than that it is. To such a tremulous wisp constantly re-forming itself on the stream, to a single sharp impression, with a sense in it, a relic more or less fleeting, of such moments gone by, what is real in our life fines itself down. It is with this movement, with the passage and dissolution of impressions, images, sensations, that analysis leaves off—that continual vanishing away, that strange, perpetual, weaving and unweaving of ourselves.

Philosophiren, says Novalis, *ist dephlegmatisiren, vivificiren.*[1] The service of philosophy, of speculative culture, towards the human spirit, is to rouse, to startle it to a life of constant and eager observation. Every moment some form grows perfect in hand or face; some tone on the hills or the sea is choicer than the rest; some mood of passion or insight or intellectual excitement is irresistibly real and attractive to us—for that moment only. Not the fruit of experience, but experience itself, is the end. A counted number of pulses only is given to us of a variegated, dramatic life. How may we see in them all that is to be seen in them by the finest senses? How shall we pass most swiftly from point to point, and be present always at the focus where the greatest number of vital forces unite in their purest energy?

To burn always with this hard, gem-like flame, to maintain this ecstasy, is success in life. In a sense it might even be said that our failure is to form habits: for, after all, habit is relative to a stereotyped world, and meantime it is only the roughness of the eye that makes two persons, things, situations, seem alike. While all melts under our feet, we may well grasp at any exquisite passion, or any contribution to knowledge that seems by a lifted horizon to set the spirit free for a moment, or any stirring of the sense, strange dyes, strange colours, and curious odours, or work of the artist's hands, or the face of one's friend. Not to discriminate every moment some passionate attitude in those about us, and in the very brilliancy of their gifts some tragic dividing on their ways, is, on this short day of frost and sun, to sleep before evening. With this sense of the splendour of our experience and of its awful brevity, gathering all we are

---

1 German translation of a Latin phrase coined by the German Romantic poet and philosopher Novalis (1772–1801): To philosophize is to cast off inertia, to bring oneself to life. The quotation is taken from Novalis's *Fragments* (1798). Pater's paraphrase would seem to expand somewhat beyond the sentence's literal meaning.

into one desperate effort to see and touch, we shall hardly have time to make theories about the things we see and touch. What we have to do is to be forever curiously testing new opinions and courting new impressions, never acquiescing in a facile orthodoxy, of Comte, or of Hegel, or of our own.[1] Philosophical theories or ideas, as points of view, instruments of criticism, may help us to gather up what might otherwise pass unregarded by us. "Philosophy is the microscope of thought."[2] The theory or idea or system which requires of us the sacrifice of any part of this experience, in consideration of some interest into which we cannot enter, or some abstract theory we have not identified with ourselves, or of what is only conventional, has no real claim upon us.

One of the most beautiful passages of Rousseau is that in the sixth book of *Confessions*, where he describes the awakening in him of the literary sense.[3] An undefinable taint of death had clung always about him, and now in early manhood he believed himself smitten by mortal disease. He asked himself how he might make as much as possible of the interval that remained; and he was not biased by anything in his previous life when he decided that it must be by intellectual excitement, which he found just then in the clear, fresh writings of Voltaire.[4] Well! we are all *condamnés*, as Victor Hugo says: we are all under sentence of death but with a sort of indefinite reprieve—*les hommes sont tous condamnés à mort avec des sursis indéfinis*: we have an interval, and then our place knows no more. Some spend this interval in listlessness, some in high passion, the wisest, at least among "the children of

---

1 Auguste Comte (1798–1857), French philosopher who founded the doctrine of positivism, which held that progress entails surrendering the pursuit of absolute truth for a quantifiable understanding of the laws of the universe; Georg Wilhelm Friedrich Hegel (1770–1831), German philosopher who was a key figure in German idealism, which held that seeming oppositions—for example, mind and nature or subject and object—could be overcome.

2 From Chapter II of *Les Misérables* (1862) by Victor Hugo (1802–85). Hugo was a widely popular French novelist, poet, and dramatist.

3 Jean-Jacques Rousseau (1712–78), French philosopher who was associated with the Romantic movement; his *Confessions* (1789) was an autobiographical account of his life.

4 Voltaire (François-Marie Arouet, 1694–1778), French philosopher and key Enlightenment thinker.

the world," in art and song.[1] For our one chance lies in expanding that interval, in getting as many pulsations as possible into the given time. Great passions may give us a quickened sense of life, ecstasy and sorrow of love, the various forms of enthusiastic activity, disinterested or otherwise, which comes naturally to many of us. Only be sure it is passion—that it does yield you this fruit of a quickened, multiplied consciousness. Of such wisdom, the poetic passion, the desire of beauty, the love of art for its own sake, has most. For art comes to you proposing frankly to give nothing but the highest quality to your moments as they pass, and simply for those moments' sake.

2. From John Addington Symonds, "Male Love," *A Problem in Greek Ethics and Other Writings* (1883)

[John Addington Symonds (1840–93) glorified Hellenic culture for its high degree of civilization and the great esteem it placed on male–male erotic relations. Symonds's *A Problem in Greek Ethics* (1883) included one of the first uses of the term "homosexual" in English although in a section of text not included in the excerpt below.]

VI

Resuming the results of the last four sections, we find two separate forms of masculine passion clearly marked in early Hellas—a noble and a base, a spiritual and a sensual. To the distinction between them the Greek conscience was acutely sensitive; and this distinction, in theory at least, subsisted throughout their history. They worshipped Erôs, as they worshipped Aphrodite, under the twofold titles of Ouranios (celestial) and Pandemos (vulgar, or *volvivaga*); and, while they regarded the one love with the highest approval, as the source of courage and greatness of soul, they never publicly approved the other.[2] It is true, as will appear in the sequel of this essay, that boy-love in its grossest form was tolerated in historic Hellas with an indulgence which it

---

1 French: All men are condemned to death with infinite reprieve. From Hugo's *The Last Day of a Condemned Man* (1829).

2 Ancient Greeks worshipped Aphrodite and her son Eros in two distinct forms: Aphrodite and Eros Ourania, the celestial deities associated with a higher spiritual love, and Aphrodite and Eros Pandemos, the earthly or common deities associated with sex and physical love.

never found in any Christian country, while heroic comradeship remained an ideal hard to realise, and scarcely possible beyond the limits of the strictest Dorian sect.[1] Yet the language of philosophers, historians, poets and orators is unmistakable. All testify alike to the discrimination between vulgar and heroic love in the Greek mind. I purpose to devote a separate section of this inquiry to the investigation of these ethical distinctions. For the present, a quotation from one of the most eloquent of the later rhetoricians will sufficiently set forth the contrast,[2] which the Greek race never wholly forgot:

> The one love is mad for pleasure; the other loves beauty. The one is an involuntary sickness; the other is a sought enthusiasm. The one tends to the good of the beloved; the other to the ruin of both. The one is virtuous; the other incontinent in all its acts. The one has its end in friendship; the other in hate. The one is freely given; the other is bought and sold. The one brings praise; the other blame. The one is Greek; the other is barbarous. The one is virile; the other effeminate. The one is firm and constant; the other light and variable. The man who loves the one love is a friend of God, a friend of law, fulfilled of modesty, and free of speech. He dares to court his friend in daylight, and rejoices in his love. He wrestles with him in the playground and runs with him in the race, goes afield with him to the hunt, and in battle fights for glory at his side. In his misfortune he suffers, and at his death he dies with him. He needs no gloom of night, no desert place, for this society. The other lover is a foe to heaven, for he is out of tune and criminal; a foe to law, for he transgresses law. Cowardly, despairing, shameless, haunting the dusk, lurking in desert places and secret dens, he would fain be never seen consorting with his friend, but shuns the light of day, and follows after night and darkness, which the shepherd hates, but the thief loves.

---

1 Ancient Greek ethnic group that included the Spartans, famous for their military discipline.

2 Taken from Oration 19.4 of *The Philosophical Orations* by Cassius Maximus Tyre, or Tyrius, a second-century CE Greek philosopher and rhetorician, although Symonds would have known the passage as drawn from either 25.4 or 19.4, depending on the edition he was using.

And again, in the same dissertation, Maximus Tyrius speaks to like purpose, clothing his precepts in imagery:

> You see a fair body in bloom and full of promise of fruit. Spoil not, defile not, touch not the blossom. Praise it, as some wayfarer may praise a plant—even so by Phœbus' altar have I seen a young palm shooting toward the sun. Refrain from Zeus and Phœbus' tree; wait for the fruit-season and thou shall love more righteously.

With the baser form of paiderastia I shall have little to do in this essay. Vice of this kind does not vary to any great extent, whether we observe it in Athens or in Rome, in Florence of the sixteenth or in Paris of the nineteenth century; nor in Hellas was it more noticeable than elsewhere, except for its comparative publicity. The nobler type of masculine love developed by the Greeks is, on the contrary, almost unique in the history of the human race. It is that which more than anything else distinguishes the Greeks from the barbarians of their own time, from the Romans and from modern men in all that appertains to the emotions. The immediate subject of the ensuing inquiry will, therefore, be that mixed form of paiderastia upon which the Greeks prided themselves, which had for its heroic ideal the friendship of Achilles and Patroclus, but which in historic times exhibited a sensuality unknown to Homer.[1] In treating of this unique product of their civilisation I shall use the terms *Greek Love,* understanding thereby a passionate and enthusiastic attachment subsisting between man and youth, recognised by society and protected by opinion, which, though it was not free from sensuality, did not degenerate into mere licentiousness.

... Presents were of course a common way of trying to win favour. It was reckoned shameful for boys to take money from their lovers, but fashion permitted them to accept gifts of quails and fighting cocks, pheasants, horses, dogs and clothes. There existed, therefore, at Athens frequent temptations for boys of wanton disposition, or for those who needed money to indulge expensive tastes. The speech of Æschines, from which I have

---

1 The bond between Achilles and Patroclus, Greek heroes of Homer's *Iliad*, has often been interpreted as amorous in nature, although Homer's text does not make this explicit.

already frequently quoted, affords a lively picture of the Greek rake's progress, in which Timarchus is described as having sold his person in order to gratify his gluttony and lust and love of gaming.[1] The whole of this passage, it may be observed in passing, reads like a description of Florentine manners in a sermon of Savonarola.[2]

... It may be well to state that the Athenian law recognized contracts made between a man and boy, even if the latter were of free birth, whereby the one agreed to render up his person for a certain period and purpose, and the other to pay a fixed sum of money. The phrase "a boy who has been a prostitute," occurs quite naturally in Aristophanes;[3] nor was it thought disreputable for men to engage in these *liaisons*. Disgrace only attached to the free youth who gained a living by prostitution; and he was liable, as we shall see, at law to loss of civil rights.

Public brothels for males were kept in Athens, from which the state derived a portion of its revenues. It was in one of these bad places that Socrates first saw Phædo.[4] This unfortunate youth was a native of Elis.[5] Taken prisoner in war, he was sold in the public market to a slave-dealer, who then acquired the right by Attic law to prostitute his person and engross his earnings for his own pocket. A friend of Socrates, perhaps Cebes,[6] bought him from his master, and he became one of the chief members of the Socratic circle. His name is given to the Platonic dialogue on immortality, and he lived to found what is called the Eleo-Socratic School. No reader of Plato forgets how the sage, on the eve of his death, stroked the beautiful long hair of Phædo, and

---

1 Aeschines' speech "Against Timarchus" (346 BCE) accused Timarchus of sexual immorality and argued for his disqualification from public speaking.
2 Girolamo Savonarola (1452–98), Florentine friar who zealously condemned sodomy and vice and prophesied apocalyptic consequences for the sins of his era.
3 Athenian comic playwright (444–385 BCE); sexual politics figure prominently in his surviving work.
4 Phaedo (fl. fourth c. BCE) was a devoted disciple of Socrates (470/69–399 BCE) who informed Plato (428/27–348/47 BCE) that he was present when the Greek philosopher killed himself by drinking hemlock.
5 Ancient district of southwestern Greece.
6 Cebes (c. 430–350 BCE) was a philosopher and student of Socrates; little of Cebes' work survives.

prophesied that he would soon have to cut it short in mourning for his teacher.[1]

3. From Sir Richard Burton, "Pederasty," in the "Terminal Essay" to *The Book of a Thousand Nights and One Night* (1885; London: Heritage Press, 1962)

[Sir Richard Burton (1821–90) was a celebrated explorer, cartographer, diplomat, and Orientalist whose *Book of a Thousand Nights and One Night* (1885) was an English translation from the Arabic of Middle Eastern and South Asian folk tales. Burton was also famous for his English translation of the *Kama Sutra*, an Indian Hindu text that is part erotic guidebook and part meditation on love, family, and pleasure. In the tenth volume of *The Book of a Thousand Nights and One Night*, Burton offered a "Terminal Note" that postulated that homosexuality was especially prevalent in the southern latitudes that Burton designated as the "Sotadic Zone."]

The "execrabilis familia pathicorum"[2] first came before me by a chance of earlier life. In 1845, when Sir Charles Napier had conquered and annexed Sind,[3] despite a faction (mostly venal) which sought favour with the now defunct "Court of Directors to the Honourable East India Company,"[4] the veteran began to consider his conquest with a curious eye. It was reported to him that Karáchi,

---

1 This account of Socrates and his student appears in the *Phaedo*, or "On the Soul," Plato's dialogue on immortality told from the thinker Phaedo's perspective.

2 Latin: execrable family of pathics, a derogatory sobriquet for male sexual partners who are the passive recipients in anal intercourse.

3 Sir Charles Napier (1772–1853), a high-ranking British army general who led the invasion and conquest of Sind, or Sindh, now the southernmost province of Pakistan.

4 The East India Company was a sprawling English trading organization that imported spices, tea, opium, textiles, and other commodities from India and other parts of Asia. Privately owned by wealthy aristocrats, the company functioned as a quasi-governmental entity with its own military troops and dramatically expanded the scope of British colonial rule, generally by force. The company effectively ruled the areas it annexed and eventually came into conflict with the British government's own colonial agendas. The company was nationalized in 1858 and dissolved in 1873 by Acts of Parliament.

a townlet of some two thousand souls and distant not more than a mile from camp, supported no less than three lupanars or bordels, in which not women but boys and eunuchs, the former demanding nearly a double price, lay for hire. Being then the only British officer who could speak Sindi, I was asked indirectly to make enquiries and to report upon the subject; and I undertook the task on express condition that my report should not be forwarded to the Bombay Government, from whom supporters of the conqueror's policy could expect scant favour, mercy or justice.[1]

... Subsequent enquiries in many and distant countries enabled me to arrive at the following conclusions:—

1. There exists what I shall call a "Sotadic Zone,"[2] bounded westwards by the northern shores of the Mediterranean (N. Lat. 43°) and by the southern (N. Lat. 30°). Thus the depth would be 780 to 800 miles including meridional France, the Iberian Peninsula, Italy and Greece, with the coast-regions of Africa from Morocco to Egypt.
2. Running eastward the Sotadic Zone narrows, embracing Asia Minor, Mesopotamia and Chaldæa, Afghanistan, Sind, the Punjab and Kashmir.
3. In Indo-China the belt begins to broaden, enfolding China, Japan and Turkistan.
4. It then embraces the South Sea Islands and the New World where, at the time of its discovery, Sotadic love was, with some exceptions, an established racial institution.
5. Within the Sotadic Zone the Vice is popular and endemic, held at the worst to be a mere peccadillo, whilst the races to the north and south of the limits here defined practise it only sporadically amid the opprobrium of their fellows who, as a rule, are physically incapable of performing the operation and look upon it with the liveliest disgust.

---

1 In 1845 the "Bombay Government" would have been under the control of the East India Company, which had recently ousted Napier from his brief installation as Bombay President. Burton implies here that the East India Company would have been hostile to any interference in the region by Napier or his supporters.

2 Sotades was a third-century BCE Greek poet of coarse, sexually explicit satire. His subject matter included pederasty, incest, and other sexual activities that the Victorians would have deemed immoral. Burton appropriates the name primarily for its association with homosexuality and pederasty.

Before entering into topographical details concerning Pederasty, which I hold to be geographical and climatic, not racial, I must offer a few considerations of its cause and origin. We must not forget that the love of boys has its noble sentimental side. The Platonists and pupils of the Academy, followed by the Sufis or Moslem Gnostics,[1] held such affection, pure as ardent, to be the *beau idéal*[2] which united in man's soul the creature with the Creator. Professing to regard youths as the most cleanly and beautiful objects in this phenomenal world, they declared that by loving and extolling the *chef-d'œuvre*, corporeal and intellectual, of the Demiurgus,[3] disinterestedly and without any admixture of carnal sensuality, they are paying the most fervent adoration to the *Causa causans*.[4] They add that such affection, passing as it does the love of women, is far less selfish than fondness for and admiration of the other sex which, however innocent, always suggests sexuality; and Easterns add that the devotion of the moth to the taper is purer and more fervent than the Bulbul's[5] love for the Rose. Amongst the Greeks of the best ages the system of boy-favourites was advocated on considerations of morals and politics. The lover undertook the education of the beloved through precept and example, while the two were conjoined by a tie stricter than the fraternal. Hieronymus the Peripatetic[6] strongly advocated it because the vigorous disposition of youths and the

---

1 Platonists were followers of the Greek philosopher Plato and believed in abstract ideas that have a palpable reality but do not exist in time or space; Sufis are followers of Sufism, a mystical Islamic faith whose adherents seek to have a personal relationship with the divine; Muslim Gnostics were members of a religious sect that believed in arriving at transcendence through an intuitive knowledge of the divine.

2 French: perfect model or ideal.

3 Platonic name for the divine creator of the world.

4 Latin: primary cause.

5 Songbird of Asia, Africa, and the Middle East that appears often in Persian poetry, where the songbird's yearning for the rose often serves as a metaphor for the soul's striving for union with God.

6 The Greek philosopher Hieronomous of Rhodes (290–230 BCE) belonged to the Peripatetic philosophical school founded by Aristotle (384–322 BCE). Only a few fragments of his works survive, preserved in the quotations of later writers. The ideas cited here are attributed to him in Plutarch's Platonic dialogue *Amatorius* (c. 120 CE).

confidence engendered by their association often led to the overthrow of tyrannies. Socrates declared that "a most valiant army might be composed of boys and their lovers; for that of all men they would be most ashamed to desert one another."[1] And even Virgil, despite the foul flavour of Formosum pastor Corydon,[2] could write:

Nisus amore pio pueri.[3]

The only physical cause for the practice which suggests itself to me and that must be owned to be purely conjectural, is that within the Sotadic Zone there is a blending of the masculine and feminine temperaments, a crisis which elsewhere occurs only sporadically. Hence the male *féminisme* whereby the man becomes patiens as well as agens,[4] and the woman a tribade, a votary of mascula Sappho, Queen of Frictrices or Rubbers.[5]

4. George Bernard Shaw, Letter on "The Cleveland Street Scandals," *Truth* Magazine (26 November 1889); *Collected Letters, 1874–1897*, ed. Dan Laurence (New York: Dodd Mead, 1965), 230–31

[George Bernard Shaw (1856–1950) was an Irish-born playwright and critic whose plays, such as *Mrs. Warren's Profession*

---

1 Burton would seem to be referencing Plato's celebrated dialogue *The Symposium* (360 BCE), although in this work it is the figure of Pausanius who speaks favorably of what evidently is, although it is not specifically named, the Sacred Band of Thebes, an elite group of 150 pairs of male lovers and soldiers in the fourth century BCE. In the *Symposium* of Xenophon (430–354 BCE), written around 360 BCE, Socrates speaks disapprovingly of the practice of placing lovers side by side in battle, a characteristic detail on Xenophon's part in that in his writing Xenophon often curbed what he considered Plato's excesses.

2 Roman poet Publius Vergilius Maro, or Virgil (70–19 BCE), from *Eclogues* 2.1, "Formosum pastor Corydon Ardebat Alexim"; Latin: the shepherd Corydon burned for the lovely Alexis.

3 Latin: Nisus, for his devoted love for the boy; Virgil, *Aeneid* 5.295

4 Latin: patient; agent. Burton uses the words to indicate passive and active sexual roles.

5 Sappho (c. 630–c. 580 BCE) was an ancient Greek lyric poet known best for her references to homosexuality among women; "tribade," "Frictrices," and "Rubbers" are slang terms for lesbians; the words have Greek and Latin etymological roots.

(1893); *Man and Superman* (1905), and *Major Barbara* (1894), skewered conventional Victorian moral pieties. A founder of the London School of Economics and a member of the Fabian Society, a left-leaning intellectual and political group, Shaw was often at odds with his contemporaries over a range of social issues, from prostitution and vegetarianism to the rights of women and sexual dissidence. When Oscar Wilde was arrested and imprisoned for "gross indecency" under the Labouchère Amendment (see Introduction, p. 28), Shaw rallied to his fellow playwright's defense. In this 1889 letter, Shaw protests the effects of Labouchère as well as the atmosphere of intolerance generated by the 1889 Cleveland Street scandal. The case—in which well-heeled men were exposed as frequenting a male brothel in the West End of London—generated headlines in the British and European press and led to the downfall and arrest of a number of prominent figures, although ultimately none were jailed (see Introduction, p. 26). The letter, one of the most explicitly pro-homosexual documents of the Victorian era, was intended for publication in *Truth* magazine (of which Henry Labouchère [1831–1912] was the publisher) but was either never sent or rejected for publication.]

SIR—I am sorry to have to ask you to allow me to mention what everybody declares unmentionable; but as a majority of the population habitually flavor their conversation with it to the extent of mentioning it at every sixth word or so, I shall not make matters much worse by a serious utterance on the subject. Go through this passage and ensure that there is only a single space between each word.

My justification shall be that we may presently be saddled with the moral responsibility for monstrously severe punishments inflicted not only on persons who have corrupted children, but on others whose conduct, however nasty and ridiculous, has been perfectly within their admitted rights as individuals.

To a fully occupied person in normal health, with due opportunities for healthy social enjoyment, the mere idea of the subject of the threatened prosecutions is so expressively disagreeable as to appear unnatural. But everybody does not find it so. There are among us highly respected citizens who have been expelled from public schools for giving effect to the contrary opinion; and there are hundreds of others who might have been expelled on the same ground had they been found out. Greek philosophers, otherwise of unquestioned virtue, have differed with us on the point. So have soldiers, sailors, convicts, and in fact members of all communities deprived of intercourse with women. A whole series of Balzac's novels turns upon attachments formed by galley slaves for one another—attachments which are represented as redeeming them from utter savagery.[1] Women, from Sappho downwards, have shewn that this abnormal appetite is not confined to one sex. Now I do not believe myself to be the only man in England acquainted with these facts. And I strongly protest against any journalist writing, as nine out of ten are at this moment dipping their pens to write, as if he had never heard of such things except as vague and sinister rumours concerning the most corrupt phases in the decadence of Babylon, Greece and Rome. All men of the world know that they are constantly carried on by a small minority of people, just as morphine injecting or opium smoking are constantly carried on; and that wherever the passions are denied their natural satisfaction (as on Norfolk Island,[2] for instance) the alternative will become correspondingly general unless it is prevented by stringent surveillance.

I appeal now to the champions of individual rights—to Mr. Herbert Spencer, Mr. Auberon Herbert, Lord Bramwell, Mr. Leonard Courtney, Mr. John Morley, Mr. Bradlaugh and the rest[3]—to join me in a protest against a law by which two adult men can be sentenced to twenty years penal servitude for a private act, freely consented to and desired by both, which concerns themselves alone. There is absolutely no justification for the law except the old theological one of making the secular arm the instrument of God's vengeance. It is a survival from that discarded system with its stonings and burnings; and it survives because it is so unpleasant that men are loth to meddle

---

1 Honoré de Balzac (1799–1850) was a prominent French novelist. Shaw here may be referencing, among other works by Balzac, the novelist's *The Girl with the Golden Eyes* (1834), which dealt with themes of sexual slavery, homosexuality, and incest.
2 Penal colony in the South Pacific Ocean.
3 These are prominent liberal-minded intellectuals of Shaw's day, the most famous of whom is the biologist, philosopher, and progressive political thinker Herbert Spencer (1820–1903). Auberon Herbert (1838–1906) was a writer; George Bramwell (1808–92) was a judge; Leonard Courtney (1832–1918) was an academic and politician; John Morley (1838–1923) was a newspaper editor and writer; Charles Bradlaugh (1833–91) was a political activist and atheist.

with it even with the object of getting rid of it, lest they should be suspected of acting in their personal interest. If the conduct which its abolition would remove from the category of crime is indeed intolerably repellent to society, persons addicted to it can be boycotted—"hounded out," as the phrase goes. But it is worth mentioning that society, instead of acting up in any such way to its overcharged protestations of horrors, only laughs contemptuously. You, Mr. Editor, or I, or any man who knows London life, could without a moment's hesitation, point out at least one gentleman and one lady as to whose character in this respect there is no more doubt than there is as to that of the latest absconder against whom a warrant is out; but we do not find that their social acceptance is much, if at all, less than that of their untainted peers.

We are now free to face with the evil of our relic of Inquisition law,[1] and of the moral cowardice which prevents our getting rid of it. When the corruption of children (which is quite on a different footing, and is a legitimate subject for resolute repression) made it necessary the other day to expose a den of debauchees, the Press was paralyzed with superstitious terror; and not a word was said until you, fortified by your parliamentary position, let the cat out of the bag. My friend Mr. Parke,[2] promptly following it up is menaced with proceedings which would never have been dreamt of had he advanced charges—socially much more serious—of polluting rivers with factory refuse, or paying women wages that needed to be eked out to subsistence point by prostitution. One result of this is that the scandals can no longer be ignored by the general Press. The only question now is, shall they be discussed with sane straightforwardness and without affectation; or are they to be darkly hinted at and gloated over as filthy, unmentionable, abominable, and every other adjective and innuendo that can make them prurient and mischievous? If the latter, the discussion will do more harm than all the practices, from the subterfuge of Onan to the peculiar continence of

---

1 A reference to the Spanish Inquisition, established in 1478 in Spain, a religious campaign that sought to preserve Catholic orthodoxy as it persecuted Jews and other non-Catholics.

2 Ernest Parke was a journalist at the politically radical newspaper the *North London Press*. He was one the first journalists to expose some of the details of the Cleveland Street Case and later vociferously objected to what he considered to be the overly lenient treatment of the men arrested in that case.

Oneida Creek,[1] which might be persecuted as "abominations" with as much reason as the poses plastiques[2] of Cleveland St. For my own part, always reserving the right of the children to careful protection against debauchees, I protest against the principle of the law under which the warrants have been issued; and I hope that no attempt will be made to enforce its outrageous penalties in the case of adult men.

Yrs, etc.

G. BERNARD SHAW
29 Fitzroy Square, W.
26th November, 1889

5. From John Addington Symonds, *The Memoirs of John Addington Symonds*, ed. Phyllis Grosskurth (1892; New York: Random House, 1984)

[Married and the father of four daughters, Symonds (see head-note to Appendix C2, p. 215) had a long-standing clandestine life as the lover of men. Unquestionably the most forthright, detailed, and sensitive exploration of homosexual self-identification in Victorian times may be found in Symonds's memoirs, which were composed in 1892 but unpublished until 1984, when they were printed in a shortened edition. The full text was published in 2017. Symonds described his conflicted life as a loving husband and father who nonetheless had deep emotional and erotic relationships with men, first during his years at Harrow with a young church chorister, Willie Dyer (1843–1905), and

---

1 Onan is a minor character in the biblical book of Genesis who was struck down by God, in some accounts for the sin of masturbation; the Oneida Community was a religious communal society founded in 1848 on the Oneida Creek in Oneida, New York. The group believed that Jesus had already returned in 70 CE, an idea that allowed members of the Oneida community to believe they could bring about Jesus' millennial kingdom and thus be free of sin. Its religious beliefs entailed striving to be perfect in this world, a theological credo known as Perfectionism. The group believed in group marriage, which would have been considered an "abomination" by most of its members' contemporaries.

2 French: nude statuary. The term here refers to popular theatrical performances in Victorian Britain in which men and women adopted the poses of classical nude sculptures.

then on a sojourn in Italy with a young, working-class Italian, Angelo Fusato (1857–1923).]

From
Painful circumstances connected with my last year at Harrow[1]

The distinction in my character between an inner and real self and an outer and artificial self, to which I have already alluded, emphasized itself during this period. So separate were the two selves, so deep was my dipsychia,[2] that my most intimate friends there, of whom I shall soon speak, have each and all emphatically told me that they thought I had passed through school without being affected by, almost without being aware of, its peculiar vices. And yet those vices furnished a perpetual subject for contemplation and casuisitical reflection to my inner self.

The earliest phase of my sexual consciousness was here objectified before my eyes; and I detested in practice what had once attracted me in fancy. Personally, I thought I had transcended crude sensuality through the aesthetic idealization of erotic instincts. I did not know how fallacious that method of expelling nature is. The animalisms of boyish lust sickened me by their brutality, offended my taste by their vulgarity. I imagined them to be a phase of immature development, from which my comrades would emerge when they grew to manhood. Nevertheless, they steeped my imagination in filth. I was only saved from cynicism by the gradual unfolding in myself of an ideal passion which corresponded to Platonic love.[3] This ideal was not derived from Greek literature; for I had not yet read the works of Plato and Theocritus.[4] It sprang up spontaneously, proving that my thought was lodged in Ancient Hellas.

While my school-fellows, therefore, regarded me as an in-

---

1 One of England's great public (i.e., private in North America) schools for boys, located in London.

2 Greek: double-mindedness. The term denotes a lack of faith or weakness of character.

3 Platonic love generally refers to non-sexual love. However, homosexuality was common and largely accepted in certain contexts of ancient Greece, and scholars have also interpreted "Platonic love" as a form of idealized affection among men. Plato's writings suggest that his views of homosexuality changed throughout his life.

4 Theocritus, third-century BCE Greek pastoral poet; both hetero- and homoerotic romantic relations are featured in his work.

sensitive student, immersed in what they called "swatting" and incapable of active good or evil, I was theorizing.

Adolescence, Life at Oxford, and the Painful Incidents

When my father learned the truth about my romantic affection for Willie Dyer, he thought it right to recommend a cautious withdrawal from the intimacy. The arguments he used were conclusive. Considering the very delicate position in which I stood with regard to Vaughan, the possibility of Vaughan's story becoming public, and the doubtful nature of my own emotion, prudence pointed to a gradual diminution or cooling-off of friendship.[1]

At that important moment of my life, I could not understand, and I've never been able to understand, why people belonging to different strata in society—if they love each other—could not enter into comradeship. But my father made me see that, under the existing conditions of English manners, an ardent friendship between me (a young man, gently born, bred at Harrow, advancing to the highest academical honours at Balliol) and Willie (a Bristol chorister, the son of a Dissenting tailor),[2] would injure not my prospects only but his reputation. The instincts of my blood, the conventionalities under which I had been trained, the sympathy I felt for sisters

---

1 Charles John Vaughan (1816–97) was a clergyman and headmaster of the Harrow School from 1854 to 1859. In January 1851, Symonds received a letter from Alfred Pretor, a fellow student at the Harrow School, in which Pretor informed him that he was having an affair with Vaughan. Symonds was skeptical until Pretor produced intimate letters that Vaughan had sent to him. Distressed by the affair, in 1859, while an undergraduate at Oxford, Symonds confided his knowledge of the relationship to his Latin professor, John Conington, who encouraged Symonds to inform his father. Symonds did so and the elder Symonds immediately wrote to Vaughan, threatening to expose him unless he immediately resigned. Four years later, when Symonds's father again threatened Vaughan with exposure, Vaughan withdrew his acceptance of an appointment as Bishop of Oxford. The Harrow scandal does not seem to have brought Vaughan ignominy, however, since in subsequent years he became Vicar of the Temple Church in the City of London and, later, president of University College Cardiff.

2 Balliol: college of Oxford University; Bristol choristers: members of the choir at Bristol Cathedral School in central Bristol; Dissenters: Protestant Christians whose beliefs diverged from those of the Church of England.

and for brothers-in-law, the ties which bound me to the class of gentlefolk, brought me to look upon myself as an aberrant being, who was being tutored by my father's higher sense of what is right in conduct. Furthermore, I recognised that in my own affection for Willie there was something similar to the passion which had ruined Vaughan. I foresaw the possibility, if I persisted in my love for him, of being brought into open rupture with my family, and would involve my friend thereby in what would hamper his career by casting the stigma of illicit passion on our intercourse.

Under this pressure of arguments from without, of sense of weakness within, and of conventional traditions which had made me what I was, I yielded. I gave up Willie Dyer as my avowed heart's friend and comrade. I submitted to the desirability of not acknowledging the boy I loved in public. But I was not strong enough to break the bonds which linked us or to extirpate the living love I felt for him. I carried on our intimacy in clandestine ways and fed my temperament on sweet emotion in secret. This deceit, and the encouragement of what I then recognised as an immoral impulse, brought me cruel wrong.

Here I feel inclined to lay my pen down in weariness. Why should I go on to tell the story of my life? The back of my life was broken when I yielded to convention, and became untrue in soul to Willie.

But what is human life other than successive states of untruth and conforming to custom? We are, all of us, composite beings, made up, heaven knows how, out of the compromises we have effected between our impulses and instincts and the social laws which gird us round.

Had Willie been a boy of my own rank, our friendship need not have been broken; or had English institutions favoured equality like those I admire in Switzerland, he might have been admitted to my father's home. As it was, I continued for some years to keep up an awkward and uncomfortable intercourse with him, corresponding by letters, meeting him in churches where he played the organ and going with him now and then to concerts. I paid the organist of Bristol Cathedral fifty guineas as premium for Willie's musical education, and thus was responsible for starting him in a career he wished to follow.... testing, and sublimating the appetites which they unthinkingly indulged.

Life in London, Marriage....

My father, dissatisfied with Bowman and Acton, sent me to Sir Spencer Wells[1].... He impressed upon me the theory that marriage ought not to be regarded as a matter of idealized passion, but as the sober meeting together of man and woman for mutual needs of sex, for fellow service, and loyal devotion to the duties of social and domestic life in common.

I felt that if I hired a mistress, or took a wife on calculation, I should be running counter to my deepest and most powerful instincts; shutting myself out from passion and ideal love, neither of which had been indulged, although my whole being panted for them. An older man, who had tried life, might do this safely, I reasoned. I, at the age of twenty-three, was far too young and too unformed for compromises. And I could not assume my good physician's plain practical standing ground with regard to the relations of sex. Illicit connections with women were out of the question. If instinct had to be followed, I must have found its satisfaction in male friendship. But this was just what I had resolved to suppress and overcome. His argument, therefore, made a strong appeal to my reason, when I considered the possibility of a suitable marriage. It seemed to be the one exit from my difficulties; and I found myself supported by my father and Sir Edward Strachey, when I talked the matter over with them. The temptation became powerful, to try.

Then, as my inspiration, the memory of Catherine North returned to me. She was connected with the best and happiest period of my past confused existence. To her I felt that I must turn. I was well aware what I was seeking from her, and what a poor self I had to offer. At least I could be frank and true with her. At least I might discover whether she would accept me, as I was, and enter upon life with me according to my modest views of matrimony.

The plan once formed, I put it into execution with characteristic impetuosity and single-sightedness. I did not stop to think or hesitate. I felt myself led and directed. To idealize the situation was for me only too easy, and to concentrate my energies upon it was obeying the impulse of my character

I called at 3 Victoria Street where Mr. North lived. He and his daughter received me hospitably ... They asked me to dinner. I hunted up common friends, especially Mrs. Mary Ewart.

---

1 Bowman and Acton are evidently two physicians; Thomas Spencer Wells (1818–97), medical professor and doctor to Queen Victoria.

All the social threads which connected me with the Norths, slender and distant, yet capable of being used, I put in requisition. And so I gradually made myself, during the later weeks of the London season, a house guest of the Norths. Catherine and I saw much of each other at operas and concerts. These were the places where we came to know each other best—and also in visits to her own house. The more I saw of her, the more I felt certain that she was the woman whom I ought to marry—for my own sake. I did not foresee the complications of life in such a marriage. I deeply felt my own unworthiness of her. But at the same time, I saw no reason why I should not present myself as fairly as I could. In social position and birth I was hardly her equal. I carried an ugly surname. But I was well enough off in property and expectations. And I knew that, although my health had placed me under disadvantages, I was a man above the average in acquirements and ability.

Angelo Fusato

In the spring of 1881 I was staying for a few days at Venice. I had rooms in the Casa Alberti on the Fondamenta Venier, S. Vio, and it was late in the month of May.

One afternoon I chanced to be sitting with my friend Horatio Brown in a little backyard to the wineshop of Fighetti at S. Elisabetta on the Lido.[1] Gondoliers patronise this place, because Fighetti, a muscular giant, is a hero among them. He has won I do not know how many flags in their regattas. While we were drinking our wine Brown pointed out to me two men in white gondolier uniform, with the enormously broad black hat which was then fashionable. They were servants of a General de Horsey; and one of them was strikingly handsome. The following description of him, written a few days after our first meeting, represents with fidelity the impression he made on my imagination.

> He was tall and sinewy, but very slender—for these
> Venetian gondoliers are rarely massive in their strength.
> Each part of the man is equally developed by the exer-
> cise of rowing; and their bodies are elastically supple,
> with free sway from the hips and a Mercurial poise

---

1 Horatio Brown (1854–1926), Scottish historian who specialized in the history of Venice and Italy; the Lido was a popular Venetian beach resort in the late nineteenth century.

upon the ankle. Angelo showed these qualities almost in exaggeration. Moreover, he was rarely in repose, but moved with a singular brusque grace.—Black broad-brimmed hat thrown back upon his matted *zazzera*[1] of dark hair.—Great fiery grey eyes, gazing intensely, with compulsive effluence of electricity—the wild glance of a Triton.[2]—Short blond moustache; dazzling teeth; skin bronzed, but showing white and delicate through open front and sleeves of lilac shirt.—The dashing sparkle of this splendour, who looked to me as though the sea waves and the sun had made him in some hour of secret and unquiet rapture, was somehow emphasised by a curious dint dividing his square chin—a cleft that harmonised with smile on lips and steady fire in eyes.—By the way, I do not know what effect it would have upon a reader to compare eyes to opals. Yet Angelo's eyes, as I met them, had the flame and vitreous intensity of opals, as though the quintessential colour of Venetian waters were vitalised in them and fed from inner founts of passion.—This marvelous being had a rough hoarse voice which, to develop the simile of a sea-god, might have screamed in storm or whispered raucous messages from crests of tossing waves. He fixed and fascinated me.

Angelo Fusato at that date was hardly twenty-four years of age. He had just served his three years in the Genio,[3] and returned to Venice.

This love at first sight for Angelo Fusato was an affair not merely of desire and instinct but also of imagination. He took hold of me by a hundred subtle threads of feeling, in which the powerful and radiant manhood of the splendid animal was intertwined with sentiment for Venice, a keen delight in the landscape of the lagoons, and something penetrative and pathetic in the man.

How sharp this mixed fascination was at the moment when I first saw Angelo, and how durable it afterwards became through the moral struggles of our earlier intimacy, will be understood by anyone who reads the sonnets written about him in my published volumes ... Many of these sonnets were mutilated in order to adapt them to the female sex.

---

1 Italian: a shock or mop of hair.
2 Greek sea god.
3 The engineering corps of the Italian army.

Eight years have elapsed since that first meeting at the Lido. A steady friendship has grown up between the two men brought by accident together under conditions so unpromising. But before I speak of this—the happy product of a fine and manly nature on his side and of fidelity and constant effort on my own—I must revert to those May days in 1881.

The image of the marvelous being I had seen for those few minutes on the Lido burned itself into my brain and kept me waking all the next night. I did not even know his name; but I knew where his master lived. In the morning I rose from my bed unrefreshed, haunted by the vision which seemed to grow in definiteness and to coruscate with phosphorescent fire. A trifle which occurred that day made me feel that my fate could not be resisted, and also allowed me to suspect that the man himself was not unapproachable. Another night of storm and longing followed. I kept wrestling with the anguish of unutterable things, in the deep darkness of the valley of vain desire—soothing my smarting sense of the impossible with idle pictures of what it would be to share the life of this superb being in some lawful and simple fashion.

In these waking dreams I was at one time a woman whom he loved, at another a companion in his trade—always somebody and something utterly different from myself; and as each distracting fancy faded in the void of fact and desert of reality, I writhed in the clutches of chimaera,[1] thirsted before the tempting phantasmagoria of Maya.[2] My good sense rebelled, and told me that I was morally a fool and legally a criminal. But the love of the impossible rises victorious after each fall given it by sober sense. Man must be a demigod of volition, a very Hercules, to crush the life out of that Antaeus,[3] lifting it aloft from the soil of instinct and of appetite which eternally creates it new in his primeval nature....

I can now look back with satisfaction on this intimacy. Though it began in folly and crime, according to the constitution of so-

---

1   Fire-breathing mythological monster made up of parts of multiple animals, generally a lion, goat, dragon, and snake.
2   Sanskrit: "magic" or "illusion," a fundamental concept in Hindu philosophy. Maya originally denoted the magic power whereby a divinity can make human beings believe in illusions.
3   Mythological warrior who wrestled and killed all passing travelers. Antaeus drew his superhuman strength from the ground, a limited source of power that allowed Hercules to defeat him by hoisting Antaeus up in the air and crushing him.

ciety, it has benefited him and proved a source of comfort and instruction to myself. Had it not been for my abnormal desire, I could never have learned to know and appreciate a human being so far removed from me in position, education, national quality and physique. I long thought it hopeless to lift him into something like prosperity—really because it took both of us so long to gain confidence in the stability of our respective intentions and to understand each other's character. At last, by constant regard on my side to his interests, by loyalty and growing affection on his side for me, the end has been attained. His father and brother have profited; for the one now plies his trade in greater comfort, and the other has a situation in the P & O service,[1] which I got for him, and which enables him to marry. And all this good, good for both Angelo and myself, has its taproot in what at first was nothing better than a misdemeanour, punishable by the law and revolting to the majority of human beings.

6. From Charles Kains Jackson, "The New Chivalry," *The Artist and Journal of Home Culture* (2 April 1894): 102–04

[Charles Kains Jackson (1857–1933) was a writer and editor of *The Artist and Journal of Home Culture*, a publication associated with the so-called Uranian poetic movement that stressed the value of male same-sex relations as a welcome reinvigoration of Platonic ideals. Along with other controversial writings endorsing homoerotic love published in the journal, the essay below contributed to the firing of Kains Jackson as editor.]

England has only now emerged into conditions favourable to a real civilization and a high moral code. For 437 years at least there has been a necessity for increasing the population, a necessity on which the national existence depended. Necessity makes its own laws, and makes its own morals. It dictates what form religion shall assume and decides what classes of a religious code shall be enforced or left inoperative by the civil law. We accordingly find that any contract in restraint of marriage during this period of defective population as compared with our neighbours has been held invalid at law as "contrary to public policy." *Salus*

---

1 The Peninsular and Oriental Steam Navigation Company, a British shipping and logistics company.

populi suprema lex.[1] We find that second marriages have always been allowed, that a celibate priesthood has been legally discouraged, that marriages however much of affection, are null at law unless "consummated," in other words that not love or fidelity, but a physical act is "of the essence of the contract." Yet the sense of humour always inherent in the English people has kept them from such curious exhibitions of nasty mindedness and truculence as marked the Jewish laws of family marriages and as express themselves in the Levitical books, in such passages as "Habeo duas filias vobis placuerit" (Gen. xix., 8)[2] and "Ingredere cum Dominus" (Gen. xxxviii., 8–10);[3] Semitic influences however, continue to secure that the work containing these cold-blooded incitements to phallic filthiness is actually allowed to be published at the leading seats of learning, as well as in the metropolis. Even health and science when their teachings clashed with this desire for population have had to go to the wall, and despite the increase of insanity resulting, the marriage of first cousins is permitted—so jealous has the State been of any restraint, even that of hygiene, on marriage.

That the next century, at all events, will have to be lived for Englishmen under widely different circumstances than the last five have been is a point which hardly requires to be enforced. Time and circumstances have conspired to remove the dangers which affected the past. Even a hundred years ago either France or Germany would have conquered England twice over if valour were merely equal. We had frightful arrears of fighting strength to make up.

Today even without our colonies we are too numerous for this to happen and it is probable that we should be assisted by England oversea. The problem therefore is shifted and from the dangers foreseen in the Middle Ages in England, from the dangers to which the Jews eventually succumbed, we have now to turn and confront the new series of perils involved in "the people exceeding the means to live contentedly."

---

1 Latin: the health of the people is the supreme law. From Cicero's (106–43 BCE) *De legibus*, which explored the author's theory of the natural laws of harmony between different social classes.
2 Latin: I have two daughters for pleasing you. In Genesis 19.8–9, Lot offers the Sodomites his two daughters when they demand to sexually assault his male houseguests.
3 Latin: go with the master. From Genesis 38, in which Judah instructs his son Onan to sleep with his brother's widow.

Again, will necessity effect our laws, our morals, the enforcement or non-enforcement of different sections of a religious code. It will not be all gain; no change ever is. But we can at least make the best of it; as can the wise of all changes. Wherefore just as the flower of the early and imperfect civilization was in what we may call the Old Chivalry, or the exaltation of the youthful feminine ideal, so the flower of the adult and perfect civilization will be found in the New Chivalry or the exaltation of the youthful masculine ideal. The time has arrived when the eternal desire for Love which nature has implanted in the breast of man requires to be satisfied without such an increase in population as has characterized the past. The methods connected with the agreeable names of Bradlaugh, Besant, and Drysdale need no notice here.[1] We need not consider the degree of viciousness involved in what is known as "French vice." It will suffice for us that it is essentially bourgeois, that it is not only lacking in the aesthetic element but is directly antipathetic thereto. To the aesthete a smirched flower is worse than no flower at all, and the intrusion of chill precaution upon the heat of passion can only result in that lukewarm condition which aestheticism rejects as forcibly as ever orthodoxy did Laodicea.[2]

The new ideal therefore will be one which unites true fancies and a lofty aspiration with a freedom from the two classes of evil already considered. The direction in which it is to be found is indicated by the natural tendencies which secure the survival of the fittest. The animal ideal is to secure immortality by influencing the body. The spiritual is that addition by which we are differentiated from the animal. And the law of evolution is addition, is change. Wherefore the human animal to which the spiritual has been added, will eventually find the line of proper and ultimate evolution is emphasizing that which has been added. The men of most influence on their fellows will be those who are the most spiritual, not those who are the most animal.

---

1 For Charles Bradlaugh (1833–91), see p. 224, n. 3; Walter Besant (1836–1901), English novelist and historian; George Drysdale (1824–1904), British free-thinker and advocate of contraception.

2 Laodicea was a prosperous ancient city located in modern-day Turkey, but Kains Jackson refers to its church, one of the flawed Seven Churches of Asia described in the book of Revelation. God calls upon Laodicea to repent for its lack of religious zeal, and presumably the orthodoxy rejected Laodicea on the same grounds.

At the same time the majority will always lag behind the more advanced type, a provision by which the perpetuation of the species is adequately secured. For five centuries in England the necessity that the race should increase and multiply has been paramount, but these five centuries of assistance have now secured their result, and we need at the present time no more than not to go back in numbers, at the same time that we greatly need to increase in the average of wealth. "Il faut traffiquer de notre superflu."[1]

The New Chivalry then is also the new necessity. Happily it is already with us. The advanced—the more spiritual types of English manhood already look to beauty first. In the past the beauty has been conditioned and confined to such beauty as could be found in some fair being *capable of increasing the population.* The condition italicized is now for the intelligent, removed. The New Chivalry therefore will not ask that very plain question of the Marriage Service. "Will it lead to the procreation of children?" It will rest content with beauty—God's outward clue to the inward Paradise. No animal consideration of mere sex will be allowed to intrude on the higher fact. A beautiful girl will be desired before a plain lad, but a plain girl will not be considered in the presence of a handsome boy. Where boy and girl are of equal outward grace the spiritual ideal will prevail over the animal and the desire of influencing the higher mind, the boy's, will prevail over the old desire to add to the population. The higher form of influence will be chosen.

The gain in human happiness will be direct and immediate. It has been obvious in the past that the praiseworthy attempts of women to be beautiful have in the next generation been half abolished by the want of such attempt in their husbands. Thus the human animal in England got "no forwarder" in physical beauty. But the New Chivalry inducing boys to be beautiful as well as girls, will remedy this. The whole species will move on, and a type of higher beauty will be evolved.

The gain in human intelligence will be direct, for love will impart with the eagerness of joy all its most treasured intellectual acquisitions, all its experiences of life. It will not fear to bare its errors to loving eyes and will not grudge even shame if so be it may save the beloved from the like. As in Sparta so once more, will the lover be the inbreather—*eispnelos,* the beloved "this lis-

---

1 French: we must traffic in our own superfluity.

tener"—*aites*.[1] A royal road to learning will be found. The gain in human physique will be direct. For the carelessness of fathers, the sexual impossibilities of mother and sisters, the more the indifference of brothers, the watchful and devoted discipline of the lover will be substituted. The boy will find exactly the words, the cautions, he requires, the incentives which best stimulate in the converse of the lover still young and strong enough to preach by act, and finding as in Sir Frederick Leighton's admirable canvas no greater glory than in guiding younger and well loved hands to the mark.[2]

That comparisons are not popular has been affirmed by many authorities and in cases where evolution is working out its silent inevitable course they are also unnecessary. There are, however, two matters wherein the New Chivalry inspires us with a new hope. It is evident that in the Old Chivalry there was always a certain absence of freewill, in other words its essential element, a refusal to take by force and for ought than love, was at best imperfect. A married woman blessed with children is cajoled by nature itself, as it were, into tolerating the husband for the sake of the children even where but for the Baconian "hostages to fortunes" no such tolerance would be possible.[3] And the marriage contract adds for the same sake a proviso which is not of chivalry or even—except for the good of the community as expressed in increase of population—of common sense. "Till death us do part" is the phrase. "Till Love us do part" is the obvious logic of the situation. The New Chivalry imposes no irksome or fatuous ties. It is genuine or it is nothing. Where love upholds its banner the heathen may rage in vain; and it is

---

1 Kains Jackson refers to the classical social system of combining pederasty with education. The eispnelos, or the inspirer, was an older man who would both love and educate the aites, or the listener, the younger man who was thought to benefit from the elder's wisdom.

2 An evident reference to a painting depicting a male youth being instructed in how to shoot an arrow, "The Hit," by the British academic painter George Leighton (1830–96). Leighton's paintings sometimes depicted classical themes with homoerotic undertones.

3 A quotation from the English philosopher and scientist Francis Bacon's (1561–1626) essay "Of Marriage and Single Life," from his *Essays* (1597), which reads in full: "He that hath wife and children hath given hostages to fortune; for they are impediments to great enterprises, either of virtue or mischief."

So strong
That should its own hands dig its grave
The wide world's power and pity shall not save.[1]

The chief drawback is that under the New Chivalry all the plots of the French dramatists would disappear. Lovers while loving would not care for the "world outside" and when they ceased to love there would be neither incongruity or scandal in their going apart.

A gain to the world of a new nature, but all the more important in an age when poverty of purse, not of population, is the danger, exists in the decrease of idleness involved by the New ideal. No woman wants to work. Every girl of the least personal attractiveness nourishes the hope of being kept in idleness. Above a certain class the proviso "by a husband" is added. But the new lovers will both work and will be the happier for both working. The newer and intenser love will see its way to avoid the separation of hours, of interests and of resources which is the inevitable destiny of ninety-nine married couples out of every hundred. The desire of the male to express itself in action, will be fully satisfied in each case, age will make no difference. The ideal partnership indeed will more frequently than not be accomplished, the elder having the greater power of physical endurance, the younger too having greater powers of physical endurance under due direction. Had it but this single recommendation, the new ideal would still be adding enormously to the wealth and happiness of the country.

... Of companionship also there is much to be said. Here it is enough to ask how much do ordinary engaged couples, how much even do husband and wife see of each other? How much may not lovers see if man and youth, if youth and boy? The joys of palaestra,[2] of the river of the hunt and of the moor the evening tent-pitching of campers out, and the exhilaration of the early morning swim, for one pleasure of life and physical delight in each other's presence, touch and voice which man and woman ordinarily share, it is not too much to say that the new chivalry has ten. Intimacy of constant companionship, of physical and personal knowledge is also a power of help and aid which cannot be put into words.

---

1 Algernon Charles Swinburne (1837–1909), "Tristram of Lyonesse" (1882).
2 Gymnasium (ancient Greece).

... The mind of adolescent manhood being the development stage of potentially greater powers, must needs be capable under stimulus and guidance, of sweeter and fuller flower than that of girlhood, sweet as is that flower, and while no woman wishes to be loved for her intellect, youth is proud to be helped to learn. Nor is handsome youth less disposed towards knowledge than youth which is not handsome.

The possibility of having to fight life's intellectual and physical battles side by side and shoulder to shoulder is full of a new inspiration, an inspiration which the old ideal could not take to itself, which the Old Chivalry never knew. When Love enters, then Possibility will become Desire, and Like will be drawn to Like by each attempting to attain for the sake of greater worthiness, to that which in the other is the Best.

That the tenderness of the elder for the younger, of one who has endured for him that has yet to endure, of the strong for the weak, the developed for the developing, is retained in all fullness, while these other things are added, is perhaps that note which gives its highest value to the New Chivalry.

7. From Edward Carpenter, *Homogenic Love, and Its Place in a Free Society*, Talk Delivered to the Manchester Labour Society (London: Labour Press Society, 1894)

[Edward Carpenter (1844–1929) was an English socialist, poet, and utopian thinker whose writings, such as *Love's Coming of Age* (1896), *Civilization: Its Cause and Cure* (1889), and *The Intermediate Sex* (1912), accentuated same-sex desire as linked to communitarian ideas and intense male companionship. Carpenter's friendships with a diverse range of progressive intellectuals included John Ruskin (1819–1900), Olive Schreiner (1855–1920), and E.M. Forster (1879–1970), whose homosexual novel *Maurice* (1914) was inspired by a visit to the home of Carpenter and his partner George Merrill (1866–1928).]

Of all the many forms that Love delights to take, perhaps none is more interesting (for the very reason that it has been so inadequately considered) than that special attachment which is sometimes denoted by the word Comradeship. In general we may say that the passion of love provides us at once with the deepest problems and the highest manifestations of life, and that to its different workings can be traced the farthest-reaching threads of human endeavour. In one guise, as the mere semi-conscious Sex-love, which runs through creation and is common to man and the lowest animals and plants, it affords a kind of organic basis for the unity of all creatures; in another, as for instance the love of the Mother for her offspring (also to be termed a passion) it seems to pledge itself to the care and guardianship of the growing race; then again in the Marriage of man and woman it becomes a thing of mystic and eternal import, and one of the corner-stones of human society; while in the form of Comrade-love with which this paper is concerned, it has uses and functions which we trust will clearly appear as we proceed.

To some perhaps it may appear a little strained to place this last-mentioned form of attachment on a level of importance with the others, and such persons may be inclined to deny the homogenic or homosexual love (as it has been called) that intense, that penetrating, and at times overmastering character which would entitle it to rank as a great human passion. But in truth this view, when entertained, arises from a want of acquaintance with the actual facts; and it may not be amiss here, in the briefest possible way, to indicate what the world's History, Literature and Art has to say to us on the whole subject, before we go on to any further considerations of our own. Certainly, if the confronting of danger and the endurance of pain and distress for the sake of the loved one, if sacrifice, unswerving devotion and life-long union, constitute proofs of the reality and intensity (and let us say *healthiness*) of an affection, then these proofs have been given in numberless cases of such attachment, not only as existing between men, but as between women, since the world began. The records of chivalric love, the feats of enamoured knights for their ladies' sake, the stories of Hero and Leander, etc., are easily paralleled, if not surpassed, by the stories of the Greek comrades-in-arms and tyrannicides—of Cratinus and Aristodemus, who offered themselves together as a voluntary sacrifice for the purification of Athens; of Chariton and Melanippus, who attempted to assassinate Phalaris, the tyrant of Agrigentum; of Diodes who fell fighting in defence of his loved one; or of Cleomachus who in like manner, in a battle between the Chalkidians and Eretrians, being entreated to charge the latter, "asked the youth he loved, who was standing by, whether he would be a spectator of the fight; and when he said he would, and affectionately kissed Cleomachus and put his helmet on his head, Cleomachus with a proud joy placed himself in the front of the bravest of the Thessalians and charged the enemy's cavalry with such impetuosity that he threw them into disorder and routed them; and the Eretrian cavalry fleeing in consequence, the Chalkidians won a splendid victory."[1]

... We may say that to all love and indeed to all human feeling there must necessarily be a physical side. The most delicate emotion which plays through the mind has, we cannot but perceive, its corresponding subtle change in the body, and the great passions are accompanied by wide-reaching disturbances and transformations of corporeal tissue and fluid. Who knows (it may be asked) how deeply the mother-love is intertwined with the growth of the lacteal vessels and the need of the suckled infant? or how intimately even the most abstract of desires—namely the religious—is rooted in the slow hidden metamorphosis by which a new creature is really and physically born within the old? Richard Wagner, in a pregnant little passage in his *Communication to my Friends*, says that the essence of human love "is the longing for utmost physical reality, for fruition in an object which can be grasped by all the senses, held fast with all the force of actual

---

1 Hero and Leander were famous lovers of Greek myth. Leander swam across the Hellespont (a narrow channel now known as the Dardanelles) every night to visit his lover, Hero, navigating by a beacon that Hero lit for him. One night, the light blew out, and Leander became lost in the water and drowned. Upon discovering Leander's dead body, Hero leapt to her own death; according to a story told by Neanthes of Cyzicus, Cratinus and Aristodemus were male lovers who heroically gave their lives as human sacrifices to purify Athens during a plague; Chariton and Melanippus were male lovers who conspired together to kill the Sicilian ruler Phalaris, a tyrant with a reputation for roasting his victims inside a bronze bull. Before they could carry out their plan, Phalaris caught Chariton and tortured him until Melanippus came forward and confessed his own exclusive responsibility for the assassination plot. Phalaris, in spite of his reputation, was so moved by the strength and selflessness of Chariton and Melanippus' love for one another that he set them both free; Diodes, or Diocles, was an Athenian warrior who died in battle while protecting his male lover, an act for which he was buried with special honors; from Plutarch's (45–120 CE) *Amatorius, or Dialogue on Love* (c. 120 CE).

being."[1] And if this is a somewhat partial sentiment it yet puts into clear language one undoubted relation between the sensuous and the emotional in all love, and the sweet *excuse* which this relation may be said to provide for the existence of the actual world—namely that the latter is the means whereby we become conscious of our most intimate selves. But if this is true of love in general it must be true of the Homogenic Love; and we must not be surprised to find that in all times this attachment has had some degree of physical expression. The question however as to what degree of physical intimacy may be termed in such a case fitting and natural—though a question which is sure to arise—is one not easy to answer: more especially as in the common mind any intimacy of a bodily nature between two persons of the same sex is so often (in the case of males) set down as a sexual act of the crudest and grossest kind. Indeed the difficulty here is that the majority of people, being incapable perhaps of understanding the *inner* feeling of the homogenic attachment, find it hard to imagine that the intimacy has any other object than the particular form of sensuality mentioned (i.e., the *Venus aversa*,[2] which appears, be it said, to be rare in all the northern countries), or that people can be held together by any tie except the most sheerly material one—a view which of course turns the whole subject upside down, and gives rise to violent and no doubt very natural disapprobation; and to endless recriminations and confusion.

... That passionate attachment between two persons of the same sex is, as we have seen, a phenomenon widespread through the human race, and enduring in history, has been always more or less recognized; and once at least in history—in the Greek age—the passion rose into distinct consciousness, and justified, or even it might be said glorified, itself; but in later times—especially perhaps during the last century or two of European life—it has

---

1   From the German composer Richard Wagner's (1813–83)
    Communications to My Friends (1851), an autobiographical work
    justifying Wagner's operatic ideas. Wagner here is referring to
    the myth of Zeus and Semele (in which Zeus took human form to
    seek human love), a narrative that Wagner claimed was a model
    for the relationship of Lohengrin, the hero of Wagner's 1850
    Romantic opera, and Lohengrin's beloved Elsa. In Wagner's opera,
    Lohengrin returns from the transcendent Grail to earth in order to
    seek redemption from the sterility and vacuity of divine being so as
    to embrace the earthly love of Elsa.
2   Latin: euphemism for anal intercourse.

generally been treated by the accredited thinkers and writers as a thing to be passed over in silence, as associated with mere grossness and mental aberration, or as unworthy of serious attention.

... This question of the physiological basis of the homogenic love—to which we have more than once alluded—is a very important one; and it seems a strange oversight on the part of Science that it has hitherto taken so little notice of it. The desire for corporeal intimacy of some kind between persons of the same sex existing as it does in such force and so widely over the face of the earth, it would seem almost certain that there must be some physiological basis for the desire: but until we know more than we do at present as to what this basis may be, we are necessarily unable to understand the desire itself as well as we might wish. It may be hoped that this is a point to which attention will be given in the future. Meanwhile, though the problem is a complex one, it may not be amiss here to venture a suggestion or two.

In the first place it may be suggested that an important part of *all* love-union, mental or physical, is its influence personally on those concerned. This influence is, of course, subtle and hard to define; and one can hardly be surprised that Science, assuming hitherto in its consideration of ordinary sexual relations that the mutual actions and reactions were directly solely to the purpose of generation and the propagation of the species, has almost quite neglected the question of the direct influences on the lovers themselves. Yet everyone is sensible practically that there is much more in an intimacy with another person than the question of children alone; that even setting aside the effects of actual sex-intercourse there are subtle elements passing from one to another which are indispensable to personal well-being, and which make some such intimacy almost a necessary condition of health. It may be that there are some persons for whom these necessary reactions can only come from one of the same sex. In fact it is obvious there are such persons. "Successful love," says Moll (p. 125) "exercises a helpful influence on the Urning. His mental and bodily conditions improves, and capacity of work increases—just as it often happens in the case of a normal youth with *his* love."[1] And further on (p. 173) in a letter from a

---

1 Albert Moll (1862–1939) was a pioneering German sexologist who wrote sympathetically of men of same-sex erotic impulses and whom he designated as "Urnings" (from "Urania" or Aphrodite). Moll maintained that Urnings had masculine bodies but feminine souls.

man of this kind occur these words: "The passion is I suppose so powerful, just because one looks for everything in the loved man—Love, Friendship, Ideal, and Sense—satisfaction.... As it is at present I suffer the agonies of a deep unresponded passion, which wake me like a nightmare from sleep. And I am conscious of physical pain in the region of the heart." In such cases the love, in some degree physically expressed, of another person of the same sex, is clearly as much a necessity and a condition of healthy life and activity, as in more ordinary cases is the love of a person of the opposite sex.

... In conclusion there are a few words to be said about the legal aspect of this important question. It has to be remarked that the present state of the Law—arising as it does partly out of some of the misapprehensions above alluded to, and partly out of the sheer unwillingness of legislators to discuss the question—is really quite impracticable and unjustifiable, and will no doubt have to be altered.

The Law, of course, can only deal, and can only be expected to deal, with the outward and visible. It cannot control feeling; but it tries—in those cases where it is concerned—to control the expression of feeling. It has been insisted on in this essay that the Homogenic Love is a valuable social force, and, in cases, an indispensable factor of the noblest human character; also that it has a necessary root in the physical and sexual organism. This last is the point where the Law steps in. "We know nothing"—it says—"of what may be valuable social forces or factors of character, or of what may be the relation of physical things to things spiritual; but when you speak of a sexual element being present in this kind of love, we can quite understand that; and that is just what we mean to suppress. That sexual element is nothing but gross indecency, *any form of which by our Act of 1885 we make criminal*."[1]

Whatever substantial ground the Law may have had for previous statutes on this subject—dealing with a specific act

---

1   Carpenter refers to the passage of Section 11 of the Criminal Law Amendment Act of 1885, also known as the Labouchère act Amendment after Henry Labouchère, the member of Parliament who proposed it. The amendment expanded the criminalization of homosexual activity beyond the act of anal intercourse and subjected other homoerotic acts to criminal penalties. Oscar Wilde was convicted and sentenced to prison on Section 11 grounds in 1895. The 1967 Sexual Offenses Act repealed the amendment.

(sodomy)—it has surely quite lost it in passing so wide-sweeping a condemnation on all relations between male persons. It has undertaken a censorship over private morals (entirely apart from social results) which is beyond its province, and which—even if it were its province—it could not possibly fulfil; it has opened wider than ever before the door to a real social evil and crime—that of blackmailing; and it has thrown a shadow over even the simplest and most natural expression of an attachment which may, as we have seen, be of the greatest value in national life.

That the homosexual passion may be improperly indulged in, that it may lead, like the heterosexual, to public abuses of liberty and decency we of course do not deny; but as, in the case of persons of opposite sex, the law limits itself on the whole to the maintenance of public order, the protection of the weak from violence and insult and, of the young from their inexperience: so it should be here. Whatever teaching may be thought desirable on the general principles of morality concerned must be given—as it can only be given—by the spread of proper education and ideas, and not be the clumsy bludgeon of the statute-book.

We have shown the special functions and really indispensable import of the homogenic or comrade love, in some form, in national life, and it is high time now that the modern States should recognize this in their institutions—instead of (as is also done in schools and places of education) by repression and disallowance perverting the passion into its least satisfactory channels. If the dedication of love were a matter of mere choice or whim, it still would not be the business of the State to compel that choice; but since no amount of compulsion can ever change the homogenic instinct in a person, where it is innate, the State in trying to effect such a change is only kicking vainly against the pricks of its own advantage—and trying, in view perhaps of the conduct of a licentious few, to cripple and damage a respectable and valuable class of its own citizens.

8. Alan Dale (Alfred J. Cohen), "A Word from the Author," *An Eerie He and She* (New York: G.W. Dillingham, 1889)

[In this preface to his novel *An Eerie He and She*, Cohen expressed his dismay at the critical reaction to *A Marriage Below Zero*, published just a few months earlier. These are his only known comments concerning the controversy generated by his novel.]

The storm that burst with relentless fury over my unprotected head, after the publication of "A Marriage Below Zero," has spent itself, and I believe that feeble little tomes can now assert themselves again.

The unconventionality of my last novel caused one of my energetic and benevolent critics to publicly declare that I was "an enemy of the human race."

Thank goodness that I was born with an ability to see the human side of nearly everything! Without that ability, I suppose that by this time, I should be Robinson Crusoe-ing on some desert island.[1]

The idea that I am antagonistic to my species and several pretty little theories to which I have been credited, speak volumes for the ingenuity of my friends.

They have attributed to me motives of the blackest description; they have found between the lines of my book, meaning of which I must truthfully say I never had the slightest suspicion. In a few instances, I was not misjudged, and these instances I shall treasure for a pleasant reading for the years to come....

---

1 *Robinson Crusoe* (1719) by Daniel Defoe (c. 1660–1731), the eponymous protagonist of which spends thirty years on a tropical island.

Appendix D: Late-Victorian Legal and Medical Models and the New Social Panic

1. From Section 11 of the 1885 Criminal Amendment Bill

[Henry Labouchère (1831–1912) was a journalist and a Liberal member of the British Parliament who sponsored an amendment to an 1885 criminal bill that outlawed sexual relations between men and underage girls. The one-sentence amendment to that law, sometimes referred to as the Labouchère Amendment, for the first time criminalized all sexual acts between men both in private and public.]

Any male person who, in public or private, commits, or is a party to the commission of, or procures, or attempts to procure the commission by any male person of, any act of gross indecency shall be guilty of a misdemeanour, and being convicted shall be liable at the discretion of the Court to be imprisoned for any term not exceeding two years, with or without hard labour.

2. From Richard Krafft-Ebing, "Case 237," *Psychopathia Sexualis: A Medico-Forensic Study*, trans. Harry E. Weddeck (1886; New York: G.P. Putnam's Sons, 1965), 423–25

[Richard Krafft-Ebing (1840–1902) was a pioneering Austro-German psychiatrist whose pioneering work, *Psychopathia Sexualis: A Medico-Forensic Study*, first published in 1886 and then in many expanded editions, introduced influential new categories to describe new sexual pathologies. In this excerpt from the work's final section, Krafft-Ebing devoted several pages to a certain "Case 237," which concerned a young man, "S.," who, although married, had continued to conduct a sexual relationship with a younger man, "G." Krafft-Ebing characterizes S.'s problem as "male love" and gives the case a date of 30 May 1888, when S. was accused by his step-father

of "immoral relations" with G., an accusation that leads to
S.'s arrest.]

S. states that it was first in the course of his legal examination
that he saw how he had been careless in his intercourse with
G., by causing gossip. His openness he explained as due to the
innocence of their friendship.

It is worthy of note that S.'s wife never noticed anything suspicious in the intercourse between her husband and G., though
the most simple wife would instinctively notice anything of that
nature. Mrs. S. had also made no opposition to receiving G. into
the house. On this point she remarked that the spare-room in
which G. lay ill was on the second floor, while the living apartments were on the fourth; and, further, that S. never associated
alone with G. as long as he was in the house. She states that she
is convinced of her husband's innocence, and that she loves him
as before.

S. states freely that formerly he had often kissed G., and talked with him about sexual matters. G. was much given to women,
and in friendship he had often warned him about sexual dissi-
pation, particularly when G., as often happened, did not look
well. He had once said that G. was a handsome fellow; it was in
a perfectly harmless relation.

The kissing of G. had been due to inordinate friendship, when G. had shown him some particular attention,
or pleased him especially. In the act he had never had
any sexual feeling. When he had now and then dreamed of G., it
was in a perfectly harmless way.

It appeared of great importance to the author to form
also an opinion of G.'s personality. On 12th December
the desired opportunity was given, and G. was carefully
examined.

G. was a young man, aged twenty, of delicate build, whose
development corresponded with his years; and he appeared to
be neuropathic and sensual. The genitals were normal and well
developed. The author thought he might be permitted to pass
over the condition of the anus, as he did not feel called upon to
pass judgment upon it. Prolonged association with G. gave one
the impression that he was a harmless, kind, and artless man,
light-minded, but not morally depraved. Nothing in his dress or
manner indicated perverse sexual feeling. There could not be the
slightest suspicion that he was a male courtesan.

When G. was introduced in medias res,[1] he stated that S. and he, feeling their innocence, had told the matter as it actually was, and on this the whole trial had been based. At first, S.'s friendship, and especially the kissing, had seemed remarkable, even to him. Later he had convinced himself that it was merely friendship, and had then thought no more about it.

G. had looked upon S. as a father-like friend; for he was so unselfish, and loved him so.

The expression "handsome fellow" was made when G. had a love-affair, and when S. expressed his fears about a happy future for G. At that time S. had comforted him, and said that his (G.'s) appearance was pleasing, and that he would make an eligible match.

Once S. had complained to him (G.) that his wife was inclined to drink, and burst into tears. G. was touched by his friend's unhappiness. On this occasion S. had kissed him, and begged for his friendship, and asked him to visit him frequently.

S. had never spontaneously directed the conversation to sexual matters. G. once asked what pederasty was, of which he had heard much while in England; and S. had explained it to him.

G. acknowledged that he was sensual. At the age of twelve he had been made acquainted with sexual matters by schoolmates. He had never masturbated, had first had coitus at the age of eighteen, and had since visited brothels frequently. He had never felt any inclination for his own sex, and had never experienced any sexual excitement when S. kissed him. He had always had pleasure in coitus normally performed. His lascivious dreams had always been of women. With indignation, and pointing to his descent from a healthy and respectable family, he repelled the insinuation of having been given to passive pederasty. Until the gossip about them came to his ears, he had been innocent and devoid of suspicion. The anal anomalies he tried to explain in the same way that he did at the trial. Automasturbation denied.

It should be noted that Mr. J. S. claimed to be no less astonished by the charge against his brother of male-love than those more closely associated with him. Yet he did not understand what attached his brother to G.; and all the explanations which S. made to him concerning his relation to G. were vain.

---

1 Latin: in the middle of things.

The author took the trouble to observe S. and G., in a natural way, while they were dining, in company with S.'s brother and Mrs. S., in Graz. This observation revealed not the slightest sign of improper friendship.

The general impression which S. made on me was that of a nervous, sanguine, somewhat overstrained individual, but, at the same time, kind, open-hearted, and very emotional.

S. was physically strong, somewhat corpulent, with a symmetrical, brachycephalic cranium. The genitals were well developed; the penis somewhat bellied; the prepuce slightly hypertrophied.

Opinion. Pederasty is, unfortunately, not infrequent among mankind to-day; but still, occurring among the peoples of Europe, it is an unusual, perverse, and even monstrous manner of sexual gratification. It presumes a congenital or acquired perversion of the sexual instinct, and, at the same time, defect of moral sense that is either original or acquired, as a result of pathological influences.

3. "Sex-Mania," *Reynolds's Newspaper* (21 April 1895)

[*Reynolds's* was a radical republican newspaper that covered the Wilde trials throughout 1895. While its sympathetic view of the Irish cause tempered its disapproval of what its 14 April 1895 headline called "The Notorious Mr. Wilde," *Reynolds's* aggressively pursued a social-purity editorial position throughout the 1890s, seeing recent sodomy scandals as related to the problem of the New Woman, the exploitation of working-class youths, and a "sex-mania" whose pervasiveness, *Reynolds's* maintained, found confirmation in the new sexology. "Sex-Mania" directly addressed the issue of women who were married to men of same-sex tastes. That the front-page piece concludes with a reference to the 1877 Somerset family scandals (see Introduction, pp. 37–42) suggests that nearly twenty years after Lord and Lady Somerset's marital separation editorial writers could reference the case in fulminating against upper-class privilege, homosexual impropriety, and, as "Sex-Mania" would have it, the vexing problem of female independence and planned pregnancy, causes on whose behalf Lady Somerset advocated in the years after her scandalous court case.]

What does all this perpetual discussion of sex mean? Wherefore this constant analysis of the passions? How does it come that the people today are filled with nothing but sex, sex, sex? Influenza is not the only new plague which has come to reside among us. Rather a more terrible plague has taken hold of the nation—sex mania.

Now what is this prevailing lunacy of sex, but a violent reaction from the Puritanical constraints and artificial up-bringing of both ...To repress every manifestation of passion is the cardinal doctrine of English home training. The result is that the schools of both sexes have become hot-beds of vice, and the Universities—public women being excluded from the University towns—are the homes of unnatural offences. All this is reflected in our literature and in the social movements of the day. The "New Woman" is, to a certain extent, a development of sex-mania: the male decadent is the victim, and the rising population are being affected physically and mentally by symptoms of the same disease.

For, after all, this perpetual brooding on sex is as much a disease or form of madness, or hundreds of other tendencies for the manifestation of which we lock people in asylums. Any doctor will say as much. Pederasty, Sadism, Masochism, Fetischism, Androgyny, Gynandry,[1] are forms of pure madness, which drive the sufferers to lunatic asylums, or to suicide ... Already, indeed, and more specifically on the Continent, these abnormal tendencies are being treated by hypnotic suggestion. Dr. R. von Krafft-Ebing, the Professor of Psychiatry and Neurology in the University of Vienna, indeed, goes so far as to treat excessive devotion to religion as a form of sex-mania. He says: "For the most part, [such devotions] rest upon sexuality which manifests itself in a sexual impulse that is abnormally early and intense. The *libido* finds satisfaction in ... exaggerated religious enthusiasm...." And no one who knows anything of the practice of our criminal courts can be unaware that the defense of uncontrollable sex tendency, amounting to partial lunacy, is being more frequently put forward as a plea in answer to offenses of this character. If the truth were known Jack the Ripper was nothing but a sex maniac in the sense of the term which we have been using.

---

1   In his *Psychopathia Sexualis* (see Appendix D2), Krafft-Ebing categorized gynandry as an extreme perversion. "The woman of this type," he wrote, "possesses of the feminine qualities only the genital organs; thought, sentiment, action, even external appearance are those of a man" (Brooklyn: Physicians and Surgeons Book Co., 1908), 333–36.

These alarming symptoms of national life are likely to spread with the increasing lunacy of the age and the ever-growing population who live on the labours of others. And to all there can be but one end. History teaches us that moral corruption has always been the forerunner of the downfall of nations. It was so in Greece, Rome, the Italian Republics, and France before the Revolution. There is no example to the contrary. So we may take it that the shocking depravity of the English idles classes at this moment is a symptom of our approaching dissolution.

Who can wonder at the depravity of the classes? Given idleness and wealth, the offspring of Bacchus and Venus will be Corruption.[1] A feature of a low state of morals among the patrician class always has been that the most conspicuous devotees of unnatural offenses have been persons already married. The inference is obvious. They have led their unloved ... spouses to the altar from motives other than affection—position, money, influence. They have simply gone into the marriage mart and bought a female for commercial reasons. What the female may be in other ways does not enter into their consideration. She may be a consumptive inane. She may powder and paint her skin ... What matters all this? There are the consolations of Cleveland Street and Pimlico ...[2]

The English classes have been justly accused of being the most hypocritical the world has known. Our society is honeycombed with corruption as a decaying cheese is with maggots ... The Magistrates and the judges of criminal courts spend a large portion of public funds in hearing charges of sexual offences against State Church clergymen and old men. Scarcely indeed is the child out of arms, but we hear of some criminal assault attempted. Our streets are strewn with the bodies of new-born babies illicitly begotten. Luxury, more cruel than war, is descending from the patrician caste: its example is demoralizing all grades of Society. And in the face of this foul dream of lust, this Walpurg's

---

1 Bacchus was the Roman god of agriculture, wine, and fertility, from the Greek god Dionysus; Venus was the Roman goddess of fertility, sexuality, prosperity, and victory.

2 A reference to the 1885 Cleveland Street scandal involving upper-class men who frequented a male brothel in London's West End (see Introduction, p. 26). Pimlico is an area of central London. Although an 1877 newspaper article described Pimlico as "genteel, sacred to professional men" and a "cut above Chelsea," in the 1890s parts of the neighborhood had become decrepit.

Night of Corruption, the State's clergy, themselves connected by blood with the criminals, are dumb![1]

We have already referred to the morals of the aristocracy. For a body so limited in numbers, the amount and the gravity of their offences against public and private morals are astounding. By what is revealed we may guess what is concealed. Every effort is made to hush up aristocratic scandals. Numerous offences of this character are the subject of private conversation, although they never find their way into the public courts or the newspapers. As to the outrages which are made public, an influential section of the Press suppress, tone down, or modify what has occurred. The same journals would eagerly publish scandalous details if they affected not a peer, but a leader of the Democracy. Upon this hypocritical foundation is our Society built. Humbug and cant are the prevailing notes of our time. The sins of the classes are condoned by the churches. The pulpits ring with no denunciation of the offences of those who arrogate to themselves the position of "leaders of Society." There is no Savonarola[2] among our clergy to enforce the moral of the lesson taught by old William Caxton,[3] "Doo after the good, and leve the evil, and it shall bring you to good fame and renomee."

On the subject Mr. Ashcroft Noble[4] has some sensible observations in the new number of the *Contemporary*:

> It is not morality, but civilization, which excludes certain themes from general colloquy; it is, again, not morality but civilization, which places certain offices in comparatively obscure and undeserved corners of our dwellings—which sends us into seclusion even to wash our hands or clean our teeth. As it is impossible to use the most fitting comparison, I can only say that

1 In German folklore, witches meet on the evening of 30 April, Walpurgisnacht.

2 See p. 218, note 2.

3 William Caxton (c. 1415–92), English printer, writer, and diplomat.

4 John Ashcroft Noble (1844–96) was the author of *Morality in English Fiction* (1886) and other works. Affiliated with the Pre-Raphaelite Circle, he was an aesthete who nonetheless authored essays with a strong moral perspective. The quotation is taken from his essay, "The Fiction of Sexuality," *Contemporary Review* 3519 (April 1895): 490–98.

the novelists of erotomania resemble the host who holds a reception and cleans his teeth in the drawing-room before his assembled guests. The success of such a book as Mr. Hardy's "Tess,"[1] which certainly does not ignore the missing "half" of life, shows that there is all needful freedom for any writer who treat sex questions sanely, truthfully, proportionally, and convincingly.

Yet what shall we say to a woman like Lady Henry Somerset, screaming in an American magazine, the *Arena*, against what she calls "compulsory motherhood"?[2] Where does the compulsion come in? Women are not forced to marry in these days nor are they bound, except in the way of business, to speak to men. She says the "unwelcome child" is her conception of original sin. It is time that a healthier blast was blown through the ranks of our Society and this ... maundering about their sex ceased. It is a sign of idleness, or of an activity unwholesome, and akin to decay. We are not overburdened with admiration for former times, but certainly the Englishwoman of the last and preceding centuries seem to have been a brighter influence, and to have induced a more healthy feeling in the community among whom they moved. It is not necessary that woman should confine herself to making jam; but if there was a little more of that kind of domestic industry, not only would it add immeasurably to the comfort and convenience of our homes, but it would provide a useful occupation for persons like Lady Somerset, who—excel-

---

1 Thomas Hardy (1840–1928), novelist. His *Tess of the D'Urbervilles* (1891), the story of the romantic travails of a "pure maiden," was controversial at the time of its publication owing to its frank treatment of such themes as rape and female sexuality.

2 The *Arena* (1889–1912) was a Boston-based progressive magazine that published the writings of Leo Tolstoy (1828–1910), Stephen Crane (1871–1900), Frank Norris (1870–1902), and Upton Sinclair (1878–1968). In the March 1895 issue, Isabel Somerset, who had been the subject of a scandal involving her husband's sexual relations with other men (see Introduction, p. 17), published an essay entitled "The Welcome Child" that argued that the "unwritten tragedy of women's life" lay in the problem of women compelled to have children who are unwanted—a problem affecting not only the "garret and the cellar" but "homes of opulence and ease." Although the term "compulsory motherhood" appeared nowhere in her essay, she writes in favor of a "mother's right to choose when to become a mother" (42–48).

lent woman as she is—is one of those depressing Cassandras[1] who, in ever-increasing numbers, are inflicting themselves upon our age and nation.

4. From Olive Schreiner, "The Woman Question," *Cosmopolitan Magazine* (1889)

[Olive Schreiner (1855–1920) was a South African novelist and feminist intellectual whose most celebrated volumes were *The Story of an African Farm* (1883) and *Women and Labour* (1911). The former is a semi-autobiographical fictional account of three youths struggling for personal freedom in the Karoo region of South Africa and the latter is a bold assessment of women's economic fortunes in patriarchally structured society. Although admired by Oscar Wilde and other aesthetes for the lyric experimentalism of her fiction, as the essay below indicates, Schreiner was skeptical about the new aestheticist coteries that held sway at century's end.]

The conception which again and again appears to have haunted successive societies, that it was a possibility for the male to advance in physical power and intellectual vigour, while his companion female became stationary and inactive, taking no share in the labours of society beyond the passive fulfilment of sexual functions, has always been negated. It has ended as would end the experiment of a man seeking to raise a breed of winning race-horses out of unexercised, short-winded, knock-kneed mares. Nay, more disastrously, for while the female animal transmits herself to her descendant only by means of germinal inheritance, and through the influence she may exert over it during gestation, the human female by producing the intellectual and moral atmosphere in which the early years of life are passed, impresses herself far more indelibly on her descendants. Only an able and labouring womanhood can permanently produce an able and labouring manhood; only an effete and inactive male can ultimately be produced by an effete and inactive womanhood. The curled darling, scented and languid, with his drawl, his delicate apparel, his devotion to the rarity and variety of his viands whose severest labour is the search after pleasure; and for whom even the chase, which was for his remote ancestor an invigorating and manly toil essential for

---

1 Cassandra was a daughter of King Priam and of Queen Hecuba of Troy in Greek mythology. She had the gift of prophecy but her curse was that her prophecies were never believed.

the meat and life of his people, becomes a luxurious and farcical amusement—this male, whether found in the later Roman empire, the Turkish harem of today, or in our northern civilisations, is possible only because generations of parasitic women have preceded him. More repulsive than the parasitic female herself, because a yet further product of decay, it is yet only the scent of his mother's boudoir that we smell in his hair. He is like to the bald patches and rotten wool on the back of a scabby sheep; which indeed indicate that, deep beneath the surface, a parasite insect is eating its way into the flesh, but which are not so much the cause of disease, as its final manifestation.

It is the power of the human female to impress herself on her descendants, male and female, through germinal inheritance, through influence during the period of gestation, and above all by producing the mental atmosphere in which the impressionable years of life are passed, which makes the condition of the child-bearing female the paramount interest of the race. It is this fact which causes even prostitution (in many respects the most repulsive form of female parasitism which afflicts humanity) to be, probably, not so deadly to the advance and even to the conservation of a healthy and powerful society, as the parasitism of its child-bearing females. For the prostitute, heavily as she weights society for her support, returning disease and mental and emotional disintegration for what she consumes, does not yet so immediately affect the next generation as the kept wife, or kept mistress, who impresses her effete image indelibly on the race.

No man ever yet entered life farther than the length of one navel-cord from the body of the woman who bore him. It is the child-bearing woman who is the final standard of the race, from which there can be no departure for any distance for any length of time in any direction: as her brain weakens weakens the man's she bears; as her muscle softens softens his; as she decays decays the people.

Other causes may, and do, lead to the enervation and degeneration of a race; the parasitism of its child-bearing women MUST.

We, the European women of this age, stand to-day where again and again, in the history of the past, women of other races have stood; but our condition is yet more grave, and of wider import to humanity as a whole, than theirs ever was. Why this is so, is a subject for further consideration.

Select Bibliography

Aronson, Theo. *Prince Eddy and the Homosexual Underworld.* London: John Murray, 1994.

Austen, Roger. *Playing the Game: The Homosexual Novel in America.* New York: Bobbs Merrill, 1977.

Berryman, John. *Stephen Crane.* London: Methuen, 1950.

Black, Ros. *A Talent for Humanity: The Life and Work of Lady Henry Somerset.* Chippenham and Eastbourne: Anthony Rowe, 2010.

Bordman, Gerald, ed. *The Oxford Companion to American Theater.* New York: Oxford UP, 1984.

Brooks, Peter. "The Mark of the Beast: Prostitution, Melodrama and Narrative." *Melodrama.* Ed. Daniel C. Gerould. New York: New York Literary Forum, 1980. 143–70.

——. *The Melodramatic Imagination: Balzac, Henry James, Melodrama, and the Mode of Excess.* New Haven, CT: Yale UP, 1976.

Buckton, Oliver S. *Secret Selves: Confession and Same Sex Desire in Victorian Autobiography.* Chapel Hill: U of North Carolina P, 1998.

Caine, Hall. *The Deemster.* 1887. Auckland: Floating P, 2014.

Carpenter, Edward. *Love's Coming of Age.* New York: Boni and Liveright, 1911.

Chauncey, George. *Gay New York: Gender, Urban Culture, and the Making of the Gay Male World, 1890–1940.* New York: Basic Books, 1996.

Cocks, H.G. *Nameless Offences: Homosexual Desire in the 19th Century.* London: I.B. Taurus, 2010.

Cohen, Alfred J. [Alan Dale]. *Familiar Chats with Queens of the Stage.* New York: G.W. Dillingham, 1890.

——. *A Marriage Below Zero.* New York: G.W. Dillingham, 1889.

Craft, Christopher. *Another Kind of Love: Homosexual Desire and English Discourse, 1850–1920.* Berkeley: U of California P, 1994.

Cvetkovitch, Ann. *Mixed Feelings: Feminism, Mass Culture, and Victorian Sensationalism.* New Brunswick, NJ: Rutgers UP, 1992.

Dellamora, Richard. *Masculine Desire: The Sexual Politics of Victorian Aestheticism.* Chapel Hill: U of North Carolina P. 1990.

Disher, M. Willson. *Melodrama: Plots that Thrilled*. New York: Macmillan, 1954.

Dollimore, Jonathan. *Sexual Dissidence: Augustine to Wilde, Freud to Foucault*. New York: Oxford UP, 1993.

Dzwonkoski, Peter, ed. *American Literary Publishing Houses, 1638–1899*. Detroit: Gale, 1986.

Ellis, Havelock. *Studies in the Psychology of Sex. Vol. 2, Sexual Inversion*. 1897. New York: Random House, 1936.

Fishkin, Shelley Fisher. *From Fact to Fiction: Journalism and Imaginative Writing in America*. Baltimore: Johns Hopkins UP, 1985.

Foucault, Michel. *The History of Sexuality: An Introduction. Vol. 1*. Trans. Robert Hurley. 1978. New York: Vintage, 1991.

Garde, Noel I. "*Marriage Below Zero*: The Very First One?" *Mattachine Review* (1958): 17–20.

Gerould, Daniel C. *American Melodrama*. New York: Performing Arts Publications, 1983.

——. *Melodrama*. New York: New York Literary Forum, 1980.

Grimsted, David. *Melodrama Unveiled: American Theater and Culture, 1800–1850*. Chicago: U of Chicago P, 1968.

Heilman, Robert. *Tragedy and Melodrama: Versions of Experience*. Seattle: U of Washington P, 1968.

Horowitz, Helen Lefkowitz. *Rereading Sex: Battles over Sexual Knowledge and Suppression in Nineteenth-Century America*. New York: Alfred Knopf, 2002.

Hyde, H. Montgomery. *The Cleveland Street Scandal*. London: W.H. Allen, 1976.

Hyland, Paul, and Neil Sammells, eds. *Writing and Censorship in Britain*. New York: Routledge, 1992.

Katz, Jonathan. *Gay American History: Lesbians and Gay Men in the U.S.A.* New York: Thomas Y. Crowell, 1976.

Kaye, Richard A. "The Return of Damon and Pythias: *A Marriage Below Zero*, Victorian Melodrama, and the Literature of Homosexual Representation." *College Literature* 29.2 (2002): 50–79.

Krafft-Ebing, Richard von. *Psychopathia Sexualis: A Medico-Forensic Study*. Trans. Harry E. Wedeck. 1886. New York: G.P. Putnam's Sons, 1965.

Leckie, Barbara. *Adultery and Culture: The Novel, the Newspaper, and the Law, 1857–1914*. Philadelphia: U of Pennsylvania P, 1999.

Londre, Felicity Hardison. *The History of World Theater: From the English Restoration to the Present*. New York: Continuum, 1999.

Lundberg, Ferdinand. *Imperial Hearst: A Social Biography*. New York: Modern Library, 1937.

Martin, Robert K. "Knights-Errant and Gothic Seducers: The Representation of Male Friendship in Mid-Nineteenth-Century America." *Hidden from History: Reclaiming the Gay and Lesbian Past*. Ed. Martin Duberman, Martha Vicinus, and George Chauncey. New York: New American Library, 1989.

McConachie, Bruce A. *Melodramatic Formations: American Theatre and Society, 1820–1870*. Iowa City: U of Iowa P, 1992.

Miller, Tice L. "Alan Dale: The Hearst Critic." *Educational Theater Journal* 26.1 (1974): 69–80.

Mott, Franklin Luther. *American Journalism: A History of Newspapers in the United States through 250 Years, 1690–1940*. New York: Macmillan, 1941.

Niessen, Olive Claire. *Aristocracy, Temperance and Social Reform: The Life of Lady Henry Somerset*. London: Tautis Academic Studies, 2007.

Nissen, Axel. *Manly Love: Romantic Friendship in American Fiction*. Chicago: U of Chicago P, 2009.

Pater, Walter. *Marius the Epicurean*. 1885. New York: Penguin, 1985.

Prime-Stevenson, Edward Irenaeus. *The Intersexes: A History of Similisexualism as Problem in Social Life*. New York: The English Book P, 1908.

Reynolds, David S. *Beneath the American Renaissance: The Subversive Imagination in the Age of Emerson and Melville*. New York: Alfred A. Knopf, 1988.

Robinson, Paul. *The Modernization of Sex: Havelock Ellis, Alfred Kinsey, William Masters and Virginia Johnson*. 1976. Ithaca, NY: Cornell UP, 1989.

Rubery, Matthew. *The Invention of Newspapers: Victorian Fiction after the Invention of the News*. New York: Oxford UP, 2009.

Sarotte, Georges Michel. *Like a Brother, Like a Lover: Male Homosexuality in the American Novel and Theater from Herman Melville to James Baldwin*. Trans. Richard Miller. New York: Doubleday, 1978.

Sedgwick, Eve Kosofsky. *Between Men: Male Homosocial Desire and English Literature*. New York: Columbia UP, 1985.

Showalter, Elaine. *Sexual Anarchy: Gender and Culture at the Fin de Siècle*. New York: Viking, 1990.

Vicinus, Martha. *Independent Women: Work and Community for Single Women, 1850–1920*. Chicago: U of Chicago P, 1985.

Walkowitz, Judith. *City of Dreadful Delight: Narratives of Sexual Danger in Late-Victorian London*. Chicago: U of Chicago P, 1992.

Weeks, Jeffrey. *Sex, Politics, and Society: The Regulation of Sexuality Since 1800*. London: Longman, 1981.

———. *Coming Out: Homosexual Politics in Britain from the Nineteenth Century to the Present*. London: Quartet, 1997.

White, Chris, ed. *Nineteenth Century Writings on Homosexuality: A Sourcebook*. London: Routledge, 1999.

Wilde, Oscar, et al. *Teleny*. 1893. London: Gay Men's P, 1997.

FROM THE PUBLISHER

A name never says it all, but the word "Broadview" expresses a good deal of the philosophy behind our company. We are open to a broad range of academic approaches and political viewpoints. We pay attention to the broad impact book publishing and book printing has in the wider world; for some years now we have used 100% recycled paper for most titles. Our publishing program is internationally oriented and broad-ranging. Our individual titles often appeal to a broad readership too; many are of interest as much to general readers as to academics and students.

Founded in 1985, Broadview remains a fully independent company owned by its shareholders—not an imprint or subsidiary of a larger multinational.

For the most accurate information on our books (including information on pricing, editions, and formats) please visit our website at www.broadviewpress.com. Our print books and ebooks are available for sale on our site.

broadview press
www.broadviewpress.com

The interior of this book is printed on 100% recycled paper.